About The Authors

Growing up on opposite coasts of the US, Jeff and Kent didn't meet each other until later in life. With over 55 years combined in the music industry; producing, touring, and performing with many artists, the pair finally met seventeen years ago. Their sense of humor collided, and they instantly bonded over the stories of their road experiences. While their careers have taken very different routes, once they crossed paths, they knew after working together that they shared a connection that rarely is seen in any industry.

Soon they realized that they had seen so much of the industry; the idea of a fictious tour could be fun to write about, with the right element added. That element was murder. Murder on a rock and roll tour loaded with satire on the industry that they already thought was humorous. They started penning ideas back in 2009; created characters and scenarios with the intension of making one another laugh. Soon they were writing one chapter after another with ideas that they developed over numerous phone calls and an occasional meeting over a beer.

As time moved on, they had what was the basic building blocks for half a novel. But both became busy with other projects and the writing process slowed down. Phone calls continued, and the ideas flowed as the two became addicted to their stories. It was agreed that at some point when they had more time, they would continue to finish the manuscript.

Then Covid Fucking 19 reared its ugly head and there was time. While not much else in the world was moving, Jeff and Kent were on the phone almost daily. Their ideas kept flowing and soon they had enough material not just for one novel, but for several. Now well into their third novel, they are proud to release their second titled, Tones, Clones, and Bones.

Jeff: "Having seen it all on the road, it was fun to take that knowledge and create something that people will enjoy. This book follows up our first book 'Are We A Bus?'. The characters continue and life moves on for them. I hope everyone that reads this enjoys it and laughs out loud just as Kent and I did while creating it."

Kent: "To say that I've lived the rock and roll dream, would be an understatement. What I have seen on tour is far funnier than This is Spinal Tap ever was. I hope to live a few more years in the arena."

Tones, Clones and Bones

Jeff Agins

And

Kent Niepert

The book is a work of fiction. Names, characters, places, and incidents either are products of the authors' imaginations or are used fictitiously. Any resemblance to actual events, locales, or persons, living or dead, is entirely coincidental.

ISBN: 978-1-7374027-3-2 (paperback)

ISBN: 978-1-7374027-5-6 (Ebook – Kindle)

ISBN: 978-1-7374027-4-9 (Ebook – EPUB)

Chapter 1

Spud Burger, the world's worst booking agent, wanted to make a statement and show the music industry that the world's greatest guitarist is back. Jurgen Weislangwolf's last tour of North America was a catastrophe. A killer following the tour killed many people along the way for no apparent reason. He left two FBI agents looking like bumbling, clueless morons as he repeatedly eluded them. After Jurgen's bass player, Heinz, was kidnapped by the unidentified assailant, the tour was canceled by the FBI. Now all of that seemed distant in the past.

Spud had scheduled a press conference weeks ago; it would be grand. Jurgen Weislangwolf, known to his fans as the Doctor of Dynamics because of his out-of-this-world ability on the guitar, would play a solo piece blasted to the shores of Redondo Beach from a boat. The Doctor would perform Beethoven's Violin Concerto third movement on his Universe Guitar. A guitar so powerful with its nine strings and forty-five frets that it could cover every note on the piano and more.

It was important to make an impact with this press conference to increase the confidence of the promoters, who were show buyers, and the fans to prove that this tour would be different than the suddenly shortened last tour. Spud had money issues and needed his commission from this tour. He was losing more of his artists on a monthly basis due to his less-than-honest business practices.

Spud purchased a flight for the Doctor to arrive early in the afternoon for the 5:00 pm press conference. He would pick up the Doctor and bring him to the press conference and then put him right back on a flight to Austria late the same day to save expenses.

It would be a spectacular display of the Doctor's ability, performing on the rear deck of the yacht that his silent partner, retired millionaire Brian Wallack, owned as they sailed up to Redondo Beach. The media would be there in force; this was the perfect plan that would lead to Spud booking additional shows at higher guarantees for the Doctor's upcoming tour of North America.

The Doctor agreed to do this as his life has not been going well since the canceled tour. He picked up odd shows in Europe and slots twice a week at the local bar in his hometown of Salzburg, Austria. His longtime girlfriend, Bea, and their eleven children have been miserable since their diet had been reduced to mostly rice and beans. He needed money that the back-to-back tours of India and North America would provide him for nearly three months. More important to the Doctor, he would get out of earshot and not have to listen to the ramblings of Bea. That alone was worth a ton of gold.

Kurt "Neusy" Neustadt and Jeb Acorns approached the marina in Santa Monica in Neusy's BMW, ready to get to work on the one-off gig. The press conference would be easy. One amp and one mic with a PA aimed at the beach from the yacht.

"Neusy," said Jeb, the Doctor's tour manager of many years. "This is it, turn in the marina here, we just need to find the boat. Spud had the equipment delivered for us this morning."

"This will be a piece of cake," replied Neusy, Jeb's friend and touring partner. Jeb trusted no one more than Neusy on the road, relying on his always-willing-to-help attitude and problem-solving ability. "What's the boat called?"

"The *Unsinkable IV*."

"What happened to the first three *Unsinkables*?"

"I asked the same question. Apparently Spud Burger crashed all three. Two into piers and one into a cruise ship."

"That makes me feel safe," said Neusy as he stepped out of the car, his shoulder-length blonde hair blowing in the ocean breeze.

"Spud is no longer allowed to operate any vessel on the water. The Coast Guard suspended his privilege of operating a boat; he had no choice but to hire a captain. Spud should be picking up the Doctor now, so we have about an hour to get the gear set up before they arrive."

"It will be great to see him again after that last tour got so ugly. Look over there! There it is, the *Unsinkable IV*. Wow, it's a big boat!"

"Damn, look at the size of that rear deck. Well, he did call it a yacht," said Jeb, whose beard had now fully grown in. Perfect gray and white to match his hair tied back in a ponytail.

Jeb and Neusy walked the dock to where the *Unsinkable IV* was berthed. It was the largest private-owned ship either of them had ever boarded. Eighty-four feet in length, six decks, and painted a brilliant powder green. They walked the gangway and were stopped by a middle-aged balding man wearing shorts and no top. His mostly gray hair, what was left of it, was slicked back. "What do you want?"

"We are the Doctor's crew," said Neusy.

"The who?" said the captain.

"The Doctor of Dynamics, Jurgen Weislangwolf!"

"What the hell is the Doctor of Dynamics?"

"We are here to set up the gear before Spud arrives with the Doctor."

The captain's face seemed to acknowledge that he knew who Spud was. He moved aside for the guys to board. "I'm Captain Noah, Brent Noah, but everyone calls me Flip."

As they boarded, Neusy gave Jeb the I-hope-this-motherfucker-does-not-flip-this-boat look. Jeb nodded, then motioned with his eyes to the left. Neusy grabbed two of the life vests off the rack on the wall and handed one to Jeb.

The embers burning in Scaggz's fire next to his tent in the mountains outside Los Angeles were ready. He had perfected his spice blend that he used to thoroughly rub his freshly caught California mountain beaver. His blend of salt, pepper, brown sugar, chili pepper, and garlic was now tweaked to perfection. He finally was able to catch these elusive rodents at will after accidentally falling on one a few months back. The secret, he discovered, is that California mountain beavers are attracted to his brother's cologne.

He placed the mountain beaver over the fire and contemplated what the next months would entail. Not since he lost his job years ago as stage manager for guitarist Jurgen Weislangwolf had he felt this much passion and enthusiasm for touring once again. On the last tour, he made his presence felt, a one-man force, while meticulously causing problems that ended the tour early. There must be more, a reason to purge more of the additional dead weight.

While Scaggz tended to their dinner, his brother Jimmy preferred to stay inside of Scaggz's VW Kombi as he was not keen on the camping idea. In fact, he despised camping. He was not sure how much more of this he could take. It had to end soon. His tour with the Doctor ended after his disappearance, which his brother orchestrated perfectly. It was the final incident that caused the tour to be canceled as the FBI recalled the visas for the mostly Austrian band. But five months in the woods with his brother, eating all sorts of wildlife, was enough.

"Jimmy," said Scaggz, "the Doctor announced his tour of India a few weeks ago and today he will announce that the next North American tour will follow right afterwards. We must go to his press conference."

"I am ready to get out of here," said Jimmy through the open doors of the van. "I disappeared as Heinz Beckenschultz, the Doctor's bass player, so now I cannot risk anyone seeing me until I make my big reappearance. I hate this up here. I haven't eaten broccoli in months. Just this shit you are always cooking. How can I go to the press conference? I will be seen."

"Patience. Isn't that what I told you in the beginning? We need patience. You will stay in the van; I will go and listen from the beach. You want to mess with him just as much as I do. Remember the audition, when he knew you as my brother and called you a hack and a poser that would never play in a touring band. Remember that always! This is the reason you reinvented yourself and took all those lessons. Moving to Austria was genius. Think about all you did to get the Doctor to notice you as Heinz. You had so much patience then. This is just like that." Scaggz cooked the rodent crispy on the outside and tender on the inside.

"OK, I must admit that this is one of the best things we have eaten since we have been up here in the woods," remarked Jimmy.

"Finish up, you'll get your wish, we will come down off the mountain and head to the beach. After the press conference, we have to go back to Minnesota where you will reappear once again as Heinz Beckenschultz." The brothers finished the mountain beaver, leaving only bones, then urinated on the fire before driving to Redondo Beach.

"I am sure glad we are only setting up these fourteen effect pedals," exclaimed Neusy as he was checking the connections for the Doctor's amp and minimal effects. "What do you know about the India tour?"

"Not much. The offers are excellent, but I think Jurgen wants to use it as some kind of motivational journey," said Jeb as he turned on the rented PA system.

"Well, whatever, as long as we get paid and can enjoy some Indian beers, I am in. Speaking of which, I am about ready for one now."

Neusy and Jeb finished their work and decided to have a couple of beers at the marina bar. "Wish all the setups were like this," said Jeb.

"You got that right. Glad it's just the two of us going to India. I can only take so much of Hocker and Marlon. Hocker is a good worker, but I need space from him sometimes. Marlon is as neurotic as they come but seemed to be OK last time out," said Neusy. Jeb gave him the eyes of agreement as they were approached by a pair resembling the Blues Brothers. "Agents Sparrow and Crow, what are you guys doing here? Still on the FBI's payroll?"

Jeb laughed as he sipped his California Wildfire Smoked IPA in the marina bar. "Agents, nice to see you!"

Agent Jathan Sparrow said, "We heard the Doctor has another tour planned." They all shook hands.

"We came out for the press conference. We heard you boys are on the *Unsinkable IV*, found out it was docked here and came out here to see for ourselves. We want to watch from the beach in Redondo and are hoping something will reveal itself, although a long shot. All that happened last time and minimal clues. You know that headquarters will be watching closely—anything happens, they will have you two on a short leash," added Agent Jester Crow, the taller, skinnier one of the pair.

"I see you have not changed your ensembles. Still rocking the Blues Brothers look," said Jeb while Neusy was drinking his Pacific Ocean Shark Vomit Lager and gagged slightly.

"It's just our regular look. Fucking people! Always saying shit like that to us. Fuck off!" said Sparrow, and the agents walked out.

Neusy ordered the seasonal Smog Free LA Lager and Jeb a Pig's Foot Stout served with a slice of bacon in the glass. They bumped glasses as the Doctor walked in. He immediately walked up to the pair enjoying their beers and said, "Jebs und Neusy, my boys, how are you two? I have missed you both." As they hugged, they both noticed the Doctor seemed to have been working out. "Jeb, you gained a little weight, but it looks good on you. Und Neusy, yah, you know without a GPS you still can drive well. I miss your driving, yah!"

Jeb looked over at Neusy, who was giving him the what's-up-with-the-compliments look. Jeb gave a head shake and eye roll to indicate he had no idea. "Yah, you two with the beer. I know you both love it. So happy that you can enjoy." The Doctor wore his stage wigs now in public. His white Mozart wig was tied back in a ponytail. Jeb noticed it was not the original that his grandfather bought at auction, but a nice replica.

Spud said, as he offered his hand to the two touring warriors, "Great to see you boys again. The Doctor seems extremely excited about this tour and what we are doing today." Then to the bartender, "I'll take the Ocean Shark and a shot of whiskey, along with a glass of red wine for the Doctor. I'm quite sure my friends here have a tab open." After the drinks were served, Jeb paid the tab before anything additional could be added.

They finished their drinks and walked to the *Unsinkable IV*, the Doctor talking the whole way. "Yah, the flight, it was so nice. I had this baby screaming a few rows ahead, but it was like music, I kept hearing melodies. This man next to me, we talked the whole way here." They were approaching the yacht. "Wow, this is a big boat. Spud, you did so well. You are the best booking agent in the whole world!"

Jeb walked up first, realizing something may not be OK with the Doctor, just as Neusy said to him, "Is he doing drugs now?"

"Something is not right," said Jeb as they passed Flip smoking a joint on the deck where they boarded.

"Yah, someone will have a good trip," said the Doctor to Flip. "Now I will check the equipment. Neusy, you go plug in my guitar."

Neusy plugged in the guitar and turned on the amp. The Doctor played a run through while Flip maneuvered the yacht out of the marina. The ride down to Redondo Beach would not take long, but Spud wanted to go out four miles past the horizon to make the arriving *Unsinkable IV* more dramatic as it appeared.

The beach at Redondo was in full party mode, packed with people spilling out onto the street and into the adjacent park. There were vendors of every type, along with celebrity impersonators from Hollywood who were there to take pictures with the crowd for a tip. Superman, Batman, Marilyn Monroe, Darth Vader, three different Elvis impersonators, as well as Spongebob and a Donald Trump impersonator. The party carried up to the pier that overlooked the beach and the ocean. The pier had various restaurants and bars that all were taking advantage of the boost in business generated by the press conference.

Scaggz had parked the van two blocks away and walked to the beach while Jimmy had to wait in the van. Scaggz was walking the beach looking for the perfect spot to watch the event when he spotted the FBI agents, who blended right in with all the impersonators.

Now with his hair grown out again and full-on beard, he doubted they would remember meeting him over five months ago. To test his theory, he approached the agents and yelled out, "I love the Blues Brothers," as he took a selfie with them. He was quick to hand them a dollar then sprinted away. He looked up over his shoulder and saw a crowd of people that also wanted a photo with the impersonators.

Scaggz, down by the ocean, still could not find the ideal spot to watch the event. He looked up at the huge pier staring down at him, loaded with restaurants and shops. He scaled the pilings and ascended to the top but positioned himself under the pier platform. From this vantage point he could see the ocean and the beach unobstructed.

"People, we are FBI!" said Agent Sparrow as they showed their badges in unison, as if rehearsed, each with a handful of dollar bills. This caused more of a stir and a cheer. More people surrounded them for pictures thinking it was all part of their act.

"I want one with the badges," said a woman with her children.

"Yes, a picture with the badges!" shouted someone else.

Agent Crow liked the attention and was putting more cash in his pocket than he had space to carry. Sparrow, annoyed, finally slapped Crow on the arm and dragged him away from the crowd. The people followed until they walked to the pier steps. Crow said, "We just need a break, people. We will be back later."

A large sigh ensued, and the people started walking back to the beach. A couple said, "Please let us be first when you come back." Crow was about to speak but Sparrow yanked him up the stairs. The agents walked up and stopped at a Mexican Cantina, ordered a taco each and made their way to the railing where they could see the ocean and the beach unobstructed just like Scaggz, who now was right below them on the support posts.

Jeb could finally see the beach at Redondo in the distance. Neusy was on the rear deck with him. They checked the systems, and all appeared OK. The Doctor appeared from below and said, "Yah, you two really are so good. I see the beach."

"You must wait to play until I tell you, we are too far from the beach for them to hear it clearly," said Neusy.

Scaggz could now see the yacht approaching, still a mile out. What a huge yacht. How did they afford that? Probably Spud Burger did something that the Doctor would end up paying as some fictitious expense.

The agents also noticed the *Unsinkable IV* approaching. "There it is. Keep scanning the beach, look for anything unusual, not normal," said Crow.

"This whole press conference is not normal. Look at all those people. You got news cameras, vendors selling who knows what, people drinking on the beach half naked, and these impersonators. Not to mention people wanting our pictures. Then you have those people in the water surfing, then coming ashore to smoke weed. Maybe we should change the colors of our suits to gray," said Sparrow.

"No way, I always have worn black since my father bought me my first suit. People are just idiots! I don't know why they are always calling us the Blues Brothers. I saw the movie back in the day. We look nothing like them, plus my skin is way too dark," replied Crow as he took off his fedora to scratch his head while Sparrow removed his sunglasses to get a clearer look down on the beach.

The *Unsinkable IV* was now a half mile from the beach. "Get ready, Jurgen," instructed Neusy. "Just a little further."

"Yah, this is amazing, that many people want to see this. Why do we not get more people at the shows?" asked the Doctor.

"Well, this is a beach, and it is like a party; look at all the people having a good time. But a lot has to do with the venues you are booked in," said Jeb, and he and Neusy both looked at Spud as he was downing his third shot of whiskey since boarding the yacht.

"Yah, well don't blame Spud, he is a good man," replied the Doctor. "Do you have a pick for me to use?"

"I put a couple on the amp," answered Neusy. As the Doctor turned around, both Jeb and Neusy noticed he had a small tattoo under his left ear towards the back of his neck that was now visible with the light wind blowing across the deck. It was just the number one.

"Strange, I never noticed he had that tattoo with all the years I've worked with him," said Jeb.

"Yeah, me neither, but it makes sense since he does not think anyone can even play on the same planet as him. Conceded asshole would get a tattoo saying he is number one," said Neusy. "OK, Jurgen, we are about where we need to be; just wait for the boat to turn so people can see you."

On the beach, the onlookers were standing up now as the *Unsinkable IV* was only 250 feet out and could no longer get any closer. Spud was unsure what the laws were but had to pay Flip an additional thousand dollars to bring the *Unsinkable IV* this close to shore. "This is it," said Flip. "We need to be quick."

Jeb once again switched on the massive PA, which gave feedback until Neusy adjusted one of the slides on the sound board. The people on the beach screamed when they heard the feedback. The *Unsinkable IV* turned parallel to the beach so that the people on the beach could now see the rear deck and the Doctor standing facing them with his hand in the air.

Neusy started the backing track. It was Bach's Violin Concerto third movement. The people on the beach were quiet. Neusy increased the volume of the PA, but still not much reaction on the beach.

The Doctor also noticed this, he turned around and adjusted his custom Galactic Amp to its maximum level of 900 watts. The onlookers screamed. Neusy, maxing out the PA, could only hear the Doctor as Spud rented a PA too small for the task at hand.

The news cameras were rolling, and the onlookers were in awe of the Doctor's playing. They were silent for the entire ten-minute length of the movement, which included an improvised section. It was loud on the deck of the yacht. Jeb looked over at Neusy to see if Neusy noticed it as well. It was clear from Neusy's what-the-fuck look that he too sensed something off in the Doctor's playing. His vibrato seemed out of time and his playing uninspired. Both so slight that the average listener would not notice during a live performance.

But they knew, they have seen the Doctor play live hundreds of times and during rehearsals the Doctor always emphasized these things. Jeb too was a victim of the Doctor's criticism when he was playing his guitar on the tour bus to kill time. The Doctor told him, "Ach, if you must play your guitar on my bus, then you must play it properly. I cannot stand to hear you play unless you play it right." Jeb never brought his guitar on tour again and now watches movies on his tablet to occupy his free time.

The Doctor finished the third movement of Bach's Violin Concerto; the crowd on the beach erupted in cheers.

"More! More!"

"That was fucking amazing!"

"Play some Centipedes!"

But that was it, Spud walked over to the microphone as Flip was ready to bring the *Unsinkable IV* further out to sea. Spud announced, "Ladies and gentlemen. The Doctor of Dynamics." The crowd screamed once again. "His North American Tour will kick off in a few weeks. Visit his website or Burger Musical Bookings International for all the tour dates. Thank you for coming out. Flip, let's get out of here."

Flip put the yacht in motion, and they headed back to Santa Monica. "Well, that went OK. I was wondering how this was going to be with this boat thing," said the Doctor. "Spud, you did well. But now I need my red wine." Jeb handed him a glass of red wine, but the Doctor grabbed the bottle from his other hand and finished it in one long sip. Neusy looked over, watching what was going on, then watched as the Doctor put the empty bottle down and grabbed the glass that was offered to him a few seconds earlier.

"What the hell is going on with Jurgen? You need to talk with him, Jeb," said Neusy. "His personality is off. He is not critical like he always is and his playing… You heard it too, I saw you. If he is on drugs, it will be a disaster. Remember when he was drinking before he went on stage. It was a nightmare. And what was with playing Bach's Violin Concerto? He was supposed to play Beethoven."

"He told me right before he went on that the backing music he gave you was for Bach. I asked, 'Why? The press release said you will be playing Beethoven.' His answer was, 'Suck my Bach!' So yes, something is way off with him. I will talk with him once he is back home. He is always more approachable when he is home and relaxed. But now we need to take him back to the airport once we get on shore."

Once back at the marina in Santa Monica, Flip berthed the *Unsinkable IV* to the relief of Neusy and Jeb. They all walked ashore. Neusy and Jeb handed Flip their life vests, who did not find it humorous. Once on the shore, the Doctor said, "Achh, that was some good red wine. I want some more."

Jeb answered, "We need to get you to the airport. Your flight home is in a few hours."

"Yah, Jeb, you are always so good with the time."

Jeb shook his head, as normally he would get the Doctor's verbal lashing. They walked to Neusy's car, said goodbye to Spud, then headed to LAX to drop off the Doctor for his flight back to Austria. On the way, the Doctor in the back seat said, "Achh, when we go to India, you both will see what is going on."

Jeb didn't want to ask; he looked at Neusy who was looking forward, not acknowledging what the Doctor was saying. "Good thought, Jeb! Let's just get him back to the airport and sort out what issues he is having when he is back home," said Neusy.

Scaggz, high up on the pier, could also tell there was something not quite right with the Doctor's playing. The Doctor was not right. He must find out what is going on. The Doctor never plays like that. Back at his VW, his brother Jimmy was in the passenger seat. When Scaggz opened the door, the smell of steamed broccoli hit him. We have to see what is going on with the Doctor. His playing was off. I am not even sure that was the Doctor playing. He was too far away to see for sure. Why did you leave the van to get that food?"

"Relax, it was right across the street. No one saw me and I was hungry. What are you going to do?"

"We're driving up to Santa Monica. We should be able to beat them up there," said Scaggz as he pulled away from his parking spot and headed up the coast.

They arrived in Santa Monica and there was no sign of the *Unsinkable IV*. They waited in the parking lot in a spot behind the restaurant at the marina. There Scaggz could see the marina but they would not notice him. Just the back of the VW to the water. Jimmy pulled a second container of broccoli out of a bag and began to eat that as the *Unsinkable IV* arrived.

They watched the passengers exit the yacht and then watched Neusy, Jeb, and the Doctor walk to the parking lot. Scaggz maneuvered his VW to the side of the restaurant, waited for the three to get into the BMW, and then followed them out of the parking lot.

Neusy drove down the coast and then across to LAX. The Doctor said, "Yah, this was fun, thank you for driving me. Neusy, see, you do not need your GPS, you made it here as if you had one."

"It's just driving to the airport; I have done it many times."

"Achh, yah, but you do it so well. Now I must stop quick for a red wine. We have a little time. Neusy let's go to the hotel over there for a quick one."

Jeb said, "No, there is not that much time. Your flight is in two hours. It is always a lot of people going through security. You can get the wine on the other side."

"Yah, Jeb, you always know what is best, so this I will do."

Neusy drove around the airport until he arrived at the international terminal and then pulled the BMW over. They all three got out and hugged goodbye. Neusy said, "Jurgen, have a good flight! We will see you in India."

"Yes, safe trip home," added Jeb.

"Yah, thanks, I will see you both in India und then you will see."

Jeb and Neusy got back in the BMW. Neusy said, "Wow, he has been working out it seems, what did he mean, 'und then you will see,' when we get to India?"

"I have no idea; I will call him. Let's go to the hotel and check in. I am glad we decided to take a couple of days here on the beach to work production for these tours. But now is beer o'clock." They drove away. They did not notice the VW Kombi behind them pull over and drag the Doctor through the open side door.

Chapter 2

The Doctor sat in his living room in Salzburg peering out of his window watching the chirping birds pecking at the ground for their morning worms while he sipped his Earl Grey tea. The Doctor was in deep thoughts about his Indian tour. This would be one of the greatest spiritual adventures of his lifetime. India, the center of the mystical and gateway to the art of transcendental meditation and yoga. What greater heights he could attain by meditation of the various planes of existence. His creation of new music and playing abilities would universally improve.

His tour of India would be a solo tour, meaning no backing band, just himself. He would play the guitar and sing. He wanted to make the music sound fuller and more textured. He thought to add a keyboard and switch between that and the guitar, but eventually decided not to go that way. Something about the birds' chirps convinced him to go another way. He sat there wearing his Mozart stage wig. A wig his grandfather had bought at an auction, and it was genuinely Mozart's wig. He channeled inspiration from this wig and wore it now off stage as well as on.

He picked up his phone and called Trenton Towers, his friend in England who invented the Metal Mind Melder (MMM), which played instruments through thought waves using a reading device called a Thought Reader Module (TRM). "Hallo, Trenton! This is Jurgen, how are you?"

"Hello, Jurgen, I am great! I heard that you are going to tour India."

"Yah. Yah! This is the plan…und why I am calling you. I have this crazy idea. I want to add extra arms to the MMM device."

"Yeah? What for?"

"Well, this is what I think, then the MMM could play some percussion und other instruments while I play guitar. Do you understand what I mean?" explained the Doctor.

"Yeah, I got it! I have been working on some new developments in the MMM technology. One new thing is I have created a type of head gear that you can wear, instead of using the TRM mounted on the wand."

"Ahhh, now that sounds wunderbar!"

"Yeah. It is! I think I could combine two MMM devices together to make one that has four arms."

The Doctor thought for a moment about the prospect. When he performed, he would resemble the goddess Shiva, from Indian mythology, who had four arms. That could be unique and quite the spectacle and appealing to the Indian people. "Yeah, Trenton, this is fantastic! How long will this take to finish these things for me?"

"I think I can get it done in two weeks' time and ship it to you in Austria so you can practice with it."

"*Schpectacular!*"

Two weeks later the newly modified MMM arrived from England to the Doctor's door in Salzburg. He uncrated it and set it up in his living room. He walked around it, looking at its four arms. Two arms could be used to play percussion instruments, the other two could be used to play bass, another guitar, or even a sitar. *The sitar is a great sound*, he thought as he went into his music conservatory, bringing out two congas and his sitar. He placed the congas near two of the arms and attached the other two arms to the sitar.

He always found Ravi Shankar's music fascinating and began to listen to it some more. After an hour, he went back into the living room, located the newly designed headgear, and he put it on. He stood in front of the MMM and concentrated on the music that he had just heard. He went into a deep trance. Suddenly, the arms began to play. The two hands on the left played rhythm on the congas. The two arms on the right fretted and strummed on the sitar. It was playing a melody that he had just embedded in his mind. It was incredible! Now he would have to create a repertoire of music to play in India before his departure date.

In addition to using his wondrous Universe Guitar, he wanted a special instrument to be used in India. Somewhat of an acoustic instrument. He browsed online to find an Indian luthier. He found one in Madras, a Mr. Zarveen Agarwal, and sent him an email of his ideas.

The Doctor had worked through the entire night, excited with the latest edition to his arsenal. Now in the early hours of the morning in Austria, he received a message on his phone stating that he missed his flight back home.

Jimmy grabbed the Doctor through the open door of the VW Kombi; Scaggz drove the VW towards the airport exit. In the back, the Doctor, dazed by what just happened after hitting his head while being abducted, laid on a mattress.

Scaggz, now back in the front seat, was rummaging through the glove box, looking for something to cover his face. "Oh, shit! That was insane!" he said. "Now what? I can't tour with him if he knows it was me that pulled him into the van."

"Relax," said Scaggz, "that is not the Doctor."

"What do you mean? You just went to the press conference. I could hear him playing from where we parked. Just look at him. It's the Doctor."

"His playing was not right, and his normal spiritual vibe was missing."

"I don't know," replied Jimmy. "He looks like the Doctor to me. Maybe he just had an off gig. He did just fly in from Europe. Where are we going now with him?"

"Well, I can't kill him till I am sure he is an impostor. Even then, he looks so much like the Doctor I would have to totally destroy the body or make sure it never will be found. For now, I'm taking him to Pointy's," said Scaggz.

"Pointy? He is still alive?"

"Alive and well and living in Palm Springs."

Mark "Pointy" Pennguiny was a competent tour manager and stage tech. He excelled in his career, working for one of the top acts in the seventies and eighties. He broke into the industry at an early age with the band Copperwood-Marks. Davey Marks, the band's founder, had known Pointy since childhood. When his band was signed and released their first album, he hired Pointy as their stage manager. Pointy was a drummer by trade, however he couldn't keep a straight tempo. While Davey would never hire him for his musicianship, he valued his friendship and knowledge of the music industry.

When Copperwood-Marks released their second album *Fences*, they were catapulted to stardom. For the next twenty years their albums went platinum, and they toured at will. Today they still exist, still all original members. They have not released an album in eleven years, but still manage to tour sold-out arenas worldwide.

After twenty-six years with Copperwood-Marks, Pointy was forced to step down from his management job when a stage collapsed, leaving half his left foot severed on an angle with only his big toe remaining. He got various gigs with bands up until the Doctor was introduced to him and asked for his insight and wisdom. He became the Doctor's stage manager and became close with Scaggz, who was the Doctor's tech at the time.

Over the years he managed to tour the world with the Doctor's slowly dwindling career. As he got older, and arthritis set in, Pointy became less mobile with his severed foot. He was not able to walk straight and always would walk to the left. As time went on, the condition got worse. It would not be unusual for Pointy to walk in a complete circle before he was able to right himself and get to where he needed to walk. As the condition progressed, he could not turn right at all.

It became problematic and dangerous while setting up a stage. In the men's room, if the toilets were on the right, he would end up using the sinks on the left. He was urinating in the shower on the tour bus when he could not navigate to the right in the confined space of the small restroom. Then he became forgetful. He would walk a complete circle, sometimes twice, and then forget why he even started moving.

Finally realizing his newly developed shortcomings, he decided to retire at the recommendation of Scaggz and the Doctor. He was devastated; this was all he knew how to do and never had stayed in one place very long. When he wasn't touring, he would crash at Davey's sister's house.

Lilith Marks, Davey's older sister by eleven years, was Copperfield-Marks' manager for their first twenty-eight years. She managed the band and then retired herself to a nine-bedroom mansion in Palm Springs that Davey bought her as a thank you for her work over the years. She invited Pointy to stay with her, where he has been living the last eight years. Over that time, they have taken in retired roadies and techs that had no other place to live once they stopped working. It became somewhat of a roadie old age home that had as many as sixteen retired road crew living there at one time.

The Doctor in the back of Scaggz's van had shaken off the daze and sat up. "Scaggz, is that you? Und Heinz, you are alive. The whole tour last time was canceled when you disappeared. Everyone thought you were dead."

As Scaggz continued to drive he said, "Ah, glad you are awake. Now let's talk. I attended the press conference today. Not a bad idea, I have to give that to Spud. So now, who the fuck are you?"

"Ahh, Scaggz, it's me, what is wrong with you? We toured so much together, have you forgotten? By the way, this van is very comfy. Why is Heinz here with you?"

"Yes, it is comfy, do you want to drive?" asked Scaggz, trying to figure out who this person was.

"Nein, I hate to drive these things. But you drive beautifully," answered the Doctor.

Scaggz pulled off the next exit on Interstate 10 and sat on the shoulder. The Doctor was looking out the windows admiring the majestic Southern California mountains. Scaggz waited five minutes then turned around and said, "Stop the bullshit or I will kill you right here! Who are you?"

"Yah, I tell you already, you know that I am Jurgen Weislangwolf."

"Stop!" shouted Scaggz. "Tell me what is going on or those mountains you are looking at will absolutely be the last thing you see."

"Ahh, OK, it is like this. I am Number One," said the Doctor.

"None of that 'I am the best guitarist' bullshit you tell me. I know the Doctor better than anyone else, and that playing I heard today was not the Doctor. The Doctor loves to drive and would have not only taken my offer to drive but asked himself to drive. Finally, the Doctor is never so complimentary."

"Achh, yah, it is true, I am not the real Doctor. He had me und another made—he was cloned. I am clone Number One. Look here behind my ear, do you see this number here?" asked Number One. "They call me the Complimentary Doctor because I am nicer than the real Doctor."

"See I knew! I know the Doctor. Why is he not here?"

"Yah, you see, he is getting lazy. He did not want to come for only this one day. He has been using us in Austria to play these small bars, so he can bring in money for Bea und his kids. I hate it! I hate playing the guitar! I don't like this life. I am glad I am not on that plane heading back. You rescued me, Scaggz."

Jimmy could not speak. He tried and nothing came out. He took a sip of his water and tried again. "How is it that you can play so well that the fans are fooled, and you know everything that he knows?"

"Well, you see, when we were born, we were born as adults in a lab, und our memories are all the Doctor's up to that point. Everything he knows und remembered, we are both the same. But our personalities from that day on have grown away from the Doctor's. He controls us, und Doctor Spiers must give us these shots to keep us alive. If we do not get these shots, we will die."

"How long until you need the shot?" inquired Scaggz.

"Achh, every two weeks. But for me it is OK, I am not wanting this life of music. I hate it. He created us to be his slaves. I just like to work out. We cannot eat food. It's these shots. Our digestive systems are not fully developed; it was a defect in the process that Doctor Spiers created. We can smell, und food smells so good. But he says if we eat food, there is no place for the food to digest und it would just rot in our bodies, und we will die. But drink we can und must. We have stomachs but that is it."

"What else is different between you and the Doctor?" asked Scaggz.

"We have nothing that identifies us with him. See my fingers, no fingerprints, und my teeth, look, they are fake. Our eyes are gray, we must wear these blue contacts so we look the same. Und we have no hair on our entire bodies. I wear this wig that is made from hair collected from the local hairdressers, then dyed und cut to look like his. Then his stage wig over it. But not his real stage wig, he never parts with that. He found me this one on the internet; it is so itchy, but he says I must wear it. This is all imperfections that happened when we were created. We are just an empty shell with his wisdom. It's horrible!"

Jimmy got out of the car and needed air as he heard all of this. Scaggz, realizing that Number One would die without that shot, made his plan more perfect. "Jimmy, get back in here, we need to go!"

"Where are we going?" asked Number One.

"To our old friend, Pointy. You can stay with him in Palm Springs," answered Scaggz.

"Yah, this is good. Palm Springs is a good place for me to die."

Chapter 3

Sludge was the lead guitarist and main songwriter in the band Petunia and Amo. They quickly jetted to the forefront of the hard rock scene in the early nineties. Sludge, whose real name is Omar Dorfman, is known for his heavy blues-inspired playing and hugely famous riffs; some of the biggest anthems of their time were from his inspiration alone.

Sludge had the perfect rock-and-roll image. His long, curly blonde hair was always up in a ponytail until showtime, when he let his hair down and transformed into his rock star personality. Always wearing jeans and a black tee on stage, the women loved him and the men wished they were him. With his famous double-billed baseball cap, he would march around the stage in total control. Sludge's Lid, as it was known, had two fronts—he would flip the cap around and always had a different message on the other side. When his fans saw him flip the cap around, they went nuts. His confidence on the stage showed and the fans ate it up. His black T-shirts were the same, always showing a message. His clothing line was now earning him as much as his music career.

Fans would attend the concerts wearing his caps and T-shirts. They were now sold at most department stores and would have one of his coined phrases from interviews over the years printed on them. The most popular ones were *I'm going to write a song about you*; *Take me to the bar and buy me a drink; That guy floats his own balloon; Not every fish leads the school;* and his biggest seller, *I'm Sludge, what have you done?*

One could not listen to a radio station for more than a half hour without hearing one of Petunia and Amo's biggest hits. They were like a machine, having only recorded three albums before the band split, but they all went to number one in the US and many other countries around the world.

Unfortunately, the band broke up after singer Marco Amo decided that it was him and not Sludge who made the band great. Marco had been on a drinking binge that lasted four months and midway through announced that he was leaving the band and taking the name with him. His band mates sued him for the name rights and it was determined after a two-year legal battle that they could continue without Marco, but the band would have to be called Sludge's Petunia and Amo.

While the lawsuit was going on, Sludge recorded a solo album that was filled with great riffs and different guest stars performing on the drums and vocals. He called the band Sludge from Hell. He toured large arenas with a band and three of the vocalists from the album. It was a huge success. The singers all took a long break from their careers to perform on this tour. The two-month tour stretched into a two-year marathon that toured the world three times.

After the tour, Sludge decided that he would take a break, and after a year he recorded a second album just called *Sludge*. He did the singing himself, and it was a more bluesy album with only a drummer and a bass player. The following tour was a mess. Sludge was booked in arenas that were empty. Not even a quarter filled. After only five shows, the tour was canceled and rescheduled into smaller venues. When the dust settled, he had only half the dates in mid-sized theaters and larger clubs.

Marco Amo, after a couple of years, resurrected Petunia and Amo with a band of complete unknown musicians and was touring stadiums and arenas worldwide. Fans knew it wasn't Sludge, but hell, it was still Petunia and Amo.

Sludge needed a comeback album after his disastrous *Sludge* album. He moved back to his hometown of Redondo Beach, CA, and after taking another year off, he got married. A year later his son was born. Not wanting to leave his wife and newborn, he didn't tour for six years. During this downtime, he wrote five albums-worth of material and entered the studio to record the follow up to *Sludge*.

The result was thirteen newly recorded songs that were somewhere in between Petunia and Amo and a more modern sound. He found the perfect singer: Nick Baronson from the Portland-based band Feculence. Nick had the range Sludge only dreamed of and took these new songs to the next level. The new band was called Sludge's Hollow and the album was just released with rave reviews worldwide. Nick had touring obligations with Feculence in Europe and Japan, which left Sludge with time before he could take Sludge's Hollow on the road.

Sludge, being a huge fan of the Doctor, attended the press conference on Redondo Beach. The Doctor was Sludge's biggest influence growing up, and the first solo he mastered was "Slap the Virgin" from the Doctor's first band the Centipedes. He had seen the Doctor perform a half-dozen times with the Centipedes back in the eighties, but never had the chance to meet him. Their paths crossed multiple times, but never close enough for an encounter. They played the same festival eight years ago, when Sludge played with Sludge from Hell, but on different days. Sludge's dream was to have the Doctor jam with him on "Slap the Virgin." He had had his band rehearse that song just for the festival, but when he arrived was informed that the Doctor had performed the day before and was already on his way back home. He was disappointed at not being able to see the Doctor that day, but now sitting right there on the other side of this bar was the Doctor's manager. What luck! Hoping that the Doctor would not be too far away, Sludge approached Jeb and Neusy.

Sludge saw Jeb answer his phone and decided to wait to introduce himself. Jeb looked at his phone and showed Neusy that the Doctor was calling.

"Shouldn't he be on his flight home?" asked Neusy.

"Yes," said Jeb, annoyed, and then into his phone, "Jurgen, what's going on?"

"Achh," said the Doctor. "My man is not on his flight. What happened?"

"WHAT?" screamed Jeb, and half the bar looked at him, including Sludge. "Your man, you mean you missed your flight!" Jeb got up off his seat at the bar and walked outside.

Neusy watched the interaction until Jeb was outside. He knew Jeb would come in fuming. Just to what degree was his concern. He continued to drink his Northern California Sweet Potato IPA. Strange named beer, he thought, and the orange tint was odd, but it tasted good. He called the bartender over and said, "I'll have another one of these, and my friend, whatever he was drinking, another as well."

The bartender said, "He was drinking the Goat Milk Lager. I'll bring them right over." When he brought the beers he said, "These beers are on that guy over there with his hair in the ponytail."

"That's great, thanks!" said Neusy. "Why is he buying us beers?"

"I guess he likes you. That's Sludge, from Petunia and Amo."

"Right on," said Neusy as Jeb re-entered the bar and made his way back to where Neusy was sitting. "I thought you might need that beer, buddy."

"Need a beer. I need ten. You're never going to believe what Jurgen just told me."

"I'll believe anything you tell me."

"He claims that was not him today, but a look-alike, a clone is what he called it. Mostly human. He said this clone did not board his flight home."

Neusy signaled the bartender, indicating that they needed another beer each. "What are you talking about? I watched him play, talked to him, and we dropped him at the airport."

"Yup, but you noticed something was off. He told me that it is not perfected, and each clone has their own personality. He called that thing Number One. There are two of them, apparently, and he has been using them to earn money playing gigs."

"How is this even possible?" asked Neusy.

"This is the part that got me yelling. You're not going to like this either, but Lord Doctor Simon Spiers has been in Salzburg over the last three months. It started when Jurgen wanted his special vitamin shots, and then he explained he had developed this procedure and successfully cloned a pig. Jurgen insisted he try it on himself."

"What? The Doctor's doctor is back? I thought he was out of the picture forever since what happened in the past."

"HE IS FUCKING BACK!" screamed out Jeb.

"Shit, the last time I saw him, he gave me that vitamin shot and my skin turned green for a week."

"Exactly!" said Jeb. "So, we now have that to deal with."

"That's fucked up!" replied Neusy. "By the way, Sludge is here, and he bought us a beer."

"Sludge? What is he doing here?" asked Jeb. He saw Sludge approaching and added, "I see him; he's walking over."

"Hi guys," said Sludge and he shook their hands. "I saw you sitting here and was hoping that the Doctor was somewhere around. I saw his press conference. Man, he can play."

Jeb looked at Neusy as he shook Sludge's hand; Neusy gave him the don't-say-a-fucking-word look. Jeb said, "He flew back to Austria already. How did you know that we worked for the Doctor?"

"Yeah man, I saw you guys on the boat with my binoculars. I was hoping to meet him. I am a huge fan of his playing."

"He will be back in a couple of months; you should come out. I'll give you all my contact info."

"Great, I would love to jam with him. I have a new album that was just released. Maybe I can play on a couple of his shows before our tour. I could even have my band open for him. That would be an honor."

"Let's stay in touch. I'll talk to our booking agent, maybe we can get a couple of shows in. It may help us a little."

They took pictures together and Sludge bought another round and then said, "I got to get home. Please don't post any of those pics online. I didn't tell my wife I was coming out here."

They agreed and, with that, Sludge left the bar.

Chapter 4

Lilith Marks lived in an 8,700 square-foot home situated up against Mount San Jacinto in Palm Springs. Her nine-acre property was meticulously cared for and highlighted her hobby of gardening. The bushes in her yard were trimmed on a weekly basis to heighten the experience. She had full-time landscapers tending to the lawn and property daily. Lilith's contribution, though she takes credit for the entire yard, was the raised flower beds of her patio behind her home.

Pointy enjoyed his days watching the news, smoking weed, and drinking beers with the other retired roadies. He'd often be seen walking in circles admiring the grounds. He took two daily walks: one in the morning and one precisely at 4:00 pm. Regardless of what he's doing, he would stop, not say a word, take his walker that helped him walk straight and walk out into the yard for exactly half an hour. He would leave the walker on the patio and walk circles the entire time. He enjoyed his retirement immensely with no worries and all the food he could want.

Scaggz rang the doorbell and Lilith opened the door with her two Dobermans by her side. She immediately recognized Scaggz from his visits. "Scaggz, wow, it's been a long time! You brought your brother as well. Hi Jimmy, come on in, who is this with you?"

"This is Number One, he needs a place to stay for a max of two weeks," replied Scaggz.

"Welcome, come on in, fellas. You know that any touring professional is welcome here. Nice to meet you, Number One."

"This is a very nice home," said Number One. "Perfect for my last few days. I love your dogs. This will be much nicer than being forced to play guitar."

Confused by what she was hearing, Lilith said, "Pointy is outside, he will be happy to see you, Scaggz."

As they walked past Lilith and into the large living room, they could see Pointy through the window walking his circles in the backyard. When they walked outside, Pointy was at the far side of his circle. "Scaggz, my boy, wait, I will get around to you in a minute."

They all watched as Pointy slowly completed the circumference of his walk. "Pointy," said Scaggz, "it's great to see you."

"Yes, Scaggz, thanks for visiting. Doctor, it's wonderful to see you again," said Pointy to Number One.

Scaggz then informed him, "This is not exactly the Doctor. It is his Number One clone. He is mostly human, but does not eat, as he has no digestive system. It is because of this that he only has a short time to live."

"That's right," said Number One. "I am far away from where I was created, und since my creator is not here to give me nutrient shots, I will die. But it is OK. I am happy to be here. These gardens are beautiful. I hate playing the guitar, can you believe that? I can play OK, but man, I am just tired of playing. Pointy, it is nice to meet you. I have all these memories of you. I feel bad that you lost your foot the way that you did. Can I do some of the gardening out here, Lilith? I can work out here in the yard. This is perfect. Thank you, Scaggz, for helping me escape, und soon I'll be out of my misery."

The four of them were looking at Number One. Although Scaggz was now feeling bad for him, he knew this was the best. There cannot be more Doctors walking around, certainly not performing. This would ruin the plan.

Pointy said, "He is a talkative one, isn't he?"

"Well, I am going back in, you're welcome to stay here as well if you like, Scaggz," said Lilith.

"Can I get your Wi-Fi code? Yes, we will stay a few days," said Scaggz.

Sitting in a coffee shop, Scaggz ordered another coffee brewed with beans from India. He picked up the pen sitting on the table for the last hour and began to write his message to deliver to FBI agents Sparrow and Crow.

Agents, it was a pleasure seeing you on the beach last week. It has been a while since seeing you on the Jurgen Weislangwolf tour last year. Thanks for the selfie on the beach at the press conference! I want to make myself clear. I am not crazy. Sometimes things just need to be set right.

You see the average person is at their best right now. Privileged and entitled to everything without working to get there. And why not, they were born into a society that is given everything and contented with being mediocre. This is the highest level they will achieve in life. Never will they aspire to anything greater or experience anything new from where they currently are. They can only see from their four walls inward without any desire to expand on their bubble. Sure, they may get a new job or a raise, purchase a larger home or a new vehicle, but it is just a continuation to their current life, an extension of the status quo they have trapped themselves within.

Like a mouse in a cage. Food, water, a place to shit, and a wheel that they run on and return to the exact spot where they started. Not knowing anything else exists, they continue the grind and are miserable, but content being miserable since their knowledge and desire are lacking. The mouse sees its whole existence in this cage, seeing past the enclosure, but not paying any attention or ambition to excel. Round and round they go, day after day, until the day they die. It is a sad existence.

The only difference that people have compared to this mouse is that people possess the intelligence and, when motivated by something other than self-worship and greed, have the ability that could aspire them to pursue the difference from a meaningless life to one of intellectual and spiritual growth. Leading them to another plane of happiness and awareness that the majority of people cannot comprehend. An existence that is not force fed by society, and the discovery that the world is an immense and diversified destination, waiting to be explored and appreciated.

Discovering the shallow, empty selfishness of people is an eye-opening experience. From the daily self-proclamation of uninspired achievements, to placing children on pedestals for reaching ordinary plateaus reached by the masses. Inferior and ordinary has become the new great. It even starts prior to a child's birth, with the gender reveal parties, and then boasting how smart one's baby is for doing nothing more than sucking on a tit and shitting themselves. Later receiving praise and awards for participation, not motivating more than just existing to be included in society's version of remarkable, leading children to depression and confusion when they become adults. It would be smarter to schedule a gender reveal party for the child's eighteenth birthday, so they can reveal what gender they strive to be after not figuring out life and being an adult.

Road rage incidences to mass shootings and the continued hatred of one another have become derivative of a society that is lacking any motivation to transcend the ugliness of a civilization that has no aspirations other than complacency. Yet the association of a society is required by most as they do not have the intelligence or strength to survive without the groundwork supporting the emptiness of their lives. Self-righteousness and then being tainted by the same society that inflated their ego is the proof that they are not more than average. Stuck in that cage going round and round on that wheel that they call life, losing just a little more with each rotation.

Society will not miss any of the people that were purged last year. I will see you on the next rotation. Remember I am always watching.

Sincerely,

Guitarman SJ

The Executioner

Scaggz, being happy with his letter, folded it and put it in an envelope ready to deliver. In another week he and Jimmy would leave town, and Jimmy would reinvent himself as Austrian bass player Heinz Beckenschultz.

Using the Wi-Fi connection at Barrel Brewers, he began to ponder ideas on how to join the Doctor on his Indian tour. Scaggz ordered another large coffee, more Indian beans to help inspire him to create the perfect plan. He perused websites about Indian culture to absorb the ways of Indian life. But most importantly he found a site that would teach him basic Hindi in less than a month. Although most Indians could speak English, he wanted to look and sound Indian in order to blend in. To do this he would have to create his greatest disguise to date.

He opened a page of popular Indian names. "Ranesh Kumar? Nah… Arjun Gupta?" he mumbled. People at the nearby tables looked up at him, and a mother with her two children in a stroller immediately walked out.

He started surfing sites about India tourism to acquaint himself with places he might visit. He realized that his skin was too light. He needed to find a way to darken his skin. The mountain beaver had that oily coat, and together with its blood he could create a dye. But there are no mountain beavers in Palm Springs. He would need to color his hair too and grow a decent beard. He searched the web for tanning products and found a few suitable brands.

Tanover—The apply once every four to seven days, depending on skin type, climate, and atmospheric condition tanning spray. Also available in pocket-sized spray bottles. One large bottle could last up to two months, said the website. He ordered the large bottle and two pocket-sized bottles for emergency touch ups and had them shipped to Lilith's house.

Since most young Indians go casual these days, jeans and sneakers should be fine. Maybe some colorful tie-dyed shirts would be good. But Scaggz really wanted something to go over the top, something unique. "Turban!" he shouted, and more people stood and walked out of Barrel Brewers.

Looking at websites for turbans, he found most of the sites taught one how to wrap the cloth around the head. Scaggz wanted something more convenient. He kept searching and found the Contemporary Turban. They had pre-rolled turbans made to order to fit your individual head size. They offered over fifty colors and patterns, and even customized prints. One could upload pictures of family members to have printed on the front.

He had to get busy with his plans as the Doctor's tour was scheduled to begin in less than one month. He decided that Jeetu Kapoor would be his name, meaning *Always a winner!*, because Johnny Scaggz is a winner.

Now to contact the Doctor's management. He sent Jeb an email.

Hello, my name is Jeetu Kapoor. I am Indian and can be of great service to the Doctor on his first trip to India. I will be his driver, translator, whatever that is needed from me. I am familiar with all the famous places of interest and can speak Hindi. I am willing to work for only $100 a week, plus my gas and hotel room. Please reply to me at your earliest convenience.

Sincerely,
Jeetu Kapoor.

After sending Jeb the email, Scaggz found the website of his old hang out bar, and just as he thought, it was open mic night at the Drenched Hog. It has been a couple of years since he was a regular, and it wasn't long after he started playing open mic nights that he started dating bartender Sylvia Bass. She was beautiful: dark skin, brown wavy hair, hazel eyes that melted his soul, with a body that was muscular with all the right curves. He fell in love. Many nights after closing they would just sit on the patio of the Drenched Hog and talk, then they would make love in his VW Kombi. In the beginning, they could only see each other on the five days a week that she worked. She had to spend some time with her kids. But then soon, even on those days, they would find time to see each other. They had plans to move away, take her kids, and live on the coast. She would leave her husband, a drunk that worked as a manager at a local hotel. She watched as he would have to drink a six pack just to leave the house and go to work. They had slept in different rooms for years. She never took his last name of Bastardo but instead kept her birth name of Bass, and Kevin Bastardo always held that against her.

Kevin got suspicious and questioned her numerous times, in which she denied seeing anyone. One day she called in sick to work and spent the day with Scaggz. Her husband stopped in at the bar but she was not there. Her car was there but she was not. She was at the beach with Scaggz. Sylvia went home that night and the next day informed Scaggz that Kevin installed a tracking app on her phone.

Scaggz pleaded with Sylvia to leave, and she just kept telling him that she couldn't. "Why not? Tell him it's over," said Scaggz at the time.

Her response was always the same: "This is just the way it is. I have to please him and do what he says."

"Is he hitting you? Threatening you? Because if he is, I will kill him!" The answer was always no. Scaggz had to only see her when she worked. He would sit at the bar, and she would leave when her shift was over. Kevin was always waiting for her in the parking lot to drive her home.

On the last night that Scaggz saw Sylvia, she said, "I can't see you anymore. Kevin won't allow it. He's watching everything now. He signs into all my apps. He is tracking everything I do."

"Just leave him already," said Scaggz in the parking lot of the Drenched Hog that night after her shift.

Just as he said that, Kevin walked up to him and said, "I don't know what she sees in you, but we are happily married and you are ruining my life. I need you to leave."

Scaggz, not knowing what to do, just stood there in the rain as they drove away together, his heart broken. That was then, before he realized that society consists of a bunch of non-appreciative underachievers. A year later his attitude changed after he killed a man that was screaming at him because his Kombi was parked too close to his Subaru. Scaggz got out of his Kombi with his blue Stratocaster and, yielding it like an ax, split the man's head open, then stuffed him in the trunk of the Subaru.

Neusy read the final words Jeb had just completed. The two sat in Neusy's home in Northern California; finally they had their book complete. Those last words staring them in the face. It had taken a long time to write the description of events that the two experienced on the road as touring professionals. Their last tour, canceled mid-way through due to being stalked by a killer. Death followed them on the road from town to town. This was a blessing for the pair as it gave them additional time to complete their book. Now they could finally turn in their manuscript.

Jeb was approached a few years ago by a literary agent at one of the concerts he was working. After several beers together and listening to Jeb's stories, the agent asked Jeb if he was interested in authoring a book of his stories. People would pay to hear this rarely revealed inside look at touring.

Jeb agreed, only if it would be together with his friend and touring associate Neusy. He had equally great versions of the events. He and Neusy have been touring the music scene for most of their lives. They met fourteen years ago and have toured together ever since. Their partnership on the road is one rarely seen in the industry. They can jump any hurdle, which is always put to the test with the Doctor, Jurgen Weislangwolf. The agent agreed and they began writing their stories.

"You really nailed it with those closing words. We see these people on the road, the fans. Mostly annoying, yet they make good stories," said Neusy.

"Exactly! I wanted to have the readers get a glimpse of what we see when it comes to the fans. I will submit this in the morning. It was fun writing this with you. Your take on some of what I remember is amazing."

"Thanks, Jeb, I have a surprise for you. I bought these last year and waited to open them. Now I am glad." Neusy had what looked like two small bottles of wine but were in fact beer in a corked bottle. 9.3% alcohol. "I bought these when they were released. Extremely limited, NC Brewery's Elephant Nut Brown Barley Wine." Neusy opened one bottle and poured them each a small glass. The two clinked glasses and drank in silence, enjoying the malty goodness of this once-only brewed masterpiece.

Neusy opened the second bottle while Jeb read his emails. "Looks like we have a Mr. Jeetu Kapoor who wants to be our guide and driver in India. We will need a driver, so this is perfect."

Chapter 5

Up on stage of the Drowned Hog, Scaggz was in his element. His ability on the guitar was well above average due to all his touring and lessons with the Doctor. He started with ZZ Top's "Sharp Dressed Man" with the house band, and everyone came inside from the smoking patio to see who was playing. When the song ended, he turned to the band and said, "I need you to keep up on this one." He then played the Centipedes classic "Slap the Virgin." After the solo in the song, which he performed note for note, he signaled to the band to stop. He played a solo that started out as a medley of songs from the Centipedes, then arpeggios, and a pull-off run that left the people in a daze. When he was finished, he signaled to the band to start again. He sang the last verse, then ended the song with a thunderous push on his tremolo bar that awakened everyone from their daze.

He left the stage with the patrons wondering why they all dropped their drinks. With the floor littered with broken bottles and glasses, Scaggz made his way to the bar on the side of the room, perpendicular to the stage. The wooded decor was badly worn but had that played in feel. Scaggz sat at the bar and Sylvia walked over to him, opening a beer so as not to look suspicious. "What are you doing here? My husband comes around all the time and watches me. I never know when he is here, he's always hiding."

"I don't care about that guy. Tell me the truth, has he hit you?"

"No!"

"Threaten you? I want to know. The way you live is not right!"

"It's just what I have to do," said Sylvia.

"I don't get it, are you suddenly happy?"

"It has nothing to do with that. I just have to pretend for now that all is OK. I will make my move one day. But he watches everything that I do."

Scaggz chugged his beer. Sylvia handed him another and walked away to tend to her bar. On the stage was a duo trying to play the blues. Scaggz watched the room. No sign of Kevin. He walked the room with his guitar slung over his shoulder and beer in one hand. Stepping on broken pieces of glass, he made his way back to the bar. His previous stool was taken but he found one closer to the front door.

He sat down and finished his beer. Sylvia took a step towards him with another beer, then stopped and handed the beer to the unexpected patron in front of her. Scaggz felt a hand on his shoulder. He turned his head and there was Kevin who immediately said, "Why are you here?"

"It's open mic night and I'm in town. Look, I brought my guitar."

"I told you to leave my wife alone. She is totally happy with me. She loves me very much. We are perfect together."

"Perfect? I guess if she is happy being married to a drunk. Go away, I want to drink another beer," said Scaggz.

The grip on Scaggz's shoulder became tighter. Scaggz looked at the hand on his shoulder as Kevin said, "You should be careful. There is a lot of broken glass on the floor. Big pieces of bottles with jagged, sharp edges that could be dangerous. I think it is best that you leave."

"I see," said Scaggz. He stood up and Kevin stepped back, expecting that Scaggz would take a swing at him, but instead he said, "OK, whatever you want. Remember, this is your wish, I cannot help you once I leave."

Kevin, confused by what he just heard, said, "I don't need your help."

As Scaggz walked away he said, "Oh! I think you'll change your mind, but it'll be too late." Scaggz walked out to his VW and waited. He waited for an hour. It was now midnight, but he continued to wait. Finally, at a few minutes before one, Kevin walked out of the bar and scanned the parking lot. He did not know what he was looking for but was content that Scaggz was nowhere to be seen. He must have taken the warning seriously.

Kevin walked to his blue Kia sedan and opened the door. He had one leg in the car when—BAM!—the blue Strat came down on his head. Not hard enough to cause damage, but enough to lay him out on the ground. Scaggz had become proficient in the art wielding the Strat as a weapon. The difference between stunning a victim and killing a victim was just a flick of his wrist.

He bent over and removed Kevin's cell phone from his pants pocket and threw it into the car on the passenger seat. He lifted Kevin, put him in the trunk, and tended to his limbs.

Kevin woke up five minutes later disoriented in the darkness of the trunk. He tried to move his hands and found that they were duct taped to his legs and he could not move at all. He tried to yell, but the tape on his mouth prevented any intelligent sounds from emitting out of his head. The car was moving quickly; he was getting tossed around the trunk.

Scaggz drove to the farthest part of town that he could where there were still buildings. He found a business park at the edge of the desert and, what luck, one of the buildings was boarded up. He pulled around the back of the building and parked the car in the center of the lot away from any potential daytime shadows. He checked Kevin's cell phone, which was almost fully charged, and receiving signal. He threw it back on the front seat and walked around to the back of the car.

When Scaggz opened the trunk Kevin was squirming, trying to wiggle out. Scaggz put his foot up over the ledge onto Kevin's chest and Kevin's eyes opened wide. He now realized what was happening. Scaggz said, "You should have asked for my help when I offered, but now I am afraid your life depends on whether Sylvia actually cares about you. You see, we are way out here at the edge of the desert. This building that you see behind me, well, it appears vacant and looks like no one has been here in a while from the overgrown bushes and trees over there." Scaggz used his thumb to indicate where he was referring to. Kevin's eyes moved from Scaggz to the trees and his eyes closed.

Kevin tried hard to push up with his chest, but Scaggz had him pinned with no chance of any movement. "Don't worry, I parked you far enough away from those trees so they won't interfere with your fate. So, as I was saying, Sylvia will wait for you after work, and you will not be there. She'll probably think that you went somewhere and got drunk. Then she'll find a way home. Maybe a taxi, or maybe I will drive her. But that is irrelevant to your situation. Then she will go to sleep, and in the morning when she wakes, guess what?"

Kevin's eyes looked directly at Scaggz as he mumbled something that Scaggz could not understand.

"That's right! You guessed it. You still will not be home. So here is where you better hope that she cares that you come home at all. About the time she wakes, the sun will have been out for…I don't know…a few hours, depending on when she wakes. Maybe I'll keep her up a little later, if you know what I mean. That may help things along in the morning. So…the sun will bake your car and inside the trunk with the desert sun. I am guessing the temperature will get to 150 to 160 degrees. So, without water, you may make it through the day, but it's a gamble."

Kevin started to shake violently, screaming behind the tape across his mouth. Scaggz raised the Strat and Kevin became still. "Exactly. If you don't stop that shit, I will have to hit your head again, but this time a little harder. My guess is that with a skull that is bleeding, possibly internally as well as externally, that you will not survive that long in that trunk. So… When Sylvia wakes up and you are not home…will she care enough to call the police? Or will she just think that you are an asshole and, as always, drunk somewhere? Don't worry, I checked your phone, you must have charged it before we had our chat at the bar. The good news for you is that if she does call the police that they will find you here, as I left your phone's location on. I know what you're thinking. What if they think the car is abandoned and don't check the trunk? That is smart thinking. But this is where you can help yourself. Do you save your energy so that you can make some sounds back here and kick the side and save yourself, or do you somehow try to free yourself and dehydrate that much quicker? Because from what I'm looking at, there's no way you're getting loose from that duct tape. I used a whole roll, so it is quite the situation you are in.

"Oh, I almost forgot, if you are rescued, there are two things." Kevin closed his eyes, so Scaggz pushed down harder with his foot. "This is important so listen. One is that if your wife cares enough to call the police in the morning, you treat her as if she were the only woman on this planet. You work hard and you provide for her, no more drinking. If I find out that you *ever* hit her, I will find you and no one will ever know where you disappeared to… The second thing, and this is equally important, is that you never mention my name regarding this arrangement we have here. When they ask for a description, you say that you got drunk and that you threatened these two guys. One looked like guitarist, Doctor Jurgen Weislangwolf, but he had no hair, and the other was wearing a Sheriff's uniform."

Scaggz removed his foot from the trunk and, with Kevin's eyes pleading *stop*, he closed the trunk. He hit the top and said, "OK, so that does it. I hope you are comfy, because it will be some time before this is open again." Scaggz walked away and could hear Kevin in the trunk kicking. He walked back to the intersection outside the business park and then summoned a Lyft to return him to the Drenched Hog.

A half hour later he arrived at The Drenched Hog and peered inside. He could see Sylvia still working, the room had mostly emptied out. He smiled and walked away back to his van.

Chapter 6

"Why do we have to drive all the way to Minnesota? I could just reappear here in California. It seems like a long, long drive," said Jimmy as he sat in Lilith's living room with Scaggz. They were watching Pointy through the window walk his circles with Number One.

"We've gone over this already. They think that you're Heinz, the Austrian bass player that was abducted at the end of the last tour. It is better for you to show back up in Minnesota. Remember…you managed to escape. You were held in a basement, but you have no clue where. You then walk into a local store and tell them to call the police. It is very important that they believe you," said Scaggz.

"What about my Austrian passport? I will need to go back to Austria since the Doctor's North American tour is still a month away."

"You left that on the bus. I'm sure the FBI have that now. Ask them when they come to talk with you. But it is important that you get that back. It's no longer evidence if you're alive and well. But it is important that they do not contact the Austrian Embassy for a new one since it's a fake."

"OK, but I'm eating my food along the way. Broccoli and real food. I'm not eating that shit that you catch in the neighborhoods. I have eaten that for months. I like it here. They have tasty food here. You missed it last night, but Lilith brought in Huang's Wings. I haven't eaten this good in months. I can recognize everything on my plate. Could I just stay here a while?" pleaded Jimmy.

"We must stick to the plan. I leave for India in a week from Chicago. We leave in two days. You better enjoy the food here."

Outside, Number One was getting weaker on each revolution of the circle Pointy was walking, until Pointy lapped him. Pointy put his arm around Number One and brought him to a chair. He noticed that his once muscular body was now very skinny. "My friend, are you OK? You are half the size you were a week ago," he said.

"Without the nutrient shots, this body feeds upon itself. I will eventually be nothing left but this skin und bones that were all created in a lab. I look the same as everyone else, but I was not born like you. I was created in a lab. This body was formed by using chemical reactions. My mass is not the same. Dr. Spiers said that if we ever separated und we could not get shots that we should find a place to die. He said it would not be painful since we do not have a real nervous system. He said that we will shrivel up und die. Our bodies, because of the mass, would decompose quickly. Within weeks," said Number One.

"Scaggz!" shouted Pointy.

Scaggz and Jimmy came running out into the back. "What is it, Pointy?"

"Your man here is not doing well."

"Already?" asked Scaggz. "You said a couple of weeks. Why so quick?"

"My last shot was about ten days ago. I was supposed to go back last week, but you were so kind as to rescue me."

Scaggz looked at Number One, who was smaller than only two hours ago. Walking with Pointy burned up most of the remainder of his stored energy. Number One filled Scaggz in with the info he just revealed to Pointy. Scaggz figured that he only had a day or two left. He would wait until Number One died, then take what was left and bury him in the desert when leaving town. "This Dr. Spiers cannot continue this cloning. I will see to this," declared Scaggz.

The next morning, Scaggz combed his freshly dyed hair along with his beard. Both looked great and, just as the box promised, intense black. He trimmed the beard in a manner that he discovered online was popular in India. He pulled up several sites on his laptop and compared it to his own beard. Perfect! He opened the box of Tanover that had arrived the day before and applied it to all parts of his exposed skin, careful to make sure he got way under the shirt line and across his mid-section, just in case those areas became exposed.

Happy with his look, he took his blue turban out of the box and placed it on his head. He stared in the mirror for five minutes, looking at himself from every angle. "Jeetu, indeed, you are born," he said to the image staring back at him.

He went downstairs to Pointy's room to check in on Number One before he left. When he entered the room, Pointy screamed and said, "What do you want? How did you get in here? LILITH! I need help!"

"Relax, Pointy, it is me, Scaggz. I am in a disguise."

"Scaggz? Shit, you had me scared. Number One hasn't gotten out of that chair all morning."

Scaggz looked over at Number One, who was slumped over in the chair. He didn't have enough energy to look up. Scaggz saw his face, which was now unrecognizable from when he first met Number One. His head was the size of large grapefruit and his body looked as if he would slide right out of the clothes he still had on. This made Scaggz angry that someone would be this cruel and create these living organisms—human in form and had the thought process to know their eventual fate. "I have to run some errands; I will be back this evening."

On his way out, he stopped in the kitchen where Jimmy was steaming broccoli. Scaggz came in and opened the steamer. "Whoa, buddy, get your own broccoli! That's mine!" said Jimmy.

"Jimmy, I have a few things to do, I will see you later."

"Johnny? I couldn't tell. You look totally different."

"That's the idea! My name is Jeetu Kapoor. I will see you later, my kind sir."

"It's too bad I'm not going to India with you. I like you like that."

Scaggz walked out and drove away in the VW Kombi.

Three hours later, Scaggz arrived at the FBI building in Los Angeles. He parked far enough away that his vehicle would not be on any of their security cameras. He entered the lobby and put the envelope and the contents of his pockets through the X-ray machine, then proceeded to walk through the metal detector. Security, being content that he did not pose a threat, told him to go the reception area around the corner.

Scaggz did what he was told and was in the main lobby of the FBI building. Above him was the second floor, which looked down on him with its balcony that was connected by a set of stairs. In front of him was a second security desk with two men behind the counter. One was busy looking at the monitors while the second one said, "How can I help you?"

"Oh yes, my fine friend, I was instructed to deliver this to agents Sparrow and Crow. Are they here, please?" said Scaggz, now fully into his Jeetu character.

"Yes, they are here, and I will make sure they get your delivery."

"No no, my friend. The delivery instructions were quite clear. I must put this directly in their hands."

"Please take a seat over there. I will call them and let them know." The man motioned to his left and picked up the phone. He pressed a couple of buttons, then after a moment said, "Agent Sparrow, there is a man here with a delivery for you and Agent Crow." Then to Scaggz he said, "They will be down in a few minutes."

"That is so kind of you, sir."

Scaggz waited for ten minutes, knowing the entire time that he was on the security cameras and would be on footage that he was sure they would be looking at once he left. This is where the disguise would be tested fully. In India, the agents will not be part of the tour, so the connection would not be made. He sat patiently, confident that his appearance in the building appeared normal.

Ten minutes later, Sparrow and Crow were there right in front of him. Crow said, "What can we do for you? You asked for us?"

"Yes sir, thank you for coming down here. I was instructed by my boss that when I made this delivery that I place it in one of you fine gentleman's hands," said Scaggz, getting more confident in his Jeetu voice.

"What do you have there?" asked Agent Sparrow. "Why could you just not leave it?"

"Well, my fine sir, sometimes when I deliver a package, I can leave it and sometimes I have to be certain that it is delivered right to the person whose name is on the envelope." Scaggz hoped that this made some sort of sense to the agents. He tried to sound like a delivery person.

"OK, well thank you... What is your name?" asked Agent Sparrow.

"My name is Jeetu Kapoor, sir."

"Thank you, Jeetu," said Agent Crow as Scaggz handed him the envelope.

"You both have a good day, my friends," said Scaggz, as he walked away.

Sparrow said, "What a polite guy. We should visit India one day."

"Yes," said Crow, "at least we'd have no Blues Brothers comments there. I doubt they know who they are. We can be ourselves without that bullshit."

"But first, we go to St. Martin after the next Doctor tour. I heard their nude beaches are legendary," said Sparrow as he opened the envelope that had no return address. He held the letter so they both could read it.

Ten minutes later they were sitting in their supervisor's office. He slammed the door and said, "Who the hell is this Guitarman SJ? He calls himself the Executioner?"

"We don't know, sir," said Sparrow. "We were at the Doctor's press conference on the beach. No one there seemed out of place or even the least bit suspicious."

"Yeah, we walked the beach and then went up on the pier. Lots of people talked to us. Nothing," added Crow.

"You guys were on the tour last year; you have no clue at all? No one at all? You did not see anyone that looked familiar at all the shows? This guy killed at how many shows? You were there at most of them. How can this be?"

"Sir, we were both watching every night. Many times, one of us in the back, which we know he entered a couple of times. But nothing. The guy sneaks around undetected, maybe in a disguise, but we didn't see any pattern and he left no clues," said Crow.

"You're telling me that he sneaks around right under your noses?"

"He must be a master of disguise, sir," said Sparrow. The agents looked at each other. Neither of them had the courage to mention Jeetu, but they were both thinking the same thing.

Scaggz decided before he went back to Sylvia's house that he would further test his Jeetu disguise. He stopped at the Drenched Hog for another open mic night. He grabbed his light blue Stratocaster guitar out of the VW and went in. There was a woman on stage singing and playing acoustic guitar. She had a nice voice.

Scaggz found an empty seat at the bar and ordered a beer. Sylvia had no clue who she was serving even when Scaggz said, "Thank you, ma'am." He left his beer and went up front to put his name down on the list for open mic. There were three people ahead of him, so he returned to his seat at the bar.

To his right were two younger guys, one with shoulder-length blonde hair and the other with short black hair, who was taller and wearing a tank top to show off that he works out. As Scaggz sipped his beer, the two kept looking at him and then laughing. Scaggz couldn't hear what they were saying. He finished his beer and Sylvia walked over and said, "Wow, you sure finished that fast. I haven't seen you before in here. My name is Sylvia, let me know if you need anything. What's your name?"

"Hi, beautiful Sylvia, my name is Jeetu. It would please me if you would give me another beer."

"Sure, Jeetu, here you go," she said and walked away.

From his right he heard, "My name is Jeeeetuuu," and then laughter. He looked over at the two, which caused them to laugh some more.

Then one said, "Jeetu, shouldn't you be somewhere cleaning cow pastures?" More laughter.

Scaggz sat quietly, drinking his beer until he heard, "Jeetu, you are next."

As Scaggz approached the stage, he heard the two he left at the bar continue to heckle him. "Get ready folks, we have an ace sitar player coming up next." Scaggz stopped, turned around, and looked at the pair. "Uh oh, it seemed he didn't like that."

Scaggz got up on stage and said to the house band, "Try and keep up, I will play some Judas Priest." Then into the mic, "Hello, my fine people! It is an honor to play for you tonight. I would most certainly like to dedicate this song to my two friends sitting back there at the bar. It is a song called, 'You Got Another Thing Coming.'"

Scaggz played the song as it was recorded on the record. The patrons were rocking to it and, when Scaggz played the solo, they got very loud, clapping their hands. When the song ended, he walked back to the bar and took his seat. He motioned to Sylvia for another beer. The two guys next to him were laughing and the blonde-haired one said, "It is a fine honor to be here at this bar." They both laughed again.

Scaggz ignored them when he saw Kevin walk in. Sylvia had reported him missing. He sat at the end again and handed Sylvia a bouquet of flowers. She smiled and looked like she really appreciated it. He sat down and she handed him a beer. Scaggz could see that he said something, and she took the beer back and handed him a bottle of sparkling water. This pleased him and Scaggz was hoping for Kevin's new lease on life to last.

He took a sip of his beer when tall guy said to him, "It is my honor to tell you that I must go take a piss. I most certainly advise you not to be here when I get back."

The blonde-haired man laughed and said, "Bro, I gotta go too," and joined his friend.

Scaggz paid his tab and said, "Sylvia, it was an honor to meet you." He walked to the men's room, where his bar mates were both at the urinals with their backs to the door. The Strat was up high over his head then BAM, BAM. The blonde-haired man fell into the urinal and tall guy fell forward, hit his head on the wall, and fell backwards. While they were both out cold, Scaggz removed their clothes and put them in a sexual position with tall guy bent over the blonde-haired man.

He exited the bathroom and, as he walked past the bar, he said to Sylvia, "Excuse me, but there are two men having sex on the floor of the men's room." Sylvia looked at him shocked and walked out from behind the bar. Scaggz passed her husband, Kevin, at the end of the bar and whispered into his ear, "Very good, you are learning. Remember what it takes to stay out of the trunk."

Kevin turned to see who was speaking to him, but all he could see was Jeetu walking out the door. Scaggz now felt good about his disguise, but the real test would be in India with the Doctor.

Jeetu's first two victims awoke in the men's room with a dozen people standing there looking at them. They were asked to put their clothes back on and were escorted out of the bar by three large, muscular men.

Chapter 7

With the death of clone Number One, Scaggz and Jimmy said their goodbyes to Lilith and Pointy, who said, "It was nice having your friend out in the backyard walking with me. I am sorry he died."

Scaggz hugged his longtime touring mate and retrieved the clone from his bed where he died. Jimmy pulled back the sheet. "Wow," he said, "shit, look at him. What happened? That is disgusting!"

"He said because of the make up of his body that he would decompose quickly, but this is insane," said Scaggz, looking down at the face that was just skin on his recently constructed bones. His body too looked as if someone let all the air out of a balloon. Scaggz put his arm under the clone's head and legs. He picked him up and the body snapped with a loud pop. Scaggz was now holding a body that was folded perfectly in half.

"That's even more disgusting," said Jimmy.

He adjusted his hands to get a grip on the changed mass and picked him up again. Another pop was heard, and the clone was still folded in half, but his legs were bent at the knees and perpendicular to his body with his head bent in the opposite direction resembling the letter T.

Jimmy held his mouth and looked away.

Scaggz tried to straighten out the clone's body, but he was locked in the position. He picked up the body once more. Jimmy gasped, but there was no popping sound. Scaggz loaded the newly formed origami into his VW van, and they were on their way.

"What are we going to do with him? He is creeping me out back there looking up front at us," asked Jimmy.

"We will have to get rid of him quickly before he starts breaking apart. As soon as we get out into the desert a bit, we'll get rid of him."

A half hour later they were far enough out in the hills looking across the valley at the San Jacinto Peak hovering high above Palm Springs. Scaggz found a spot nestled in the mountain surrounded by several rock formations. They exited the VW and Scaggz moved the body to its final resting place. "You're not going to bury him? Just throw him in there?" asked Jimmy.

"He is decomposing very quickly; did you see the dust under his body in the van? He is lighter now already than when I put him in the van."

He moved the branches on a bush at the mouth of a small cave and placed the clone behind the bush just as the clone's neck made a popping sound. As Scaggz put the branches back across the opening, he saw the clone's head rolling down the incline deeper into the cave. He decided it was better not to mention that detail to Jimmy.

After a few hours of sleep outside Salt Lake City and after a freshly caught rabbit on the grill, the brothers arrived in Spearfish, located in the rolling hills of South Dakota. The town was a combination of motorcycle enthusiasts, motorcycle clubbers, vacationers in RVs, and people that have lived their entire lives in Spearfish. With all the woods surrounding the town, Scaggz decided it would be a good place to set up camp after picking up a few items in town. Scaggz, still half looking like Jeetu with his skin now not completely dyed but lighter with blotches of darker and white areas, parked his van in town. He was hoping that his skin would get close to his normal color by the time he had to fly to India, since he now looks nothing like his picture in his passport.

Walking down the street of Spearfish the short distance from his van, he was getting looks from everyone. Bikers eyed him as he walked down the street; older couples stepped out of their RVs, crossing the street to stay away from him; and with Sturgis only twenty minutes up the road, the locals had the attitude that they have seen it all. Scaggz found a store where he could buy batteries for their lights and a case of bottled water. Food would be supplied by whatever the forest was offering.

He exited the store and was walking back to the van when two motorcycles rode past him. Each driver threw a paper fast-food bag, containing trash and a plastic bottle, at him; one hit him in the leg. He watched the bikers, with their ladies on the back screaming like they just scored a touchdown, park three hundred feet up the road at a bar that had other motorcycles parked outside. He picked up the bags and threw them in the trash can on the corner near his van.

Scaggz put his new purchases in the van, along with the two bottles of urine that had fallen out of the bags thrown at him. He cleaned the ketchup and remnants of the bikers' meals off of his leg, and to Jimmy seated in the van, he said, "I have to go back to that hardware store, I just realized I need more supplies."

"Now what, what are you going to do?"

"Teach some rude people to respect the environment." Scaggz walked back to the store garnering the same looks as earlier. He stared everyone down, which made the RVers cross the street more hurriedly to move away from him. He also received a couple of middle fingers from the next wave of bikers passing him by.

He returned to the van with several spools of rope along with duct tape, a water rifle with pump action, and a bag full of items Jimmy could not make out. He opened a chest in the back of the VW and found what he was looking for. He filled the water rifle with the entire bottle of chloroform he had in his chest.

"Do you see those bikes up there?" Jimmy nodded, not wanting to hear anymore as Scaggz said, "I'm going to walk up there. In exactly fifteen minutes, drive the van and park it behind the bikes. When I come out with my new friends, drive up to where we are standing."

"I really don't want to be part of this."

"Don't worry, all you have to do is drive up there, grab this water rifle, and hit them in the chins and their shirts. They will go down right away."

Jimmy sighed and nodded his head in response.

"Don't forget to pump it first."

Scaggz walked up to the bar. He immediately spotted the two bikes that rode past him and entered the bar. The bar was loud; there was music playing and lots of shouting. Two pool tables in the back had half the occupants entertained. Scaggz walked the room until he spotted the two he was looking for. He approached the bar and ordered a beer. He checked the time and waited fifteen minutes, watching his prey. They both were with different women than the ones on the back of their bikes. Just two pricks showing off for women. They would learn proper etiquette.

"Hey guys," said Scaggz to the two bikers at the bar.

The smaller one with a long gray beard said, "Who are you?"

"I was admiring your bikes. I saw you guys ride up."

"You did, huh?" said the smaller one's friend, who was looking down at Scaggz.

"Yeah guys, you have the gold Harley, and you the blue one with the impressive stereo."

"Yup those are our bikes," said the taller one.

"Beautiful machines! How did the tank on the gold bike get that ding? That looks nasty, hope you did not tip the bike. I did that once and my leg is still not the same."

"WHAT?" said the smaller one. "It's not dinged."

"It was when I was looking at it on my way in here."

The small one slammed his beer down on the bar and headed towards the exit with his friend and Scaggz right behind. He kicked the door open and ran to his bike. "What are you talking about? It looks fine!"

"Oh, this is yours? My mistake, I thought the one over there was yours," said Scaggz as the van skidded up next to them. Jimmy released the contents of the water rifle right on target.

The two bikers started to approach the van but fell about three feet short. Scaggz opened the side door and dragged them both inside, secured his two prisoners, then walked around to the driver's side. As Jimmy moved over to the passenger seat Scaggz said, "Nice shooting."

"Where are you taking them?"

"Into the woods. Not sure exactly where, but once we find the location it will be clear."

Scaggz drove the van to the outskirts of town and followed a sign that showed camping sites were in that direction. As he rounded the corner, an RV was stopped above a storm sewer on the opposite side of the street. "What is that smell?" asked Jimmy.

"Do you see that RV up there? Well, they are releasing their wastewater into that storm sewer. Apparently not wanting to pay for the hookup at the camp site."

When the RV pulled away, the VW Kombi van followed. They were back in town at the hardware store. "If those two ever wake up back there, hit them again with the water rifle," said Scaggz. "I am going to need more supplies, looks like we will have another two joining us."

Scaggz opened the back of the van and put in another bag of supplies and a small plastic kiddie pool. When the occupants of the RV exited the hardware store and walked to their motor home, the middle-aged man was waving at his wife in response to her yelling at him. Scaggz started the van and followed them out of town towards the campsite that was indicated on the sign that they just passed once again.

"What the fuck is this?" said one of the bikers in the back. "What the hell are you doing?"

"Now!" said Scaggz, and Jimmy hit them both with another dose from the water rifle. There was silence once again as they passed the campsite and watched the RV turn down an unpaved road in the woods a couple hundred feet from the entrance to the campgrounds. Scaggz parked the van and watched with the lights off. He saw the RV park farther down the unpaved road. He walked to where they were parked and waited in the brush on the side of the road.

The man exited first followed by his wife, who was talking before they came into view. "I don't see why we can't stay in the campground. I was all for saving on the hookups, but it would be nice to use their pools and a shower with good water pressure."

"You wanted to see the country. With all the money we spent on this RV, I can't afford the cost each night of paying for a spot to park it when we can park here for free. You can walk back to the RV park and use the pool. Just walk straight through the woods, they will never know."

"I am not walking through the woods at night. You're an asshole!"

"That may be, but you are getting the vacation you never could afford all those years till I came into your life."

Scaggz left the arguing couple and started his preparation. "I will be back in a little while. You know what to do if our guests wake up, right?"

"Yes, how long will this take? I really hate doing this kind of stuff."

"It will take as long as it takes to teach these people that there are consequences for their blatant ignorance for disposing of their bodily fluids all around town."

An hour later, Scaggz returned with two large containers that he put behind the van. "How did it go?"

"I had to hit the guys in the back again, and the couple up there have not stopped yelling at each other since you left."

Scaggz drove the van up the road and parked on the side near the clearing where the RV was set up. With the water rifle in hand, he rounded their camp site and found a spot sitting under a bush on the back side of the RV. "Look, you are just as comfortable sleeping in the RV here or over there. Stop the complaining. I went along with this whole RV thing for you."

"For me? You were just as happy to get away. I said we can dump the tank to save on the hookup, but I wanted to be in the park. I like meeting new people."

"New people, then why didn't you just go to a resort so you could be around people? Or a cruise. Oh, that's right, until we got married you couldn't afford to do anything. Living with your daughter. I bet she's happy that you're out of her house. Her poor husband having to deal with you every day."

"You're such a jerk. I would never have marr—"

"Enough out of you two," said Scaggz as he came around the front of the RV holding the water rifle in front of him. "You two have this beautiful RV and you can't enjoy life together. What is the point, then, in going out in it? But that is your problem. What became my problem is all you assholes that think because you have an RV you can do what you want. The north side of town now smells like piss because of you."

The woman screamed. Her husband said, "Relax, he has a water gun. Nothing to worry about." He reached for the door of the RV as a stream of liquid hit him in the face and drenched his shirt. The woman screamed again as her husband fell to the ground. She turned to run but was unable to as she fell into a deep sleep.

The two bikers were first to wake up. They were bound to a fallen tree in front of the RV, unable to move at all with all the duct tape and ropes that surrounded their bodies. The smaller one tried to talk, but the object in his mouth made it impossible and he sounded like a child playing a trumpet for the first time.

"Don't even bother. I know you cannot see with your eyes duct taped like that, but what is in your mouth is a funnel. It is in there pretty good. I was able to make a perfect seal with Gorilla Glue while you were out. Have you ever used it? It is strong stuff. In case you don't know who I am, I am the guy you threw your trash at. Pretty funny, hitting the dark-skinned guy with long hair walking down the street with your bottles of piss and what was left of your totally unhealthy meal. All you had to do was throw your trash in the can on the corner, but instead you bikers think you own the town and it is OK to do this. In case you care, I picked up your trash and threw it away for you. I did save the bottles of piss. I don't know which one belongs to either of you. But also, not my problem."

The RV couple was starting to come around. They were bound as well but hanging upside down from a tree branch with their heads resting in the kiddie pool. "OK great, we are all here now. I know you are wondering why you are upside down, and I will get to you in a minute. Just please wait till I finish with these two gentlemen. OK guys, so you are now each wondering why there is a funnel in your mouth. If I was you, I would use my tongue to block the end of the funnel. Here goes, the first bottle of piss goes to you. Kind of gross, even more so since it could be your buddy's."

Scaggz poured the bottle into the smaller man's funnel. "There you go, that should be full of bacteria, sitting out for a few hours. Not sure you want to swallow any of that." The man tried to move but he was bound too tight. He could not make a sound, now holding back the contents of the funnel with his tongue. The second biker was making sounds through his funnel, trying to move, but he too was tightly bound. Scaggz poured a small drop from bottle number two into his funnel. The biker coughed and then went silent. "Exactly. Now that I have your attention, here comes the rest of the bottle.

"OK my friends from the RV. You can see that as much as you were trying to move while I was tending to my buddies over there, that I have you both tied up pretty good. So here is the thing: you should have stayed in the RV park. It is very nice. I was able to take a quick shower there and the people were very nice. I told them that I am taking an advanced science class and needed some wastewater from their RVs.

They were so helpful. Do you see these two containers here? I was going to tape your eyes like the fellows over there but thought maybe you could use the time to communicate with each other. That's why I have you tied up like that facing one another. I know with your mouths taped shut you cannot talk, but isn't sincerity all in the eyes?"

The couple's eyes opened wide as Scaggz opened the first container of wastewater. The color blue could be seen. "OK, I am going to fill the pool with these two containers. You are probably thinking that I am going to drown you with this waste. But that is not true. I will pour enough into the pool so that the two of you will have to pick your heads up off the bottom of the pool to keep from drowning. Your teamwork will be key to staying alive." Scaggz poured the first container into the pool. The woman tried to scream but could not. Her husband's eyes got big trying to tell her to keep calm and work together. "Good, I see you are already communicating." Scaggz poured the second container into the pool. "OK, so that is about six inches of liquid. You only have to keep your faces above that to survive. Easy, right? So the point of this exercise it to teach you all a lesson in proper etiquette. There is a trail that runs right there behind you from the campsite. They told me there that it loops around and is part of the campsite. Two-mile trail that runs partially along the creek back there. I was told that it is very popular in the morning. So just hang tight and you will be OK once people walk by and see you. Once you all get cleaned up, that walk sounds nice, I recommend it to you." With that, Scaggz and his brother got into the van and drove away.

"I don't understand why you just can't let people like that be," said Jimmy. "Your plan to fuck with the Doctor makes sense since he not only fired you but refused to hire me all those years ago and called me a hack with no talent. But I showed him, he hired me as Heinz, I took lessons just to get back at him, changed my look, and he does not remember me as your brother. But why fuck with these total strangers?"

"Those people are the problem with society. Self-righteous assholes! Someone has to step forward and take charge. So I did that. The Doctor and his touring party will soon meet Jeetu while you reappear as Heinz. The plan is perfect!"

Chapter 8

The next day, the brothers arrived in Moorhead, Minnesota, the scene of Jimmy's disappearance as Heinz the bass player only months before. Jimmy finally was able to show his face in public again. "I don't ever want to do this again. I was content being Heinz and playing in the Doctor's band, eating how I like to eat. This was not what I originally wanted to do. You said to fuck with him for firing you and for calling me a hack."

"You have gotten quite good on the bass after all those years of practicing. But isn't that what motivated you? I remember how down you were that you were not good enough to play in the Doctor's band."

"Yes, that is right. It kills me that I need to use a different name and that people think that I am Heinz from Austria. I get it, he's an asshole that needs to be put in his place."

"Yes, we are now all a team. I belong on the tour to keep it balanced and am the one who was with him all those years when he was playing to minimal crowds and the occasional festival. He still needs me around now even if he does not realize it. I will protect him from the evils of the music business. I have gotten quite good at weeding out the bad. In the beginning it was all about revenge, but now, I am the Doctor's executioner."

"OK, I just don't want to be part of all of that. I can fill you in on plans when we're on the road, but the water rifle was about as far as I am willing to go this time out."

"I get it, we're different. OK, once we find the ideal location for you to camp, I will leave you the tent and camping stove. I find it easiest to use the spear I made to catch the small animals. Remember to show up as Heinz when we discussed, it will be the perfect time towards the end of the Doctor's India tour. That way, with the North American tour right around the corner, you'll already be in the States. Tell him that you're up for it. I am sure he plans to rehearse before the tour, thinking he needs a new bass player. He must do it here and not in Austria since it doesn't make any sense to fly American drummer Tommy over there. He will take you back in the band once he knows that you're still alive since you played in on the last tour."

"Yes, I know what to do. We went over it so many times."

"If you come out too soon, they may insist that you fly back to Austria. Then the Doctor may take the replacement bass player."

"I don't know, I think earlier is better as they need the visas for us all coming from Austria."

"Once I am with them in India as Jeetu, I can judge better. Keep your phone on. Look, there is a good place. You're still close enough to get cell reception and be in the woods."

Scaggz found a spot in the small clearing in the woods a mile and half out of town. "OK, I have you all set up. Remember what to do. You go into the police station and say you escaped."

"Yes, I know what to do."

The brothers hugged goodbye. "OK, see you when I get back. I have to get to Chicago for my flight to India in two days."

Neusy and Jeb arrived at Chicago O'Hare Airport separately a day before their flight to India. Once they collected their luggage, they met by the rental parking lot. Jeb had already completed the paperwork and waited in the car for Neusy. As he waited, he punched in the address for their destination in the car's GPS. The passenger door opened. "So, tell me why we have to be here a day before our flight? Pop the trunk so I can put my bag in there."

When Neusy entered the car Jeb said, "The Doctor wants us to visit the Rock and Roll Clog Makers since the tour last time was canceled and he wasn't able to pick up his new clogs."

"That's why we are flying out of Chicago, because of freaking clogs?"

"No, no, my friend. This will make you happy. I insisted because of the distance to India that we will only fly business class. That way we can stretch out and lay down, drink some good beers, and eat well. The cheapest flights were through Chicago. I was assuming the flights were cheaper through Chicago, but now you have me thinking that perhaps he planned it this way to pick up his clogs."

"Business? Nice call, Jebsy! But it wouldn't surprise me, you know, if he had us come through here to pick up his clogs. The guys could have shipped them to Austria, though."

"Yeah, I guess he could have had them shipped to him. But here we are."

"I see you have your GPS working, very good, unlike me always getting reamed by the Doctor. Every time someone uses a GPS around him, I have to hear about it."

"Haha, that's the way it is. Anders' house is about a half hour away. We should be there soon. Let's get this over with quick, get back to the hotel by the airport, drink a beer, and get out of town tomorrow. I hate Chicago."

"Yeah, me too, always something here when we tour through. These guys are cool, though. I enjoy when they come out to the shows."

The clog makers were friends since high school. Gustav Johansen, a woodworker that was bored with making cabinets and furniture, started turning wood on his lathe. After turning a few bowls, he was bored with that as well. Soon he was making strange objects that he would call lamps. Although they were just wood and had no electrical components, he put lamp shades on them and insisted that they be called lamps. His friend Anders Olsen saw the lamps one day when visiting Gustav's house and after an hour arguing that these were not lamps because they were missing the actual components that distinguished a lamp from a sculpture, Anders talked Gustav into allowing him to take a couple of the shaded wooden objects home.

Two days later Anders returned to Gustav's house with the two lamps fully operational, with a main light and smaller colored lights in the base of the units. The two formed Rock and Roll Lamp Makers and sold their lamps online. Being fans of bands from the eighties, each lamp then had a theme of one of their favorite bands. They would attend concerts and gift the lamps to the different artists and created a name for themselves. Five years ago, Gustav was watching a cable network that aired a five-part series on the history of clogs. He was mesmerized by what he was watching. When the show ended, he immediately called Anders. When Anders picked up his phone, the first word they both said was, "Clogs." Anders too had watched the same cable network. The two put aside their lamp business and have concentrated on making clogs and improving on the classic design.

"OK, this is the street where Anders lives. Keep an eye out for his house," instructed Jeb.

"Did he tell you what his house looks like?"

"He just said that we can't miss it. Wow, these are huge houses. Didn't think those guys had that much money."

"Right there, do you see that?"

"You mean that ten-foot clog on the front lawn of that house? Nope, I don't see it."

"Dude, there are kids climbing on that clog. Shit, one just went inside."

"Is that a window near the top?"

"Jeb, I think we are looking at the world's only two-story clog," said Neusy as they drove up the driveway.

Anders came out of the house with his shop apron on. "Boys, welcome to my home. It is an honor that you two are here. You guys are like, famous, everyone knows you are always on the road with the Doctor. Come over here to the clog playhouse, I want to get a picture with you." They walked over to the large two-story clog as a child came down a slide out of the back.

"Thanks for the picture, guys. Come on in, let me show you what we have. Gustav is not here; he is in his woodshop putting the final additions on a new pair we designed for the Doctor. He wanted a pair that had a couple of tambourine jingles built into the heel. Which is what we are all about, bringing the clog to the next level and the twenty first century."

They walked in. Neusy gave Jeb a look that clearly stated that the Doctor is fucking nuts. Jeb could not agree more.

"This way, guys, my workshop is in the basement. We are working on all sorts of new products." When they reached the bottom of the steps, Anders rolled a suitcase from the corner of the room then lifted it onto an empty table. "Everything the Doctor wanted is in here, obviously other than the pair Gustav is working on. He lives close; I am hoping that he will be here soon."

"Suitcase? He asked me to pick up a couple pair of clogs that he wanted," said Jeb.

Neusy looked at the now open suitcase that had many wrapped items in it that he was assuming all were clogs. "What all is in here?"

"We have several pair of the clogs that we made the Doctor in the past. He also wanted four pair made of different woods. He liked the distinct sound that each made when he walks. We were on the phone for almost two hours. I went through all the different woods and demonstrated their different sounds, or pitches as he called them. He chose the alder, maple, swamp ash and walnut. We made him our traditional clogs with my custom leather upper, but he wanted enough bare wood on the bottom to really enhance the sound they generated. He also wanted each wood in our new hybrid clog."

"Uhhh, hybrid clog?" asked Neusy.

"Yes exactly, you see the base, here is one here." Anders lifted a package from the suitcase and opened it gently. "The base is wood, but we have a material that we sandwich in between the wood to cushion the step. In this case here we use cork. Do you see this line running through the center? It's cork. We also have a version where we use rubber, but he felt it would muffle the sound they made. Then on the uppers, he wanted two pair slip-ons and two that were full boot where the upper is full."

"How much does this suitcase weigh? All this wood has got to be heavy?" asked Jeb. "There are weight restrictions for the flight."

"Yes, we are aware of this. The Doctor mentioned fifty pounds and that we should put as many clogs as possible that he wanted in there, keeping it just under fifty pounds."

"Fifty pounds of clogs?"

"Yes. We also are including a couple of pairs of our new clog sandals in both blue and white, as he likes. We will be displaying these as the center of our booth at this year's Mid-West Clog Fest next month."

"Neusy, aren't you glad you packed light? This way you can drag around fifty pounds of clogs," said Jeb, smiling. Neusy just gave him the keep-it-up-and-you-will-get-a-clog-up-your-ass look.

"Ahh, Gustav just texted me. He is on his way. Follow me into the workshop. I want to show you all we are working on." Anders led them through a door and turned on the light, illuminating a large space with workstations all around the perimeter of the room and, in the center, various leather working tools with a workbench that had a few prototypes on it.

Neusy and Jeb stood there taking in the entire room. It was larger than either of their living spaces at home. Neusy looked at Jeb, who was fixated on what was on the center workspace. "Yes, come here guys. Jeb, you noticed this, I see. We are working on something that will one day make the lives of leg amputees far better." He picked the prototype up off the work bench. "This is a design for a friend of Gustav. He lost his leg in a car accident many years ago and was never happy with any of his prosthetics.

"We designed this from the ground up and then were able to build on what we already designed. The clog here on the bottom is the same design as our hybrid with rubber between the layers of wood. The heel portion also is rubber below the center line, creating a cushion. The clog is attached to a prosthetic leg that Gustav turned on his lathe. Look at the detail. But what is unique is that he designed it using his friend's existing leg as a model. See the ankle joint? If you take that apart, you will see it is built just like a human ankle joint. He hollowed out the wooden leg and built a model of his friend's joint using an X-ray supplied to him. The cartilage and ligaments I fashioned out of leather and rubber. He will be coming tomorrow for a fitting. Gustav finished the leg in the same color as his friend's existing leg. You see here, it is all one piece with the clog."

"I really don't know what to say. I have never seen anything like this before," said Neusy.

"Exactly. We will be debuting this at the Clog Fest and a medical trade show in two months. It's very exciting! Over here, guys, is the next thing we are working on using wood fibers that are formulated from the waste in Gustav's shop. They are spun into these fibers here and we can make clothing out of it; it is all our own proprietary methods on custom-made equipment. See here are the first prototypes of T-shirts, and on the table there the matching men's boxer briefs."

"You guys are insane. I want a pair of the underwear when you are done," said Jeb.

"No problem, Jeb, I think those boxer briefs on the table there would fit you. They are thirty-four waists," said a voice at the door.

Standing there was a man that stood 6'3" with long brown hair and an eight-inch full beard who looked nothing like his equally tall but clean-shaven partner. "Gustav, it's been a while," said Jeb. "Yes, thirty-four waist, you are correct."

They hugged and Gustav said, "Great, then take a pair. Hopefully you like them and can give us an endorsement."

"Of the underwear? I guess I could."

"Excellent. Here, I brought the final pair of clogs for the Doctor. These are the ones he wanted that are made of alder with extra exposed wood on the bottom and the tambourine jingles in the heel. He said that he could keep perfect percussion beat with this if designed right. We took a full month to make this perfect for him. I'll put them in your suitcase over there."

"OK, great guys, this is quite the set up here. We must get going and check into the hotel and prepare for the India tour. We leave tomorrow."

"Yes," said Gustav. "India should be a blast for you guys. We hope to see you on tour here soon. You don't have a little time to come to my house? I want to show you my setup. Equally impressive."

Neusy rolled his eyes and said, "Thanks guys, appreciate it, but Jeb is right, we have work to get done and only a little time before we have to fly out."

The clog makers walked their guests out to their car. They all hugged goodbye as another child came flying out the opening of the large clog on the lawn and slid down the slide screaming.

"Damn that suitcase is heavy," said Neusy as they were driving away. "I'm glad you used that story about having to do work. Those guys, while nice, they just don't stop talking."

"Exactly, I saw you catch right on."

"I am looking forward to trying on the boxer briefs. They are soft; it's amazing they can make sawdust into fibers."

"Yeah, but do me a favor, if you're going to make me drag around that suitcase all through the airports, can you at least take out your pair of wooden underwear?"

Chapter 9

The next afternoon Jeb and Neusy were in the business lounge at O'Hare Airport waiting for their flight to India. "Fuck, I'm glad to get rid of that suitcase. That thing was heavy. Now we have to roll that all around India. By the way, thanks for the honor of being able to be keeper of the clogs for the Doctor. It's really appreciated," said a sarcastic Neusy.

"Relax, soon we will be on the flight. Good food, beers, and relaxing with no worries for twelve hours with flight attendants catering to our needs. The only way to fly long distances. But for now, have another beer. We have an hour before we have to be at the gate. Forget about the clogs." Then to the passing bartender Jeb said, "we'll take another two Al Capone's Empty Vault IPAs."

"Right on! Cheers, my friend, to an excellent India tour and adventure."

"Yes, my friend Neusy. Cheers! Plus, we have that driver, Jeetu, who will be helping us. He can help you with the clog case."

In the same terminal, Scaggz just cleared security and was walking to his gate. He passed a business lounge and wondered what flying in business was like. He had only flown economy and this trip was no exception. Being that he had secured his role on the tour as an Indian man, he could not ask for a flight to be purchased for Jeetu. The cost of the trip was challenging for him. He saved enough money for the ticket by doing odd jobs, giving guitar lessons, and the occasional pick pocketing of an unexpected tourist when he would venture into town from the woods where he and Jimmy were camped.

He arrived at the gate and was unable to find a seat in the waiting area. The flight was fully booked, and he was stuck in a middle seat on the plane. His only hope was that the people on either side of him would be small and not be in his space. He waited in line until a woman that worked for the airline went through checking everyone's boarding pass. "You are in the second to last boarding group. Please wait on the side until your group is called," he was advised. As to not stand out, he did what he was told as the business class passengers were allowed to board.

"Haha, Neusy, this is great! Right through on the plane, we will be drinking a beer while all these people are boarding." Scaggz heard the familiar voice of Jeb walking right behind where he was standing.

"I must say, Jebsy, you called this one right." Scaggz walked away, not wanting to be seen. How could this happen? They, too, were in Chicago flying to India. He had chosen Chicago for just the reason that they should be flying from the West Coast.

The two were in their seats on the plane, already sipping a beer, when Scaggz, sitting forty rows behind them, found his seat. There was a small Indian woman sitting in the window seat. She smiled at Scaggz, and he sat in his middle seat. Perhaps this would not be too bad.

"Well, it looks like I'm sitting here next to you. You don't snore while you're sleeping do you? Haha, just kidding. I make this flight once a month for business. We will get to know each other quite well." Scaggz was looking up at the extremely large man putting his bag in the overhead bin. As he sat down, he extended his hand. "My name is Travis." Scaggz just looked at him. Something in Scaggz's eyes made the man pull back his hand. "OK, not everyone likes the handshake. I get it. Just a warning, when I fall asleep, I tend to drool. Just nudge me if I am drooling on you."

Scaggz stood up. "I have to use the restroom."

"No worries, hold on, it's a little hard for me to get out of these tight seats. OK, made it. Haha! I will stand and wait for you. That took a lot of effort to get up."

Scaggz walked to the front of the economy section and could see into the luxurious business section. Everyone was drinking either champagne or whatever drink they desired. They each had a small plate of crackers and cheese while the rest of the people were herded into the sections behind them. He saw Neusy and Jeb toasting with their beers until the curtain was abruptly closed in front of him and he was instructed to go back to his seat.

Scaggz's seat mate was still standing when he returned. "OK, that did not take too long. Me, when I go, it takes a lot longer. I have a condition that it always takes me a little time to get the flow going." Scaggz sat down in his seat and leaned towards the woman, who positioned herself up against the window wanting no part of the two men to her right.

After takeoff, the large man managed to get himself out of his seat and walked to the restroom. He returned fifteen minutes later. "See, just like I told you, it takes me a while. Whew, I can't wait till they serve us some food." He sat down and Scaggz once again leaned towards the woman, who now covered herself with a blanket to somehow give herself a more protected space. Ten minutes later, "Oh, I have to go again." The man stood and walked off.

Scaggz followed the man but could not get past the flight attendant, who at that moment decided it would be best to start serving drinks. He waited for her to pass with her cart and found the galley near the bathrooms. He peered around the corner. The flight attendants were at the rear of the section working their way to the front. After ten more minutes, the large man, who called himself Travis, emerged from the restroom. "Hey, you had to go as well. Sorry it took me so long."

Then the man heard the only additional words that Scaggz would say the entire flight, which would be the last words that he ever heard. "Look what they have for us in here. I think you will really enjoy this." The man walked into the galley just in time to get the full force of the metal coffee pot coming down on his head.

After an unscheduled stop in Philadelphia for unannounced reasons, Scaggz enjoyed the remainder of the flight sitting in an aisle seat with the middle seat empty. The small Indian woman going home scated by the window also seemed to enjoy the additional space and emerged from her protected shelter.

Chapter 10

The plane arrived in Madras, India, at the southernmost tip of the country, in the evening of the next day. Jeb and Neusy collected their luggage and waited in the luggage area. The Doctor arrived on his flight from Europe around the same time, the excitement rushing through his veins as he stepped into the terminal. "How did it go with the clog makers?" he said when he saw Jeb and Neusy. The Doctor stood in front of them in his Mozart wig and long coat that looked like it was from the same time period.

"No hello? Just where are the clogs?" said Jeb, giving Neusy the that's-fucked-up look. Neusy returned the well-that's-the-Doctor nod.

"Yah… Yah… Hello. I see you guys und we talk all the time on the phone. Do we always have to do these tedious hellos und goodbyes?"

"We never made it to the clog makers; time was too short."

"What? You're kidding. You always kid me."

"We got fifty pounds of clogs, what is wrong with you? Why would you need so many clogs?"

"You will see, each one has a purpose. Plus, one day when I have the complete set, I will use them in a seminar to demonstrate perfect timing und how different percussion notes determine the mood of song writing."

They stood there looking around the terminal for their guide, whom they had never seen nor met. They were looking for someone holding up a sign that had "Doctor" written on it. Jeb and Neusy followed the Doctor about and gazed at all the dark-skinned, native people in the terminal.

"Man, are we the only white people here?" asked Neusy.

"Keep it down, don't talk too loud," whispered Jeb.

"Dude, this is kind of scary…" replied Neusy.

"Don't worry, Indian people are very friendly," answered Jeb.

The Doctor wandered, looking for an unfamiliar face to approach him or to see someone with a sign to catch his attention. His two companions continued to follow him. "Achh! Where is this guy?"

"I don't know. Maybe we should go outside and see if he's there," said Jeb. "It would have helped if he would have emailed a photo of himself."

Jeb looked at Neusy and motioned his head to the left toward the exit doors. Neusy replied with a nod.

The three travelers ventured outside the main terminal into an area with multitudes of people standing by their cars. It was pitch black outside with minimal lighting and difficult to see into the distance. There were not any discernible faces that could be recognized.

"Wow, man, this is fucking creepy!" said Neusy.

"It's like that Beatles movie," said Jeb.

"Which one?"

"Yellow Submarine."

"Why do you say that?" asked Neusy.

"You remember the sea of holes?" asked Jeb.

"Yeah."

"Well, this is like the sea of eyes and teeth," replied Jeb.

"Dude, that's freaky! You're not helping matters here."

"I have never seen such a sight in my whole life. This is amazing!" said the Doctor. "Where is this guy? What is that over there?"

On the left, they could make out a sign wavering about in the air that read, "Over here, Doctor."

"Achh, yah, that must be him!"

"Come on, Neusy, grab the suitcases. I will move the MMM box. The Doctor can manage his own Universe Guitars."

The three scurried over to meet the fellow holding the sign. "Hello! You are the Doctor. My name is Jeetu Kapoor."

They scanned Jeetu from head to toe in his colorful, green, tie-dyed T-shirt and blue jeans. Medium height, short black beard, his hair was covered by a blue turban, but he was not as dark skinned as most of the people they had already seen in Madras. They followed their new guide through the darkness to a psychedelically painted VW bus. "Here we are, gentlemen. Our chariot of mystical fire."

"Wow! That's cool!"

"What a paint job!"

"I did it myself," said Scaggz as Jeetu, hoping it would seem as if he was here in India longer than his travel companions. The reason for his tardiness was caused by the fact that he himself had just landed with Jeb and Neusy and he had to find the man delivering his VW. As agreed, the man was waiting for Scaggz away from the terminal so as not to be seen by his waiting passengers. He had to hastily apply his tanning spray once inside the van and then drive around to the terminal to meet his arriving guests.

"I love it! It reminds me of the sixties," said Neusy.

"Let's get moving, my kind friends. It's late and we have to get to our hotel."

"Great! Don't forget in the morning we have to visit Mr. Zarveen Agarwal about the new instrument."

"Yes, my friend…I know."

Scaggz, as Jeetu Kapoor, was feeling like he pulled off his greatest caper. The three travelers had no idea who he was. Especially the Doctor—years of service under him and not a clue. "Kind sirs, I will take us to the hotel so that you may rest yourselves and prepare for tomorrow."

"Thanks, Jeetu!" said Jeb.

Scaggz was really liking his new name. He drove them off into the black night toward their hotel. In the morning, everyone joined together in the hotel dining area for the continental breakfast of breads, cheeses, cereal grains, but no meat products.

"Achh! I like to eat this way every day!" said the Doctor.

"Why is that, sir?" said Jeetu.

"Because I don't eat meat!"

"Then most Indian cuisine shall be to your liking, my good Doctor! Most Indian people don't eat meat. And we have many special curries for you to try."

"I don't like things too spicy!"

"My dear Doctor, we have many curries that are not very spicy at all. Everywhere in India the cuisine changes from region to region. In the Northwest, we have very special breads and cheeses. You will see, my good sirs! But now we must leave or we will be late. Follow me, kind sirs." The information that Scaggz had researched in the weeks prior to his flight to India were just flowing out of his mouth. Full into his Jeetu character, he led his traveling party to the VW and smiled.

"How far is this guitar maker?" asked Jeb.

"My GPS says about one hour from here."

"Achh! A smart man uses a GPS like we do in Austria. You can learn from this man, Neusy."

Neusy looked at Jeb seated next to him in the back of the VW van and gave him the what-a-dick look. Jeb held his middle finger out low behind the Doctor seated in front of him. The weather was hot in southern India, as it normally is most times of the year. As they drove, they looked out the windows at many kinds of trees they had never seen before. They noticed people piled their trash on the streets.

"Why do they put the trash on the streets?" asked the Doctor.

"Because we don't use trash cans. We burn the trash every week."

"WHAAAT? Und the plastics? Und the metals?"

"Everything gets burned."

"What an environmental nightmare!"

"Welcome to India, my dear Doctor!"

They saw a cow nosing through a trash pile on a road. Between the cow's legs was a little dog chewing on some trash bits. "Achh! That's awful! I have to vomit!"

Jeetu pulled the van over to the side of the road; the Doctor opened his door just in time. The little dog saw this, moved towards the van, then stood looking at the Doctor. The little dog then looked at Jeb in the back seat through the window. Jeb looked at the dog, smiled, and nodded. The little dog licked the Doctor's vomit. The Doctor nauseated by what he was watching, vomited again on the dog's head. The little dog wandered away wondering what was in that weird tasting food those nice people gave him. Jeetu fired up the van and they continued down the road. "We are almost there, kind friends."

The guitar shop wasn't anything like what they expected. A very primitive-looking shack nestled in some tall trees, a few cows wandered around. Beautiful green grass surrounded the shack, a color of green not often found in nature. A little fat man waddled out of the shack to greet the visitors. "Greetings, good sirs! My name is Zarveen Agarwal, the master lute maker."

"Und I am the Doctor!"

"I'm Jeb, the tour manager."

"I'm Neusy, the assistant."

"And I am Jeetu Kapoor, their faithful guide."

"Nice to meet all of you! I do not wish to be rude, but my shop is small, it is best that only the Doctor and I enter to see the instruments."

"That's okay, no problem," said Jeb.

"A gracious welcome to my shop, my good Doctor, please follow me."

Although Zarveen's shop was small, he made use of every space inside. He had many types of instruments hanging on the walls, even things hanging from the ceiling. There was a work bench for assembly and the back wall had shelves with tools and instrument parts. Then Zarveen led the Doctor through a rear door and into a smaller shack. In this area was a collection of exotic woods. The Doctor was impressed. Then, off to the side, he saw it. The new instrument that he had ordered. It looked like the sun and the rays of light were the necks of each of the instruments. It was made of various exotic woods that were mostly of darker color. They created the perfect balance. The instrument had six necks, each the same length, which included a 6-string guitar, a bass, a 12-string guitar, a sitar, a mandolin, and an Indian lute. The instrument was mounted on a stand, and the center of the instrument was at the Doctor's waistline.

"Achh! Zarveen, it is remarkable!"

"I am glad that you like it, my dear Doctor."

"How do I use it? I mean to change necks?"

"It is quite simple, the guitar spins on the stand and then you just grab which neck you want to play. I also have a belt buckle attachment so that you can wear it."

"Achh! That is wunderbar! Let's give it a spin!"

The Doctor approached the instrument and stood behind it. He gave it a spin and grabbed the 12-string. He strummed pretty chords; Zarveen was soothed by what he heard. The Doctor spun it again and grabbed the sitar. He began to bang out an Indian melody. To Zarveen, the Doctor played perfectly as a sitar was intended. He spun it again and grabbed the 6-string guitar. He did what he does best on that one, his fingers were one with the instrument, fire dancing from one end to the other. Zarveen had never seen such skill or heard such melodies.

"Zarveen, you have made me the perfect instrument!"

"Thank you, my kind Doctor!"

"What do you call this instrument?"

"It is called Viswadjit, or 'Conqueror of the Universe,' and you, my friend, will be known as Gandharva, or the 'Celestial Musician.'"

"Achh! A thousand thanks, Zarveen! I have one more question: how do I transport it around?"

"I have made a special case for you. You see it is round, and it has two arms that extend out that you can attach to the rear bumper of the car. Then you can tow it anywhere."

"Yah yah! Zarveen, you are a genius!"

They walked back into the main shack; the Doctor noticed another unusual instrument on Zarveen's work bench. It looked exactly like an umbrella. "What is this? It is most irregular und interesting."

"Oh, that is called the Expando. You see all of the necks fold out and make the same type of instrument that I made you, but this one is more portable. When you are done playing it, you fold it up like an umbrella. I still am making some adjustments. Not ready yet."

"You are a remarkable man, Zarveen."

Zarveen put the Viswadjit into the six-foot round case and rolled it outside to the VW van. He showed them how the two arms folded out and helped them connect it to the rear bumper of the van. It resembled a steamroller but much thinner. Jeb, Neusy, and Jeetu all looked at each other in confusion. They had no idea what was inside of the case. They got into the VW, heading off to Hosur, and waved goodbye to Zarveen.

The first concert was scheduled in Hosur, in central India, in a Seventh Day Adventist compound.

"How long until we reach Hosur, Jeetu?"

"My GPS says about four hours, so you best relax and have a rest, friend Jeb."

"Achh, yah. A good sleep! I will be refreshed when we arrive."

About two hours into the journey, Jeetu pulled off the road at what looked like a little café in a shack. "What's up, Jeetu? Why have we stopped?" inquired Jeb.

"Time for an Indian coffee, my friend Jeb."

"This doesn't look like a coffee shop; it looks more like a trading post from the old West."

"No, no, my friend, most cafés look like this along the roads. Come along, you must try Indian coffee." They jumped out of the van and took seats outside the little venue. "Four Indian coffees, please!" said Jeetu.

"I'll have an espresso," said Neusy.

"No, you can't have that…there is only one style of coffee here," said Jeetu.

"Okay then," said Neusy.

The girl brought out the coffees. "My goodness, very good." The Doctor was impressed.

"Yeah, wow! Why does it taste so good?" asked Neusy.

"The way we make coffee in India is like this, first we use very fine coffee powder and then, instead of water, we pour in boiled milk."

"Wow! This is great!" said Jeb. "How much longer until we reach Hosur?"

"About two more hours."

"Better get moving, I want to have a good look at the compound."

The four got back into the van and continued down the road. The Doctor was looking at wildlife roaming outside as they traveled. "What is this? A monkey?"

"Yes, it's a monkey."

"So cute!!! I want to see more of these monkeys."

"Don't worry, you will see many more monkeys, and camels, and elephants. Also, snakes, giant bats, and maybe some tigers."

"WUNDERBARRR! I love animals."

Scaggz thought, *I love them too, in my belly.*

"Speaking of monkeys, have you heard from Marlon? Wonder what he's up to in the States. Getting really high and trying to make his marriage work, would be my guess," said Neusy.

"You didn't hear? He and his wife split up after he got back from the last tour. He is probably getting extremely high. But he's looking forward to getting back on the road. He's constantly texting me," replied Jeb.

"No shit, he split from his wife? Last tour he couldn't stand being away from the family, now he wants to be out again on the road? Classic Marlon," said Neusy.

"Yah, Marlon, he visited me in Austria. I'm teaching him a few things. Made him more of a man," said the Doctor.

"Oh yeah?" asked Neusy. "What did you teach him?"

"Well, he learned how to clean my house. It made him a man. He is there now."

Neusy gave Jeb the that's-fucked-up look. Jeb held his middle finger low behind the Doctor's seat.

The road to Hosur was very dry, dusty, and barren, with not much vegetation. Obviously, India wasn't getting a lot of rain. Patches of green here and there could be found in central India, but not much. But one thing they were seeing was an abundance of white marble temples. "What are these little white stone buildings we keep seeing?" asked Neusy.

"Those are Indian temples."

"Wow, they are all made of white marble?"

"White signifies purity to Ganesha."

"Who is Ganesha?"

"He is one of our gods."

"How many gods are there?"

"They say about 30,000. Shiva, Krisha, Brahma, all are gods. There are statues of some of the gods inside those temples."

"This is very confusing! I only believe in the one true God!" said the Doctor.

"Good for you, my friendly Doctor. Well, it looks like we are almost there, one more turn and two kilometers."

"Great, I'm tired of sitting," said Neusy. The psychedelic van turned toward black-iron gates connected to eight-foot-wide concrete walls that continued around the compound in either direction. A guard approached the van and asked what they wanted. Jeetu told him they were there to perform a concert. The guard opened the gates. They drove in towards a huge white building, almost like a government state building. Jeetu stopped the van and Jeb got out. He looked up at the large white building. Then a man came outside.

"Good day, my friends! I am Arjun Gupta. I am the manager of this facility."

"Hello, I am Jeb Acorns. We emailed each other about one month ago. This show was arranged by Spud Burger."

"Yes, everything is in order. Do you require much electricity for your show?"

"Not too much, we have an electric guitar, a small amplifier, an acoustic guitar, and a robotic machine that plays various instruments."

"Okay, all sounds good! However, I must warn you about the power in India. We always have power outages! But we have a small gasoline-powered generator that I suggest you use during your performance."

"Okay, thanks, that sounds very useful."

"Indeed…and another thing, Mr. Jeb, this is a Christian community. The people don't like loud rock music or suggestive lyrics."

"No problem, Arjun. The Doctor has prepared some very nice classical pieces, as well as his own interpretations of Indian music for tonight's performance. Where can we set up?"

"Drive your car behind this building and you will see the stage."

Within seconds they were there in front of a stage that was set on top of picnic tables with plywood. It was three-feet high, twelve-feet wide and six-feet deep. There were mini disco lights and other colored lights mounted on a mini rig that went vertically in the front, and then a long twelve-foot rig that crossed the front of the stage. There was a single mic stand in the front and small columns of speakers on each side of the stage, with cables that ran to the back to a small table with a mixing board for the sound and a small board with switches for the lights. They saw the small gasoline-powered electric generator sitting on the ground next to the stage. Jeb told Neusy to set up the equipment, simple detail, would take only minutes.

Jeetu opened the back of the van and helped Neusy carry the equipment to the stage. He had a flashback to his last show with the Doctor when he broke a guitarist's leg from the band playing before the Doctor. He pounced on him from a catwalk above the stage after the guitarist stepped on the Doctor's cables. He was fired after that incident in Munich. Jeetu started breathing hard, which caused him to almost break character. He put down the amp he was carrying and took a couple of deep breaths. Neusy saw this but didn't say a word. Jeetu picked up the amp and walked it to the stage.

They positioned the MMM in the middle of the stage about five feet back from the front. They set the sitar up in two hands and positioned the conga drums near the other two arms. They set the headset thought reader on a stool. Then near the front of the stage, off center, they set up the new instrument on its stand and two small amps, one for the MMM and one for the Universe Guitar.

The Doctor instructed Neusy, "Bring me three sets of clogs. The one with the tambourine sound und the slip-on black pair with the walnut wood, also one with alder." Neusy scrambled off. "Now you will see something." When Neusy returned, the Doctor put on the walnut-base clogs. He played his acoustic guitar and kept a beat on the stage with his clogs. "You hear this? The walnut makes a nice warm sound when I play the clog on the stage."

"Play the clog?" said Neusy. Jeb gave him the let-the-Doctor-continue-this-will-be-funny look. Neusy smiled and gave Jeb a nod.

"Yah, now I play the one with alder." The Doctor once again played the same chords, and with the alder clog kept beat once again. "Ahhh so finely tuned, those boys make a nice clog. You hear the difference? This one is a sharper, more precise sound. Not quite as warm." The three of them nodded as they absorbed this new knowledge.

The Doctor unwrapped the clogs with the tambourine jingles. They made a tambourine sound as the Doctor shook them. "Achh, yah, this is exactly what I wanted." He put on the clogs and played the chords once again on his guitar. He kept beat again with the clog, but in between lifted his foot and shook the clog. It sounded like a tambourine when he alternated feet. He looked like an Irish river dancer but lacked the stamina. "This is perfect. Now do you hear the different clogs und how full the sound is with the tambourine clog? I will have them make me more of these in each wood. Wow, I will have to exercise my legs, this is quite the workout."

Jeb looked at Neusy, who returned a glance, indicating Jeb was correct, this was quite entertaining. The Doctor handed Neusy the clogs and went off and stood back in the distance looking at the stage, trying to get the vibe of the concert area. As he turned and looked around him, he could see the huge, white building behind the stage. There were bungalows in all of the areas behind him. He saw fruit trees, other trees, shrubs, flower gardens, and a parking area. He could see clothes lines tied between trees with laundry hanging on them. It was a small paradise inside the walls of the Adventist community and an absolute dry, desolate, wasteland outside the gates.

"Hallo, Arjun! How many people will be here tonight?" asked the Doctor.

"We should have about 300, Mr. Doctor."

"Okay, this is good!"

Jeetu asked if he could run the sound and said that he had experience before at a small discotheque. Jeb told Arjun that Jeetu could manage it, and he knew the musical pieces that the Doctor was going to play.

Jeb didn't have a lot of merchandise for India, mostly small items, including CDs, key chains, head scarves, and guitar picks. They couldn't bring boxes of T-shirts and larger items on the plane as they already had to help move the Doctor's guitars, amps, effects, and their own suitcases of clothes and personal items. Jeb asked Arjun for a small folding table for the merch and set it up off the side of the building where the people would enter the grounds.

Two grey rhesus monkeys were now visible through the trees and were pulling on the laundry lines, causing white garments to fall to the ground. Then they ran down and back up into the fruit trees. Fruit was flying overhead as they threw it at each other. "Achh! What darling little monkeys!"

"My good Doctor, the monkeys are very troublesome. We set up cages through the compound and trap them."

"AAACHHHH! The poor things! What do you do with them?"

"Well, we catch them and then we drive them to the jungle and send them back into the wild."

"Okay! That's OK then!"

Jeetu looked at the monkeys running around. He had never eaten monkey but thought they would make excellent BBQ. He was formulating a spice rub in his mind.

"I ain't never seen monkeys before, only at the L.A. Zoo," said Neusy.

"Me neither," said Jeb. "They sure are crazy little bastards!"

The stage was set; everyone ate the few snacks provided to them by Arjun. The guests began to gather inside the grounds. About 7:30 pm most of the people were there, standing and mingling. Jeb gave the Doctor a nod so he knew it was time to go on the stage. The Doctor nodded in agreement. He walked to the stage and took his Universe Guitar out of its case and plugged it in. He took the headgear and placed it on his head. He approached the mic.

"Guten Abend, my new friends! I have picked some very nice classical pieces to play for you tonight. Let's start with some Beethoven."

Bamm bamm bamm bahh! Bamm bamm bamm bahh! Everyone knew Beethoven's 5th Symphony, but no one ever saw or heard it done like this. The Doctor stood in front of the MMM and the arms on one side played the percussion while the arms on the other played the bass line on the sitar. The Doctor held and played the main melodies on the Universe Guitar. It sounded full for just one player. The Doctor looked like the Goddess Shiva with her multiple arms moving about playing on both sides of him. The crowd, not being hard rockers or metal heads, quietly ooohed and aaahed, nodding their heads to the rhythm of what they were hearing, then politely clapped after the songs were finished.

"I am glad you all liked that piece. Und now here is something by Ravi Schankar!" He played the piece beautifully. Some wept but they all cheered a little louder. When the piece was done, he took off the Universe Guitar and carefully set it down on the back of the stage. He then stood behind the new instrument and spoke.

"Tonight, I have something special. This is called Viswadjit. I will play my own composition of Indian melodies und use this new instrument." He first put his hands on the 12-string and started strumming. He thought of a rhythm; the MMM started to play the percussion on one side. He thought of the bass line; the MMM played that on the other side as he strummed along on the 12-string, making beautiful delicate chords. Then he suddenly spun the Viswadjit and the necks flew around in a fury. He grabbed the sitar and began a faster, upbeat melody. The MMM followed along with his thought patterns. The people all knew the melodies that he played. He gave the Viswadjit another spin. He grabbed the mandolin and started another familiar melody. The people clapped along to the rhythm with the MMM.

The mandolin's double-ringing, high-pitched sounds started making the monkeys in the trees go crazy. Fruit catapulted out of the trees at the guests, and the monkeys began ripping down the laundry. One brave monkey ran up to the stage, climbed up on the light rig, and swung back and forth, singing along in high-pitched monkey sounds. The Doctor watched the monkey swing about over his head wondering what was going on. The monkey was going nuts, screaming and swinging frantically. The Doctor quickly spun the Viswadjit and grabbed the 12-string neck again. He played a slower, more peaceful medley and the monkey began to calm down. He climbed up on top of the lighting truss, sat in one place, and nodded his head back and forth. Jeb looked at Neusy at the side of the stage and gave him the it's-OK nod. Neusy nodded back as he was hit in the head by a piece of fruit.

In the morning, Jeetu saw they captured a grey rhesus macaque monkey in a cage. He asked the groundskeeper what would happen with the monkey. The groundskeeper said that they would release the monkey back into the jungle. Jeetu asked the groundskeeper how to get to the jungle. The man gave him a hand-drawn map, then Jeetu said, "Can I take him and release him? It would be an honor."

"Well, I don't know… It can be a bit dangerous; these monkeys can be viscous and unpredictable."

"I have a gift with animals, they trust me. I think I can handle it."

"Okay, I guess it's alright."

"Can you help me load the cage in my VW bus? I will bring back the cage later when I collect my group after breakfast."

After the monkey in the cage was loaded in the VW bus, he drove away from the complex. About an hour later, Jeetu arrived in the jungle. He was hungry and it was time for a feast. He parked off the main road in between some trees. He opened the rear door, pulled out the cage, and set it on the ground. Then he pulled out a mini BBQ grill and set it up. "Oh boy! This is going to be great." He pulled out his Bowie knife and prepared to open the cage. The monkey sensed something bad was about to happen and began to grunt and hiss. As soon as Jeetu undid the latch to the cage, the monkey bolted against the door and was free. It took off for the trees. Jeetu was right on its tail and pursued the monkey relentlessly. "You little fucker are not going to get away from me!" The chase lasted less than a minute when the monkey shot up a tree and landed on the first level of branches. THUD!!! The monkey fell to the ground with Jeetu's Bowie knife thrown deep into its back. "Told ya! You little fucker! You weren't going to spoil my breakfast plans."

Scaggz, the hunter, now pulled out his blade and threw the monkey's dead corpse over his shoulder and walked back to his van. He prepared to skin the monkey for the BBQ. Even though he never skinned and prepared a monkey before, the process was the same as all the other animals he captured and cooked. He had something special in mind today, though. He took out his knife and cut around the top of the monkey's head and peeled back the skin. He then brought out a cordless grinding tool and sawed around the skull.

Once the brain was exposed, Scaggz delicately removed it, seasoned it with cumin and other Indian spices, wrapped it up in foil, and set it on the BBQ. The rest of the body was sectioned into ribs, thigh meat, and a rump roast. He fired up the coals and, when it was perfect, he set all the meat on the grill. The foil wrapped brain would be his dessert: monkey brain flan.

After Scaggz had his monkey BBQ, complete with the brain flan, he drove back to the compound and returned the cage. "How did it go?" asked the groundskeeper.

"Delicious," said Jeetu.

"What?"

"I mean great. I opened the cage and he ran up a tree."

Jeb and Neusy were first out and loaded the VW with help of Jeetu. "Where did you go, Jeetu? We were worried about you," said Jeb.

"Oh, I was helping the groundskeeper to take the monkey in the cage back to the jungle. I needed a little time for myself."

"Okay, well, let's get a move on," said Jeb, and they finished loading up.

The Doctor emerged from his bungalow and walked toward the van. "Yah, that was fun, but next time we need to put in rider that monkeys should be put in cages."

The load up was quick, and all said their goodbyes to Arjun.

"Nice show, my kind sirs."

"Yes, we enjoyed it too!"

The next destination was Bombay, to the British, or Mumbai to the Indians. It would take about eight hours to drive there from central India. "Well, take care, Arjun, maybe we will see you again one day," said Jeb, and they all got in the van and drove outside into the wasteland.

In the van, Neusy and Jeb both noticed that Jeetu smelled of BBQ. Neusy looked up in the trees and Jeb said, "It would not surprise me."

Chapter 11

After a long grueling journey across the Indian terrain, they arrived in the bustling city of Bombay. Bombay was like the New York City of India. It was dirty and smelly with many vagabonds wandering around begging for money or picking pockets. Some locals even cut off limbs so one would feel sorry for them and give them some money. In India folklore, one could be reincarnated in the next life. However, it could be into a cow or a monkey, not necessarily a human.

Jeetu drove down the busy street looking for their hotel. "There it is over there! The Maharajah Palace," said Jeetu, and he whipped a heavy U-turn and parked in front.

"Let's go, guys, let's get checked in," said Jeb, happy to get out of the van after the high-speed U-turn.

They piled out of the car, Jeb and Neusy grabbing their suitcases while the Doctor got his. Jeb and Neusy walked into the hotel; the Doctor stood on the sidewalk, suitcase next to him, looking at his surroundings. Lots of commotion, car traffic, foot traffic, busy like most large cities. Jeetu said he would look for parking and come back. He found a spot and ran back to find the Doctor still standing on the sidewalk. "Where are the others, Doctor?"

"They have gone in the hotel to check us in."

"Well, what do you think of Bombay?"

"I don't know, I haven't seen enough of it yet. But from here it looks like many other cities that I have been to before. But that curry aroma smell is enticing."

"Yes, that makes India different than other cities."

"What is that over there? Turban Masters."

"Do you want to have a look?"

"Yah, I think so."

Jeb and Neusy came outside. "What are you waiting for? Don't you guys want to get into your rooms?" asked Jeb.

"Nein, I want to go across the street there und look in that shop,"

"Well, here are your room keys. I am going to my room to relax a while. Eight hours in that van is a long time and my body is aching."

"Me too, let's go, Jeb. Maybe later we can look for a bar and have a couple brewskis."

"Yeah, good idea! Good thing the show isn't until tomorrow night, I'm too beat to set up things tonight."

"I know what you mean." Jeb and Neusy left and went to their hotel rooms.

"Well, let's go, good Doctor, I will go with you in case there is a translation issue."

Jeetu and the Doctor ventured across the street and into the turban shop. It was a stunning display of very fashionable turbans, some in the traditional colors and styles and others in more modern colors and designs. Now, most Indians that wear a turban usually wrap it on their heads each day, but in modern times some people want convenience and don't have a lot of time to wrap their turbans each morning. So more and more turban shops have appeared. As they looked, they noted the pricing on a small card next to each turban on the shelves. Very plain ones, similar to the one Jeetu was wearing, started at 3,000 rupees, or $60 US. Others went as high as 30,000 rupees, depending on what kind of fabric, wrapping style, and if it had a semi-precious stone woven in the front. Ones with precious stones could escalate the cost greatly.

The Doctor was particularly interested in two different turbans on the higher shelves: one a cosmic violet purple color with thin curvy silver pin lines and the other a royal blue color fabric with sparkles. Both ran about 25,000 rupees. The short, dark-skinned, long-bearded shopkeeper, who wore a bright red turban with a giant shimmering 30-karat ruby mounted in the front, came up towards the Doctor to greet him.

"Good day, my fine sirs! My name is Yogikarishi. But you can call me Yogi, like the bear. Where are you from, my good sir?"

"I am from Austria. My name is Jurgen Weislangwolf, but you can call me the Doctor. This is my guide, Jeetu."

"I see that you are interested in two of my finest turbans."

"Yah, yah… They look quite exquisite!"

"These are all made by my father in the outskirts of town. We only use the finest fabrics!"

"Wow! Look at that magnificent red stone in your turban!"

"Thank you, my good Doctor! That is a very rare 30-karat red ruby mined in the Himalayas."

"How much would something like that cost to mount in my turban?"

"I'm afraid that this one would be quite expensive, about 1,500,000 rupees."

"Acht du lieber! That does sound expensive."

"It's about $30,000," replied Jeetu.

"Well, I really think I like the cosmic purple fabric turban."

"A fine choice, my good Doctor."

"How about a discount for him, Yogi Bear? You know, he is a world-famous guitarist on tour here in India," said Jeetu.

"Really, well, let me think… I don't normally give a discount on our turbans. At Turban Masters, we spend a lot of painstaking hours selecting the finest fabrics, and then many more hours to warp them." Neither the Doctor nor Jeetu said a word. "Well…OK, I can give you 10% off."

"Deal! I like a bargain!" said the Doctor.

"You better try it on, my dear Doctor."

"Yah, yah…we wouldn't want it too tight or loose, would we?"

Yogi took the cosmic violet turban from the shelf and set it on the Doctor's head. It was too big and fell to the bridge of the Doctor's nose, covering his eyes.

"Achh, what a shame! Too big."

"No problem, my dear Doctor, all my turbans have a distinctive feature exclusive to my family's secret. Please turn around and hold the turban up comfortably above your eyes."

The Doctor did so. Yogi reached for a small tab of purple fabric with a black edge and gave it a sharp tug. ZIIIPPPP! The turban instantly fit the Doctor's head perfectly.

"Wow! That is amazing! I wonder if I could get a nice stone to go on it?"

"I have some stones over here. Dark blue sapphires are a bit expensive; however, these lighter colored blue topazes are cheaper and would be a good contrast color to the cosmic purple fabric."

"What about these lavender colored ones?"

"Oh, those are even cheaper! I can give you this 15-karat one for 5,000 rupees."

"That's about $100," said Jeetu.

"And of course, the 10% discount again on that stone?" Yogi frowned but nodded his head. "OK, can you mount it for me?"

"Sure, just give me a few minutes and I'll do it for you."

Jeetu and the Doctor waited as Yogi mounted the stone on the turban with a special jewelry clasp. The Doctor looked in his fanny pack and pulled out a wad of Indian rupees. "How much is that, Jeetu?"

"It would be 27,000 rupees including the 10% discount." Jeetu helped the Doctor count out the money and they handed it to Yogi.

"Thank you, my good sirs! And wait, let me get you a nice hat box to carry it around in."

"Thank you, Mr. Yogi Bear!"

The Doctor decided to wear it outside then said goodbye to Yogi and they left the shop. They were not on the street for more than ten seconds when a thief, watching the transaction from outside Turban Masters, ran by and snatched the turban off the Doctor's head. Instinct kicked in and Scaggz emerged. He immediately chased the thief leaving his Jeetu character behind. The Doctor, in shock that his new turban was already missing, thought Jeetu was one fast runner.

The thief ran into an alley behind the stores and hid behind old, discarded cartons waiting to be picked up. Scaggz turned into the alley and cautiously slowed, moving like a panther stalking his prey. The thief saw him coming. He waited and then appeared from behind the cartons with a curved eight-inch blade, lunging at him. Scaggz sidestepped as he grabbed the thief's arm, pushing it past him, then punched the knife-wielding hand with a leopard knuckle punch. The thief dropped the knife. Scaggz followed it up with a throat punch and the thief fell lifelessly to the ground. Scaggz took the knife, carved out the thief's eyeballs, and stuffed them down the dead man's throat. He pulled down the stacked cartons onto the thief's body, picked the turban up from where the thief dropped it, and left the alley to rejoin the Doctor. Minutes later, Jeetu was with the Doctor again.

"My goodness, Jeetu! What happened to the thief?"

"Oh, he was afraid when I was running after him. He dropped the turban and disappeared into a crowd. Here you are, your turban."

"Jeetu… I am fortunate to have you along with me."

Neusy and Jeb were in the hotel bar enjoying a beer. Jeb ordered the Throwing Monkey Fruited Pale Ale and Neusy had the Curried Lager, both brewed locally by Smells Of Bombay Brewing Company. Their bottles were painted in the same manner as Jeetu's van. "Only the finest local ingredients," it stated on the bottles.

"How is that beer?" asked Jeb.

"Not bad, only a hint of curry."

"Who would have thought? Anyway, this seems to be going OK. That Jeetu seems nice and attentive."

"Yes, glad he contacted us."

"The Doctor said they spoke about a half dozen times on the phone. He got to know him well. He knows the set, it seems, so all is good."

An hour late the Doctor walked in with his new turban on his head. Neusy was taking a sip of beer and burst out laughing, snorting beer out of his nostrils all over the bar. Jeb also found it funny and was happy he was not drinking his beer at that moment. Neusy said to the bartender, "Sorry about that."

"No, no, it is no worries, I'll clean it up," remarked the bartender just as police cars were heard coming from multiple directions. Everyone in the room stopped what they were doing. Jeb and Neusy each ordered another beer from the same brewery, but Jeb wanted to try the Sacred Cow Brown and Neusy the Rolling Stoned Red. They clicked bottles and drank the fresh beer.

Someone ran up to the bartender on the other side of the bar and whispered into his ear. When the bartender walked around to where Neusy and Jeb were sitting, Neusy asked, "What happened?"

"Oh, this is not good. Never happens around here, my kind sirs. But someone was killed in an alley behind those buildings across the street. His eyeballs cut out and were found in his throat."

Neusy gave Jeb a worried look. Jeb said, "I'm sure just a coincidence. Besides, on the last tour, all the murders happened at the concerts. He just bought that ridiculous turban so he was not near any alley."

The next morning, the whole group met up for breakfast in the hotel dining room. Complimentary continental breakfast was offered, and the Doctor wore his new turban for all to see. "What the heck is that? We saw it yesterday; it looks ridiculous on you," said Jeb.

"Yah, it's my new turban… It is part of my spiritual journey. I must look und be the part of who I am to become."

"Huh?" said Neusy.

Typical Doctor gibberish, the two thought to themselves. "And how much did you spend for that thing?"

"It was 27,000 rupees, or $540 US Dollars," said Jeetu.

"I don't know how you are ever going to get out of debt and make money if you keep wasting money on useless junk. I don't want Bea calling me to send her money from this tour or the next one in the US. In fact, I never want her calling me again," said Jeb, annoyed, referring to the Doctor's girlfriend in Austria.

"Achh, yah. I knew you would say these things, Jeb, you are such a downer sometimes. You have no vision… Achh."

"Well, I try to help you manage your money a bit, but you never listen to me. What would your Bea have to say about it?"

"She needn't know about the cost, und I can say it was a gift by an Indian fan."

"OK, whatever…let's finish up here so we can get to the venue and get set up for the concert tonight."

"Jeetu, you can drive them to the venue, I have something to do. You can come back for me later," said the Doctor.

Jeb and Neusy climbed into Jeetu's van and they took off. The Doctor sat in the hotel lounge on a purple sofa waiting. After a while, a man walked into the hotel lobby. He was in his early seventies with grayish, receding, black-dyed hair and moustache wearing spectacles and a blue-gray business suit. His name was Lord Doctor Simon Spiers of London, England. He was Jurgen's pediatrician when he was a young lad. Later he developed special vitamin cocktails made from flowers near Antonio Vivaldi's grave in Italy. The Lord Doctor discovered that the flowers contained DNA of Vivaldi and greatly enhanced his musical abilities. In fact, after an injection, the Doctor would only play Italian music for days. More specifically, *the Four Seasons* or *Violin Capriccios di Paganini.* The vitamin shots keep him exhilarated for two weeks but afterwards he felt weak and uninspired. He walked over to the purple sofa. "Hello, Jurgen, I'm here."

"It's about time. I am running low of energy. I really need my vitamin shot."

"Well, I have that…but something new as well."

Doctor Spiers injected Jurgen with the vitamin shot and within seconds he felt rejuvenated.

"What's this new thing that you mentioned?"

"You will no longer need me to fly in to give you the vitamin shots. I have developed the formula into easy-to-take tablets."

"Yah, that is good!"

"In fact, I have a bottle here I can give you now. This will last you six months."

"Wunderbar! Bravo!"

"I have also shipped a box of vitamin tablets to your home in Austria. They should be waiting for you when you get back. Now we have another matter to discuss."

"Yah, I know…it's about the clone. Where is the clone, now?"

"It is in New Delhi. We have him booked in several clubs and we should make out pretty well."

"I hope no one hears about me playing these other shows in India at the same time."

"Well, we will always be on opposite sides of the country, so it is unlikely for anyone to find out. Besides, that other Indian booking agent, Tamissvara, isn't well known. These are small, indiscrete, out of the way places. Oh, one more surprise: Tamissvara is sending four boxes of the Doctor T-shirts to sell at the show tonight."

"Yah? Where did he get those?"

"His family are in the silk-screening business. Before we arrived, I sent him images of you to create the T-shirts. We are going to sell them at the clone's shows too."

"Achh! Brilliant, Dr. Spiers! But we must not tell Jeb or Neusy about the other shows with the clone."

Jeb and Neusy had the stage and merch booth set up. They instructed Jeetu to go back to the hotel to collect the Doctor. Showtime was scheduled for 8:00 pm at the TATA Theater. TATA was a moderate theater with 1,010 seats. Tonight, the famous singer, Sheila Chandra, would join the Doctor on stage during the concert. Since the Beatles had been extremely popular in India, a Beatles medley would be performed. It was nearly 6:30 pm when the Doctor arrived at the TATA.

"Well, you took your sweet time getting here, Jeetu."

"I'm sorry, good Jeb, the road near the hotel was blocked by a caravan of camels and a few elephants."

"Oh, just a few elephants…imagine that."

"Well, we are here now. Yah, where is the singing lady? We need to talk about the songs," asked the Doctor.

"She should be here soon."

Sheila entered the theater with her 6'7" bodyguard at 6:45 pm. They walked down to the stage where the Doctor and the others were standing.

"Hello! I'm Sheila! How are you?"

"Hello, Sheila! I am the Doctor. My, you are very lovely, my dear."

"Thank you!"

"That is a beautiful dress, Sheila," said the Doctor.

"Thank you! That is a magnificent turban!"

"Yah, danke. We need to discuss the song list."

"You got the text from me about which songs I know, yes?"

"Yah, yah… All of those songs I can play."

"Okay, George Harrison songs are the most popular in India, I would like to do more of those. How about 'Here Comes the Sun' and 'While My Guitar Gently Weeps?' The latter would give you some nice guitar solos to play."

"Yah…agreed! Good choices. Yah!"

"And let's do the John song, 'Across the Universe.' It touches on a bit of Hinduism. The people will like that one too."

"Okay, we do it. What about the finale piece? It should be up tempo, yah?"

"Hmmmm? How about 'Hard Day's Night,' that's a good one."

"Okay, this will be fine, Sheila!"

"Let me get a photo of you both together for the Doctor's website," said Neusy.

"Achh! Maybe we go backstage until showtime, yah?"

"Certainly, Doctor!"

"Achh! You can call me Jurgen, my dear!" The Doctor was in full on charm mode. Jeb gave Neusy the I-am-going-to-puke look and Neusy responded with an upward eye roll signaling he felt the same way.

The theater had nearly filled its capacity; it would be a good show. Jeb had the merch table set up and was ready to go when a delivery man came up to his table with four boxes on a cart.

"What's this?"

"Special delivery for Jeb."

"Oookaaaay, that is me?"

Jeb opened a box. The Doctor T-shirts, where did they come from? They didn't bring any along because they had enough things to carry between the three of them. Jeb took out a T-shirt and looked at it. "Wow! Pretty good design and good photo of the Doctor," he said to Neusy. "It almost rivals my own designs." He read the label: Made in India. Something strange was going on. "Oh, well, I will just sell them, anything for a buck… Hahaha." Neusy agreed with a nod, then motioned to the stage with his head. Jeb nodded and Neusy walked to the backstage area.

Showtime, the curtains opened; the Doctor stood on stage behind the Viswadjit and behind him was the MMM— one side had congas and the other held a sitar. He looked radiant in his beautiful cosmic purple turban. He began to play. Song after song, spinning to different necks, the audience enjoyed the spectacle of it all. After all, he did look like the Goddess Shiva with the MMM playing the other instruments behind him with its multiple arms moving. The addition of the sparkling lavender amethyst in his turban bouncing off beams of light into the eyes of the spectators added to the effect.

"Guten Tag, Mumbai! I am pleased that you have enjoyed what I have played so far. But now we have a special surprise, which isn't really a surprise because it was well advertised. Please welcome Sheila Chandra!"

The audience roared as Sheila came out onto the stage dressed in a stunning red sari with gold sequenced designs about it. "Good evening, my dear fans! I am very happy that you came out to see me and this wonderful gentleman, the Doctor."

They began the Beatles medley. Standing ovations came after each of the George Harrison songs. And then they played 'Hard Day's Night.' Sheila's powerful voice ripped through the theater. The people were powerfully moved, yelling, screaming, loving every second of it. After the song was finished, another standing ovation was received.

"It was a wonderful show, Jurgen! But I have to go now, I have another engagement tomorrow and a long way to travel."

"Achh, yah… Well, all's well that ends well! It was nice playing with you, Sheila."

Shelia and her bodyguard left the theater. Unfortunately, more than half the room left with her. Jeb was bewildered, he wasn't going to sell as much merch now. However, there were about fifty people or more lined up at the merch table, so maybe he would make some cash.

The Doctor played on with the remaining people enjoying his playing. It was not as upbeat as his shows with his band, and because of this, the merch sales were lower. Jeb, though, was pleased that the addition of the T-shirts did help. The Doctor did something to make money. This tour was going quite well.

While the real Doctor played his concerts in Mumbai, clone Number Two, or as he was known, the condescending clone, was playing in New Delhi. His first night would be at the famous Haus Khas Club. Very suitable for Number Two. He didn't have Jeb, Neusy, or Jeetu to rely on. Most of his set ups were done by the agent, Tamissvara, which means the Lord of Darkness.

Tamissvara was promised an extra 10% above his agent fee to help the clone set up his gear, which wasn't very much, just a little amp and a cheap Universe Guitar copy that was made in Indonesia. No MMM machine would be used. Simple logic was that the Indian Doctor fans would be happy enough to see the Doctor play, although this wasn't really the Doctor. Everything was ready to go at the Haus Khas and Tamissvara motioned the clone to go on stage.

"It is time for the show! You better take the stage, Mr. Doctor."

"Yah, yah. What's the rush? I'll go when I'm ready, Tamissvara."

Number Two exited the green room and took the stage. "Guten Abend, my New Delhi friends! Well, you're not really my friends, but that's okay. I will play some classical music for you, und you will enjoy it! Here is Tarrega's 'Capricho Arabe.'"

Clone Number Two could play much better than clone Number One. The concentration on his face was intense, careful not to make mistakes. However, some feelings and textures were different from the real Doctor. A little bland, but well absorbed by the crowd. The song ended in applause.

"Und now a little Indian folk melody improvisation I came up with, because I am a genius und all of you, unfortunately, are not." The clone played his Indian improvisation piece. This one went off quite well and his feeling and mood were correct. The crowd was swaying their heads and grooving with the clone. Again, the song ended in mass applause.

"I knew that you would like that! How could you not? Only morons wouldn't like the genius I put into that piece." The show went on, song after song, and the people really liked it. "Well, it is time to end the show, thank God! I will now play my final piece, 'Leyenda' by Issac Albeniz."

This piece is one of the most difficult to play in Spanish music and the clone's expert dexterity in his finger style really showed through on this one. The piece was played perfectly.

The song ended in the loudest applause of the night. "That was great! Fantastic!" Then, "More! More!" roared from the crowd. But they would get no more.

"Well, that's it! Und now a little meet und greet. I really don't like meet und greet because I don't really want to meet or greet any of you. But my manager said I have to do it. So let's go!"

The clone went to the side of the club where he could sit down at a small table and meet the line of people that lined up along the side wall. Tamissvara had a table next to the clone's table with bootleg Doctor T-shirts, DVDs, and CDs for sale. He was also promised an extra 30% of all merch sold, as he used Indian factories to make all the merch products and would bring the stuff to each show. But these extra shows and merch were part of the grand scheme of things to generate the extra income for the real Doctor and to help Dr. Spiers continue his clone program.

The fans approached the fake Doctor and each began to say hello and ask a few questions. "You were marvelous, Mr. Doctor!"

"Yah, yah, I know, I always am! Now move it along!"

Tamissvara then encouraged the man to buy some merch. The man bought a T-shirt for 1,500 rupees, or $30 US.

"Wow! You were so great tonight! I have waited a lifetime to meet you, Mr. Doctor. I have been a fan a long time."

"Yah? Just to let you know, I am great every night because I am the Doctor of Dynamics. No one can play like me. Now move along!"

Tamissvara made a DVD and T-shirt sale this time.

"Yah, what do you want?"

"I just wanted to meet you and shake your hand. Maybe some of your inner energies will flow into me and make me a better player."

"You can meet me, but you cannot shake my hand or touch me. Und no matter what you do in life, you will never be better or play like me!"

The disgruntled fan walked away and didn't buy a T-shirt.

Tamissvara looked at the clone and said, "Hey Doctor, cut out the condescending trash talk and insults. I am trying to sell some merchandise here and make some extra money."

It wasn't easy for the clone to be nice to people, something that carried from Jurgen's actual traits but amplified in Dr. Spiers' cloning process. The actual Doctor could be very rude and condescending, but usually only with people he knew, not with fans.

After Tamissvara warned him, the clone tried to be nicer, but sometimes he would slip.

"How are you, Mr. Doctor? It is an honor to meet you and hear you play tonight."

"Yah, yah, danke!"

"Will you stay in Delhi long? We have special food in Delhi that is only found here."

"Yah, well, you know, I don't eat so good in India. I have a special diet."

"What kind of diet?"

"No Indian food diet! Would you now buy a T-shirt or a DVD? I really like making extra money. Thank you, bye-bye!"

Tamissvara made another sale. This time a T-shirt, CD, and a DVD.

"That's it, Doctor…keep being nice to people."

"I am getting tired und I want to go und rest soon, Tamissvara."

Tamissvara stood up and made the announcement. The meet and greet would end soon and only two more fans could meet the Doctor.

"You were so great! I have been a fan for a long time."

"Yah, yah! I've heard it all before, dankeschön!"

"Can I get your autograph?"

"Achh! I hate autographs. Prescriptions is what I call my signature. I don't want to…"

"Please, I'll do anything."

The clone looked at Tamissvara and they both nodded and grinned at each other.

"Well, I tell you what, I'm very tired und want to sleep now. But if you und the next person in line each buy two T-shirts, two DVDs, und two CDs. I will sign those things for you. Und then I must sleep."

The happy fans were more than willing to do what the Doctor said. They bought their things and the clone signed them. Tamissvara was pleased that the night had been very successful with the merch sales, which added a hefty profit in addition to the club's payment.

"If we can do this well every night, we will make the big bucks."

"Achh! I'm very tired. I must get to my hotel room now."

"Okay, I'll grab the amp and your guitar and we'll leave."

"Yah, I hope Dr. Spiers arrives soon."

The next day, Number Two, feeling more tired and weak, had another show. "This will be great fun tonight, Mr. Doctor."

"Yah? Und why is that?"

"The Odeon is a very unique and fun place."

"Und what is so special about it?"

"Well, it's like a school classroom. It has a blackboard and books everywhere. The guests in the front can sit in a primary school desk and the people in the back just have to stand."

"Yah, yah! Sounds like great fun. NOT!!"

"And you can be their teacher, kindly Doctor. At the Odeon, it is customary to teach good manners and a moral lesson to the students."

"Yah, I will give them a moral lesson already. But good manners they will not get." As they entered the club, the clone was carrying the small amp and cheap Universe Guitar in a gig bag on his back and Tamissvara carried two merch boxes stacked on top of each other almost blocking his eyesight. They took in the surroundings. It was just as they had been told, like a school classroom. A large blackboard was hung on the wall behind the stage. There was a teacher's desk on one side of the venue. There were also 25 desks in front of the stage. All of the walls had bookcases full of books and shelves with toys, crayons, a few globes, and other useful teaching aids. Off the one side there was a whiteboard with dry erase makers in various colors for guests to write their names or draw pictures on.

Tamissvara set down the merch boxes on the teacher's desk and began to set up the amp on the stage. The manager came to greet them. "Hello, my good friends, I am Gupta Bedi and welcome to the Odeon Club."

"Yes, hello! I am Tamissvara. Where can I set up these fine T-shirts to sell?"

"Over there, next to the ancient history bookcase. We are expecting a good crowd tonight. And we hope the Doctor can teach them some lessons."

"Yah, yah! I will teach them how great I am!"

"And don't forget to teach them a moral lesson."

"Yah, I will teach them to not bother me or ask me too many questions."

"Okay, good gentlemen, we open the doors in thirty minutes and the show will start promptly at 8:00 pm."

"Okay, very good! How are you feeling, Doctor?"

"Achh, you know, Tamissvara, I am feeling very weak. I hope Dr. Spiers shows up tonight."

"Well, hang in there, Doctor. He should be here soon."

The venue had close to two hundred people and the front 25 desks were already occupied by VIP guests. Tamissvara told the clone to get ready as it was almost 8:00 pm. The clone walked up on the stage with his cheap Universe Guitar and approached the mic.

"Guten Abend, Delhi! It is time for a little Ravi Shankar!" The clone played a well known number by Ravi Shankar. The mood was good, the rhythm was right. The crowd was right and enjoying the authentic Indian sounds the clone played on his cheap Universe Guitar. Even though the guitar was a cheap copy, it played decent and had good tone. It also had some EFX built in, such as an echo and a looper so that the clone could make additional textures and rhythms.

"Und now, I will play an instrumental version of 'Something' by the Beatles."

"Why don't you teach us a lesson first?"

"All right, here is your lesson… Don't interrupt me while I am playing!"

The clone began to play an interesting version of "Something." The crowd loved it, mostly because George Harrison wrote it, and he was all of India's favorite Beatle. The crowd clapped ecstatically and hollered at the end of the song.

"How about another lesson, Doctor!" yelled one fan.

"Yah, here is one… Be quiet or I'll sentence you to Saturday detention in the camp, yah? Und now, some 'Moonlight Sonata' by Beethoven." The clone masterfully finger picked his version of the sonata. The people were in indescribable bliss. Never had such an artist played in New Delhi before. An artist of such magnitude that could cover Indian music as well as Western classics. The clone played a wonderful set of mixed music. It came time for the last song.

"It is now time for the last song. Und now here is my version of Vivaldi's 'Summer.'"

"How about another lesson?" stated one of the guests seated in the front row of desks while four others nodded in agreement.

"Yah, okay. You five go over there to the white board und each write ten times, 'I will not bother the Doctor during his show.'"

The guests did as they were instructed. Once again, the clone ended the show to thunderous applause in the small room. The clone was exhausted from his lack of nutritional shots so he decided to go back to his hotel room.

"There will be no meet and greet tonight! Please let the Doctor through. I will be here if anyone needs a T-shirt or a DVD."

"Everything was great, my good friends."

"Thanks, Gupta. The Doctor is very tired, can you get a driver to bring him to the hotel?"

"My pleasure, Tamissvara."

Several fans began to block the exit way. Some were insistent to get an autograph.

"Hey Doctor, how about an autograph?" said one fan.

"Nein, nein. I am exhausted, let me by."

"Come on, dude! We waited forever to see you! Come on, just an autograph," said another.

"Und you will wait longer. I am leaving."

"Come Doctor, here, sign this concert flyer for me. Don't be such a baby."

"Achh, so you want me to sign your flyer, eh?"

The clone took the man's flyer, put it in the back of his stretchy pants, and rubbed his ass with it. The clone made his way outside to get into the car that was sent for him. The driver brought him to the hotel and the clone slowly dragged himself to his room. Being very weak, he dropped down on the bed and closed his eyes.

A few minutes later a knock came at his door and he slowly got up to answer it.

"Here you are, Number Two!"

"Dr. Spiers! I am almost dead! I need my shots."

"And that you shall have, my fine creation. Pull down your pants."

"Why did you wait so long to come?"

"I had problems with the train schedules from Mumbai. But I am here now, and everything will be all right."

The clone dropped to the floor in exhaustion and his breathing slowed. Dr Spiers helped him up and guided him towards the bed. The clone lay down.

"There, there, my little clone. The Doctor is here now." He pulled Number Two's pants down to his knees. Along with no digestive system, he had no rectum or anus, only a round mass where one is usually split. Dr. Spiers injected the clone with three very large shots into his round mass. One red vile, then a yellow vile, and lastly a blue vile, which altogether had what the clone needed to stay alive.

After a good night's sleep and the rejuvenating shots, the clone was feeling alive. Tamissvara came to his room to discuss the evening's performance.

"How are you feeling this morning, Doctor?"

"I am feeling much better. I received my special sauce mixture last night."

"Okay good! Tonight's show is in a theater, it's a lovely place."

"Yah, okay…"

"There will be a guest singer that wants to do a Beatles medley with you."

"Yah? Und what songs are they?"

"'Across the Universe,' 'My Guitar Gently Weeps,' and 'Helter Skelter.'"

"That's not a problem."

"Are you coming down for breakfast?"

"Nein, I don't eat the India stuff. I will practice the songs for a while und see you before we go to the theater."

Tamissvara left and then the clone had another visitor come knocking on the door. "Good morning, my little clone."

"Achh, Guten Morgen. Don't call me your little clone. I am the Doctor!"

"Well, actually, I am the doctor. I am your doctor, Doctor Spiers."

"Yah, yah. You are the great Lord Doctor! My creator…blah, blah, blah."

"Well, you don't have to be rude… Oh, I forgot, you are the condescending one, not at all like the other more socially acceptable clone."

"Yah, why did you make two of us? I should have been enough."

"Well, because with the two of you we can make a lot more money than with just one of you."

"Yah, I guess that makes sense."

"Tonight, we have to leave right after the meet and greet. The real Doctor will come to Delhi to play at the Taj Mahal. We cannot be seen in the same city at the same time."

"I'll be ready to leave right after the show."

The time neared 6:00 pm. Tamissvara came to collect the clone and bring him to the venue. Doctor Spiers would also go with them in the taxi. Tamissvara did not know for what purpose Dr. Spiers had joined them, only that he collaborated with the Doctor.

Tamissvara, Dr. Spiers, and Number Two arrived at the theater. They entered a beautifully decorated theater, the kind that the real Doctor would appreciate. But to the clone, it was just a place to play in. He did not care about the décor or fashion. He just wanted to play and insult people. The place had not opened to the public yet and was basically empty, except for the manager and a few staff members. The manager came to greet them, as expected.

"Good day, my fine sirs! I am Sadavir, the manager."

"Hello, Sadavir! I am Tamissvara and this is the Doctor!"

"I am a doctor, too. My name is Lord Doctor Simon Spiers."

"My goodness gracious, two fine doctors at my place. How wonderful! It certainly will be a great evening. Especially when the Doctor, ahem…the Doctor of Dynamics, plays the medley with Benny Dayal, one of India's famous pop stars."

"Yes, it will be most memorable, I'm sure," said Dr Spiers.

Sadavir led Tamissvara to the area prepared to set up the merch. The clone walked over to the stage, set up his amp, and plugged in the cheap Universe Guitar to experiment with the acoustics of the theater. It sounded amazing. Unlike the other venues, this place had superior acoustics. Doctor Spiers sat in the front row of seats and listened as the clone played. He smiled as he admired his own work.

"Number Two, you are definitely the finer of the two."

"Yah, yah! I know that!"

"Your condescending attitude is your only flaw."

"Yah, it's not a flaw," said Number Two.

At 6:30 pm, the pop singer Benny Dayal arrived. "I must warn you about the Doctor. He has had a rough journey here in India. He gets a bit…well, let's just say cranky," said Dr. Spiers.

"Okay, I'll keep that in mind."

"Hey Jurgen! The singer is here. This is Benny."

From up on the stage, Number Two responds, "So you are a famous singer here in India?"

"Well, I don't like to brag, but yeah!"

"I hope that you can sing as well as I play the guitar. If not, it won't sound too good."

"Well, I'll do my best. Do you want to try the medley?"

"Nein…I will be perfect."

"Are you sure? Why don't we try it once?"

"Achh! Okay, let's get it done with!"

Benny climbed up on the stage and grabbed a mic. First, they tried the first verse and chorus of "Across the Universe." After a few lines of Benny singing, the clone stopped playing. "What's the matter?"

"Achh, you don't sound anything like Lennon."

"Sorry, I'm Benny, not Lennon. Let's keep going."

They tried the next song, a verse and a chorus of "While My Guitar Gently Weeps." Again, after a few vocal lines he stopped playing. "What's the matter now, Doctor?"

"Achh! That's the worst George Harrison voice I ever heard."

"Well, you don't exactly sound like Eric Clapton either. Let's keep going."

They tried the final song, "Helter Skelter." The clone again stopped playing mid-way through the song. "What's the matter now? I don't sound like Paul McCartney?"

"Nein, my balls itch. I have to scratch my balls." Dr. Spiers was wondering why the cloning process created balls and no digestive system, hair, or an ass.

"How lovely. I guess it will be okay tonight."

"Yah, you will be okay, I will be outstanding," said Number Two as he adjusted his wig.

The doors opened and the people waiting outside were coming in. It looked like it would be a full house. Tamissvara was ready to sell merch. He was feeling good about these recent shows and was raking in the cash, just as Jurgen and Dr. Spiers had planned. Soon the theater was filled and the announcement to commence came over the speakers. The clone took the stage and began to play. First, he played Bach, then Mozart, and then some Spanish music, and finally some

Indian music. Then came the time everyone was waiting for. "Please welcome our very own Benny Dayal." The women went nuts and the men were just as happy. Benny approached the mic.

"The Doctor and I have worked up a little Beatles medley for all of you. And here we go, a one, and a two—"

"Nein, nein… I will do the counting here. A one, und a two, und a three."

The medley began and Benny sang beautifully. They continued into the second song; people were crying and weeping. Then the third song, "Helter Skelter," was in your face. The clone played a mean and hard sound as Benny belted out the lyrics. The people were fanatical and screamed loudly. "We hope that you liked our show, good night."

People were already lined up at the merch table, buying up things. Benny and the clone walked back to the merch area to greet the guests.

After a brief period of handshakes and hellos, Dr. Spiers came over to the clone and reminded him that they had to leave. Dr. Spiers told Tamissvara to pack up the merch and it was time to go. The clone took his little amp and guitar, and the three headed toward the door. Tamissvara already had a driver and a car waiting to drive them to Rajasthan. They left the theater abruptly, while the fans wanted more.

"How long until we reach Rajasthan, driver?"

"About seven hours or so."

"Well, we might as well try to get some sleep in the car. Tomorrow is a big day in Jaipur. The Concert for the Tigers. Then the next morning, we will make a detour and visit the tiger reserve," said Tamissvara, thinking he would show the Doctor some things he had never seen.

It was about midnight as they drove out of the city. At the last signal, as they drove out, a colorful VW van drove into the city through the same signal. The driver of the VW got a glimpse of someone with the Doctor's features in the passing car. But how could that be? The Doctor was in his van. Then he thought about clone Number One who he had left in Palm Springs.

Jeb, Neusy, Jeetu, and the Doctor slept well at their hotel. They all joined together for breakfast in the hotel dining hall. "Achh! I never can get enough of these continental breakfasts in India. This food is fantastic!"

"Yeah, it's all right. I was a bit reluctant about Indian food, but I have been very surprised by how good it tastes," said Jeb.

The whole time, Jeetu was eating slowly and not speaking. His eyes kept moving back and forth between the people he shared the table with. He was thinking about when they pulled into town. That guy in the other car sure looked like the Doctor. Then he thought again about the clone in California.

"Tonight is going to be special! I will play Mozart's *Requiem* at the Taj Mahal." Very appropriate since the Taj Mahal is a mausoleum dedicated to the beloved wife of the emperor, Shah Jahan, in 1631 AD.

After breakfast was finished, the group made their way into the van once more. The Taj Mahal was a magnificent site, one of the most beautiful and unique buildings in the world of architecture. There was a stage already set up in front of the water ways with the domes of the Taj Mahal just behind the stage. There were lighting trusses and sound equipment set about the stage. As they parked the van near the stage and began to unload, a man approached them.

"I am Baha Udeen. I am the curator of the Taj Mahal. I hope that the stage is set up to your liking."

"Yes, it looks fine, thank you," replied Jeb.

"We will start letting people in at 7:00 pm. I trust that will be fine."

"More than fine, Baha, more than fine," said the Doctor.

Neusy was already setting up the equipment while the Doctor, in his turban, just stood and stared at the magnificent Taj Mahal.

The concert went off perfectly while Jeetu spent the entire time in town searching for what he believed was the second clone that Number One mentioned to him. Unsuccessful, he reapplied his tanning spray and headed back to the Taj Mahal to pick up his passengers.

Chapter 12

After leaving the hospitality of Baha Udeen, the real tour hit the road for Udaipur, the Lake City. Besides the concert that was planned on a barge on the lake, the Doctor would meet his first guru to help explain about transcendental meditation. This was a big day for the Doctor.

Udaipur would take them about five hours to reach. Scaggz was having trouble staying in his Jeetu character as his thoughts about a second clone raged. Luckily for him, everyone in the van was busy and did not speak to him. Neusy had in his ear buds and listened to some tunes, Jeb was reading a new fiction novel, and the Doctor sat in front next to Jeetu and enjoyed the Indian landscape, which was very arid and dusty, dotted with a tree here and there. Eventually they got to the base of the mountain that would take them upwards to Udaipur.

The landscape changed to taller evergreens lining the winding, two-lane mountain road. There were a few cars going up in front of their van and some cars going down the opposite direction. To their left was the mountain and to the right was a cliff that extended downward. "Well, about forty-five minutes and we shall be there, my friendly Doctor."

"Achh, that is wunderbar! We are making good time."

Fifteen minutes later, the cars traveling in front of them came to an abrupt stop. Jeetu slammed on the brakes. Jeb flew forward and bumped his head on the back of Jeetu's seat; his fiction novel flew out the driver's window. Neusy did the same on the Doctor's side. The Doctor and Jeetu had braced themselves for impact.

"What the hell happened?" asked Jeb.

"The cars in front just stopped."

"What the hell?" said Jeb. The cars were jammed up as far as the eye could see. This couldn't be good. How long would they be stuck on the narrow mountain road? Would they get to Udaipur in time for the Doctor to meet the guru?

"I'm going to take a walk and see what's happened up ahead," said Jeetu.

"Yah, a promising idea, Jeetu. Maybe I go for a walk with you." The two exited the van and walked uphill. Jeb got out to look for his book on the road while Neusy just sat in the van listening to his music.

About one hour passed and no sign of the Doctor and Jeetu. "I wonder what those guys are up to."

"I don't know. What could be taking them so long?"

"I'm getting hungry…" As they looked out of the van, they could see other drivers and people outside their vehicles. They could hear all kinds of Indian music blaring out of the different cars and trucks. It was a mix-matched catastrophe of sounds, not at all in sync. They saw some people taking out portable stoves and cooking, right there on the steep mountain road. Some of it smelled rather good. It was a mountain road tailgate party. Very strange, indeed.

"Hey Jeb, do you want to walk around and see if anyone will offer us something to eat? I'm starving."

"Yeah, maybe so… It's getting monotonous just sitting here."

Jeb and Neusy got out and walked uphill. They hoped to see the Doctor and Jeetu. They walked past many people sitting around outside their cars, some had chairs and sat listening to their music. Others were cooking. They came near a man cooking yellow curry and had some naan bread.

"Excuse me, good sir, but my friend and I are hungry. We have been on the road for four hours without a morsel to eat," said Neusy.

"Sure, you can eat with me… I have enough for three… Not quite done yet, needs a few more dashes of spices."

"Thanks, that's really nice of you! My name is Neusy, and this is Jeb."

"Hello, my name is Kim. Nice to meet you two! Where are you from?"

"We are from the US. We are on a musical tour with Jurgen Weislangwolf, world class guitarist from Austria."

"Wow! That sounds interesting! So how do you like India so far?"

"It's okay…but we could do without this traffic jam," said Jeb.

"Yeah, this sucks!" agreed Neusy. "I wish we could get some cold beers. It's been a while since we had some good, cold beer."

"Well, it just so happens…" Kim pulled out an ice chest from his trunk. "Here, you guys, have one on me!" He had twelve bottles of beer packed in ice. Jeb and Neusy couldn't believe it. "This is brewed by my brother's brewery on the other side of the mountain. He was a shepherd, inherited the family business. That was never for me. I became an engineer. After a few years, he too realized he was not meant to be a shepherd. He took his love of beer and opened a brewery he named the Drunk Shepherd Brewery." The three popped open the cold brews. As Kim tended to his curry, Jeb and Neusy touched bottles and drank their Shedding Sheep Crisp Lager, brewed by the local brewery.

Kim took out three bowls and spoons from his car, put curry in each one, and handed two bowls to Neusy and Jeb.

"Thanks, Kim!"

"Here, take some of this naan bread, you dip it in the curry. My wife made it this morning."

"Wow! This is fantastic!"

"Yeah. Really good!"

Jeb and Neusy looked at each other and both smiled and winked. This was the best curry and naan bread they had had on the entire trip. Better than all the hotel curry and better than all the restaurant curry. The beer added to the experience as Kim made sure the two never had an empty bottle. As they ate, they could see the Doctor in his purple blouse and wig blowing in the air as he and Jeetu walked downhill. They finally met together. "What took you guys so long?"

"We had to walk a long way until we saw the problem."

"And what is the problem?"

"There is a truck that crossed the center line to try and pass a slower car ahead of him. But his engine conked out and his truck is diagonally blocking the road. Cars cannot go up and cars cannot go down."

"Fuck! That's just great!" said Jeb.

After another hour and a half, the local army regiment arrived to deal with the problem. They were able to get the cars coming down the mountain from Udaipur to back up the hill, leaving enough space to push the truck blocking the road off to one side of the two-lane mountain road. Then by directing traffic, they allowed ten cars to go up and then ten cars to go down. Cars started to move in both directions. This process took a long time. After ten hours total, they made it to Udaipur. It was now 4:00 am. Jeetu's GPS ran out of power and they had no idea how to find the hotel. They drove up and down the darkened streets in search of their hotel. They saw soldiers sitting on a corner. "Excuse me, sir, we are looking for the Royal Udaipur Hotel."

"Waaah, I think it's down that way about one kilometer."

"Nooo, it isssn't, Abmed. It is that way about two kilometersss."

"These guys are drunk. It is forbidden for soldiers to be drunk on duty. Shame on them!" said Jeetu.

Feeling lost and like they would be spending the night in the VW van, they eventually saw a laundry truck. Jeetu ran after it when it passed the van. "Wait! Wait!"

"What's the matter?"

"We are lost. We are looking for the Royal Udaipur Hotel."

"Well, follow me, good sir, I am going there now to deliver fresh bed sheets."

Jeetu returned to the van and informed the others about the stroke of luck they just had. Within one minute they were at the hotel and parked the van. They grabbed their travel bags and entered the lobby.

"Hello, do you have a reservation for Jeb Acorns, plus three?"

"No sir! Sorry we don't."

"What? I made the reservation two weeks ago."

"Yes, that may be true…but it was canceled at 12:00 am."

"What are you talking about?"

"It's our policy, if the guests do not check in before 12:00 am, the reservation is canceled."

"My God, well please, give us three rooms."

"Sorry, sir, the hotel is fully booked, there are no rooms."

"What the hell are we going to do?"

"There is a small hotel across town called the Natini Inn. They are not a seven-star hotel like us, but it should be suitable. They might have some rooms; I can call them and find out."

"Yeah, that would be great," said Jeb.

The desk clerk made the call. "They have three rooms available, and you will speak with Mahesh at the desk."

"Okay, how do we get there?"

"You can follow our laundry truck driver; he can show you the way. It is next on his route."

After a decent rest at the small but cozy Natini Inn, the travelers assembled for another continental breakfast in the dining room. Discussion of the day began to commence.

"I have to meet with this Chenmay Chemmal about tonight's show."

"Achh, yah… I also have things to do."

"Like what?"

"I must meet Swami Dharma."

"Swami Dharma? Who the hell is that?"

"He is my yoga guru… He will instruct me in transcendental meditation."

"That sounds really important. You better not miss him," Jeb sarcastically remarked.

"Jeetu, do you know how to get us to the lake where we are to perform?"

"Yes, I charged my GPS last night and already plugged in the location."

"Yah, Jeetu, text me this location und I will send it to Swami Dharma."

"Well, we better get a move on."

"Nein, not quite yet."

"Why not?" asked Jeb.

"Achh! I am going in for seconds, the cheese und naan bread are fantastic here."

"You better slow down on all that cheese; you are developing quite a gut and love handles."

"Yah, yah, Jeb. You are always the party pooper."

They left the Natini Inn and made their way to the lake where the performance was to be held. As they stood in front of the palace, they looked across the deserted land. Then Chenmay Chemmal arrived, the promoter. "Good morning, good sirs, I am Chemmal."

"So where is the lake?" asked Neusy.

"You are looking at it, kind sir."

"What? There is no lake here!" snapped Jeb.

"On the contrary, you are looking at it. It has just dried up,"

"Dried up? On the Udaipur website it shows a nice lake in front of the palace. There is nothing here."

"Yes, well, that is an old picture. To tell the truth, Udaipur hasn't had any significant rain for years, and the constant use of water to take care of the population, well…so the lake has dried up."

"How are we supposed to have a concert on a barge in the middle of the lake if there is no lake?"

"There is the barge over there. See it?"

In the distance they could see a red-and-gold colored structure that looked like a small house but was the barge.

"There is where you will set up your equipment for the show tonight."

"Great!" said Jeb.

While Jeb and Neusy continued to discuss the plans for the setup with Chemmal, a man with long black-and-gray hair and a long beard wearing an orange robe appeared. It was Swami Dharma.

"Good day, my good sirs. Who is the Doctor?"

"I am the Doctor!"

"Greetings and good tidings, dear Doctor, I am Swami Dharma. We communicated online about your desire to learn the ways of transcendental meditation."

"Yah, that's what I am here for."

"But first a donation for my organization. Let's say… 50,000 rupees."

"Achh! How much is that, Jeetu?"

"It's like $1,000 USD."

The Doctor opened his fanny pack and counted out the money. After the transaction, Swami Dharma motioned the Doctor to follow him to a secluded place. Jeetu was instructed to wait with the others as this journey was only for one. After walking about fifteen minutes to a secluded spot, Swami Dharma and the Doctor sat under a banyan tree.

"The first step is to sit in the lotus position like me."

"Achh! Yes this is possible, but very uncomfortable."

"In time you will get used to it. You must do it every day for short periods of time. Now put your palms facing upwards with them resting on your knees and close your eyes."

"Ah, so. Like this?"

"Yes, that's right. Now clear your mind of all thoughts. Think of peaceful things: a bustling stream, birds singing in the morning, a cool wind at the end of a hot day."

"Yah, I feel the peace."

"Yes, that's right, feel the peace. Now listen. To be able to transcend into the different spiritual planes, you must concentrate on being one with the universe. One that belongs to the whole. Continue to feel the peace."

"Yah… I feel it."

"On different planes you can learn new creativity."

"Yah, that is what I want, to create new music the world has never heard before."

"And you will. Keep concentrating; think about that music that you want to create. The music must be shared freely without profit to yourself. A true devotee to transcendental yoga must not concern themselves with material things or money."

"Yah, I understand… It is so peaceful in here."

"Just keep thinking, feel the peace."

The Doctor rocked back and forth. He tried to stand but could not get up. His hands were frozen on his knees and his voice became high pitched, "Achh! It is dark in here! I want to get out! I want to get out! I am trapped in here… Let me out!"

"Just think, you want to go home, and something familiar like your Universe Guitar and you will return to the current plane of existence."

"Achh, yah…now it is better. So much peace in the void. Then I transcended to another plain and it started getting scary and dark… I was seeing my home and Bea….she was destroying one of my guitars…… So, this is the basic way to transcendental yoga meditation?"

"Yes, and to supplement to your growth you must follow these precepts. You must let your mind go. You ended up in the dark place by not letting go of things that you experience in life and fears that haunt you" He handed the Doctor a card with the precepts printed on one side.

Know your gods: Brahma the Creator, Vishnu the Preserver of Life, and Shiva the Destroyer of the Old Body.

Learn to use the seven Chakras or energy spots in your body.

Get yourself a Bhagavad Gita and read it daily.

Practice your yoga and meditate daily. Leaving the world behind.

Abstain from sexual immorality, alcohol, drugs, and do not consume animal flesh.

The Doctor read the steps, letting them sink in. He turned the card over. On the back was an advertisement for Swami Dharma's meditation practice and a coupon for a local restaurant.

"If you follow these precepts, you will find what you are looking for." The Doctor spent two hours with Swami Dharma. He felt he learned much in a short period of time. He felt satisfied.

"Is there anything else that I can do on this journey while I am here in India?"

"If you go to the Holy City of Varanasi, you can look for my spiritual guru, Gururaj. He can help you wash your sins away and purify yourself in the Ganges River. I can text you his phone number."

"Yah, that sounds good! Thank you!"

The Swami Dharma walked the Doctor back to where the others were and said goodbye.

"So how was your spiritual journey?" snarked Jeb.

"Achh! Most enlightening! The most important two hours that I have spent on this trip." The Doctor looked as if he was drunk, still shaken up by his experience.

Neusy looked at Jeb who shot him the all things will pass look and said, "well, we have important things to do, too, like getting set up for tonight. You see that barge out there? There is no electricity. They have sent someone in town to look for a gas-powered generator so we can have sound and power for the MMM."

"Achh! Don't worry, Jeb…all will work itself out."

"Not only that, but you also see the speaker columns on the barge? They forgot to connect cables from the speakers to the mixing board. They forgot the cables in town. Someone has to find the music shop owner and get them; he is out to lunch."

"Achh! Don't worry. It will work itself out. You must feel the peace!"

After an hour, the cables arrived. With no power still they weren't able to check the equipment. People started to arrive with chairs and blankets and were setting themselves up in the dry lakebed. No one seemed to have a ticket but the people kept coming.

Finally, a half hour from showtime, a generator arrived and Neusy was able to get all the equipment set up and powered. Neusy found Jeb, who set up a makeshift merchandise table on the left side of the barge. He said, "Jeb, I guess we are not doing any sound check now with all these people."

"It is very strange. They arrive, and no one is here to check tickets. They just arrive and find a place to sit out there."

"Have you been up on the barge? The stage is quite unusual."

"Yes, I noticed it. It will be a challenge for him tonight up there."

"Should we mention it to him?"

"No," said Jeb. "Let him figure it out on his own. It should be humorous."

Chenmay Chemmal arrived again with four other men. "Ahhh, I see that you are all set up. Where is Sir Doctor?"

"He is inside the palace sleeping. Are we ready for him?" asked Jeb.

"Yes, very soon. We will now walk through the people sitting out there and collect money from them."

"Don't they have tickets?"

"No, we are extremely informal here. They come in, and then prior to a show we collect from them. We watch while the show is going on, and if someone arrives, we collect money from them."

After the money was collected, the Doctor was summoned. Since the barge was never attached to any secure mountings or on any foundation, it was unstable and would sway as someone walked across its decking. The barge was left to settle where it was when the lake dried up and just set in its current location.

The Doctor found out during his first song that the more he moved the more the barge became unstable. He learned quickly that he needed to play perfectly balanced in the front of the stage. Neusy had to come up on the stage while he played to hold the MMM in place. Its movement caused the deck to sway even more, and it moved out of position.

As the Doctor played, he decided that the show would be shorter than normal. The cramp he developed in his leg from having to hold the same position for an hour and a half was no longer tolerable. He also thought that adding legs to the MMM would be something that he should talk to Trenton Towers about so he could make it move around the stage.

After the show, the Doctor left the stage and, with pain shooting in his leg, said to Jeb, "Tell Spud not to book barges anymore." He walked off into the palace as his phone rang.

"Jurgen, it's me, Dr. Spiers. We are in Jaipur now."

"Yah. How are you und the clone doing?"

"You will be pleased to know we had enormous success in Delhi. We are making money."

"Yah, that was the plan."

"We have been selling lots of T-shirts. By the way, did you get the T-shirts that I sent to Mumbai?"

"Yah! Jeb received them… Tee-hee, he had no idea where they came from."

"That's good! Two shows here and then we'll be on the road again. I want to take a detour. There is something I want to see on our day off."

"Yah, we have a few shows left, und then we will fly back to Austria und then to the US from New Delhi Airport. I have told Jeb that we too will do something productive on our day off und not just sit around drinking beer like they like to do."

"I will go to the bank and wire transfer to your Austrian bank your portion of the money that we made in Delhi and what we will make here in Jaipur. Tata for now, Jurgen!"

"Yah, auf wiedersehen," and they hung up their cell phones.

"Let's go and get set up for tonight, Number Two."

"Yah, yah! Let's go."

"Tamissvara is waiting in the car outside."

The HOP ON rooftop lounge at the Las Vegas Hotel was a very nice venue. The music of the Doctor and the soothing night air would be very pleasing to the Jaipur locals.

"Guten Abend, Jaipur! The Doctor is in," said Number Two. "YAAAH!"

Neusy had the stage broken down and ready to load up the van. He was standing next to the barge with Jeb waiting; they were looking for Jeetu. He spent most of the show watching small rodents running around, formulating curry spices for each. He finally was able to catch a black rat. After skinning it, he found his spice ingredients in the kitchen of the palace and made a small barbecue around back, out of the view of the concert goers. He arrived back in time to bring the van around for the load out. Both Jeb and Neusy once again smelled smoke on Jeetu and were starting to wonder what he was doing during his free time.

Chapter 13

"How long to get to the Sariska Tiger Reserve from Udaipur?" asked the Doctor.

"About three more hours," replied Jeetu.

"I can't wait to see all the wonderful animals, especially the tigers."

"Yes, they have many animals that you probably have never seen," replied Jeetu. He was visioning the feast waiting for him at the zoo.

Jeb again was deep into his fiction novel and Neusy into his music. This was the way they passed the time on the long cross-country drives. The smell of barbecue emitting off Jeetu was making them both hungry.

"How long to get to the Sariska Tiger Reserve from Jaipur, driver?" asked Dr. Spiers.

"About two hours, my friend," replied the driver.

"I don't know why you have to look at a bunch of wild animals," spoke the clone.

"You don't understand, we can't see these things back home."

"You can go to a zoo and see them."

"That's not the same! These animals will be in the wild, roaming freely."

"Big deal…no thrill for me," said the clone.

It had always been Dr. Spiers' dream to see the Royal Bengal tigers of India, and the reluctant clone wasn't going to hold him back. When they arrived, they exited the car and asked the driver to wait for them a few hours. They walked into the ticket office.

"Three-hour drive in a safari wagon and a guide: 2,500 rupees per person. That's the ticket! We will take two!" Dr. Spiers bought tickets for himself and the clone. They met with their tour guide, Aish, and got into his safari wagon.

"You gents are in for a treat today. We are going to see many wonderful creatures roaming freely in nature."

"That's sounds great!" said Dr. Spiers.

"Whoopie!" said the clone sarcastically.

"Well, let's not keep the tigers waiting!" said Aish, and off they went. The safari vehicles were open cab, no roof, to get the best feeling of nature and the animals. Next to the driver was a dart pistol that shot tranquilizer darts for use when a tiger or a boar got out of hand. It also could be used to tranquilize the annoying monkeys, if need be.

The countryside was dry and mostly brown. There was the beginning of green trees dense in patches, which would lead them to the jungle. The dirt roads were well traveled on by the safari wagons. At some parts of the road the trees swept over from both sides, making tunnels. Running across the front of their wagon, a family of boars ran to the other side.

"Wow! Look at that, a four-horned antelope!" exclaimed Dr. Spiers.

"I have an idea what they can do with those horns," remarked the clone.

"Where are the tigers?" asked Dr. Spiers.

"You will see them, there are many!" replied Aish.

Jeetu reached the gate. The sign read, "Sariska Tiger Reserve."

"We are here! Everyone wake up!" The sleeping travelers woke up and exited the van. They went into the ticket office. They each bought the three-hour package and went outside to meet their driver.

"Good day, my fine sirs! My name is Taksheel. I will be your guide."

"Yah, we are here to see the tigers."

"And you will, my fine friend! Let's get into the wagon and get going!"

The Doctor, Jeetu, Jeb, and Neusy all piled into the safari wagon with Jeetu in the rear third row by himself. The Doctor loved the fact that it had no roof. He removed his Mozart wig and put it into his pocket. His long hair fell out and was blowing into Jeb's mouth in the back seat.

"Hey Jurgen! Pft. Can you tie your hair…pft…up with a rubber band or something?"

"Where are the tigers?" asked the Doctor.

"You will see! We have Royal Bengal tigers here, they are special. But we have many animals here, not just tigers. Rhesus monkeys, Hanuman langurs, hares, wild boars, chousingha or four horned antelope, chinkara, nilgai, sambar, golden jackals, striped hyenas, caracal, and leopards. There are a few different snakes as well."

"Ach du lieber! I have never heard of most of those animals."

"Pffftt…Jurgen, your hair."

"Yes, my good Doctor, all belong to India and seldom seen in your Western zoos."

Both Jeb and Neusy were interested in the Doctor's planned activity for the day. Where else could they see all these fine animals in one place anywhere else other than

Africa? It didn't take the Doctor long to convince them to see the tigers. Jeetu looked about from the rear of the wagon looking for his lunch.

"Look there, a family of rhesus monkeys swinging in that tree there," said Taksheel.

"Yah! The cute little monkeys."

"Pffttt… Just like the little…pffftt…bastards at your show in… pffftt…Hosur," said Jeb.

"Yah, just like those!"

Jeetu looked at the monkeys. Pretty good, tasty, but he needed to change the spice rub next time. Exceptionally good brain flan. He would wait; he wanted something new on the menu today.

The wagon continued to drive; Taksheel stopped. "There you are, my Doctor friend! A four-horned antelope with his horns lowered. Pointing them at that tiger. One false move and the tiger will have a tasty meal."

"Nein, nein! Bad tiger, leave the antelope alone."

Jeb removed the hair from his mouth.

"On the other hand, the chousingha could gore the tiger with those sharp horns."

"Nein, I can't bear to watch."

"We better drive away then," said Taksheel.

As they drove farther into the jungle, more and more animals could be seen. They saw wild boars fighting off some striped hyenas. They saw leopards chasing hares. They saw monkeys and langurs playing tag. So much to see in the reserve. The Doctor was on the edge of his seat looking out the front windshield!

A safari wagon passed them going the opposite direction. No one paid any mind to it other than Jeetu. Something caught his eye for sure. Another Doctor was riding in the back seat. Jeetu, in the third-row seat with no one paying attention to him, rolled out the back and went after the other safari wagon.

The wagon stopped down the road. He crept up close but stayed behind a row of thick trees. "I have to take care of these clones," he said to himself as a tasty looking mouse passed near his feet. He could hear what the driver was saying.

"Look over there, Dr. Spiers, behind those trees: a family of tigers."

"Yeah, they are beautiful! Maybe we can get a closer look."

"Achh! Why bother?" remarked the clone in the middle seats. "These animals are boring me."

Jeetu crept up to the back of the safari wagon and climbed into the back row unnoticed. The driver drove closer until they were twenty feet away from the tigers.

Aish pulled out the tranquilizer dart pistol just in case a tiger rushed at them. "We have to be very quiet not to upset the tigers."

"What if a tiger comes for us and you miss with your dart gun?"

"Not to worry, Dr. Spiers. This dart gun is the newest model. It carries ten shots," replied Aish.

"That's good news," replied Dr. Spiers.

"Please shoot me with that, this is lame," said Number Two.

Jeetu leapt forward from the rear of the wagon and grabbed the dart pistol from Aish.

"Surprise!" Jeetu yelled and fired three shots. A tranquilizer dart found a home in Aish, Dr. Spiers, and the clone. Within seconds the sedative easily took effect, being formulated to take down a 400-pound animal. The three victims slumped over in their seats. Jeetu pushed Aish out of the driver's seat onto the ground below. He sat behind the wheel and drove closer to the tigers.

"You wanted to get a closer look at the tigers, didn't you, Dr. Spiers?" Jeetu said as he gave the tranquilized doctor a swift kick. He flew out of the wagon onto the ground. The two adult tigers looked at the body then sniffed at it. Jeetu slid between the seats and gave the clone a push. The clone lay on the ground near Dr. Spiers. Jeetu saw the clone had a number 2 tattooed behind its left ear. He wondered if there were more. Well, one thing was for sure, Dr. Spiers wouldn't be around to upset nature any more than he already had.

The tigers looked at the clone and sniffed it. It didn't smell the same as the human lying to their right. The male gave it a sharp bite in the face, ripping off most of its features. The clone oozed a red liquid that the tigers had seen before but it tasted different. He spit out the plasticized, lab-grown skin. The tigers bit into Dr. Spiers and continued until there were only bones remaining while the red liquid from the clone slowed then stopped. The dry, lifeless clone resembled a raisin.

For the next few days, the clone would be the center of attention to many passing animals. The animals would decide that they've had better and would wonder why anyone would leave them this disgusting tasting food. The clone will quickly dry up and, after a few days, the only remnant that would remain would be dust blowing in the jungle breeze.

Jeetu had to find his way back to the others. He turned the wagon around and drove to find them. After twenty minutes he saw them in the distance driving into a tree tunnel. He sped up his wagon and got as near as he dared. He stopped his wagon and, in one swift move, jumped out and ran along the side of the road until he caught up with Taksheel's wagon. With a mighty leap he made it onto the back bumper and slowly crawled into the back where he once sat. Jeb was spitting out the Doctor's hair and, because of the bumpy road, they did not feel the added weight of their lost passenger.

"Well, my friends, we are just about finished with our tour. Right up there is where you entered. It was a pleasure to drive you all," Taksheel said. He was pleased to see Jeetu sitting in the back. Many people that have left the wagons during a safari were never found. In the last year he had lost two, and one more would have meant termination.

When Taksheel stopped the car, Jeb was the first out. "Pffffttttt… Taksheel…is there water for sale in that office? Pffffttttt, I need to rinse out my mouth."

"Yes, right inside there are bottles, you all can help yourselves."

"Yah, you guys go, I have to check my phone." The Doctor did not receive the message he expected. He called Dr. Spiers and the phone went right into voicemail.

Chapter 14

"Achh! We are finally here, the holy city of Varanasi. I must find Gururaj!"

"What's that? It sounds disgusting," asked Neusy.

"Nein, not what but who. Gururaj, the master of the teachers, the one that will help me in my journey of transcendental meditation."

"Oh, brother!" quipped, Jeb.

"You must be willing to learn und absorb new things to make progress with your spirit," stated the Doctor.

"I just need to make progress with your tour and income with the shows," remarked Jeb.

Varanasi was a very colorful and festive city. Probably the most colorful of all the places the travelers visited on this tour. The buildings, shops, and houses were painted in bright oranges, yellows, and greens and lined the Ganges River. The famous ghats, or steps in Varanasi that sloped downward to meet The Ganges River, could be seen along the riverbanks stretching northward a long distance.

There were religious ceremonies held every day on various ghats, the most famous being the Dashashwamedh ghat where the Ganga Aarti ceremony, important to all Hindus, takes place. During the day, many Hindus bathe in the river to cleanse themselves of sins and purify the soul. This was Jurgen's intent. He felt it was a last step in his transcendental ways. But first he needed to locate Gururaj, the spiritual mentor that he was referred to. The meeting place was set at the Scindia ghat at 9:00 am.

"I see a man with an orange robe waving at us, Doctor. Maybe that's your Gururaj," said Jeb.

"Yah, I think you're right. Let's go to him." The travelers walked toward the man in the orange robe.

"Hello, I am Gururaj, you must be the Doctor? I am the one that taught Swami Dharma, your first mentor. You will finally end your journey here in Varanasi, my friend. What did you learn from my sibling in Udaipur?"

"Yah, I learned to be at peace with the universe und myself. To meditate daily on the Hindu precepts und concentrate on a peaceful existence with nature und the universe. I learned that I need to stop thinking about Bea and go to the place she cannot enter. Also, read the Bhagada Gita und eat no animal flesh."

"That sounds about right. I do not know who this Bea is, but you must take your journey alone. So, it seems that you have learned well. Follow me down the steps to the river. It is time to wash your sins away and purify your soul. This will be your final step, and it will be good karma to boot."

"Good karma to boot? What the hell does that mean?" Neusy asked Jeb.

"I have no idea. But a boot is what the Doctor needs." Neusy smiled at the thought of Jeb's boot kicking the doctor in the rear.

Gururaj led the Doctor down to the river. Before the washing in the river, Gururaj instructed the Doctor to sit with him in the lotus yoga position on the last step of the ghat and meditate.

"Ohhmm! Ohhmmm! Ohhmmmm! Ohhmmmmmm!"

"Okay, you may now enter the river."

The Doctor took off his outer clothes and stood in his purple briefs next to the river.

"Okay, jump in! I am a busy man," said Gururaj. The Doctor removed his Mozart wig, set it on top of his clothes, then plunged himself into the Ganges River. Gururaj, Jeb, and Neusy watched from the shore.

"Uugghhh! That is fucking disgusting!" bellowed Jeb.

"Why, what's wrong?" asked Neusy.

"Look at that filthy, disgusting water! I would never go into that river, not even if you paid me."

"Ah, man! You're just not a river person."

"Do you know how many germs and bacteria and disease could be moving about in there? I bet people shit in that river. The Doctor better get a good shower at the hotel, and afterwards he better rub himself down with rubbing alcohol, or any alcohol."

"Dude, you're extreme!"

"Oh God! See…look at that! A family of turds are drifting down towards the Doctor."

"What?"

The Doctor popped his head out of the water feeling satisfactorily cleansed in his new spirit. A turd brushed by his neck and through his streaming hair and floated downstream.

"Oh shit! I don't want to go near him! He will make me puke!"

"Oh, come on, Jeb! It was only a few small tree twigs."

"Neusy, I'll tell you something. Never, ever, go in swimming pools, Jacuzzis, hot mineral springs, or dirty, nasty rivers. You'll live a lot longer. They are all just large bathtubs with people's dirty, disgusting body sweat, oils and stench and their asses, dicks stewing in them while they are shitting and pissing at the same time."

"You're crazy man!"

"Maybe, but it is all true, my friend."

The Doctor stood waist deep in the water and the light of the sun gleamed off his large, bulbous forehead, momentarily blinding Gururaj, Jeb, and Neusy standing on the ghat. The Doctor waded back to the beginning of the ghat.

"Your journey is complete! You are now one with Lord Brahma, Lord Vishnu, Lord Shiva, and a whole lot more."

"Achh! That's a lot to keep track of."

"From now on you will be known as Gaganmurdha!"

"Yah? Und what does that mean?"

"It means one who has a sky-like forehead."

Jeb and Neusy giggled. Neusy gave Jeb the can-you-believe-this-shit look, and Jeb returned the now-I-need-a-beer nod. The Doctor could hear them and was not too pleased. "Und what is so funny?"

"Oh, nothing, your shininess!"

"What?"

"Oh wait, I'm blinded! I can't see. Quick, put on your turban!"

"Yah, yah, your jokes are not that funny!"

"Maybe you would like to see the holy ceremony tonight at the Dashashwamedh ghat. It starts at 6:00 pm. The priests will chant and walk around the candle lights; you can chant too."

"Yah, I would like to see this."

"Oh, man! Can't we get a beer somewhere, Jeb?"

"I don't know, we better watch the Doctor, he might get lost or something."

"Hey Doctor, I think you better go to your hotel room and take a shower first. Get cleaned up for tonight."

"Yah, this is a good idea. That river didn't smell too good."

"You're telling me," said Jeb.

The next morning was the last show of the tour on the banks of the Ganges River on the outskirts of Varanasi. The show was at 5:00 pm. The outdoor stage had no electricity, and the Doctor would have to play an acoustic guitar and nothing else. He made it known that no more acoustic shows should be booked without his approval. There were also no microphones, so he could only speak to the audience. The small amphitheater on the bank of the river was sold out at its capacity of 150 people, all tightly seated.

"Yah, thank you for coming. This is a little different for me. Can you all hear me?"

A couple of people applauded. Jeb and Neusy, with a beer in their hands, were looking around the small amphitheater. As they drank their beer, Neusy said, "Where is that Jeetu?"

"I don't know. There's something familiar about him, but I just can't place it. I know I've never met him. But just the way he carries himself. Reminds me of most stagehands that we run into. Always moving and looking around."

"Yeah, I know what you mean. They're always looking out for trouble."

The Doctor finished his shortened set of only an hour and as he walked off the stage, said to Neusy, "Tell Spud no more acoustic shows."

He went back to the VW and checked his messages. Still nothing from Dr. Spiers.

Chapter 15

Back in Minnesota, Jimmy spent his first night in the woods chasing anything that moved with the spear his brother had left for him. After four unsuccessful hours, he lit a fire to heat up water for a lemon ginger tea that Scaggz had left along with a few leftover items he had in his van. Among them were an expired box of crackers that Jimmy was sure should not be soggy but were and a roll of breath mints. Having decided that the crackers were probably best not eaten, Jimmy opted for the tea while he rethought his options in the woods.

The next morning, Jimmy walked the mile and a half into town with his backpack and found a small grocery store not very far in. It was small, more like a convenience store, but had everything that Jimmy could want. The store was narrow but long, with refrigerators on the side opposite the cashier counter and a row of freezers in the rear. Without any proper way of keeping things cool, he bought what he needed for the day and a bag of ice. When he returned to his campsite, he dug a small hole near his tent and filled it with what he had brought back in his backpack: packaged sandwiches, yogurt, and chicken pieces to cook over his fire in the evening. He covered his stock with the ice and covered the ice with branches and leaves he found in the woods.

He sat in the small camping chair Scaggz had also left for him. Eating a yogurt, he reflected on his accomplishments of the morning. The three miles to and from town outweighed his four hours walking aimlessly in the woods, chasing small animals, with an empty stomach as his reward. He sat there looking at his makeshift cooler. "Nature has everything one needs, except dinner, apparently," he said, and chuckled to himself.

After another lemon ginger tea, he walked to a stream he came across in his hunt the day before. He took off his shoes, sat on a rock, and enjoyed the water rushing around his legs. On the other side of the stream a family of badgers was drinking on the bank. "You guys are lucky that you were not here last night." The badgers did not respond, although the largest looked up at him as if he knew what Jimmy had just said. In an instant they were gone.

An hour later, Jimmy returned to his campsite and found that nature's cooler was not very secure. There was an open yogurt container near his tent next to an empty sandwich wrapper. He moved around the remaining ice, but there was no sign of the chicken he brought back for dinner. Thinking that the badger's earlier look at him was not so innocent, Jimmy decided he needed a better plan.

He walked into town and found the hardware store. There he bought rope and a proper small cooler. On his way back to camp, he stopped at the grocery store and secured dinner for himself, along with some eggs and bacon for breakfast and more ice. He returned to camp and set up a more secure way to store his food, something he saw on a survival show a few years back. He filled his cooler and tied one end of the rope around the handle and the other end over a tree branch. When the cooler was ten feet in the air, he tied off the rope to a lower branch. Satisfied that it was safe, he took a nap in his tent.

When he woke, it was already dark. He found his flashlight and was content that his campsite would suffice for the twelve days before he would show up at the police station as Heinz, the abducted Austrian bass player that had just escaped capture.

For the next four days he ventured back into town in the morning, only stopping at the small grocery store. Careful not to be seen, he was quick in and out. For those four days the cooler in the sky trick worked well for him. It was the fifth day with his new system, or sixth day in the woods, that he encountered trouble. A far cry from the twelve days that was planned.

It happened so quickly. When he was in the small grocery store, as he opened a refrigerator to pick out a couple containers of yogurt, a man with long black hair wearing a Jurgen Weislangwolf tour shirt from the previous tour walked behind him. The man had a six pack of Moosehead beer in his hand and was humming the melody to the classic Centipedes song "Slap the Virgin" when he saw Heinz.

"Heinz Beckenschultz?" said the man as he approached Jimmy, who did not pay any attention to the man as he was not in his Heinz role.

"Heinz, you're OK! This is great!"

Jimmy turned around and the first thing he saw was the Doctor staring at him from the man's shirt.

"I knew that it was you, Heinz. What the hell happened to you? I heard that you were kidnapped or something. People thought you were dead. Wait till I tell my friends you are alive. You're great! That was awesome on the last tour! You played while being stuck in the storm sewer. Your sounds were beautiful on the stage."

Jimmy stood there staring at the man in the Jurgen Weislangwolf shirt. He walked past the man and said, "My name is Jimmy, I don't know this person you are speaking of."

"Yeah, dude, you're him… Heinz Beckenschultz from Austria."

"Nope, Jimmy from California is the name," and Jimmy walked away to the small produce section. The man dropped his six pack and ran out of the store.

Jimmy found a couple florets of broccoli to his liking and moved on to find chicken wings to add to his purchase. He would feast tonight; Scaggz with his critter hunting can keep it. As he was getting ice out of the cooler, he heard it again. "Heinz Beckenschultz?"

"NO! I am Jimmy," he said and turned around to see the man in the Jurgen Weislangwolf shirt standing there with two uniformed police officers.

"See," said the man in the Jurgen Weislangwolf shirt. "Look here on my phone. That is Heinz Beckenschultz. He was abducted last year. I bet he was tortured and doesn't know his name. Look right here, an update on the Doctor's website from a few weeks ago saying that they still have not heard word from him after he went missing from last tour. Right here in Moorhead!"

"Well, it does look an awful lot like him," said the younger officer.

"Yes," said the other, "but it is not a crime to buy groceries here in Moorhead."

"No…no, what I am saying is this is Heinz Beckenschultz. He has been brainwashed into thinking that he is someone else. I don't know what happened. Look, it was in the paper… Here is the story. You guys need to call someone. He is delusional. People are worried about him. The Doctor is going to tour North America again in a few weeks. At least bring him in. Look here in the article. The FBI were involved, you should call them. They will know."

The man in the Jurgen Weislangwolf shirt made an argument that the police officers could not disagree with. This man in front of them with the backpack did look just like the man in the pictures being shown to them. The officers looked at each other. "We can't arrest him, Jim," said the veteran officer.

"Yeah, but we can take him in just to question him. If it is the same guy and he went through a traumatic experience, perhaps he is blocking out who he is because of this. Then he needs help. It is our duty. Let's bring him in and call those FBI agents and let them clear it up."

Jimmy panicked, dropped his backpack and the groceries he was carrying, and screamed. "AAAAAHHH this is not happening!" He ran around the back of the aisle and down the next and, with the exit in sight, ran into the younger officer, who simply moved over five feet from where he was standing to intercept Jimmy.

Sitting in the back of the police car with the door open and drinking a water, Jimmy was sobbing. "I don't know what to do, why don't you believe me… I just want to go back into the woods."

"Son, you are not arrested, the store owner said you have been coming around the last couple of days, polite and paid for your items and then left. But we must be sure. You do look like someone that was reported missing. We brought it up on our computer. So, we will go into the station and sort it all out. Nothing to worry about."

An hour later, Jimmy was sitting at a table, freshly showered. The officers insisted that he shower in the locker room they had on premises since he was pretty ripe, and it was hard to endure the ride back to the station with him. Now sitting there in fresh sweatpants and a police auxiliary T-shirt, Jimmy was drinking a coffee and eating a day-old donut.

The officers read the reports and called the FBI. They were informed that agents Sparrow and Crow were in route to Moorhead, having to drive to Phoenix first to board a flight to Minnesota. They were not pleased at all, being summoned back to work while on the beach in Puerto Peñasco, Mexico.

They were expected within the next day. The officers found humor in the FBI agents' names.

Jimmy spent the night at a hotel in Moorhead paid for by the city. It turned out that he would spend the next several nights in that same hotel with a police guard outside keeping an eye on him. The mayor insisted this when he heard of what happened. He too remembered the incident from the last tour and was quoted several times in the newspaper article that the officers read.

In the morning, the officers arrived and took Jimmy out to breakfast. He was to remain in his hotel room until the agents arrived in town, which ended up being two days later since they missed their flight the first day in Phoenix.

When the agents finally arrived, they were too tired to go to the police station and scheduled time there the next morning. They visited Jimmy's room and confirmed that, yes indeed, this man staying in the city-paid hotel room was in fact Heinz Beckenschultz.

Jimmy was quite enjoying the time in the hotel. It certainly beat being in the woods. He was starting to enjoy the officers' company, as well. They picked him up three times a day and took him to meals. This was the best he had ever been treated. Not even on tour where he was supposed to be catered to, did he get amenities like this. The truth was that on tour he got zero amenities and had to sleep in a small bunk on the tight space of the bus.

When the agents were properly rested, they were picked up along with Jimmy and brought to the police station. Jimmy was wearing a different pair of sweatpants and a re-elect Michael Sandman for mayor T-shirt. The agents each wore board shorts and Hawaiian shirts since they only packed for the beach.

Jimmy, with three days to compile a new and amend to what would have been his original story, felt extremely confident, although Scaggz would not be liking this new development.

"Well Heinz," said Sparrow, "we are happy you are alive, first off."

"Yeah," said Crow. "Now why don't you tell us what happened. Or at least what you remember."

"It's slowly coming back to me. I was held in a small room, food and water brought to me every day. It was dark. The only time I had light is when I was brought food…when the door opened."

"What did this person look like?"

"I don't know, each time he looked different. One time he would have a rubber mask on, the next a bandana covering his face. One time he looked like the Doctor. He even looked like the two of you. Another time he was dressed as a woman. He was in a sheep costume one time. I stopped looking after a couple of weeks. I just wanted to die. I couldn't even speak anymore. He kept calling me Jimmy. Said I was Jimmy from California."

"How did you escape?" asked Sparrow.

"We found your campsite in the woods," said one of the officers.

"There was a two-day stretch a couple of weeks ago. He left and told me that I was on my own. On my own, I am thinking, I'm locked in a room. But he left me with enough food and water for the time he was gone. I managed to eat it all in the first day. I figured it would give me more strength, better than the rations he was giving me to keep me weak. But nothing. I could not get out."

"That's how they do it," said Crow. "They get you to the point of breaking, brainwash you."

"When he returned, he said everything was all set up. He dropped me in the woods calling me Jimmy. I believed it, but now after staying in the hotel and away from it, I now see it, the whole thing what had happened. He said this would be Jimmy's new home in the woods. He gave me a spear, told me to hunt. I couldn't, so I went into town and got groceries."

"I don't get it, where did you get money?" asked the young officer.

Before Scaggz left him in the woods he withdrew a few hundred dollars from his bank account. Jimmy buried this money away from the camp site as instructed. Scaggz insisted that he go in the woods without any ID. Now Jimmy understood why. "I found some small jobs cleaning windows and odd jobs in town that gave me a little money. I panhandled the rest. Is that bad? I had no idea what I was doing. It was all a blur, but now it's much clearer for me. Thank you for rescuing me."

"The Doctor has a tour coming up in a couple of weeks. We will call him tomorrow and tell him that you're OK. It looks as if he is in India now. The mayor here in Moorhead is very nice. He said that you can stay there in the hotel until your passport arrives. It is in L.A. in evidence at our field office," said Sparrow. "We have to go back there and get proper clothes. We will send it back to the police station here. We are scheduled to follow the tour again after what happened last time out."

Jimmy spent the next several days in Moorhead as a guest of the mayor. He used Jimmy as a campaign centerpiece during these days, constantly making appearances with him and taking photos at different locations and shops. Jimmy didn't mind it so much. It was better than camping in the woods. He was elated that they all bought his story, and he was kind of a hero now.

Chapter 16

The next morning after the show in Varanasi, Jeetu collected Neusy, Jeb, and the Doctor. It was a two-hour drive to the airport. They were heading to Austria after a successful mini tour of India. The Doctor, for the first hour, was constantly monitoring his cell phone, but nothing from Dr. Spiers. He now knew something was not right. Dr Spiers would never disappear. He now feared that Number Two was gone as well.

"Why do you keep looking at your phone?" asked Jeb. "That's not like you. You always comment on us doing that."

"Yah, I look at my phone, but it is not ringing."

"Haha!" said Neusy. "Perhaps we should call Bea and tell her that you are missing her calls." Jeb gave Neusy the nice-Jab look. Neusy smiled back.

"Yah, you are not funny," said the Doctor. "Pay attention to Jeetu here, Neusy. Do you see how he has the proper GPS? Always use this device und you will be on time. You Americans have no respect for being on time."

Jeb gave the Doctor the middle finger behind the seat while Neusy nodded in agreement. "Well, I do have to say," said Jeb. "Jeetu, you have been nothing but professional. We enjoyed your company and guidance."

"Yah, this is true," said the Doctor. "The next time we come to India, we would like to hire you once again."

"Yes, my fine friends, it would be my honor," said Jeetu, who was tired of being polite and was ready to be Scaggz once again. "I will certainly follow your tour in North America. I am sure it will be a good one."

"Yah, thanks Jeetu."

"Hello, this is Jeb," he said as he answered his cell phone.

"Hello Jeb, this is Agent Sparrow."

"Agent Sparrow, how are you today? We are in India, heading to the airport."

"Yes, I know, Jeb. Good news, we found Heinz Beckenschultz." Agent Sparrow filled Jeb in on what had transpired in Moorhead.

"Wow," said Jeb, "he was found buying groceries in a store in Moorhead by a fan that recognized him? He was living in the woods, just left there by his abductor. That's crazy… Yes, I am sure the Doctor will want him on the tour. I will make arrangements and send them to his hotel. Thank you, Agent Sparrow." As Jeb hung up the phone, the van skidded off the road and stopped in a shallow ditch.

"What the…? Is everything OK, Jeetu?" asked Neusy. "What happened?"

"It is so nice to hear that your dear Heinz was found. I am overjoyed," Jeetu said as he was trying to hold back Scaggz from making an appearance. *Fucking Jimmy…no direction!*

"Achh! It is good to be back in Salzburg!" said the Doctor as he exited the plane.

"Doctor, is it true that Mozart was born here?" asked Neusy.

"Oh yah! His house is not so far from here. It is now a museum."

"Wow! I'd like to see it," said Neusy.

"Yah! Well, another time, I am hungry now. Let's go eat!"

"Yeah, really! I'm kind of tired of India and Indian food," said Jeb.

"I'm ready for some meat! Bring on the sausages!" cried Neusy.

"They're called wurst here," said Jeb.

"That's the wurst thing I ever heard," said Neusy, chuckling.

"Yah, yah! The funny Amerikaner, always with the jokes."

"Well, what do we do now? Stand around the airport all day?" asked Jeb.

"Nein, nein. Marlon is coming to collect us."

"Marlon?"

"Yah, Marlon! Remember, I told you I would make a man out of him while we were in India. He has been here cleaning my house."

"Oh yeah," said Neusy.

"Yah, he will come get us in my BMW wagon; my Fiat is too small for all our stuff."

Marlon finally arrived and walked into the terminal. Everyone was happy to see him, but he did not see the tired travelers and walked past them. He walked into a bar and sat down and ordered a beer. Neusy and Jeb looked at each other. "How did he not see us and walk right past us?" asked Neusy, watching Marlon in the bar chug the entire beer.

"Stoned," replied Jeb. "He is obviously stoned, but he has his moments."

They quickly walked into the bar before Marlon had a chance to order a second beer. "Marlon! How the hell are you?" asked Neusy.

"I'm wunderbar! How was India? It must have been fascinating," said Marlon.

"It was interesting. But the good thing is we made some money instead of losing money," said Jeb.

"That's good! I want to see pics. The good ones," said Marlon. "I have been busy here; I cleaned the Doctor's house several times over."

"Achh! How is my house, Marlon? Is it spick und span? I hope that you have cleaned it properly…every day. Yah?"

"Yes, Doctor! I have kept it exceptionally clean," replied Marlon.

"Das ist gut! I will give it the white-glove inspection later."

"I'm hungry, let's go somewhere and eat," said Jeb.

"Achh, yah! We must go to Nellie's und have a Veganschnitzel."

"Arrgghhh! That doesn't sound good at all!" said Jeb. Neusy put his hand up to his mouth as if he was sick.

"Achh! It is terrific!"

"We want meat! We want wurst und potatoes und sauerkraut und some beer!" replied Jeb, imitating the Doctor's voice.

"Yah, yah! Nellie can make all of those meaty things for you guys!"

"Enough chit-chat let's go! Raus, macht schnell!" said Jeb.

"Achh! Jeb, I didn't know you know so much German."

"There's a lot of things that you don't know, Doctor," replied Jeb.

The boys made their way out to the Doctor's custom purple-colored BMW in the parking lot. Marlon opened the back hatch and then put in their luggage, MMM box, EFX pedal case, and the Universe Guitar inside. They all got in and Marlon fired it up.

"Achh! Marlon, do you know how to get to Nellie's?" asked the Doctor.

"Yes, I go there all the time, and I even have it in the GPS already," replied Marlon.

"Yah! Good! You have become a man already. You can learn from this man, Neusy."

Neusy looked at Jeb in the back seat and flipped the finger to the Doctor from behind his seat, then made a fuck him gesture on his face.

"Achh! I miss Jeetu! He was a great guide und helper in India. I wish he were here with us," said the Doctor.

"Yeah, he really was a major help and friend, too!" said Neusy.

"Who's Jeetu?" asked Marlon.

"Yah! Jeetu Kapoor. He was our everything man in India. I'm sad he is not here."

"You'll see him again one day," said Neusy.

"We are thinking of replacing you on the tour with Jeetu," said Jeb.

"What? No...please tell me that you are kidding," said Marlon.

"It's true, he works twice as fast as you and he doesn't smoke the weed."

Neusy laughed at the hard time that Jeb was giving Marlon. Then he added, "I think he was smoking something else."

"What, hash?" asked Marlon.

Neusy and Jeb laughed, thinking about how Jeetu often smelled like fresh barbecue.

"Come on, guys, tell me. You aren't really replacing me. I just did all that work at the Doctor's house."

"Yah, yah, Marlon, they think they are funny, but they are not," assured the Doctor, which produced two more middle fingers of appreciation from Neusy and Jeb.

Within thirty minutes and two more middle fingers, they had arrived at Nellie's. The Doctor opened his door with delight and led the way.

"Guten Tag! How many?" said the hostess.

A large fat Austrian woman with blonde hair popped out from the kitchen. "Ach du lieber! Jurgen Weislanwolf! My God, how long has it been? Please come with me, I give you the special table."

"Yah! Nellie! It is so good to see you! Yah, it's been a long time."

"What have you been doing with yourself, Jurgen?"

"Achh, yah! Well, we were just in India for a couple of weeks. You know I had a tour there."

"Yah? How is that place?"

"It has some fascinating things, you know. Tigers und bats und snakes und this und that. But most of the place looks dry and deserted."

"Not at all like your beautiful, green home here in Salzburg, yah?"

"Yah! Home sweet home!"

"HAHAHAHAHAHA!!!!" The two Austrians laughed in unison.

"Yah, that is all not that funny," commented Jeb.

"Sweet Home Salzburg, you should write a song," added Neusy, and the two of them laughed.

Nellie said, "Why do they say that?"

"I have to listen to that all the time. They think they are funny."

Nellie led them to a lovely round table in the back of the restaurant. Neusy and Jeb laughed harder at the comments from the Doctor. There were deer antlers hanging over the table with lights connected in the horns. There was a suit of old armor on one side of the wall and shelves with many ornate beer steins decorating it. Pictures of Mozart and old Austria were also on display. There was a nine-foot-long Bosendorfer concert piano that had belonged to Nellie's departed husband, which separated the main room from the special area. The lighting was not too bright and perfect for polite conversation.

"So, Jurgen! What is it going to be? Your favorite, I imagine."

"Yah! You must have my mind fully read. Veganschnitzel with vegan gravy, red cabbage, und potatoes au gratin with ranch dressing."

"Ugghhh! How about the bratwurst with sauerkraut and home fries," said Jeb.

"I'll try that one," said Neusy.

"I'll have the salmon salad," said Marlon.

"Salmon salad? WTF Marlon? Are you getting weird on me?" asked Jeb.

"No, I am just tired of sausages all the time," explained Marlon.

"Und Nellie, please bring us some of your homemade black bread und butter."

"Of course, Jurgen."

"What do you fellows want to drink?" asked Nellie.

"What do you recommend?" asked Jeb.

"Oh, well. You must have the town favorite, Egger Beer," replied Nellie.

"Egger Beer? That reminds me of my old friend Steve Eggers in California that passed away," said Neusy.

"Okay, then. Four steins of Egger Beer," said Jeb.

"Make mine a Viennese red wine, Nellie," said the Doctor.

"Ein moment, gentlemen," Nellie said as she walked away. Within one minute she brought the beer and wine to the table.

"Well, here is to our dear departed friend, Steve Eggers!" Neusy said as he raised his stein.

"Here! Here! Here's to Steve Eggers. Rest in Peace, brother!" said Jeb. The food was delivered, and the boys dug in. It was great food and very filling.

"How is that salmon salad, Marlon?" chuckled Jeb.

"It's great. They put some fruits of the forest mixed into the vinegar," replied Marlon.

"Achh! Pass me some of the hot mustard, Jeb."

"Here you go!"

They were all laughing, eating, drinking, actually having a great time together, until the Doctor's cell phone rang. He looked at the screen. "BEA." *Oh no, not now…not at dinner.* Reluctantly, he answered the phone.

"Yah, Bea? How are you?"

"Are you here yet? I need some money."

"Nein, I am not in Austria yet, we are still in India. Our flight has been delayed."

"Well, I need money. I don't have any special mustard for my sausages I just cooked. I am going to throw them in the trash; they are not the same without that mustard."

"Nein, nein. Don't throw them away like that! A poor little piggy gave his life so you could eat him und have nourishment."

"I don't care… I want my mustard; I want some money. Your daughters also have no lipstick and mascara. We are women with needs! You better get home quickly and bring me some money."

"What did you do with the money Jeb wired you last week?"

"It's all gone! There are expenses around here, you know! We all have different cycles and always buying our private things."

"Yah, I don't want to know these things. How has Marlon been?"

"He is as quiet as a mouse, always cleaning the house."

"Yah, that is good! I have to go now, Bea, they are calling me over to the desk now. Bye-bye." The Doctor hung up the phone.

"Achh! We were never here. You understand me, yah?"

"Okay, anything you say," said Jeb.

"Achh! Okay, Marlon, we don't go to the house tonight, we stay at Uncle Georg's house."

"We have a show tomorrow, Doctor, don't forget," said Jeb.

"Yah! Das ist gut! That will be two days I don't need to see Bea. Und my name is not listed on this show, so she should not find out that I was here early."

After a pleasant sleep at Uncle Georg's House, the boys were up eating breakfast, drinking, and discussing the plan for the evening's show at the Der Klang von Musik Club. Uncle Georg's House is the name of the local hotel in town. Jeb paid Georg for the rooms and joined the breakfast. "I didn't budget a hotel here in Salzburg because you live here. You should have mentioned yesterday that Uncle Georg is not really an uncle."

"Yah, don't worry about these things. We would have to deal with Bea. She is on a rampage now; I can hear it in her voice."

"Yea," Marlon said, "it's best to not be in the house when she is like that. I left when she started complaining to me about the Doctor. Lots of beer in town."

After a better-than-expected breakfast served by Uncle Georg, they left and spent time in town at various shops, trying to hang low and not run into anyone that knew Bea. Marlon posted a picture of all of them on social media and immediately was instructed to remove it.

Later at the Der Klang von Musik Club, "What a wonderful theater!" said Neusy. *The Sound of Music* is playing here tonight. It said so on the poster I saw as we walked in."

"Yah, I used to come here with my parents und watch *The Sound of Music* shows."

"Look at the beautiful carved woodwork in here on the walls, and look at those lush, red, velvet curtains with gold fringes," exclaimed Neusy. "But why are we here? I thought you had a show tonight?"

"Yah, the show will be here. The manager, Hubert Franzmeier, offered me a lot of money to play with the actors tonight."

"Yeah, where is that guy? I need to speak with him," said Jeb.

"Did I hear someone mention my name?" Hubert spoke as he walked toward the group.

"Mein Gott! Hubert, you old fool! How are you!"

"I'm great, Jurgen, you Doctor you!" Hubert chuckled along with Jurgen.

"Hello, I'm Jeb, the manager. Can we talk about the stage set up before you two get all reminiscent?"

"Achh, yah! Sure, follow me, I will show you the stage area," Hubert said.

"You can set the Doctor up on this side. Here are the electrical plugs flush with the stage."

"Achh! Neusy, be sure to set the voltage to 220V. We are in Austria, you know, yah?" said the Doctor.

"Yeah, I know… Who do you think I am? Teddy Red?"

"Yah, I know, but we must always be careful. Maybe I have him clean my house next."

Neusy and Marlon went outside to get the small amp, EFX pedals, and Universe Guitar out of the car. They brought it in and set up the equipment.

"Now, Jurgen, you know that the singers and actors come out and play in these areas, so try to stay on this part of to stage," said Hubert.

"Yah, yah! I know. I have been coming here since I was a child."

"Since we both were children, Doctor," He chuckled again, along with Jurgen.

"Hey Hubert, let's talk about the payment, okay?" asked Jeb.

"Yah, yah. I didn't forget. Advance payment. I have it here in my pocket. 5,000 euros."

"Great, thanks!" said Jeb.

Later when the stage was set, people started to fill the 500-seat theater. Austrians were very polite and not too loud, so they didn't expect the same kind of fanfare they would get as in the USA. When the theater was filled, the lights were lowered. Then Maria came to sing the opening song. The spotlight trained on her. Then a guitar could be heard playing the beautiful chords and accompaniment for her voice. The spotlight came on the Doctor. Half of the people in the audience knew who he was and were surprised. Maria began to sing. "The hills are alive with the sound of music…" It was hauntingly and beautifully done with just voice and guitar. At the end, the first standing ovation came. Unusual for a first song.

As additional actors took the stage, the Doctor knew every song in the story by heart and played them effortlessly. The Doctor played a very lively and unique version of his own personal favorite song, "My Favorite Things." Again the crowd gave a standing ovation. It was now time for "Edelweiss." The family von Trapp actors assembled in the living room set to act out the famous scene. They waited for their father to enter the room with his guitar to sing for them. A shock came to the Doctor and the rest of the audience when the singer was not the usual singer in the cast. It was the Doctor's old bandmate from the Centipedes, Holger Stormburg. The Doctor looked in amazement at Holger and Holger back at him. They gave each other a nod and the Doctor finger-picked the melody of "Edelweiss." Holger's strong, golden voice rang out through the theater. His voice was so powerful he didn't use the microphone. "Edelweiss, edelweiss! Every morning you greet me…" The audience couldn't contain themselves. They all stood up during the whole song and sang along. It was unbelievable to have the singer and the guitarist from the Centipedes on stage together after so many years, even if it was only to play "Edelweiss" together. Even Jeb got teary eyed as he double checked and counted the money that Hubert gave him.

After the show, Jurgen embraced Holger and spoke some pleasantries on stage. Many fans lined up in front of the stage to say hello from below. What a fantastic night!

Later that night, the Doctor decided they would stay at Uncle Georg's one more night before they would fly to the US to prepare for that tour. He didn't want to go home and see Bea and his children. He would think of some excuse why he wasn't coming back to Austria and had to fly directly to the States. He would say there was a special concert. He asked Jeb to wire transfer a few hundred euros to Bea's account.

"Achh! We will go to the US tomorrow. Jeb, make the arrangements. We will not go to my house."

"Okay, whatever you say," replied Jeb.

"What about me, Doctor? What about my things at your house?" asked Marlon.

"Achh! You don't need to worry about the small things in life, Marlon. Those things were only temporary, material things. You will get new things in America. Yah?"

Chapter 17

The Doctor, Jeb and Neusy, along with Marlon, arrived in Newark, NJ after an uneventful flight. Waiting for their luggage and equipment, they anxiously anticipated the arrival of Cal Crabs to collect them with the tour bus and bring them to their destination in Connecticut. The economy flight with a changeover in London had left the travelers drained. The other band members—Nathan Lieber (singer/guitarist), Tommy Triple T (drums), Torsten the Viking (keys), and the reborn Heinz Beckenschultz (bass)—had arrived two days before and took a bus to Norwich. They spent the last two days rehearsing as instructed and were awaiting the Doctor's arrival.

The weary travelers in Newark had collected their luggage and equipment and now waited for their ride. Marlon, pacing without his marijuana, had already checked the laws of New Jersey and found out that there were no dispensaries nearby, although he was happy to learn that they had passed recreational use of his favorite pastime. He walked the entire length of the terminal asking anyone that looked as if they smoked weed if they indeed did smoke weed. He returned to the group as empty as he had left, with the addition of a couple of pissed-off looks and a "fuck you" issued by an older man with long hair.

"Where the hell is Crabs and Hocker? We should have seen them by now," said Jeb after two hours, referring to their bus driver and foul-mouthed stagehand who rode along in the bus from California. Cal Crabs was an always calm veteran of the road. When not driving the Doctor in his tour bus, he drove a big rig, hauling anything that anyone was willing to pay him to do so. Crabs racked up an astonishing 200,000 miles a year between the two interstate behemoths.

"Why don't you call him before Marlon gets his ass kicked," replied Neusy, watching Marlon continue his search as he was hit with the cane of an old lady he thought might be carrying.

"Yeah, I better do that now," said Jeb, watching the same scene unfold as he pulled out his cell phone. "Yo, Cal, bro…where are you? It's been two hours since we arrived here in Newark."

"Howdy, Jeb, got a stroke of bad luck here. The tour bus broke down in Ohio. I won't be there for another day," replied Cal.

"What the fuck! Now what do we do? … Later, dude, keep me informed." Jeb ended the call. "Fuck! It's always something on these tours."

"Achh! Now Jeb, put your mind at peace! Remember what my guru taught me in India. Feel the peace," said the Doctor calmly.

"Yeah, yeah! Easy for you to say! Everything always falls on my shoulders, not yours!" snapped Jeb.

"Achh! I know what to do. We can call the Pliers brothers; they live in New Jersey."

"But they don't live in Newark, they live in Long Branch. We'll be waiting another two hours for them to get here," said Jeb unhappily. He and Neusy watched Marlon scream and run aimlessly back towards the terminal exit after hearing it would be another two hours at the airport without scoring anything to smoke. He came to a stop when he ran into the automatic doors designed only to open from the inside.

"Yah, I call them now." The Doctor made the phone call to his old friends Rusty and Hal (Needle Nose) Pliers. The brothers owned fifty-eight buildings in the greater Atlantic City area. They built up a lucrative business over the years as landlords, mostly low-rent buildings, but it paid the bills and kept the boys busy. They came into millions from their uncle at a very young age: Rusty was seventeen and Hal only fifteen.

Since that time some thirty years ago, the Pliers brothers have been doing OK for themselves. They're a two-man business, too cheap to hire anyone for anything. The boys spend their time chasing tenants for rent, evictions, maintenance on the units, and the odd time anyone moves out, a total remodel of the unit. These units range from single-family homes to apartment buildings with twenty apartments in them. The intense landlord duo never finished high school. They both quit faster than the ink had time to dry on the massive checks they received. They bought their first unit a week later and never looked back.

The only issue the two have is that they have absolutely no business sense. Rusty, with his low voice and laid-back surfer demeanor, is always ready to catch the next big wave. He is six feet tall with low-cropped brown hair, which is odd since everyone calls him Rusty. But since his head is always at the ocean, he really does not spend much time on wanting to collect the rent. So, when a tenant tells Rusty that they don't have the rent, Rusty usually forgets to go back and collect it as it interferes with his surfing. Tenants love this, and while Hal suspects that this is not the way to run a business, he does trust his older brother's business methods in general. Only a few of the tenants have figured this out and don't abuse the free month's rent more than a couple of times a year. Their business practices are a constant concern for their accountant, but he too has figured out how to overcharge the brothers to straighten out their neglected books. Once a month they would hand him a shoe box full of receipts of all types—rent received, expenses, and deposits—to which the accountant had to fabricate an anecdote believable to the IRS.

Whether swinging a hammer on the remodels, replacing roofs, or just the general maintenance on the units, it kept the brothers in good shape. Hal, the younger brother, looks like he is five years older than Rusty with his mostly gray receding hair line, his abnormally long nose, and his poor posture. His lack of intelligence is puzzling to most. How he can get up in the morning and put on his own pants, much less be a partner in a successful business, is a question that is often asked. It was a good thing he came into that money. But with each of their own faults, the brothers love one another and are always by each other's side; they would not have it any other way. Perhaps this is the reason neither of them has married: they are loners and the only family they have left.

However, when the Doctor comes to town, these two drop everything to spend some time with him; they come alive. They first met twenty years ago when the Doctor toured the States. It was at a small show in Asbury Park. The brothers, being huge fans, approached the Doctor's management to make an offer. The offer was to have the Doctor play a private show at the boys' home. With the next day an off day, management agreed to the $20,000 fee the brothers offered. It was more than any individual show paid on the tour. Actually, it was about what a week's worth of shows paid on that tour! It alone made the tour profitable when the budget initially showed a loss. Since that time, the brother's and the Doctor have remained close.

The Pliers pulled up with a black cargo van. The boys jumped out; Rusty and Hal had big smiles on their faces.

"Achh! Rusty, Hal, how are you guys?" said the Doctor, and then he and the brothers embraced.

Rusty said, "Good, how are you?"

"Yeah, man…how are you, dude?" asked Hal.

"Achh! I'm fine but very tired. You know we were in India for several weeks und then we went to Austria for two days."

"Well, we'll get you where you need to go. Where do you need to go, anyways?" asked Rusty.

"Norwich, Connecticut," said Jeb.

"Norwich is about four hours from here," said Rusty.

"Man, we are beat. We need some rest. Any suggestions?" asked Jeb.

"Well, we have some vacant apartments you guys could sleep in. We are still working on them, but at least you can sleep until tomorrow. Then we can drive you up to Norwich," replied Rusty.

"That sounds like a plan, let's go," said Jeb. Marlon, seeing the van approach, walked back over a little wobbly and holding his head after another encounter with an exit door. Neusy was wondering where he had been all this time after he met with the first terminal exit door in such a violent manner.

Rusty and Hal helped them load their luggage and equipment into their work van. There were no seats in the back because the van was used to move their tools and equipment, along with rolls of carpet and cabinets.

"Dude, where are the seats?" asked Jeb.

"There are none, we had them removed. This is a work van, you know."

"That's going to be dangerous as fuck riding on the bare floor like that!" cried Jeb as he looked at two bags of tools that were sitting in the back.

"Well, sorry guys… The Doctor can ride up front with me. Hal, you sit with the others in the back," said Rusty.

Jeb thought to himself, beggars can't be choosers. It wasn't very comfortable. The shocks in the van weren't good and the guys felt every bump in the road, often bouncing up and down against the bare metal walls and floor trying to avoid the luggage and equipment bouncing around with them.

"Ouch, ouch, ouch! This fucking sucks!" said Jeb as a bag of tools bounced up and landed on his foot.

"Yeah, not very comfortable," said Neusy.

"We'll be there soon," said Hal.

"I think I sprained my pinkie. You guys don't have any weed, do you?" asked Marlon, never having met the brothers before.

"No, man," said Rusty. "We don't touch that stuff; it makes you stupid. We don't even drink." Marlon was deflated.

Jeb gave Neusy the thank-god-the-last-thing-these-guys-need-is-additional-stupid look. Neusy nodded and replied with the these-guys-are-ridiculous eye roll as Rusty pulled the van into the apartment complex parking area.

"We're here, guys! Let's move 'em out!" said Rusty.

"I'm fucking hurt all over," cried Jeb with a painful facial expression. Neusy had the same expression but couldn't speak.

"Achh! That was a wonderful drive, Rusty. So here we are? This is your building?" asked the Doctor.

"One of many, but in this one we have two vacant units," replied Rusty.

"Yah! That's nice! You know, I don't like to sleep with the others. I want one room for myself," explained the Doctor.

"Well, one room has some furniture from the previous tenant and an army cot that Hal likes to sleep on after we finish working for the day. The other unit has an air mattress on the floor. There is some shampoo and soap in each unit. I will see if I can find you some towels and bed sheets," said Rusty. "Grab what you need and follow me."

Rusty led Jeb, Neusy, and Marlon to room 201 upstairs while Hal took the Doctor to room 107 downstairs.

Rusty opened the door. The three looked inside the unit. It smelled like fresh paint. Some drop cloths with white splatters were bunched up in one corner. The kitchen, with old, worn walnut cabinets, had a stove but nothing else. There was a small black coffee table, an old, tattered grey sofa, a double bed, and a green army cot with no other furnishings. "Here you are, the best I can do," said Rusty. "I'll go to the storage unit and find some sheets and some towels."

"Hey Rusty, we are starving. Are there any places to eat around here?" asked Jeb.

"Yeah, Pizza Brigade is still open and they deliver."

"Dude, can you order us one pepperoni, one garbage pail special, and a veggie deluxe for the Doctor?"

"Sure, man, no problem… Anything for you guys, we love helping out," answered Rusty.

"I'm still looking for some weed," said Marlon, looking at his phone. "There is a dispensary two miles away. Would the pizza guy stop there for me on his way here if I tipped him well?"

Neusy and Jeb gave him the shut-the-fuck-up look and Marlon sat back on the couch.

"Oh Rusty, also, could you get us a six pack of something? And some bottled water for the Doctor?" asked Neusy.

"Sure, man. Just relax. I'll be back, let me check on the linens and stuff."

"Right on! Thanks!"

"Well, here it is, Doctor," said Hal.

The Doctor scanned the room. Nothing. As bare as Old Mother Hubbard's kitchen, with the kitchen cabinets recently ripped out. Just fresh white paint throughout the unit. The bathroom had the vanity ripped out, no sink, only the mirror. The shower was functioning. Off in one corner of the living room there was a half-inflated air mattress.

"Achh, yah! Better than nothing."

"Sorry, Doctor. It's all I have that is vacant," replied Hal. "I'm sure that you're tired. I'll let you get some sleep. Rusty and I will take you guys out for breakfast in the morning."

"OK, Hal. Danke! Gute Nacht!"

Hal said goodnight and closed the door behind him.

Thirty minutes later the pizzas arrived. Knock, knock, knock! "Yah, what is it?" asked the Doctor behind his door.

"It's me, Neusy. Open up."

"Yah, what do you want? I'm tired," he said as he opened the door.

"Here is a veggie pizza that Rusty ordered for you, and here are some bed sheets and an air pump to inflate the mattress."

"Achh. Great! Danke, Neusy! Gute Nacht." The Doctor closed the door. He threw the bed sheets on the mattress and sat down in the lotus position on the floor, opened the pizza box, took out a slice, and ate it.

Neusy returned to room 201 and let himself in. "Dudes! The Doctor got fucked! We are living high on the horse," said Neusy.

Marlon, puzzled, looked at Jeb as he tried to get comfortable on the cot. "What the fuck are you talking about?" questioned Jeb.

"All he has is a half-inflated air mattress. We have a double bed, couch, and a cot," remarked Neusy. "Let's have some pizza and beer."

"What kind of beer is it?" asked Jeb.

"Long Branch Brewery, it says; must be a local beer. It is a variety pack." Neusy took a Pigeon Beak Lager and handed Jeb the White Specked Boardwalk IPA. They clicked bottles and took a sip. Marlon was already asleep on the couch.

Chapter 18

The morning came quickly, and Rusty and Hal came back in the work van to pick up the guys for a quick breakfast in an ocean-side diner. Then they would be on the road to Norwich for rehearsal with the band. The guys braced themselves in the back of the van the entire ride to the diner. Jeb and Neusy secured the bags of tools with their legs to prevent them from moving. When they exited, they were rubbing their backs and heads. Marlon was trying to stop his nose from bleeding after the beating he took when he saw it right there across the street: Long Branch Edibles. Then, right under the shop name: Pre-rolled sale! He walked alone across the street.

A half hour later they were all back in the van. Marlon returned in time to meet the guys as they exited the diner. He was hungry but satisfied that he found his weed. The hunger would have to wait until the next stop.

The Doctor happily chatted with Rusty up in the front while Jeb, Neusy, Marlon, and Hal tried to chat in the back on the floor to keep their mind off the bumps.

"Hey, Jeb! Where exactly are we going?" asked Rusty from the driver's seat.

"Let me look on my phone, wait a minute," said Jeb, and the phone bounced out of his hand. He picked it up. "OK, here it is: 21557 Pachuawak Avenue, Norwich, Connecticut."

"OK, got it in my GPS now," replied Rusty.

"Achh, you see, Neusy, you also learn from this man."

Neusy refrained from flipping him off in fear that Hal might tell the Doctor. Jeb nodded at Neusy, reassuring him that there would be many more moments to flip off the Doctor.

Hours passed and they pulled into Norwich. Rusty followed the directions on the GPS that led them to Magic Mayhem Music Studios. They could see their band mates kicking it with some mineral waters in the parking lot in front of the rehearsal building. The Doctor told Rusty to park next to the guys. "Achh! What's up with you guys, why aren't you rehearsing?" asked the Doctor.

"Umm, well, the power is out," replied Tommy, the band's drummer.

"What? So, what is the prognosis?" the Doctor asked in medical terms.

"They said about an hour it should be restored."

Hal opened the side door and Jeb slid out of the back of the work van, stretching his back after the four-hour assault. Neusy exited and did the same. The band members watched it unfold, wondering how many more would exit the back of the van. Marlon exited and the band all shook their heads in agreement. Marlon looked at Jeb and Neusy and said, "It wasn't that bad in there. I liked the ride. Thanks guys for the ride. Wow, I am hungry. I am going over there to that deli."

"Why don't we head over to the venue for the show tomorrow and check it out while we are waiting," suggested Jeb.

The four band mates joined Neusy and Jeb and climbed into the back of the cargo van. After Marlon arrived with a fresh sandwich, there were seven people in back and two in front. Hal slid in and the door closed. Jeb gave Rusty the address to the club. He drove everyone there. When they arrived, they saw nothing that looked like a club, only a three-story office building with a Mexican restaurant on one side of the building entrance. "What the hell?" Jeb said. "Where is the club? Let me call this guy."

Jeb called the contact number on the contract. The person that answered told them to enter the office building and either use the stairs or the elevator to the basement and there they would find the Norwich Nostalgia Venue. He also said the door was open, but no one was there at this time.

Jeb, Neusy, and Marlon took the two flights of stairs as the rest of the guys took the elevator. They walked into the venue below. The main door was open, though no one was around. Dimly lit with a musty smell, the room had old beer signs. Pink and blue neon lights illuminated the orange-painted walls, plastered where band posters from previous shows hung. On one side was a twenty-five-foot dark wooden bar with glasses hanging down from the suspended rack and a few beer taps. Adjacent to the bar was a pool table, and across, on the opposite side of the room, was the three-foot-high stage in the center of the back wall with a column blocking the left side of the stage. The main problem with the stage was it was only eight feet wide and six feet deep. Typical of Spud Burger's choice bookings.

"Achh! This stage is too small! This will never do; we have a five-piece band. How are we all going to fit up there? And look at that stupid column on my side of the stage," complained the Doctor.

"Shit! That fucking Spud! We gotta get rid of that guy! What the hell are we going to do now?" said Jeb.

"Maybe we can set up the Doctor's amps on the floor on the left and he can stand on the floor," suggested Neusy.

"Nein, nein! That is a terrible idea! I don't stand on floors. The people must look up at me."

"I have an idea!" said Rusty. "My brother and I can find a home center, buy wood, and build a stage extension."

"Hey, that might work," said Jeb. "The show isn't until tomorrow. We would have to hurry it up."

"Alright, Hal and I will get it done, don't worry! The Pliers brothers are on the job. We will buy the stuff and build it. Do you see now why we always travel in our work van with tools?"

Rusty took out a notepad from his pocket and Hal pulled off a tape measure that was clipped to his pants belt and they took measurements of the stage.

The Pliers brothers left and the band sat around the venue and stared at the empty surroundings. They talked and waited, then they waited some more. Marlon ate his sandwich and went outside to smoke another joint. Two hours gone, where could they be? They were getting bored with no instruments and running out of topics to speak about. Another hour passed; Jeb was getting aggravated. They'll be here all night trying to build a stage by the time they get back. They won't be able to rehearse. Jeb walked back upstairs to go outside for a minute. What he saw blew his mind. The Pliers brothers had already built the stage sections in the parking lot. There were three three-foot-tall sections. Two were eight feet by four feet and the Doctor's side was an L-shape about eight feet by eight feet. It was an amazing feat, what the two brothers had accomplished, thought Jeb. "Wow, Rusty, what can I say?"

"Then you like it?"

"It is frickin' awesome! Just one question."

"Yeah, what's that?"

"How are we going to get it downstairs?"

The two brothers and Jeb all looked at each other. The sections were too big to fit into the elevator so they would have to hump them down the staircase, which was in flights that changed directions. They would have to turn the ends carrying the stage sections.

"Let me go get Neusy and Marlon to help us with this," said Jeb.

"I am right over here," said Marlon, walking out of the shadow and exhaling a cloud of smoke. "You guys are cool to do that. Are you sure that you don't want any weed?" The brothers did not respond.

Jeb went downstairs to get the guys. "You guys need to go upstairs and give us a hand. You aren't going to believe this," said Jeb.

Back outside, Rusty started explaining how they were going to do this. "Alright, Jeb, you and Neusy grab the back end of this section. Hal and I will get this end. Marlon open the door for us."

Marlon opened the door and the other four picked up a section and walked it in the building. They got to the staircase and Rusty barked, "Right!" They made a right turn and Jeb and Neusy backed down the stairs with Rusty and Hal up top guiding the load but not bearing the load.

"Hey, guys! It's fucking heavy! We're losing it down here!" yelled Jeb. "We're going to get smashed down here. Marlon! Get your ass over here!"

Marlon ran behind where Rusty and Hal were standing on the staircase. "What do you want?"

"Lay on your back and squirm your way down here under the stage section and help us hold this thing. Hurry up!" screamed Jeb.

Marlon did it, getting on his back and sliding under the stage section perched on the steps.

"Get a hold, Marlon! Hurry up!" said Neusy.

They got the section steadied and stood it up on the first landing. "Fuck, that was close!" gasped Jeb.

They made the turn with the section and continued down the second flight of stairs, this time being more prepared. They got it done easier than the first flight. Once down, they humped it into the club and set it on the right side of the stage, then went back upstairs to grab another section. Jeb asked Torsten and Heinz to help them make the job easier. He knew those two were more fit than Tommy and Nathan, plus Tommy just wouldn't want to do it. Now there were six people handling the next section. It went much better than before. They got it downstairs, walked it in the club, and set it in front of the main stage. One more piece to go. Back outside, they got a hold of the L-shaped section. Jeb had an uneasy feeling about this one. He could foresee trouble trying to turn the bend in the staircase. The guys got it to the first landing, and as Jeb had predicted, they couldn't turn the bend. Four guys on the bottom and two up top, they couldn't turn the bend. Now what, wondered Jeb.

"Alright, you guys, set it down on the landing! Hal, go to the van and get the Sawzall." Hal did as he was told and brought back the saw and plugged it in. Sawdust filled the stairwell, and everyone began choking on it. The guys below ran downstairs and abandoned the section. Once Hal had sawed through the leg of the section above, the lower section slid down the lower flight of stairs and BOOM! The section hit the floor below. Luckily, Jeb, Torsten, Heinz, and Neusy were far enough back they didn't get hit by the runaway stage section.

"Fuck! That was close! What the fuck, Hal? Were you trying to kill us?" yelled Jeb from downstairs.

"Sorry, dude!" Hal yelled from upstairs.

Rusty and Hal easily slid the upper section of stage that they just cut off down to the bottom and the two pieces were moved to the stage and set in place. They set the two pieces on the Doctor's side of the stage and around the column on one side. Using his drill and wood screws, Hal reconnected the runaway section to its partner and then installed it in front of the stage.

"The power has got to be on by now at the rehearsal room," said Jeb.

"Achh! I'm hungry!" said the Doctor.

"Well, what do they have around here?" asked Jeb.

"There is a Mexican place upstairs, maybe we can get something there?" said Rusty.

"Well, let's get everything to go, we don't have time to waste if they are going to rehearse," said Jeb.

"Achh! All I want is a bean-and-cheese burrito! No meat! Und some fresh salsa und chips."

"All right! Keep your pants on!" Jeb snapped at the Doctor.

Everyone got something to eat: al pastor and carne asada burritos, chicken and fish tacos with plenty of chips and salsa, and one bean-and-cheese burrito. The guys were famished from having to wait most of the day in the basement club. Marlon wasn't particularly hungry but still managed to eat more than anyone else. The bumpy, moving van made their feast quite messy. Food was all over their faces, clothes, and on the floor of the van.

They arrived back at the multi-room rehearsal studio and prepared to go inside. The Doctor grabbed his Universe Guitar case in one hand and his still-wrapped burrito in the other. Neusy grabbed the pedal board case and Jeb grabbed the MMM case. They entered the studio lobby. The manager said the power was back on, but they would need to wash the food off their faces and clothes before they could enter the clean rehearsal room. There were standards that must be met, and one is no food allowed in the rooms. He gave them towels and wipes and asked that they not sit on anything till they were cleaned up. One by one they went into the single restroom and cleaned themselves. A half hour later, they were all at their instruments and waited for the Doctor, who was outside talking to Bea on his cell phone. Patiently, they waited.

The band has remained the same now for the last few years, though the others were unaware that Heinz Beckenschultz on bass is Johnny Scaggz's younger brother Jimmy.

On guitar and vocals was the incredibly fit and handsome Nathan Lieber. The thirty-year-old Austrian, who was 6'1" tall with medium-length blonde hair, freshly added curls, and masculine blue eyes, was now in his sixth year in the band. Unfortunately for him, he picked up a curse that lasted his whole tenure in the band. He discovered early on that women just don't care for the second guitarist and has spent the last six years lonely.

Torsten the Viking was half-Danish and half-Austrian. Also thirty years old, he was exceptionally tall, standing at 6'9" behind his custom keyboard stand. When he was younger, he would have to sit to play because his hands could barely reach the keys when he stood. Playing in rock bands and sitting in a chair while the rest of the band stood rocking out gave him a complex. He felt after all the years of classical training and development of a style of playing that was superior to most keyboard players, he never received the credit he deserved because no one could see him behind the keyboard while sitting. What people did see was his four-foot-long braided red hair whipping around over his head as he passionately moved about the keys. Then when he was twenty-three years old, a rep from a famous German keyboard stand manufacturer caught his performance during a Christmas show he performed in Frankfurt. The rep signed him as an endorsee and promised that he would never have to sit behind the keyboards again. They designed a custom keyboard stand for Torsten's multiple keyboards. Now he stood behind the keyboards like he was a captain guiding a ship and took on the stage name of Torsten the Viking. On many nights when he felt that a show inspired him, he would wear his Viking helmet as he guided the band into battle.

Drummer Tommy Thompson was nicknamed Triple T after his toupee got caught on one of his cymbal stands many years ago. He was hired as a replacement for the original drummer of a rebooted seventies band's comeback tour. The original drummer decided that he deserved more than a split of the proceeds and formed his own version of the same band with all hired musicians. The name Tommy "Toupee" Thomson was born after the video went viral of Tommy losing his wig and trying to set it right on his head during the song. People talked for years about the chubby drummer's spastic movements. A California native, Tommy was a drummer that was a hired gun. He's played on many albums and been hired to play on countless tours. He was hoping that he was already contracted for another tour when the Doctor's next tour was scheduled. Unfortunately, he was not in as much demand as he used to be and had to take the gig because he needed the money.

While Neusy and Jeb set up the Doctor's equipment, the Doctor finished his phone call and stood in the hallway outside the rehearsal room. "Achh! Wait, I want to eat my burrito now. I didn't want to get all messy in the van like you swines." He unwrapped his burrito and took a bite. Then he took another and spit out the next piece on the floor. "AWWWGGG! That dummkopf girl! There is a piece of animal flesh in my burrito! Revolting!" screamed the Doctor.

"What kind of flesh is it, pork or beef?" asked Marlon.

"Achh! You are a dummkopf, too. How would I know? I don't eat meat, so how could I tell the difference between one animal to the next?" yelled the Doctor.

"Oh, there are distinct differences," remarked Marlon.

"Achh! I don't care about the differences in the tastes of animal flesh! Dummkopf!" The Doctor angrily threw his burrito into the room and it splattered against a wall. Some of it ricocheted into Marlon's hair. He was pleased to find both bacon and chicken and ate them both. The manager saw this and yelled down the hallway that he was adding a $250 cleaning fee to their rental.

"Now, now, Doctor, feel the peace!" said Jeb.

"Yah! I must meditate." The Doctor sat on the floor in the lotus position once again and closed his eyes. "AAAMM!" he chanted loudly. "I will join you in a minute."

The band began to play "Slap the Virgin."

The Doctor raised his hands and spoke. "Nein, nein! Very bad! Heinz, erratic tempo again. Tommy, you are behind the beat. Let's get it right." They started again; the Doctor stopped them again. "Torsten! You know better than that! Don't jazz up the song with that chord, keep it straight!"

"Sorry, Doctor," said Torsten.

They went at it again. This time they made it through the song and the Doctor did not stop them. They tried another classic Centipedes song, "Bitchy Wife." After thirty seconds the Doctor stopped them.

"Achh! What is this? After so many times we played this song you guys forget everything, yah? I have to go up there und direct now, hummm?"

The Doctor stood up, got his Universe Guitar out, and prepared to play. "Achh! OK, let's stop fucking around here!" said the Doctor sternly.

"Language!" shouted Neusy from across the room.

"Achh, yah! Always the funny guy, Neusy!"

After the rehearsal, the guys were tired and ready to sleep. They packed up their gear and loaded it in the van, climbing in after.

"Where to, Jeb?" asked Rusty.

"South Eastern Hotel. Wait for the address, I'm looking for it," said Jeb. "OK, here it is. Let's go!" As the van started moving, the phone bounced out of Jeb's hand into leftover salsa on the floor.

Rusty drove out of the rehearsal studio's parking lot and was on the road. Within a few minutes they were at the hotel. They were all looking forward to a good night's sleep.

Chapter 19

"Jeb, it's Cal. Where are you guys?"

"Cal, where the hell are *you*?" said Jeb.

"We are here in Norwich."

"I'll text you the address of the hotel we are at!"

"OK, me and Hocker will be right over. Hang tight, we are rolling!"

Jeb was relieved to hear that Cal and Hocker had finally made it to Norwich. Rubbing his bruised shoulder, he would not have to bounce around in the back of the van any longer. Plus, all the equipment needed for the show was in the trailer that Cal was pulling.

Jeb was standing outside the hotel when he saw the tour bus enter the parking lot. He watched the bus approach and stop right in front of him. The door opened and a large man led by a beer gut exited and walked by. Jeb looked up into the bus, and behind the wheel, sitting in a modified old barber chair, was Cal Crabs. At eye level to Jeb, he first saw the rattlesnake-skin boots, then as he looked up, he saw his friend of many years. Cal, a tall thin man with a muscular body, long stringy brown hair, and bulbous eyes like Marty Feldman was wearing a hemp-woven cowboy hat, a blue denim sleeveless shirt and blue jeans stained by the many cups of coffee he had been drinking on his drive.

"Cal, you old cowboy, we thought you'd never get here."

"Yeah, we had bus troubles. But here we are. Now we are a bus!"

Jeb looked at the man that had just exited and was now standing next to him in the parking lot of the hotel. "Hocker, what's up, fucker?" Jeb asked his old touring buddy.

"The same old shit, shithead!" Hocker said as he spit some red chew on the street.

"Well, the guys are all eating in the hotel dining room. Why don't we get the instruments and the MMM out of the van and put them into the trailer. Then after they are finished eating, we can get the luggage out of our rooms and head over to the venue and get set up," said Jeb.

"Whose van is this?" asked Hocker.

"It belongs to the Pliers brothers. When you weren't there to pick us up in Newark, we had to call them to bring us to Norwich. By the way, thanks for the call to let us know; Marlon was flipping out and almost got his ass kicked several times," explained Jeb.

Jeb slid open the van door and grabbed the Universe Guitar. Hocker grabbed the MMM and Cal grabbed Heinz's bass case and Nathan's guitar case. The back of the van was full of food scraps, stains, and paper wrappers. In the corner near the Pliers' tool chest, which had loose screws and wood pieces around it, was a half-eaten burrito. Seeing the burrito, Hocker picked it up and finished it off, throwing the wrapper back in the van. Jeb pretended not to notice but smiled.... typical Hocker.

"What a pigsty! You guys have been riding in this?" asked Cal.

"Looks like you were fucking living in there. Sure glad you had me ride from California on the bus," said Hocker. "It was very peaceful on there without you assholes."

"Yeah, we had no choice. It was uncomfortable as fuck! Marlon fucked up his pinkie yesterday," said Jeb.

"Aww, poor baby," said Hocker.

"Here, it looks like they're coming out now," said Jeb.

The band, Marlon, Neusy, and the Doctor all came outside. They all had their luggage and travel bags and were ready to get onto the tour bus. They were all happy to see Cal—no more riding in the back of a van, no more sleeping in vacant apartments—now they were all packed into the comforts of the tour bus. It was still early, and they didn't need to be at the venue to set up for a couple hours. The Doctor decided it would be nice to take a short drive to the beach for a breath of salt air and some morning meditation.

"Achh! Cal, my old friend, you finally made it."

"Yeah, Doctor! I'm here! All your worries will melt away now. Hey Marlon, how are you, little buddy?"

"I'm better now that you are here, Cal. I fucked up my pinkie riding in the back of that van yesterday."

"Well, now you can have your old comfortable bunk back on the tour bus, Marlon."

"Who are you two? I don't know you guys," asked Cal.

"I'm Rusty, and this is my brother, Hal. We are old friends of the Doctor."

"No kidding, I'm an old friend of the Doctor. Nice to meet y'all."

"Achh! Cal, I want to go down to the beach for a while," said the Doctor.

"Well, hop in and let's get rolling," said Cal.

"We will follow you in the van," said Rusty.

Cal plugged in the nearest beach into his GPS, and they were on their way. As they passed William Backus Hospital, they could see doctors, nurses, and other people walking around, going in and out of the hospital as they drove by. Looked like a busy place. Marlon was thinking that there must be good drugs in that place. After a while longer they arrived at the beach.

"OK, everyone out. How long do you want to stay here, Jeb?" asked Cal.

"We need to load in at the venue at 3:00 pm, so let's get out of here by 2:00," said Jeb.

"Alrighty, partner!"

"Achh! The seashore! I love the seashore," the Doctor said as he grabbed a towel from the bus and was on the sand.

Nathan, Heinz, and Torsten all had their towels and exited the bus, mumbling in German. Neusy, Hocker, and Marlon followed, then Cal and Jeb. Everyone was heading out on the sand towards the water. The weather was nice as it was nearing fall and not too hot. The Doctor found his spot, stretched out his towel, sat in the lotus position, closed his eyes, and listened to the seagulls crying.

The Austrians decided on a swim. "On your Karl Marx, get sets, gooo!" Nathan cried out and they all barreled into the water. Jeb, Hocker, Marlon, Neusy, and Cal found a spot and laid out their towels and plopped themselves down. Jeb began to tell Cal and Hocker about the adventures with the Pliers brothers. Cal and Hocker found the stories amusing. Jeb wasn't so amused as he told them the details. Jeb saw the Pliers had arrived and were making their way across the sand towards them. They stopped talking about them.

"Hey, guys! We're here!" said Hal.

"Yeah, I can see that," said Jeb.

"We were thinking to catch the show tonight and then head back to Long Branch in the morning," said Rusty.

"That's fine! I'll put you on the guest list. After all, you guys were a big help all the way through," said Jeb.

The brothers smiled at each other and Hal said, "Yeah, well, you know, we are all old friends here."

"Hey Marlon, go to the bus and grab some sunscreen, otherwise we are all going to get burned up," said Neusy.

Cal asked about India and Jeb told him and Hocker about some of their experiences. Marlon got back with a full bottle of sunscreen, and they all screened up.

"Marlon, you better bring the bottle to the Doctor and tell him to screen up. We don't need him all burned up before the show tonight. And yell at those crazy Austrians to come in and get some screen on as well," instructed Jeb.

Marlon did as he was told and ran off like a trained little dog. After a few hours of listening to India stories, it was time to get to the venue to set up. The Doctor had meditated the whole time and the Austrians stayed wet, enjoying the water. Jeb told Marlon to call the Austrians and the Doctor and tell them to get ready to leave. After the Austrians showered off with the public beach showers, they were ready to go.

"Achh! What a wunderbar day! I am ready to play tonight," said the Doctor.

"Yah! Yah! Alles Gut! Today was wunderbar!" said Nathan.

The other Austrians nodded their heads and smiled. "Make sure y'all dust the sand off yourselves with your towels and then shake off your towels before you get on the bus. I don't want any sand on the bus. You guys got it?" yelled Cal.

Everyone agreed and dusted themselves off as best as they could and got on the bus. Tommy the drummer, not wanting to lie in the sand, was watching TV in the front lounge of the bus when the boys entered. He shut off the TV, and in his tight whites and no shirt, walked back to his bunk. He laid down and shut the curtain to his bunk. Jeb and Neusy first on the bus saw Tommy bend over and get into his bunk.

"Ahh the pleasures of being back on the road," said Neusy. Jeb smiled and the two sat down on one of the couches located in the front lounge.

"Yah Yah Neusy," said the Doctor as he made his way past and walking through the bunk area. Opening the door at the back of the sleeping area he then disappeared into his bedroom, nicknamed the ICU.

The bus was like most tour buses. A front lounge area with seating and a table located in the front that Jeb used as his tour manager station. In the back of the lounge was a small kitchenette with a refrigerator that contained mostly leftover meals and beer. Opposite the kitchenette was the toilet and small shower used when a hotel shower was not available. Behind the toilet was a door leading to the sleeping area that contained twelve bunks. The bunks were three high and each side of the bus contained six bunks. The bunks were just large enough to crawl into and lay down. Then behind the bunk section was a rear lounge that gives the occupants more space to stretch out. Unfortunately for the occupants of this bus, the Doctor long ago modified this lounge into his private bedroom. While the rest of the band and crew were packed in tight up front, the Doctor always was comfortable in his private space.

Jeb gave Cal the address and Cal plugged it into his GPS. The Pliers brothers followed the bus to the venue in their van. Once at the venue, Jeb, Neusy, Hocker, and Marlon began the usual routine of getting equipment and merchandise items out of the trailer. They hauled the gear and merch down to the basement of the building. The Pliers brothers showed up and Jeb asked them to help carry the drums downstairs. Today when they entered the club there was someone to greet them.

"I'm William Backus III," said the man.

Jeb thought for a moment and remembered the hospital with the same name that they had passed by earlier in the morning. "Hi, I'm Jeb, the Doctor's tour manager. Are you related to someone at that hospital down the way?" asked Jeb.

"Yeah, my grandfather was the founder of it," replied the man.

"Are you a doctor?" asked Jeb.

"Well, no. Actually, I am the hospital administrator. This venue is a hobby business of mine. I just bought it recently and haven't had time to renovate it yet," explained William.

"Well, maybe you can talk to those two guys over there. Rusty and Hal Pliers. They helped us build those stage extensions yesterday."

"Wow! Look at that! I didn't even notice that. It looks so much bigger than before," said William.

"Rusty, Hal, come here and meet William," Jeb called out.

The two brothers engaged in conversation with the owner and Jeb got busy setting up the merch table. He told Marlon to continue bringing in the merch. Hocker and Neusy were up on the stage, setup almost complete. No need for the MMM tonight so one less piece of equipment to set up. The Doctor wandered in.

"William, let me introduce the Doctor to you," said Jeb.

"Achh! Guten Tag!"

"What kind of doctor are you?" asked William.

"Achh! I am the Doctor of Dynamics."

"I have never heard of that field of medicine," said William.

"Nein, nein, not medicine, but sound and music. I am the doctor of those things."

"Oh, great! First time meeting a doctor of your caliber. It is a pleasure," said William.

"Yah! Likewise, William."

Jeb finished the merch area with Marlon while Hocker and Neusy finished the stage set up. When finished, Jeb said to Neusy, "You know what time it is? It's beer thirty, as Hocker would say." The two walked over to the bar.

"What do you guys want?" asked William, standing near the bar as Hocker and Marlon arrived.

"Anything nice and cold," said Neusy.

"Here, you guys might like this Narley Norwich Home Style Brew. It's made at a micro-brewery right here in town," said William.

"Right on!" said Hocker. "I always enjoy trying new things. In fact, I have tried 366 different beers in my years of drinking. You might call me the Doctor of Brews." Hocker proudly displayed a grin from ear to ear that Neusy found disturbing.

"More like the Doctor of Drunkenness!" said Jeb, smiling at Neusy.

"Hey man, that was uncalled for!" whined Hocker.

"Am I wrong?" asked Jeb.

"No! Just, it wasn't cool, that's all," said Hocker, whose face now returned to the wretched form that Jeb and Neusy were used to.

"Well, you guys will see a lot of doctors here tonight. A lot of my colleagues are coming tonight after work. And the opening band tonight are doctors too," said William.

"You mean the band are all doctors?" asked Marlon.

"Yes. Well, actually, one is a nurse, she plays bass," said William.

"What are they called?" asked Jeb.

"The OBGYNs," said William.

The doors opened right on time and the opening band was on stage precisely at 8:00 pm, as the schedule for the night indicated. Jeb was shocked. This was a rarity; normal course of events usually would have the first band start late for whatever was the reason of the day. Most of the time out of their control and because of some local issue. It could be anything from the first band arrived late, to the sound man was nowhere to be found, or the people involved getting the show started were busy drinking and had no time to start the show. Many times, a club owner would start late to allow his occupants more time to purchase drinks and pad his pocket. But tonight was right on time. Jeb was wondering if it was because they were all doctors whose schedules were important.

OBGYN's set list was interesting. All the songs that they played were covers of songs that were about doctors. They kicked off with Van Halen's "Somebody Get Me a Doctor." After forty minutes, OBGYN closed their set with Mötley Crüe's "Dr. Feelgood" and UFO's "Doctor Doctor."

Neusy, Jeb, and Hocker enjoyed the set and the several beers that were poured for them. Marlon got stoned and was introduced to songs he never heard before, spending the entire set asking Jeb what song OBGYN was playing and looking it up online, only to be disappointed in the morning that he really did not like those songs when he was sober.

The Doctor played a set that was inspired by his meditation session on the beach. He effortlessly tore through his classics and closed the show with "Slap the Virgin."

The North American tour was successfully on its way. After settling up and getting paid by William Backus III, who remarked how professional Jeb and his crew were, Jeb returned to the merch booth where Marlon was conducting the meet and greet with the Doctor. Professional? That was the first time Jeb had heard that, but there was Marlon diligently handling the meet and greet without him and had the line almost run all the way through. This would be a great tour. One that would erase the bad stigma from the last time out. Jeb stood there watching Marlon work. He turned to the stage. Neusy and Hocker already had it broken down and were loading out the equipment. Humming like a machine. Even the Pliers brothers were busy taking measurements to extend the stage further and build a second bar in the back.

After the merch and equipment were loaded back into the trailer, the band and crew all sat around the bar for one last round on the house from the overjoyed owner having his first concert in his venue being a success.

"All shows should be like this. Nice and easy with good people running the club," said Neusy to Jeb. "Well, almost perfect, look who just walked in."

Jeb turned around and was watching Agents Sparrow and Crow approach them. "Right on time, guys."

"We missed our flight and had to take the next one out. Apparently, it's Comic Guild award weekend in Los Angeles and the Porn Awards in Hollywood. The airport was full of people in costumes, both superheroes and porn stars. We couldn't get to our flights. People wanted to take pictures with us thinking we are those fucking Blues Brothers," said Crow.

"We couldn't get away. I have never seen an airport like that. We even got a picture taken with a transgender male that said he was up for the Tightest Sack Lifetime Achievement Award, along with Wonder Woman and Ant-Man," added Sparrow.

Neusy gave Jeb the we-are-done-in-here look and the two walked up the steps out into the parking lot. Cal had the bus fired up and was preparing for the drive to Salem, waiting in the driver's seat, his comfortable old barber's chair he had retrofitted to the bus.

Scaggz was sitting outside his VW Kombi near Salem, MA, grilling a weasel he managed to trap earlier that evening after returning from the club where the Doctor would perform the next day. While talking with the bartender at the club, he felt that the Doctor would be fairly treated at a low level. He liked the layout of the club.

On his way out of the club, he walked through part of the kitchen unseen, but witnessed what appeared to be the manager teaching a young employee the art of topping off the liquor bottles.

"What you have to do," said the manager, "is make sure that on the vodka, gin, and house whiskey is pour out a third of a new bottle to an empty and fill it up with water. Keep the third bottle in this cabinet back here, and when you empty another third into it, then top it off as well. On the top shelf stuff, the whiskey and the tequila or other bottles of what people like to do shots, we have to be careful. Always pour five shots out of a new bottle of the good stuff, then fill the rest up with water. They will never know. But if we dilute it too much, these assholes taking the shots will know because of the burn factor."

Scaggz took a good look at the man speaking and planned on watching him the next night. The Doctor would be safe while Scaggz is on the tour. He now waited on Jimmy to text him on how the first night went without him there while he cooked the weasel.

Chapter 20

"Achh! Jeb, I'm not going in that place!" said the Doctor, sitting in the lounge of the tour bus parked behind the Salem Witch Trial Club.

"You have to. Just go in and look around," said Jeb.

"Nein, nein, nein! I don't like warlocks und witchcraft. I don't like these things! They can wreak havoc in your soul!"

"But it's the theme of the club! It's just play acting. It's like a big Halloween party."

"Achh! I don't like Halloween, either. My grandmother always told me to stay away from these things, they are evil. Nein, nein, nein! I don't go in!"

"OK, you sit here and meditate and calm down. Feel the peace! You have to play inside tonight, we have a contract and we need the money," said Jeb, and he went into the venue.

Neusy and Hocker were already working out the stage set up and Marlon was bringing in boxes of merch.

"Hello, I'm Magistrate Jonathan Corwin IV. I run this place."

"Hi, I'm Jeb, the tour manager."

"When can I meet the Doctor? I'm a big fan, you know."

"Well, the Doctor is having a nap. You can meet him later."

Jeb began to worry. He knew the Doctor could be very stubborn and unbendable with certain things. He thought about what to do. He didn't want to have a conflict with the club because the Doctor refused to play. He had to make it happen, somehow. This Jonathan guy seemed like a nice person.

"Hey, Jonathan, can I get a beer and relax a minute?"

"Sure, Jeb, right this way. Why don't you try this one, Magistrate IPA. It's made by my family."

"Really? I love home brews. I am a brewer myself."

"Well, you'll like this one. Not too bitter, with a hint of chocolate and raspberry."

"Great! Thanks!"

"All done with the setup, Jeb!" said an elated Neusy. "This place is kind of cool. A little creepy, but cool. The stage being set up like gallows is a bit odd. But hey, it's the theme of the day, I guess."

"I'm bushed, I need a beer," said Hocker.

"Hey, Jonathan, can I get two more Magistrate IPAs for Neusy and Hocker over here?"

"Sure, Jeb, just a minute… Here you guys are, enjoy!"

"Wow! That's good stuff!" said Hocker.

"If you guys will excuse me, I have some things to prepare for the witch trial tonight and some of the other activities," said Jonathan.

"Witch trial?" said Hocker.

"Yes, witch trial. It's like a reality game. And I am the magistrate who passes judgment on the witches, just like my grandfather."

"Your grandfather?" asked Neusy.

"Yes, didn't you know? My tenth-great grandfather was Magistrate Jonathan Corwin I. He sentenced nineteen witches to death on the gallows. Well, if you'll excuse me, I have to get my work done."

"Fuck! Witch trials, scary stuff!" said Hocker.

"Yeah, that's just great! I already have a big problem with the Doctor," said Jeb.

"That is creepy stuff. What's up with the Doctor?" asked Neusy.

"He doesn't want to play in here tonight. He is all freaked out about warlocks and witchcraft already. That's all I need to tell him is that they are going to have a witch trial in here tonight to send him over the edge," whined Jeb.

Jonathan Corwin returned to the bar. "I forgot to mention, we all have to dress up tonight. There is a costume room over there. You can choose to be a witch, warlock, a villager, a reverend, a witch hunter, or a magistrate," said Jonathan.

"OK, thanks, Jonathan," said Jeb, and when he turned around Jonathan was gone.

"Fuck! What are we going to do about the Doctor?"

"I have a crazy idea," said Neusy.

"I'd listen to just about anything at this point," said Jeb.

"Why don't we use the MMM. Put a costume on it and one of Tommy's wigs. The Doctor can wear the thought transference headset in the tour bus and think the music. The MMM can play all the songs with the band. No one will know it isn't the Doctor. Everyone has to wear a costume anyways, right? The MMM will have a costume too," explained Neusy.

"You know, you come up with some wild shit sometimes, Neusy, but I like it! This just might work," said the elated Jeb. "OK, this is what we do: Hocker, go to the trailer and bring out the MMM, take it to the green room and set it up. Neusy, go to the costume room and grab something appropriate. Then you two dress up the MMM."

"Wait a minute! This MMM has four arms. What to do about that?" said Neusy.

"Just put two arms through the sleeves of the costume. Hang the other two arms down inside the coat of the costume. No one should notice," said Jeb. "Leave the MMM in there until show time, and then you guys bring it out when it's time to play, when the stage is dark."

"Alright, Jeb. It will work, don't worry," said Neusy. "What about the face?"

"I'll go in the bus and print out a photo of the Doctor's face on my printer. You tape it on the MMM's center vertical truss rod, then hang Tommy's wig on top of the truss and put a hat on it. We will put a scarf over the face and just leave the eyes open. It's a dark club."

"I'll tell Jonathan not to disturb the green room. You guys lock the door while you're inside working in there. I'll go explain things to the Doctor and the band on the bus."

Scaggz had prepared to be at this show for some time. He had been following the tour schedule online, but this was the first place that he would be able to get in to see the show. He already knew about the theme of the venue and decided to play an executioner. He already had his costume made up in his van. With his hood covering his face, no one would recognize him. He would stay inside his van until the doors opened and then go inside.

Agents Sparrow and Crow arrived and were instructed to change into one of the costumes in the costume room next to the entrance. On cue the agents held up their badges and informed the person at the door that they were FBI agents assigned to the tour because of murders that plagued the last tour. The bouncer at the door was not impressed and told them they must wear a costume or leave. They held up their badges once again and insisted that they speak with the club's manager. Magistrate Jonathan briefed the agents on the policy of the club and of the importance for the paying customers that the illusion is unbroken. So, if they wanted entry, since they were not on the guest list it would cost each one $25 and they must wear one of the costumes or there was no entry.

The agents once again held up their badges to the bouncer, who remained unimpressed until the agents finally presented an agency credit card and were charged the $50 to enter. They were led to the costume room where the only costumes that they were comfortable wearing were out-of-date colonial suits that were part of costumes of George Washington and Thomas Jefferson, complete with the wigs, which they refused to wear and were told they then would have to leave.

The two agents were finally in position, Crow on the side of the stage dressed as Thomas Jefferson and Sparrow in the back of the venue looking a lot like George Washington but wearing sunglasses in a dark club.

"Welcome to the Salem Witch Trial Club!" announced Magistrate Jonathan Corwin IV. "Tonight, we have a special evening indeed. Tonight, besides our normal fun time, we have the Doctor of Dynamics here to play some classic rock and roll!"

"YAAHHHH! BRING IT! BRING ON THE DOCTOR!"

"But first let me explain the game for tonight. Everyone has signed the waiver to play, so here we go. Anyone can accuse someone of witchcraft. A husband can accuse a wife. A wife a husband. A villager can accuse a reverend or a magistrate. A child can accuse a grandparent. Anyone accused will stand trial before me here on the stage. Then I will pronounce judgment."

Jonathan looked around the room of costumed patrons, many with a beer in hand and enjoying the vibe. In the back of the club was a super-sized carnival water dunk tank. The kind that someone would sit inside on a board and another would throw balls at a target on a lever. If the target was struck, into the water tank the person sitting inside went. They got dunked and soaking wet. Except in this case the tank was filled with beer. 1,000 gallons of beer was freshly poured in before show time. A great new way to get drunk. The billboard leading into town advertised the club, promising lots of colonial fun and the only place in New England where dunk drunk was a real thing.

Once plunged into the beer, it was hard not to get a bunch in your mouth while being submerged. Also, the tanks were decorated to look like the gallows used to hang witches several centuries before. There were even faux nooses hanging down out of an overhead rigging structure. Designed by a famous yo-yo company, they had plenty of length, and with a simple pulley system, reeled down and up similar to the mechanics of a yo-yo.

Once the magistrate pronounced judgment, the patron would be led back to the dunk tank and sat inside on the plank. A faux noose was placed around their neck, and then patrons could throw balls, one by one, at the target and try to execute the witch. Whoever hit the target and dunked the witch won a free drink. It was great fun.

"Let the games begin!"

"My wife is a witch!" yelled out one man dressed as a typical villager.

His wife, dressed in a colonial black-and-white dress, gave him the evil eye. She wasn't very keen on playing or getting wet.

"Bring her forward!" spoke The Magistrate. "Confess, woman!"

"I am not a witch! But I confess that my husband is an asshole!" said the woman.

"What say you, jury?" asked the Magistrate.

"GUILTY!" yelled out the crowd.

"Take her to the gallows!" said the Magistrate.

The woman looked at her husband. "You'll pay when we get home tonight, fuckhead!" Her husband didn't care; he laughed, spilling his beer everywhere. She was led away, placed in the dunk tank, and a faux noose was placed over her neck. People lined up and began to pitch balls, one guest after the next. A man dressed as a reverend approached the throwing line. A retired major league pitcher, he threw the ball, and although he could not get the velocity he had in his prime, hit the target with a ninety-mph fastball. The noose reeled down on the pulley and into the beer tank the woman went, choking down some beer as she went in.

"This man is a warlock!" shouted out a thin, skinny man in a colonial jester's outfit. It was Marlon looking at Hocker.

"Oh, you little dick!" said Hocker. "I'll get you!"

"Bring him forward!" said the Magistrate.

"I don't want to play! Fuck this game!" Hocker was not pleased.

"Oh, come on, Hocker, you like beer!" said Jeb.

"I don't want to get wet!" said Hocker.

Neusy, Jeb, and Marlon began to tease him.

"Pussy!"

"Pantywaist!"

"Sissy!"

"Alright, fuckers!" Hocker conceded.

"This man has been accused of witchcraft. What say you, jury?"

"GUILTY!"

Hocker was led back to the dunk tank. He sat on the plank and became more obnoxious.

"Fuck you! None of you will knock me down in here! You can't even throw a ball, you pussy, Marlon!"

The people lined up once again and started taking turns throwing the ball. Fifteen people all missed; it kept on going.

"Fuckheads! You all suck! Kiss my fat ass!"

Marlon walked up to the line.

"Marlon, you couldn't hit the broad side of a—" SPLASH! In went Hocker, gulping down beer as he went under, but in his case it was intentional. He tried to drink as much as he could before resurfacing. His head came out of the beer. He let out an outrageously loud burp. "UUURRRRRPPPP!" He sipped the surface of the beer around his neck and dove under once more, consuming as much as he could.

"What great fun! Yes?" said The Magistrate from the stage, and the crowd agreed.

"Well, it's getting close to show time so have another beer and get ready for the Doctor and his band, the Surgeons." The Magistrate stepped off the stage and went into the crowd to mingle with some friends.

Jeb told Neusy to tell the band to get ready to come on stage, then he and Marlon walked the MMM onto the stage with their backs to the crowd so no one would stare too long at the MMM. Fortunately, the lighting wasn't very bright in the room, so it helped conceal the MMM.

Jeb readied his cell phone to call the Doctor in the tour bus to get ready with the TRM headset and his thoughts of the music. Nathan would cover all of the singing tonight and the song introductions. "Guten Abend, Salem!" shouted Nathan. "We are going to rock your socks off tonight! Here we go! 'Slap the Virgin'!"

The Doctor could hear what was going on through Jeb's cell phone, which he left connected. As he thought, the MMM's arms began to move and play. It looked okay, it just couldn't walk or move around the stage like the Doctor would. The people dug on the music and the place was pumping. The people dressed in their colonial clothes, banging their heads, was a very strange sight. Scaggz, dressed in his executioner's outfit, was watching the show from one side of the room. He noticed something strange was going on with the Doctor. Why doesn't he move around? Why isn't he making normal facial expressions?

"And now, 'Dogs That Bark'!" They started to play the intro theme. The MMM played the harmony guitar parts with Nathan. Beautiful! Then he began to sing. As he sang, he saw a beautiful girl in a typical colonial dress. She was cute. He wanted to meet her after the show. He started thinking about what they could do later. He got a bit too close to the MMM and one of the arms inside the costume began to wag its finger back and forth inside the costume. Darting back and forth in the crotch area of its pants. No one really noticed. No one except for Scaggz, who thought it was another clone. He thought he handled the problem in India, but it looked like Doctor Spiers had created more. Scaggz lost his composure and jumped up on the stage and tackled the MMM. He began hitting and kicking it. He ripped the clothes off of it, revealing it was a machine and not a man. The band stopped abruptly and stared at this man kicking the shit out of the machine.

Scaggz looked out from the stage and all around him. Everyone was staring at him and didn't know what to make of what had just happened. He jumped up and bolted for the front door. After crashing into a man dressed like George Washington, he disappeared quickly outside. Magistrate Corwin walked over to Jeb and said, "We need to talk!"

Jeb instructed the crew to load out quickly so they could leave Salem behind and move on to New York City, which was highly anticipated. The crew broke the stage down and loaded out in record time. Cal fired the bus up and waited. Jeb returned with only half of the guarantee that he settled on after a lengthy argument with Magistrate Corwin, which Scaggz witnessed from the same spot in the kitchen he hid the day before.

"Jebster," said Cal, "are we a bus?"

Jeb counted heads and responded, "We are a bus."

Cal put the bus in gear, and they exited the Salem Witch Trial Club parking lot, leaving Scaggz alone to deal with Magistrate Corwin.

Chapter 21

As the bus started its four-hour journey to NYC, Scaggz had already put together what he thought would be a fitting punishment for a person who seemed to think cheating people out of their money was OK. Tied up in the back of the VW Kombi was the employee that Magistrate Corwin was showing how to top off the liquor bottles a day earlier. Scaggz waited patiently for The Magistrate to exit the building. Scaggz knew he would be the last to leave. While his prisoner tried to wriggle out of the duct tape and ropes he found himself in, Scaggz assured him that he had nothing to worry about and was going to use him to make a point. But those encouraging words did nothing to calm the man tied up in the back of the VW.

"Ahh, great," said Scaggz to his prisoner. "Here comes Magistrate Corwin now. The show is about to start. Wait here, I'll be back soon."

Magistrate Corwin saw the raised blue Stratocaster guitar, but he was late to move out of the way. When he awoke, he was two feet off the ground, tied to a stake, with the young man from the back of the VW tied to a similar stake ten feet away from him. He could not see much in the dark parking lot but noticed that they both had a small fire at the bottom of the stake.

"What's this?" asked The Magistrate, "a joke? That small fire down below, ha ha, I get it. You have an issue with our club. It's just a gimmick; we don't really have witches or carry out sentences as they did back then. It's all just for fun."

Scaggz, now standing in front of him, placed four bottles of vodka on the ground. "This has nothing to do with your club, but more to do with you since you think it is OK to cheat people out of their money. I will show you a new way. I have here four bottles of your house vodka. See?" Scaggz held up one of the bottles. "So, two of these bottles have the special treatment you like to give your customers, which is watered down drinks for their hard-earned money. Now watch what happens." Scaggz threw two bottles into the fire at the feet of the employee tied up next to The Magistrate. The fire flared, then sizzled out.

"You see, those bottles there had enough water in them to put that fire out."

The employee was trying to scream, but nothing came out of his mouth.

"Don't worry," said Scaggz, "I will cut you loose in a few minutes. You have nothing to worry about. Now Magistrate Corwin, you do have something to worry about. You will now see what a bottle that is not watered down will do. You are cheating people out of their money. So here we go." Scaggz threw one of the unopened bottles into the fire at the feet of The Magistrate. POOF! The flames ignited and Magistrate Corwin could feel them on his legs. Then the second bottle hit the fire and the flames rose to his waist. "Now, I think that you can see the difference. I am going to cut down your friend here and he will get you help. I thought about killing you, but then you would not learn the lesson today. So when you have the urge to cheat someone out of the alcohol that they purchased, or cheat a band out of their money, you have a reminder when your legs heal up why it's best not to do what your instincts are."

Magistrate Corwin screamed as the flames ignited his stake and rose quickly. Scaggz drove away, and in his rear-view mirror saw the employee extinguishing the flames with a bucket of water.

As the bus approached NYC, the Doctor was up front looking out the window educating anyone that was still awake to the wonders of America's largest city. "Yah, there is no place on Earth like the Big Apple, New York City. The original great melting pot of the United States. New York's many cultures existing together is quite impressive."

The tour bus arrived at the outskirts of Manhattan. They parked across the river in New Jersey and waited until afternoon to be picked up by a private shuttle bus to escort them to the venue. This particular venue provided all of the backline equipment that was needed, so there was no need to transport the band's amps, speakers, keyboards, or drum set to the venue. That was quite convenient and one less thing for Jeb to worry about, parking the bus in Manhattan.

The venue, called DEAFMUTE'S, is owned and operated by Charley Deafmute Collins, a famous old-school, black, blues guitarist from the 1960s. Deafmute wasn't always deaf, but after years of playing sixty-watt Fender twin amps miked up with two extra PA speaker cabinets pumping out an extra couple thousand watts propped up right next to his head, he lost his hearing midway through his career. He eventually had to quit playing because he couldn't follow along with the band. Although, it is said that he can play with others by feeling sound waves through his body. He was a smart man, he didn't do drugs, he wasn't an alcoholic, nor did he smoke. He saved most of his money and decided to invest it in the stock market. Eventually he had enough money to buy his own nightclub. He was very successful in creating the DEAFMUTE'S merchandise line of handy kitchen products like the patented Deafmute deep fryer and the Deafmute cocktail blender. He also created Deafmute's margarita mix, Deafmute's cornbread mix, as well as T-shirts, beer koozies, bottle openers, head scarves, guitar picks, cigarette lighters, etc.

Everyone knew about DEAFMUTE'S night club in Manhattan, it was quite renowned for blues music. The one troubling thing; it was three levels underground in a skyscraper office building.

"Where is that shuttle bus?" complained Jeb.

"You got to be patient, my man," replied Cal Crabs.

"It'll be here in a New York minute!" replied Hocker, smiling as he spit into an empty beer bottle.

"Smart ass!" said Jeb. "It sucks that we can't just drive the tour bus into Manhattan," said Jeb.

"There are just too many cars here. It's a clusterfuck! There is no place to park the bus legally, so we have to do this," replied Cal.

"Big Apple clusterfuck!" said Neusy.

"Hahaha! That's funny," replied Marlon as he rolled up a number to puff on outside.

Just then, the Doctor emerged from his suite in the back of the bus and wandered up front to the lounge area of the bus. "Achh! Morgen! Why are we just stopped here?"

"We can't drive the tour bus into Manhattan; we have to wait for a shuttle bus that is being sent to our location by the venue," stated Jeb.

"Yah! I see… Well maybe I should grab a snack." The Doctor began his ritual of opening all the kitchenette cabinets and the small refrigerator. Spying, once again, a cold piece of veggie pizza in the fridge, he quickly popped it into his mouth, and it was gone.

"You know, in just a short while you can get a fresh, authentic, New York pizza. Why do you eat that nasty, two-day old shit?"

"Achh! Ahgugu! Blahct, Ahgugu!" he muttered with food in his mouth.

"Hey guys! I think that's the shuttle bus outside there," said Cal.

"Attention everyone! The shuttle is here! Grab your instruments, sticks, backpacks, whatever, it's time to go!" shouted Jeb. "Marlon, you grab three boxes of T-shirts. Neusy, Hocker, you guys grab some CDs, DVDs, beer koozies out of the trailer, whatever we can sell tonight."

Neusy, Hocker, Marlon, and Cal went outside first. Nathan and Heinz grabbed their guitars and headed out. Tommy was still in the restroom. Torsten was still in his bunk. The Doctor was back in the ICU gathering his things.

"Come on, Torsten, get out of your bunk, we're leaving!" yelped Jeb.

Torsten rolled out of his bunk and looked for a new shirt to put on. "Come on, Tommy! We don't have all day! What are you doing in there, jerking off?" said Jeb.

"No, I'm brushing my teeth, I'll be right out," said Tommy as he adjusted his wig in the mirror in the small room.

The Doctor emerged from the ICU with his guitar and a stuffed animal under his arm.

"What the hell is that?" asked Jeb.

"Achh, yah! I am bringing Mr. Platypus with me today. He has been cooped up in the ICU for a long time," said the Doctor.

"Oh, brother! Why don't you bring Mr. Giraffe and Mr. Crocodile along, too, while you're at it?" asked Jeb.

"Achh! Because they were naughty, they are grounded!"

"Jeez! Alright, let's go! Come on, Tommy, you're the last one!"

Finally, everyone got off the tour bus. Jeb closed the door behind them, and they were all on the shuttle bus headed into town.

"Wow! Just look at this city! It's Huge!" said Nathan, peering out the shuttle bus's window.

"Yeah! One of the greatest metropolises in the world," said Neusy.

"Yah! Look at all those skyscrapers. I cannot even see the tops of them from this shuttle," said Torsten.

"Achh! I'm hungry!" moaned the Doctor from the front seat next to the driver. The whole band flipped him the finger behind his seat.

"After we check out the venue, we can go look for some food," replied Jeb. After going through two hours of slow-moving traffic, the shuttle arrived at the venue. The band and crew exited the shuttle bus in front of the Grand Terminex Office Complex, a sixty-five-story building in the heart of Manhattan.

"Ach! Where is the club?" asked the Doctor.

"We have to go inside the lobby and use the elevator," said Jeb.

The reception desk guard asked the large group of guys what they were doing there. Jeb told them they were the main band on the schedule tonight at DEAFMUTE'S. The guard pointed at the last elevator of six in a row and instructed them to push level B2.

The ten guys stuffed themselves into the elevator and descended to B2. They exited the elevator and found themselves in an underground parking structure. A large sign with DEAFMUTE'S written on it instructed them with a directional arrow to the club entrance. They came to the entrance of the venue; in eight-foot-tall blue and pink neon lights it read DEAF on the left side of the double doors and

MUTE'S on the right. They walked in and saw a couple of men playing dominos at a table.

"The show isn't until tonight, guys," remarked the tall, fat, grey-haired black man.

"Oh, well, we are the band! I'm Jeb, the manager!"

"Well, y'all, come on in," said the other man playing dominos.

"Can we have a look around?" asked Jeb.

"Sure, no problem."

"Where can I set up our merchandise?" asked Jeb.

"Right over there, next to our own merchandise area," said the man.

Marlon, Hocker, and Neusy all took their boxes of merch over to that area and began to help Jeb set things up on a table that the man provided for them.

The band walked over to the stage to check it out. After the merch was set up, Hocker, Neusy, and Marlon walked over to the bar to see what the beer menu looked like. The Doctor walked over to look at the "Wall of Blues" off to the left side of the venue. There were photos of all of the blues greatest artists. B.B. King, Albert King, Loretta King, King Allenby, Rogers King, Billy Jean King, Willie Dixon, Robert Johnson, Blind Melon Nelson, Buddy Guy, George Guy, Who's That Guy, and of course, Charley Deafmute Collins. The Doctor was very appreciative of the blues and the great people that created it before the roots reached the European theater.

The band perused the large thirty-five-foot-wide stage with purple and gold curtains on both sides. Eight floor monitors would provide a good mix for everyone and seemed satisfactory. Torsten, Heinz, Nathan, and Tommy were quite pleased with the stage and the back line of equipment that was provided. One unusual feature was all of the speaker cabinets and amplifiers had steel frames built around them, anchoring them to the floor. Odd, the guys thought. It would be pretty hard to steal things out of this place. They noticed the drum set and cymbal stands also had special frames holding everything down. Strange!

"Wow! That's the nicest Ludwig drum set that I ever saw in a night club," remarked Tommy as he stood in awe of the six-piece gold-sparkle Ludwig kit with Paiste cymbals.

"Yah, it's very nice! I should have no problem pumping out the bass with that 1,000-watt Ampeg Pro Head and two double cabinet stacks!" replied Heinz.

"Und look, two full stacks of 100-watt Marshalls on both sides of the drum riser. Und, even two Fender Super twins over there. Und there is a golden mic stand and golden mic for me to sing out of in the middle," said Nathan.

Torsten climbed on the stage to look at the keyboard set up. There were six keyboards formed in a C shape mounted on a customized metal carriage. Everything was there that any keyboardist could want. Top-of-the-line Kurzweil 88-key K3 Pro, a vintage Moog, an Oberheim OB-Xa, a Yamaha DX7, a Roland Infinity 9000, and a vintage Hammond B-3 organ. The coolest thing was there was a pedal that operated a hydraulic lift that adjusted the whole keyboard carriage to any height comfortable for the keyboardist. A feature very much appreciated by the very tall Torsten.

Back at the bar, the other guys were looking at the beer marquee. A very nice selection, indeed. Jeb noticed that between all of the liquor bottles and serving glasses there were white foam pads. He said, "That's odd! I've never seen those things before." Jeb looked back toward the front door, and before he could utter a sound, one of the men that were playing dominos walked back to the bar.

"You must have read my mind," said Jeb.

"Well, you know. We like to keep our guests happy. Deafmute insists on it," said the man.

"Will we get to meet Deafmute?" asked Marlon.

"Sure enough! He will come in later before the doors open," replied the large man.

"Cool! He's a blues legend!" said Neusy.

"What do y'all want to have?" asked the man.

"I'll have an Apple of My Eye Lager," said Hocker.

"I'll have a New York Minute IPA," said Jeb.

Both Neusy and Marlon nodded their heads in unison to Jeb's answer. The man handed each fellow a bottle of what they asked for. They all clicked bottles, took a sip, and then the whole venue started to shake, violently in fact. Hocker tried to sip his beer but much of it splashed out of the bottle on his face and down his shirt. The other guys clenched tight onto their bottles. On the wall behind the bar, the glasses and bottles stayed virtually motionless with the white foam pads between everything.

"What the hell was that? I never heard of New York having earthquakes," said Jeb.

"That was no earthquake, my man. That was line six," said the man.

"Line six?" asked Neusy.

"Yeah, line six. The subway runs by us about 100 feet away. We are down deep underground here. This was never designed to be a club, but it works."

"I'd like another beer, please," said the half-drenched Hocker, handing back his empty bottle.

The band members bounced across the room when it happened. They looked at each other and ran back to the bar. The Doctor was also shaken up a bit and made his way to the bar.

"Was ist das? An earthquake?" asked the Doctor.

"An earthquake! Let's get out of here before the whole building comes down on our heads!" yelled Nathan.

"Calm down! It's just the subway train," said Jeb.

"How are we going to play with that going on, hmmm?" asked Torsten.

"Well, now is a good time to practice. Let's do a soundcheck," said Jeb.

The boys opened their guitar cases and took out their instruments. Tommy grabbed his drumsticks from his backpack. The Doctor grabbed his Universe Guitar as Torsten jumped up onto the keyboard platform and adjusted the carriage to his height. Everyone plugged in and turned on the equipment. The sound man wasn't there yet, so Jeb went behind the mixing console and figured out how to turn on the house system by himself. Agents Sparrow and Crow arrived and were talking to the domino-playing men.

"Achh! Alright boys, let's try 'Bitchy Wife'." The band began to play. They got through the first verse and then the first chorus. All was good, no issues. They got through the second verse and the second chorus. Again, no problems. Guitar solo time. The Doctor began the solo, then it happened again: the subway train came through. Everyone was bouncing erratically on the stage. The agents bounced up to the bar where the crew were seated, holding onto the bar so they would not bounce off of the stools.

The Doctor almost bounced off the stage on his right side. He quickly planted his right foot and went into a low kung fu stance to the left and performed his solo. The others also gained their footing and steadied themselves. Torsten had it easy because he could steady himself between the keyboard carriages. Tommy had a rough time of it. The subway train passed, and they finished the song.

"Wow! That was crazy!" said Nathan.

"Yah! We better run through a few songs und prepare our stances for tonight! This is one soundcheck that will be very important!" said the Doctor. "Und Tommy, watch your rhythm tonight! You already have your problems with timing!"

Tommy, unhappy hearing that, flipped off the Doctor from under his snare drum.

The show was cut short on account of the subway bouncing the band around. Unfortunately, on a Friday night, extra trains were running, and it made the performance more challenging.

The agents were careful not to mention to the band and crew what had happened in Salem after they all left. Not only did they not want to worry the guys, but Sparrow believed that the man that crashed into him running out of the venue was the person that they were looking for. It was a difficult conversation with their supervisor, but they managed the damage control.

For Sparrow and Crow, this was the greatest assignment either has had since joining the FBI. They had a job to do and needed to show their supervisor that they were making some progress in the case, otherwise they would most certainly be reassigned. What they didn't know was that no one wanted the case, and the FBI really didn't have the manpower to take productive agents and have them on a case for the length of time chasing a tour around the country involved. But they were in full-on touring mode now, enjoying the best of every city.

While Sparrow and Crow had the club locked down, Scaggz was able to park his VW in the garage adjacent to the club. He bought a ticket, and with an old all-access pass, wearing a baseball cap and fake beard, he wandered around the backstage area while the show was going on.

Having worshipped Deafmute when he was growing up, he wanted the chance to meet the man. When he finally had his chance, he went on for five minutes telling Deafmute how big of a fan he was growing up and that, because of him, he learned blues guitar. Deafmute could not follow what Scaggz was saying because the fake beard covering his lips made lip reading impossible. He waived Scaggz over to the domino table and challenged him to a game. Scaggz, never having played before, beat Deafmute in two consecutive games. Deafmute stood and walked away, telling his security to watch Scaggz closely.

The agents never noticed the encounter at the domino table as they bounced past it several times during the evening. Watching the room move past them in the dark was a challenge, and their report noted that the suspect was not in the venue.

Chapter 22

The next day they were scheduled to conduct a radio interview and musical performance at New York rock station, 106.9 WNNY. The shuttle bus once again brought them into Manhattan from New Jersey. The group made their way into the lobby of the radio station building, got into the elevator, and went up to the fiftieth floor and into the lobby of 106.9 WNNY radio. Its name was etched right on the glass doors they walked through into the reception area. The receptionist asked who they were, and Jeb told her. She said to wait while she notified the station manager.

"Hi, I'm Bill Farlow, station manager of 106.9 WNNY radio."

"Hi, I'm Jeb! We spoke a few days ago. This was kind of last minute for us, but we made it."

"Wow! You have a large band here!"

"Well, only five guys are in the band, the other guys are the road crew. By the way, this is the Doctor, Jurgen Weislangwolf."

"A great honor, sir. I have heard many wonderful things about you, like you are one of the greatest guitarists in the universe."

"Achh, yah! This is true! I am that," replied the Doctor.

"So, you are okay with doing a short interview with our DJ and a little acoustic guitar? It will be drive time, so a lot of listeners," said Bill Farlow.

"Acoustic guitar?" asked the Doctor.

"Never mind that, Doctor. Let's look around first," said Jeb.

"OK, let me show you guys around. Follow me." Bill Farlow took them back into the broadcasting area. "Ahh! Here is our famous radio personality, Jerry Joe King! Jerry, come over here, let me introduce you to the Doctor, Jurgen Weislangwolf."

"Hello there, Jurgen! I've been a great admirer of you and the Centipedes' music for years. I never thought that I'd see the day when I would meet you or have you on my show," said Jerry Joe King.

"Yah, well! I am happy to be here, too! I hope millions of New Yorkers will hear us play today."

"I have a very nice Martin D-45 for you to play some songs for us on," replied Jerry Joe King.

"Achh! That is an acoustic guitar."

"Yes, exactly! For the acoustic set after the interview," replied Jerry Joe.

"Nein! Nein! Und a Kapital NEIN! I will not play an acoustic show on the radio! It's the whole band or nothing," said the angry Doctor.

"The radio station is not set up for that kind of volume, Doctor," replied the station manager.

"It's the whole band or nothing," said the Doctor.

"Oh boy! We did this once before, but it got very loud and our mics couldn't handle the volume," said Bill Farlow. "I guess we can try it again."

Bill called some workers to go into the storage area to find some amps, drums, and a keyboard. The broadcasting room had a small six-channel, 200-watt powered PA mixer and only two 200-watt speakers mounted on stands at ear level. The PA was substandard to what the Doctor would normally expect, but he insisted on playing with his whole band so he would use what they had. The workers began to set up the equipment as the band watched them work. After the four-piece Rogers drum set was set up with the hardware, the tiny stage looked even smaller. Barely enough room for the band to stand on it. Torsten would have to stand on the floor, but with the keyboard stand on the stage it leveled out perfectly for his height. There was just enough room for Nathan and Heinz to stand on the stage. But what about the Doctor?

"Achh! I do not like to stand on the floor! The Doctor must be elevated so the people look up at me and I look down on them."

"I'm sorry, but there is no more room left on the stage with that drum set taking up most of the space," replied Bill Farlow.

"Well, then take the drums off the stage and set him up to the left of the stage," snapped the Doctor. Bill Farlow instructed the workers to move the drum set off the stage and onto the floor.

"Achh! Yah! Now that looks better," said the Doctor as Tommy scratched his head, rolling his eyes.

"Hey, can I set up a merch table in here?" asked Jeb.

"Sure, no problem," answered Bill Farlow.

"Achh! Always thinking dollars and cents, yah?"

"You know it, Doctor!" said Jeb.

Jeb sent Marlon, Neusy, and Hocker downstairs to the shuttle bus to grab the boxes of merch that he had enough foresight to bring along. Once they got back, Jeb called Marlon over and got busy. They decorated the whole wall by taping the T-shirt designs under the radio station logo. They were also given a folding table to set all of the CDs, DVDs, key chains, beer koozies, and other items that they had. The secretary and a few other office people walked in to see what was happening.

"Wow! What's going on here? Is this a full-out rock concert?" asked the receptionist.

"Yes, you might say that!" replied Jeb.

"Who are the band?" she asked.

"Jurgen Weislangwolf, ex guitarist of the Centipedes," answered Jeb.

"Hey Katy, Jeannie, come back here! They are having a rock concert in the studio. It's Jurgen…how do I say that name again?" said Alice to Jeb.

"Vise-lahng-volf," replied Jeb.

The other girls also looked amazed and excited to see a show in the studio.

"Is all of this stuff for sale?" asked Katy.

"Yep! Everything!" said Jeb.

Katy got on her cell phone and called her friends in marketing to come up. Jeannie got on her phone and called up the guys in monthly programming. Alice then got on her phone and called her friends that worked in other businesses in the same building to come for the concert. Jeb was watching everything going on and had dollar signs flashing in his head. Within a New York minute, the broadcasting studio had seventy-five people in it and a few more were walking in every second. Bill Farlow and Jerry Joe King were also stunned. They never saw anything like this happen at 106.9 WNNY Radio.

"Doctor, we better get started with the interview. I need all of you people to be quiet during the interview! You can applaud and scream if you like once the band starts playing," said Bill Farlow.

The Doctor took a seat next to Jerry Joe King and they positioned a mic in front of his mouth. The band remained on the stage and the large crowd that had assembled stood wherever they could find space.

"Good day, Tri-State! This is Jerry Joe King coming at you all with a HUGE surprise today! Today I have one of the greatest guitarists from the rock world, or any world for that matter. Most people know him as the Doctor of Dynamics; here he is, the former lead guitarist of the Centipedes, Jurgen Weislangwolf!"

The room couldn't hold back their excitement and roared out, "YAAAHHHH! THE DOCTOR! WHOOOHOOOO!"

"Achh, dankeschön, Jerry! It's good to be here in New York und speaking with all of your fans!"

"So, Doctor… You are originally from Austria, yes?"

"Yah, yah! I am still from there. Well, what I mean is that I still live there. But I am here in America for my world tour."

"Wow! That's great! Have you toured anywhere else this year?"

"Oh, yah! We were in India for a couple of weeks. Well, my three favorite people played together in India: me, myself, und I. Hahaha!"

The room was silent.

"Wow! How exciting! What was India like? The food, the people, the country?"

"Achh! It was mostly a spiritual journey for me to find the inner me und write new music the world has never known. The food was nice, a bit spicy sometimes, but mostly vegetarian, which suits me. The people were very friendly. The country was a little dried up for my liking."

"Wow! That sounds fascinating! Do you think that you reached that inner self that you were looking for and that is helping write new music?"

"Oh, yah! My inner self can transcend into many planes of the universe now, und I am conceiving brand-new music now."

"That is a fantastic instrument that you are holding. I have never seen a guitar like that. What is it?"

"This is my Universe Guitar! I designed it myself, yah. It can play every note on the piano und even notes that dogs can hear but not people. I call this guitar King Saturn!"

"Unbelievable! Why do you call it that?"

"Achh! You see the body floats around the neck like a ring? No one knows how it does that…only me."

"It certainly is a gorgeous guitar, Doctor! You are a genius for creating it."

"Yah, I know!"

"It's been a long time since you played with the Centipedes, and your music has certainly changed over the years. Why did you leave the Centipedes and how did your music change after that?"

"Achh! Yah, well, it's a complicated und long story. I don't want to get into the whole thing, but there were a lot of creative differences und personality issues. Und my creativity was being held back, yah? You know I am classically trained on piano, violin, cello, clarinet, and oboe, as well as the guitar and most recently bassoon. I just couldn't use all of my knowledge and skills in the Centipedes style of simplistic rock music. It was time for me to go."

"Do you still speak with any of the other Centipedes?"

"Oh, yah! I recently spoke with the singer Holger Stormburg. Und Rotten Rugermayer, the bassist, is still my old childhood friend."

"That all sounds super, Doctor! Now, I think it's time for a word from our sponsors and to get ready for your concert in our studio. This is Jerry Joe King speaking for 106.9 WNNY Radio in New York. We will be back with some live music from the Doctor of Dynamics, Jurgen Weislangwolf."

The Doctor joined the band on stage and plugged his Universe Guitar into a 100-watt Marshall. Nathan was also lucky enough to get a 100-watt Marshall amp, as there were only two in the storage unit. However, Heinz had to run directly into the PA mixer, which usually gave a very poor sound for the bass. Torsten was provided an older Roland keyboard and it was plugged directly into the board. Nathan was in front of the mic and they got ready to play.

"Hello, radio fans! This is Jerry Joe King at 106.9 WNNY Radio in New York and we are ready to rock the Tri-State area with the Doctor!"

The crowd in the room was about ninety-five people and they all screamed out in excitement. "YAAAHHHH! ROCK WITH THE DOCTOR! ROCK WITH THE DOCTOR!"

"Wow! We have never had anything like this in the history of 106.9 WNNY Radio! Let's do it! Ready, Doctor?"

"Oh, yah! Hallo, New York! How about some 'Nails in My Coffin'?"

The Doctor started the lick, the band joined in, and the room was rocking. The 100-watt Marshalls overpowered the PA system. As most musicians know, tube power is louder than solid state power. And given that the Doctor was playing the Universe Guitar, it added even more DBs than normal, making it extremely loud for the somewhat small broadcasting room packed with so many people. It was so loud the engineers had to dial down the mic preamps to lower the online distortion level. It was so loud that Nathan's vocals could barely be heard. The same with Heinz's bass and Torsten's keyboard parts. But the crowd didn't mind, the whole room swayed, head banged, and held up the devils horns as the band played. It was rather odd seeing short-haired salesmen in suits head banging and displaying the horns. The song came to an end and Jerry Joe King announced another commercial break.

"Wow! That is unbelievable, Doctor! I think we have time for one more song," said Jerry.

"OK, I know just the song, yah!"

"This is Jerry Joe King from 106.9 WNNY Radio in New York bringing you the rockingest music on the planet. We have time for one more from the Doctor of Dynamics, Jurgen Weislangwolf. Ready, Jurgen?"

"Oh, yah! Here is another oldie but goodie, 'In Your Pants'."

The crowd started screaming again. The business suits started their head banging ritual again. The band rocked them hard and loud. The engineers had to dial down the preamps even more as the VU meters were still redlining.

"WOW! That was great, Doctor! Thanks again for coming on 106.9 WNNY and rocking us out! And now, another word from our sponsor."

Sparrow and Crow, unaware of the radio interview, were well on their way to Allentown, Pennsylvania when they heard the Doctor on the radio. They immediately pulled their rental car off the interstate, and after debating that it would be over an hour back to NYC, decided to continue to Pennsylvania. Sparrow sent a group text to Crow, Jeb, and Neusy stating that these scheduled appearances must be reported to the agents. Jeb and Neusy looked at their phones and gave each other the fuck-them look and ignored the text. Crow added that if they did not comply with the request, they would have their visa pulled and the tour would be canceled. Neusy sent a thumbs up response and Jeb the OK sign.

The drive-time concert was over, and people were still on an adrenaline rush. People were mobbing Jeb and Marlon at the merch booth, buying up everything in sight, and then rushing over to the Doctor and other band members to sign their merch. Jeb's idea paid off. He might even take in an extra thousand dollars or so for the day, plus advertising live for free on one of New York's most famous radio stations. A truly historical day for 106.9 WNNY Radio and the Doctor and the Surgeons.

A man with an off-colored beard and a baseball cap bought the newest tour shirt from Marlon and asked why the two men dressed as the Blues Brothers were not at the radio station. Marlon, having just smoked a joint, thought it was cool that this man knew of the FBI agents. Marlon informed the man he had no idea, and he should ask Jeb that question. Scaggz decided to take his T-shirt and not push his luck. Besides, he had to search for his old boss from when he worked at a radio station in California before becoming a stagehand for touring artists and later working for the Doctor before being fired from that position as well. Bill Farlow had very little patience back then when he was younger, and before firing Scaggz, made his two months of employment a nightmare to the point that Scaggz gave up his dreams of working in radio. What a stroke of luck that Bill Farlow was in NYC.

The party continued well into the night at the radio station. There was wine and beer served, and when they ran out, more was delivered. There was catering brought in all by the station manager before he went missing. The band and crew stayed until midnight, with Jeb and Marlon selling more merchandise every time a new bottle of wine was opened.

The employees stayed all night, as well, and were more than happy to drink and eat on the station's budget, something that they were not at all accustomed to. Half of the employees lived outside the city and decided to spend the night in their offices. The party was dwindling as more people either left or stumbled their way to their office for sleep, so it went unnoticed that Bill Farlow was not there when the band and crew left. In fact, no one noticed that he had not been at the party since 8:00 pm, until the next morning when the receptionist was in the kitchen and opened the closet to make coffee. There was Bill Farlow with his head crushed and shoved into one of the Marshall speaker cabinets used the night before during the drive-time concert.

The agents, upon hearing about the demise of Bill Farlow, had to drive back to NYC all the way from Allentown and work with NYPD in what was captioned as the Drive-Time Murder on the news. Back in NYC, it was determined after interviewing the employees that partied hard the night before that the Tour Killer did once again go unseen the entire evening and there were no leads.

Chapter 23

"Are we a bus, boy?"

"Yes, Crabs, we are a bus," said Jeb.

"OK, hang on, we are rolling!"

Cal drove the bus away from New York City and headed south toward Philadelphia. A quick stop over to see the Liberty Bell and grab some famous Philadelphia cheesesteak sandwiches before re-routing to Allentown. The Doctor, sound asleep in the ICU, was hungover from his wine binge with the radio show people late the night before. The Austrians, Tommy, Jeb, Neusy, Hocker, and Marlon were sitting in the lounge drinking coffee as they were all more in control of their drinking.

"Oh, boy! I can't wait to sink my teeth into a genuine Philly cheesesteak submarine," exclaimed Neusy.

"I know a place that is the bomb! Fat Frank's Cheesesteak Emporium," replied Jeb.

"Do they serve beer?" asked Hocker.

"Of course they do," replied Jeb.

"I love cheesesteak," said Tommy. "My mouth is watering already."

"Yah, it sounds great! I love beef with cheese," said Torsten.

"Oh, yah, und don't forget the pepper," replied Nathan.

"Do they serve broccoli?" asked Heinz.

"No," said Jeb, giving Neusy the help-me-now look. "Hey, Tommy, did you look in the mirror this morning?" asked Jeb.

"No, why?"

"Something's wrong with your hair. It doesn't look straight."

"What?"

"Yeah! It looks like the left side of your bangs are two inches longer than the right side of your bangs."

"Oh shit, I better check. Excuse me," Tommy said as he tried to crawl over Heinz's legs to get by the lounge table and make his way to the restroom.

"Don't forget to wash your face, too, Tommy! You have some eye sand!" remarked Jeb.

The group chuckled.

"Funny, guys!" said Tommy as he entered the bus restroom to straighten out his wig.

"What's up next, Jeb? I mean show wise," asked Hocker.

"We have a show in Allentown."

"I'm ready for a beer! Anyone else?" asked Hocker.

"No, too early for me!" said a stoned Marlon.

The rest of the group all shook their heads, agreeing it was too early for a beer.

"OK, your loss!" remarked Hocker as he made his way to the fridge. He found himself an Empire State Lager that someone bought. He opened the bottle and took a sip.

"Hey, man! That's one of my beers," said Tommy.

"And I thank you for it. By the way, your hair still isn't straight," replied Hocker.

"OK boys, we are in Philadelphia! Hey, Jeb, give me the address of where that cheesesteak place is," said Cal.

"I just texted it to you. Look at your phone."

"Got it!"

"Well, I better wake up the Doctor. You guys better get ready, change your clothes, wash your faces, just get ready." Rapping on the ICU door, Jeb called out, "Ding, ding, ding! Jurgen, time to get up! Time for lunch and Liberty Bell."

"Achh! My head!"

"Did we have a little too much wine last night?"

"Yah, maybe soooo…"

"Do you want some Tylenol?"

"Nein, I do not like to use hard medication."

"Hard medication? What are you talking about?"

"Yah, you know, that stuff is bad for your liver und kidneys, not to mention what it does to your brain."

"Well, we wouldn't want anything to happen with your brain, now would we? OK, well, get dressed, we are almost there." Why do I even bother, thought Jeb.

"Yah, yah…okay." The Doctor closed his door.

"OK, boys! We are here at last!" said Cal as he stopped the bus in Philadelphia.

Marlon and Hocker were the first two out the door. They could smell the delicious cheesesteak odor coming from somewhere. The Austrians were out the door next. When the smell hit them, they also were enticed. Cal exited and stretched his arms up in the air after sitting and driving so long. Jeb, Neusy, and Tommy joined the others on the sidewalk.

"Where is the Doctor?" asked Torsten.

"He is moving a little slow today," said Jeb.

The Doctor exited the bus and closed the door behind him. He strode out of the bus in style, wearing a newly bought frilly lavender blouse, black jeans, a black wind breaker, and a pair of his new clogs.

"There it is across the street! Fat Frank's Cheesesteak Emporium," said Jeb. "This place rocks!"

"Achh! It sounds terrible! You woke me up for this? Shredded cows on bread with cheese?"

"They actually have a sandwich that you can eat, Jurgen. It is only cheese with green peppers and onions on a whole grain roll," said Jeb.

"Oh, that sounds fine then! Und some pomfrits yah?"

"Und some pomfrits, Jurgen," replied Jeb in a soft, relaxed voice.

The group wandered into Fat Frank's; all gave their orders then sat down. To Hocker's delight, everyone was also ready for a lunchtime beer, except for Cal, who still had to drive. Hide the Bell Lagers all around.

"Achh. My word, this is the best cheese sandwich I have ever had!" said the Doctor.

"Yep, even without meat, this place is the bomb."

The Austrians were all chewing in unison, almost like they were keeping time with each other's bites. It sounded like a small group marching. Tommy had finished his sandwich and debated whether or not to have a second one. He found himself drumming out a beat on the table that was in time with the Austrian's rhythm. Jeb and Neusy watched it unfold, looked at each other, and then finished their sandwiches. Tommy saw this and stopped his banging on the table.

"Maybe we should all order more for the road? We can put them in the bus for later," said Marlon.

"Hey, that's a good idea, Marlon!" said Neusy.

"Yah, Marlon, you think more like a man. I want to order two more cheese sandwiches."

Jeb said, "Order what you want and let's get going! The Liberty Bell is our next stop."

"We actually don't have to drive to it, Jeb... It's just down the street," said Cal.

All of the orders were ready and put into a box. Twelve sandwiches in all. Marlon was sent to take the box back to the bus and put it all in the fridge while the rest of the group waited for him to return.

When Marlon returned, the group of ten walked down Market Street to see the Liberty Bell. As they stood in the shrine of the Liberty Bell, they began to read what the signs had written on them. A wonderful account of American history could be learned by the Austrian members.

"Wow! That's a big bell," said Marlon.

"Yeah! A very important part of American History," said Neusy.

"Achh! Look at that crack! Why are they displaying a broken bell?" said the Doctor.

"Yeah, Hocker! Pull up your pants dude! The whole world can see your crack!" Jeb snickered and laughed.

"Haha! Mr. Smart Ass!"

"Achh! They hid this bell from the British in 1777 under the floorboards in a church in Allentown," remarked the Doctor as he was reading about this piece of American history. "It must have been very difficult to move by the horse und buggy."

"Yah, quite right! Herr Doctor!" said Torsten.

"They rang the bell when they first read the Declaration of Independence in 1778," said Heinz, reading along with the Doctor.

"Und they stopped using it when it developed the crack," said Nathan.

"I think Hocker's crack is still developing, the fatter he gets—OUCH! You fucker!" said Jeb as he received a punch in his arm by Hocker, who found this humor annoying.

"How do you like that crack, Jeb?"

"I don't! That fucking hurts, man."

"Well, now, maybe you will lay off the stupid insults, jerkoff."

After the guys had seen enough, they headed back to the bus.

"Are we a bus, gentlemen?" The familiar cry rang out from the barber's chair driver's seat. "Next stop Allentown!"

"Yah, yah, Cal, let's just get going, yah," said the Doctor. "I am going back for a little nap and visit with my animal friends."

Hocker was ready for another beer. Twelve large sandwiches now occupied the shelves when he opened the fridge, but no beer was to be found. As he turned around, he saw the beer, soda, mustard, mayonnaise, relish, ranch dressing, and two boxes of day-old pizza on the counter.

"What the fuck, Marlon?" barked Hocker. "The beer is warm."

"Sorry, dude! I had to make room for the sandwiches. That fridge is very small. Those are more important, I think. You can get beer anywhere," said Marlon.

"Alright, you are buying me the first cold one when we get to Allentown," said Hocker as he grabbed a warm beer and disappeared into his bunk.

"So, what's this place called, Jeb?" asked Marlon.

"The Blue Collar Workers Club. It's a theme club based on working Americans," answered Jeb.

"That sounds like us, doesn't it?" said Neusy.

"Well, some of us," said Jeb, looking at Marlon who was rolling another joint.

"Hey, can one of you guys make me some coffee?" asked Cal.

"Sure, dude! I'll make some," said Neusy as he got up and walked over to the coffee maker. He made a full pot and poured the entire contents into Cal's oversized travel mug.

"Whooohooo, now we are rolling," said Cal.

"What do you think the turn out will be in Allentown, Jeb?" asked Marlon.

"I have no idea. But it is another Spud Burger booking, so your guess is as good as mine," replied Jeb.

They arrived in Allentown, a somewhat remodeled city from the older factory look to the modern new age buildings that now stood. Cal announced that they were nearing the venue. It looked like they would be right on time for the load in.

"Here we are, guys! The Blue Collar Workers Club," said Cal as he got up and went outside to stretch out.

"Alright, let's go in and have a look," said Jeb. The four, including Cal, entered the club to announce their arrival. They were approached by a fast-moving middle-aged man wearing a suit.

"Hello! My name is George. Which one of you is Jeb?"

"I am! Can my guys start bringing stuff in?"

"Sure! As you can see, the stage is over there…the bar over there."

"Where can I set up my merch table?"

"Over there, next to the pool tables is fine."

"OK, guys, let's get this done. Neusy, go wake up Hocker and start unloading the equipment. Marlon, start bringing in the merch," said Jeb. "Interesting place you have here, George! Looks like a museum of sorts."

"Yes, thanks, Jeb. It is kind of like that."

Jeb scanned the room and saw many displays in the club, including mannequins dressed in various working clothes operating machines and equipment.

Each area of the club looked like a different factory. On the left side there were mannequins operating looms, sewing machines, and silk spinners. On the right side of the room, it looked like a wood furniture manufacturing company with mannequins building cabinets, chairs, dressers, armoires, and tables. Coal miners, saddle makers, leather tanners, arms and cannon makers were all mixed into the display. Even a mini brewery was there to commemorate the beer-making history of Allentown. The central theme was an iron foundry, with forging equipment, booms with iron chains hanging from the ceiling, and a giant cauldron with a glowing red light inside to represent molten iron. One mechanized mannequin pulled a chain that tipped the cauldron and another swung a sledge. Mannequins attended all the equipment. Each area of the club had a sign describing the type of work that was being displayed and the approximate year that it represented.

"Wow! Quite a place here, George! Really nice! The Doctor should be pleased with your venue."

"Thanks, Jeb! Very kind of you to say!"

"By the way, where did you get all of these mannequins? They must have cost a fortune. I know they are not cheap," said Jeb.

"Oh, well, I own a mannequin factory. My family has been making them for many years. We used to supply all the major department store chains. But when stores started to switch to these unisex mannequins with no distinguishable features to show it was a man or a woman, I got stuck with all of these. So, I used most of my old traditional mannequins to decorate this place."

"Very smart thinking, George! Hey, I was wondering, do you have a male mannequin that I could have? To take with us on the road?"

"I think I can find one for you in the storeroom. Why do you want the mannequin?"

"Well, I just have an idea how I might use it some time. I can keep it in one of the empty sleeping bays on the bus."

Scaggz watched the crew loading out equipment from across the street through his telescope. He saw the agents pull up and park about fifty feet behind the tour bus. He watched them as they watched the crew. Scaggz already knew what the club was like inside and decided he would dress as a coal miner and smudge charcoal briquettes all over his face and hands to disguise himself. He had time; he would now have a little nap in the VW and wait until show time. Wanting to be his best for the show, he fell asleep thinking these guys have seen nothing yet—the best is still to come.

Neusy and Hocker finished loading in the equipment. From the stage, they observed Marlon as he brought in the last box of T-shirts before helping Jeb set things up in the merch area. "What a great club," said Hocker. "I bet they have some good working man brews here. I am working and I am a man. Yuk! Yuk! Yuk!"

"Yeah, did I ever tell you the story about my grandfather, Hocker?"

"No!"

"Well, he came from Harrisburg, not too far from here," replied Neusy.

"What did he do? What kind of work?"

"He was a line-o-type operator in a printing company."

"What the hell is line-o-type?"

"It is where they used a little piece of lead with a letter on it and had to put the small pieces of lead together in a frame to make words and sentences. Then they would put ink on the lead pieces and print it on newspapers."

"Wow! That's old school! They use computers to do all of that now."

"Yes, sir, much easier today. But less pride in workmanship. You know my grandfather learned a lot of words from doing that type of work. If he didn't know the meaning of something, he looked it up in the dictionary. And they never spell checked his work at the printing company."

"Really! He must have been really smart."

"He was! Everybody that met him thought he went to college because he used a lot of fifty-cent words."

"Your grandfather used words like 'ho' and 'dope' and 'bitch-slap'?"

"No, you knucklehead, fifty-cent words are words like loquacious, you know, educated words. Not the rapper, dumbass!"

"What the hell is loquacious?"

"It means that you talk too much."

"Haha! You educated fuck, you!"

"Hey, are you guys almost finished over there?" yelled Jeb from across the room.

"Just wrapping up the drum set now!" shouted Hocker, which Tommy would have to rearrange before soundcheck. Hocker failed to realize the importance of learning Tommy's setup and never set the drums up the same from night to night.

"Well, it's beer-thirty-five! See you at the bar," shouted back Jeb.

Hocker and Neusy soon joined Jeb and Marlon at the bar.

"First beer is on you, Marlon," said Hocker, reminding all about the warm beers on the tour bus.

"Yeah, no problem, big boy with the crack… Hahahaha," said Marlon grinning, feeling like he was one of the guys.

"Mind your tongue or I will sit on you, you puny fucker."

"Nice talk, Hocker."

"This is a cool place. It looks like an industrial revolution museum," said Neusy as he looked around the room of machinery, props, and mannequins dressed as workers. Several mechanized mannequins were turned on and moved realistically, along with the machines they were operating.

"Wow! Did you see that? Those mannequins are moving! So cool. I smoked a joint earlier and thought they were real people in costumes. I was talking to one of them for ten minutes before I realized it was a robot," said Marlon.

Jeb's mouth dropped and Neusy gave him the help-me-now eye roll to the left.

"Yeah, it's like the Pirates of the Caribbean ride, but with factory workers," said Neusy.

"Hey, what is that contraption that goes along the back of the bar there?" asked Jeb.

"That is the major highlight of the bar. A Rube Goldberg machine," answered George.

"What does it do?"

"It pours the perfect beer every time. But it takes four minutes for all the levers, wheels, and pulleys to go through the motions, and then finally for the softball to roll down and depress the lever that pours the beer from the tap."

"I've got to see that in action," said Jeb.

"Follow me," said George.

"What kind of beer can I get?"

"The Rube Goldberg device serves only the house beer. Patrons pay eight dollars to watch the machine pour their beer."

"It seems like a slow way to serve everyone."

"Well, it's just a novelty, really. Not everyone wants to wait, and they can order from many other beers that we stock."

"Oh, I see. Well, let's give it a shot. I want to watch it work."

"OK, here we go."

George pulled a small rope that released a softball. The softball rolled down a track and hit a lever with a hammer on the other side. The hammer swung down and hit another lever, releasing a weight that lowered on a rope attached to a pulley that raised up one end of a seesaw. When the other end lowered, a mini bowling ball rolled down and struck a bowling pin, causing it to fall backwards onto a balloon, which shifted its interior air towards the back. It then touched a switch that spun a wheel. The wheel had one cog that spun around and touched a hair-trigger that set off several wooden levers escalating upwards to the top of the wine rack. The last lever set off a boxing glove on a spring that, when realized, punched a mannequin head on a lever. The head hit the last softball on top of a ramp, which rolled down and hit the beer tap at the bottom, consequently pouring the beer into a mug.

"That's just the craziest thing I ever saw, George!" Hocker and Neusy arrived as it finished pouring Jeb's beer.

"Wow! That's fucking crazy! Can I get one of those too?"

"Me too!"

Hocker watched and waited as the magnificent contraption ran through its cycle. At last, his beer was poured.

"Mmmmm! That's good stuff. What do you call this beer?"

"That is our house beer, The Underarm Sweat of an Iron Worker Lager."

"This is great stuff. Neusy, you have to try one."

Neusy watched and waited his turn. Four minutes passed and he had his beer. Perfect foam head on top. Everyone enjoyed their beers as they conversed with George about his amazing club and his Rube Goldberg mechanism.

An hour after the doors opened, the club was packed. With the mixture of mannequins and humans, one couldn't tell how many actual live beings were in the venue. People mingled and enjoyed the drinks awaiting the show. Many just watched the Rube Goldberg device run its course while others ordered their drinks. Some were hoping it would malfunction, but it never did. Marlon was walking around the room taking selfies with all the mannequins. He mistook a man in a dirty coal miner's costume as a mannequin. He thought it was the coolest mannequin he had ever seen, being able to hold a conversation like that. After five minutes the man finally convinced Marlon that he was a real person. The man bought

Marlon a beer and Marlon continued taking pictures until Jeb found him and instructed him to stay focused on his work.

Scaggz felt he fit right in disguised as a dirty coal miner that just got off work with dirt and grease on his face. Scaggz noticed the agents on the other side of the room near the workers making cabinets. They were looking around but not in his direction. They walked over near the coal mine exhibit, and he snuck over in that direction. He stood near them and gently slipped a piece of paper into Agent Sparrow's pocket from behind and walked away.

"This is one of the most interesting venues that we have seen, Jathan."

"Yes, indeed! It certainly is."

"It pretty much covers all the different types of trades that built up this area during the turn of the century!"

"Surely, it does at that. Hey, look at that contraption over at the bar."

"Yeah, let's go have a closer look."

Agents Sparrow and Crow walked over to the bar to watch the marvelous thing at work as people ordered their beers. They were just as fascinated at watching it as everyone was. Sadly, they couldn't order a beer while they were on duty.

It was time for the Doctor and the Surgeons to take the stage. Jeb and Marlon were already busy with pre-show sales of Doctor T-shirts and CDs. The Doctor made his greeting, and the band began to play "Wine in My Liver." The sound was loud, the crowd was digging it, moving and grooving with the music. "Bitchy Wife" was next up. The crowd was getting louder. Scaggz felt strange, something was off with him, but he couldn't figure out what. Some of the people started to look not real to him, plastic faces, some weren't moving. More clones among the humans? Then some of the faces looked like the Doctor, but in working man's clothes and uniforms. They were watching him. "CLONES! THE CLONES HAVE INFILTRATED US!" he screamed out loud. He ripped the head off a mannequin working a loom that was near him. When he realized it was only a mannequin, he ran straight towards the door, stepping on a few toes along the way. No one paid much attention to him; it was a rock concert and certainly not the strangest thing they had seen. Outside, Scaggz began to unwind and was content with his time in the venue. But did he step on one of the agents' feet?

The agents made their way outside the venue through the crowd, but they could not see Scaggz. He had vanished. On their way back inside, as Agent Sparrow reached for his badge, he found a note that read: *New York is a great town. You missed out on all the fun!*

Chapter 24

After a successful evening in Allentown, the tour was on the road again heading to Maine. A rare festival show was next, and headlining the festival quickly became the most anticipated gig on the tour and expectations were high. Especially for Marlon.

"Achh, Jeb, Spud Burger told me that the Hemp Harvest Festival in Maine attracts 40,000 people. It will be perfect for us to make a lot of money und for more people to know my music, yah?"

"You have to take anything Spud Burger says with a grain of salt. He has promised a lot of things in the past and many times things don't turn out the way he says. But one thing is for sure, he always sees any cash before any of us do."

"Yah, yah…always the pessimist, Jeb. I believe him this time. Something tells me he's right about this festival."

"Well, I don't believe jackshit what that guy says. Sure, I am all for you making money."

"You have to set your mind at ease, like what I learned in India from Guru Darma. Be at peace with existence and good karma will come your way."

"Yeah, you go ahead and believe that, and I will call things as I see them."

After an intense discussion with the Doctor, Jeb decided to go online and research the Hemp Harvest Festival. He found a lot of interesting fall festivals in Maine. Some had oysters and lobsters that all appealed to Jeb, for sure. Many games and contests at the festivals. Some had tree chopping contests, and after you chopped down your tree you had to make a little tent from the logs to live in during your stay. Almost every festival had fun family games, contests, and events, along with massive feasts. Pumpkins, squashes, berries, apples, strawberries, maple syrup, all kinds of great stuff. Various types of bands and music were played at these festivals, and yes, thousands of people would go to these festivals in Maine and have a great time.

But what about the Harvest Hemp Festival? Jeb already had in mind what went on there besides the usual. He continued to read about the founders, the events, the food, the sleeping arrangements, and of course anything to do with live musical events. It said the duration was three days, which sounded okay. What's that? The Marijuana Growers of Maine Bud Showdown? That might be of interest to Marlon, maybe even Neusy. 40,000 people expected during the three days? That doesn't mean at one time, Jeb thought, and certainly not all at the show. Typical Spud bullshit.

After three more large mugs of coffee and an equal number of stops for Cal to pee, the tour bus finally pulled into the entrance of the 300-acre farm. They were directed into a secure area for bands and VIP guests.

"All right, boys! We are here!" shouted Cal in an excited voice.

"OK, Neusy, Hocker, Marlon, come with me," said Jeb as he exited the bus.

"What is it, beer thirty?" asked Hocker, following Jeb's lead.

"No, it's time to call this guy, Billy Utters, to find out where everything is, like the stage, the toilets, the food, and get a festival schedule of events."

"Billy Utters, that's a funny name," said Marlon as he exhaled his latest roll. "It will be interesting to hear him utter his answers."

"Hahaha," laughed Neusy. "Maybe he has tits like a cow."

"Awhaha! That's fucking ridiculous," said Hocker.

"Alright, guys, knock it off! Don't crack jokes about this guy, he has to pay us when we're done," snapped Jeb.

The guys looked around. It was a huge farm, bigger than most they had seen. It was beautiful and green, with the fall colors dancing in the trees. The air was fresh and clean, with the fragrance of fresh pumpkins, strawberries, and apples mingling with the salt air of the sea.

Hundreds of people were enjoying the festivities, but it didn't look like 40,000 people yet, or even thousands as the Doctor imagined. It was still early in the morning; maybe more would come during the day. Jeb reached Billy on his cell phone and Billy came to meet them outside the tour bus. A man with long brown hair and a beard, pink tie-dyed T-shirt, puka shell necklace, and blue jeans approached the guys in an olive-drab army jeep.

"Which one of you is Jeb?"

"I am," said Jeb.

"I'm Billy! I will show you guys around."

"Great! The first thing I need to see is the stage, and second, I need to know where I can set up our merch table."

"Hop in! I'll drive you guys over to the stage."

"Are there any beer stands?" asked Hocker.

"Of course, some great craft brews can be found everywhere."

"Any chance of stopping by a beer stand before we get to the stage?" asked Hocker.

"You guys should try the hemp wagon," said Billy.

"The hemp wagon?" asked Marlon.

"Yes, the hemp wagon. You sit in the wagon and it drives you all around the farm. You can see everything! The fruit orchards, the weed fields, the barn, the lake, food concessions, the contests, the staging area, a lot to see," Billy went on.

"Why is it the hemp wagon, do you get stoned?" asked Marlon.

"You can if you want to, but it's because you sit on bails of weed instead of hay, as in a traditional hayride. If you want to smoke, you can. That's what this festival is all about!" said Billy.

"That's my kind of ride! And my kind of festival," said Marlon.

"I'd rather have a beer on my hemp ride," said Hocker.

"Well, I think we should see the stage first," said Jeb.

Billy drove them over to the stage. It was big, very big, as at a regular rock and roll festival. About fifty feet wide by forty feet deep and five feet tall with massive columns of quadruple-stacked speakers in quadruple-vertical rows on each side of the stage. Huge pro lighting rigs surrounded the stage and above. There was a twenty-foot-deep staging area behind the main stage that extended the full length of the stage. This allowed bands to store and move their equipment around before and after their turn to set up and play.

The mixing desk was about 300 feet back on top of an ice cream truck. The system was rated at 50,000 watts. They would have various bands playing all through the day, and the Doctor and the Surgeons were set to go on at 10:00 tonight and at 9:00 the next night. Jeb asked Billy to drive him back to the bus and he would have Cal drive the bus to the stage so they could get their gear set up in the backstage area nice and early.

After the bus was moved, Hocker and Neusy began to unload the things they needed: drums, amps, keyboards, effects, etc. While they did that, Jeb spoke with the band on the bus.

"Alright. Listen up! It's pretty early, so we can all go out and enjoy some events and food. But remember, we go on stage at 10:00 pm, so be back here to get dressed and ready for the show by 9:00. You all have my cell number if you need me or have a problem. There are supposed to be tens of thousands of people here today, so don't get lost in the crowds, this is a huge place. Be sure to be back at 9:00 pm. All right, have fun, guys!"

The Austrians wanted to try the canoe racing over on the lake. The Doctor wanted to see the animal petting zoo and pet the livestock. Jeb and Marlon planned to set up a huge merch area next to the tour bus. They were going to set up everything they brought, which was a lot. Jeb spent a good hour hanging up the different T-shirt design on the side of the tour bus. With three folding tables of the Doctor's CDs, DVDs, beer koozies, key chains, guitar strings, guitar picks, posters, and other items, Jeb thought he would make bank at this place, or at least he hoped to. After Hocker and Neusy were finished on stage they came over to Jeb in the merch area.

"Hey, man, Neusy and I are finished. Since we are on last, we had to set up first. I did not connect the Doctor's cables or effect pedals so that the animals on before us don't fuck with them. We're going to find the beer stands and maybe find something to eat," said Hocker.

"OK, good idea regarding the effects. Too many times we run into issues with those assholes. Alright, let me know if you find any good beer or food. Also let me know how the crowd looks where you go. Spud told us to expect 40,000 people, I highly doubt that, but it would be nice if there were 10,000 or better," said Jeb.

"Yeah, alright, Jeb. Let's go Neusy." The two walked away.

Billy drove the Doctor over to the petting zoo in his jeep. "Do you want me to wait for you, Doctor?"

"Nein, nein! Billy, I can find my way back to the bus later."

"OK, have fun!" Billy drove away. The Doctor ventured into the petting zoo enclosure. He pet many animals and spoke to them. Baby calves, baby horses, baby sheep, baby goats, chickens, ducks, and geese, even llamas. He had a wonderful time. Scaggz continued to watch him from a distance. However, petting wasn't what he had in mind.

Chapter 25

"Wow! Look at that, Jathan, that looks fun," said Agent Crow.

"What, you mean those people trying to run while holding a pumpkin between their knees? It looks stupid!"

"I wouldn't say that they're running, more like waddling."

"Hey, I challenge you to waddle against me. Who cares if anyone really wins the race? I bet you a BBQ rib dinner and beers that I can cross the finish line before you do!"

"Yeah, you're on punk!"

It indeed was very silly to watch people trying to straddle a pumpkin between their legs and carry it thirty yards. But that was one of the fun family events at the festival. Most people couldn't even make it ten yards without dropping the pumpkin. At which point, one had to stop and place the pumpkin back between their legs before trying to run again. Scaggz was watching them through his telescope.

Scaggz went to his VW Kombi and took out a four-foot piece of PVC and his hand-rolled paper darts. He walked over to the side of the pumpkin race where the spectators stood and cheered on the contestants. He stood near a tall tree with bushes next to it.

As parents gathered with their children to enter the pumpkin race, a loudmouthed individual was talking in a loud boisterous manner. "All of you little punks are going to lose! I have run this race and won three years in a row. Hey, judge! You might as well give me the trophy now!"

"OK, Ellis, just pipe down. We'll see what happens. Be nice to the kids."

Since childhood, Ellis Pipewater always considered himself superior to anyone else. He always boasted about himself and his accomplishments. Ellis was a local realtor and quite successful; he made a small fortune and still saw himself as the high school quarterback that was the star of his school. After he graduated, he had a scholarship that lasted only one semester. He learned quickly that being a high school football star meant nothing once you were out of high school. The competition was tough at the college level, and after one season of being sacked forty-eight times he decided to return home and work on his father's farm. He told anyone that would listen that college ball was no more difficult for him than high school. It was unfortunate that he had to quit in order to help his family on the farm, as his father was getting older. A year later his father died, and the farm was sold. After the mortgage was paid off, there was almost nothing left. He and his mother rented a one-bedroom apartment over the hardware store in town.

He was working part time at the hardware store when real estate legend Richard Norton walked in to buy mouse traps for a home he had just listed. Richard was amazed how everyone that walked in would talk to the ex-high school football star as if he was a retired professional football player. Richard hired Ellis for the PR that it brought his firm and soon he was holding open houses that featured the failed college player. People flocked to the events to get their picture taken with the quarterback that had brought them their only state championship.

Richard fast tracked Ellis to acquiring his real estate license. Soon anyone that wanted to sell their house in the county wanted Ellis, the high school quarterback that brought a championship to their part of the state, as their real estate agent. Ellis was able to buy a house for himself and was happy to inform his mother that she would have the small one-bedroom apartment all to herself as he just purchased the 5,200-square-foot, six-bedroom home that had belonged to the Fosters, who had made their fortune in the maple syrup business.

His mother spent the last years of her life never leaving the apartment after she fell down the steps and broke her hip. Ellis visited her in the hospital and promised that he would do all of her grocery shopping so she would not have to walk down the two flights of steps. When his mother returned home, he brought her the groceries as he told her he would, but after that decided to pay the clerk at the store to make the delivery. Within a year his mother died a lonely death. She never saw her son again, who was too busy holding parties at his large home to be bothered to visit the apartment over the hardware store.

"OK, contestants! Everyone grab a pumpkin from the pile and line up over here," said the judge. The race was about to start. The contestants, mostly children with a few adults, lined up on the line with their pumpkins between their legs.

Nothing looked more ridiculous to Scaggz than to see these two middle-aged men in black suits straddling pumpkins between their legs and trying to run with them. The whistle blew, the racers started to move. Twenty-two people tried to waddle with their pumpkins. The silliness of it. Scaggz loaded a paper dart into the tube and took aim at Agent Crow. Blap…right on his neck at fifty feet. What a shot.

Agent Crow dropped his pumpkin. "Ouch! Damnit!" Picking up his pumpkin, he started waddling to catch up to Agent Sparrow.

Blap…Agent Sparrow was hit and dropped his pumpkin. Agent Crow took the lead in their private race against one another.

Scaggz was laughing to himself. "What idiots! They look so stupid," he said out loud. He continued to hit them with paper darts and made one or the other drop their pumpkin and waste time. The race was already over between the other runners and a winner had already been declared. But for Agent's Sparrow and Crow, they continued until Agent Crow crossed the finish line and won.

"Yeah! You owe me lunch and beers!"

"Fuck! I can't believe it! You are much shorter than me. I should have won. Somebody kept throwing things at me. I kept dropping my pumpkin."

"Yeah, me too. Very strange. Well, I'm hungry! Time to eat!"

The judge reluctantly announced the true winner at the finish line. "Once again, four years running, Ellis Pipewater is our first-place winner."

"I told you little bitches! I am the champion! At forty-one years old I am still as fast as I was in high school. You kids had no chance. And you two guys wearing suits, you are pathetic!"

The Austrians walked over to the lake where the canoe races and other water events were taking place. Feeling competitive, the guys signed up for the canoe race. They could hear someone talking loudly in the group of contestants gathered near the edge of the lake.

"All of you are going to lose! You all suck! It is that simple! I was also the rowing champion in high school, along with my still-standing and well-known records and stats on the field. No one will ever beat or come close to me."

"You talk the talk, Ellis, do you walk the walk?" replied someone else in the group who seemed to know loudmouth Ellis Pipewater.

"Let's go, you pantywaist! You'll be crying in the end when I win another trophy! I'm running out of space at my house for all these trinkets…and it's a big house. It's a good thing that I bought the largest house in town."

"And if you lose, Ellis, you are buying everyone here a beer."

"When I win, all of you are buying me beers all day!"

Torsten, Nathan, and Heinz all decided to race against this loudmouth and hopefully teach him a lesson. They detested boasting loudmouths; it is not what people do in Austria. They weren't the only ones that didn't like loud obnoxious asses. Scaggz, now also at the lake, was watching. He hoped one day to rid the world of these dimwitted strains on society that constantly spewed such gibberish. It pained him to hear this imbecile speak.

He also decided that he would enter the race. He blended into the crowd very well in his hippie clothes and baseball cap with his newly grown-out goatee. He had been watching this jerk since the pumpkin race and decided he was going to take action.

"OK, everyone! Welcome to the canoe race. The first one to row to the end of the bend of the lake, row to the left and down the bend, then back to where we are now will be the winner and receive this grand trophy."

The distance of the course was about five hundred yards. The thirty-five people competing each found a canoe floating in the water, grabbed an oar, and prepared for the starting whistle. The Austrians were all seated in their canoes. Scaggz was on the opposite end in his as the remainder of the contestants found a canoe.

"You all better be ready for this. Eat my wake… jerkoffs," said Ellis Pipewater.

The whistle blew and the racers were off. Some started with a brisk, vigorous pace and others at a modest rate of speed. Ellis Pipewater was leading all the others with Torsten close behind him. Scaggz, who was a decent rower, was purposely in third position.

"Haha! How are you guys doing back there! I will be champion again this year. You guys suck," shouted Ellis as he rowed at a brisk speed. Torsten maintained a modest speed behind Ellis, as he didn't want to exert all his energy in the beginning of the race. Nathan and Heinz caught up to Torsten.

"This is great fun, yah?"

"Oh, yah! Let's not waste our energy, we still have to go around the bend and then come back here."

"Yah, you are smart, Torsten."

Other rowers were still not as far ahead as the Austrians. In fact, not everyone could row a boat straight and drifted, getting in other rower's paths. Scaggz was rowing quickly and passed the Austrians, who had slowed a bit while they were talking. Scaggz was gaining on Ellis as they were ready to turn the bend. The Austrians weren't too concerned in lagging behind. They would save their energy for the final lane back to the finish.

Scaggz neared Ellis's canoe, and as they started to go around the bend—WHACK! Scaggz struck Ellis on the side of the head with his oar. Ellis fell back unconscious in his canoe. He dropped his oars in the water and the canoe slowed down almost to a stop. Scaggz then paddled to shore and ran off in the trees.

"Hey, did you guys see that?" asked Nathan.

"Yeah, that guy just hit loudmouth in the head with his oar," replied Torsten. "Scheisse! That must have hurt,"

"Yah, let's go see if he is alright," said Torsten.

The Austrians rowed up next to Ellis's canoe. He was moaning and lying on his back in the canoe.

"Hey, man! Are you alright?" asked Torsten.

"Ohh, my head. Whaat haappened?" moaned Ellis.

"Some guy hit you on the head with his oar."

"Hey, you guys continue the race, I will guide him back to shore," said Heinz.

"OK, see you later! Hope you feel alright there," said Torsten.

Torsten and Nathan resumed rowing as other rowers were nearing their position. Scaggz, already ashore, peered through the trees to see what was happening. He saw his brother helping the guy get to the shoreline.

Torsten and Nathan quickly made it around the bend in the lake as the other rowers were still far behind them. Then in the final leg, it was Torsten and Nathan neck and neck, releasing their saved energy for the end. Torsten won the race. He got a trophy and was very proud. Who could beat a Viking in a rowing contest anyway?

The agents arrived at the lake when Scaggz introduced himself to Ellis, but they could not see around the bend. "We have to be on our toes today," said Sparrow. "This fucking guy is trying to get into our heads. Another note in Allentown a few nights ago."

"We can never tell them back at the field house about this kind of shit. It makes us look bad," responded Agent Crow.

In reality, it was exactly what their peers expected from these two. The only reason they were chosen to follow the Doctor is that there was no one else available for a long assignment like the tour. Sparrow and Crow had their moments, but they rarely solved any of the assignments that they were given. If it were not for the rescue of the kidnapped daughter of a visiting sheikh six years ago, they would have long been dismissed. But the story made all the news broadcasts for days. The sheikh was so grateful that he now makes substantial donations every year to the FBI Agents Association and pays for their Christmas party at one of the five-star hotels in Beverly Hills, including rooms for all the guests. Firing the pair was not an option since for sure it would cut off the funding the bureau has become accustomed to because of the sheikh's heroes.

No one wanted to work with the pair, and soon they were given a substantial amount of vacation time, which they would use to lay on a beach somewhere in the world. None of the other agents complained that the pair were given so much vacation time. They all knew that having them on the payroll was to their own benefit and welcomed the break from having the two wander aimlessly around their offices. When murders began happening on the Doctor's tour last time out, it was unanimously decided that Sparrow and Crow were perfect for this job as it would keep them away for an extended period of time.

Unbeknownst to them, they were being put under surveillance. Scaggz was now in a location where he had a wide-angle view of most of the area and with his telescope had spotted them walking up.

Scaggz watched as the agents wandered the grounds of the Hemp Fest; people were taking pictures with the pair. Every few steps a stoned hippy was taking a photo of the two thinking that they were in costume and part of the festival. After an hour, the agents decided they would go back to their hotel and wait until it was dark to return.

Ellis Pipewater could not see a thing clearly with the sack over his head. He also could not do anything about the sack because his hands were tied behind his back. He did, however, know it was still daylight as light filtered in through the hemp-woven sack. He also could tell that he was lying on the floor of a canoe and the canoe was moving. His head hurt but things were becoming a little clearer for him. He remembered the man with the baseball cap talking to him on the shoreline right before his lights went out.

Now drifting out in the lake, he could not move. If it wasn't for the eleven-year-old boy that he insulted before the race, no one would have noticed. The boy understood that he would not win the race against adults, but he was ecstatic and could not stop repeating himself to his parents that he did beat the asshole who was trash talking him before the race. After his parents reminded him that using that language was not appropriate in their family, the boy realized that he did not see the asshole finish the race. He left his parents' side and walked to the finish line of the race, and that is when he saw what looked like an empty canoe in the lake. He mentioned to the judges that were packing up their station that one contestant never finished the race and the canoe out there on the lake was probably his.

Ellis Pipewater was rescued by the lifeguard on duty. The lifeguard knew who he was. Ellis warned him not to mention this incident and that he must now leave as he was late for the hemp sack race.

All day various bands and diverse music played from the stage. Country music, bluegrass, blues, and rock all could be heard. The Maine Lobster Broilers Blues Band was currently playing. There were still two hours before the Doctor was scheduled to perform. The band minus Tommy and crew went on the hemp wagon ride around the farm.

It was a very large wagon and it was filled with bales of hemp that served as seats, complete with a familiar skunky smell. There was room for all: Hocker, Jeb, Neusy, and Marlon sat in back. Marlon already had a joint rolled up ready to smoke. The other three each had a bottle of beer. The Austrians and the Doctor rode in the middle and up front. The wagon driver, Wilson, grabbed the reins on the four-horse team and started off.

First, they went around the back side of the lake. There were many trees and fields of marijuana, corn, apple trees, all ready for picking. Farm workers were finishing up their day, bailing up dried-out marijuana plants and straw to be used around the festival. Marlon was in awe with all of the weed just in reach. The fields seemed to go on forever. The wagon traveled near the barn and grain silo, and there was a hemp sack race going on. Ellis Pipewater could be seen shaking his fist at all of the competitors before he got into his sack for the race.

Then they came upon the colonial mansion where the owner's family have lived for generations. Past the mansion was a large building that the tractors, plows, reapers, and automobiles were stored. They rode around the parking area with only about five hundred cars parked in it. Jeb was a bit disappointed but wasn't surprised. After all, it was a Spud Burger event.

The hemp wagon made it back and parked near the stage. The band all got out and went onto the tour bus to get dressed for the show. Jeb and Marlon went over to the merch area where Cal was sitting, watching the goods.

Sparrow and Crow arrived at the tour bus and were greeted by Jeb. "Agents, good to see you tonight. Happy to report that all has been well for days."

"That is good news," said Sparrow, not making mention of the drive-time murder back in NYC after the bus was well on its way to Allentown. "We will be positioned on both sides of the stage during the show. Anything goes on, we will see."

"OK great," said Jeb.

Neusy was mimicking the agents behind their backs. Jeb smiled and nodded in approval.

"We are going to walk around and get a feel for the festival," said Crow.

"Thought you would have gotten here earlier than now," said Jeb.

"We tried that, but the stoned crowd thought we were an attraction."

As the agents walked away, Neusy gave Jeb the we-are-in-trouble-with-these-two-guys look.

The Maine Lobster Broilers Blues Band was almost done playing their set. Marlon lit another joint and started to get into the blues band. "Blues is such an underrated style of music," he said.

"Underrated by whom? There are entire festivals and clubs dedicated to the blues," replied Jeb.

"Well, maybe just me, then." The Maine Lobster Broilers Blues Band finished their set with Marlon dancing next to the bus.

"It is our great pleasure to welcome the Doctor of Dynamics, Jurgen Weislangwolf and the Surgeons to rock the festival," said the man that was managing the stage after Neusy and Hocker had checked the gear.

"Guten Abend, Maine!" spoke the Doctor. "We are thrilled to be here und to celebrate the Hump Harvest Festival with all of you!"

"It's hemp, not hump," called out Hocker from the side of the stage.

"Yah, yaah. I know it's hemp. Yah, you all like the hemp," said the Doctor, and the smaller-than-expected crowd cheered.

"Und now here is 'Bitchy Wife'!"

All of the hippies shouted and waved. "WAAHHH! THE DOCTOR RULES!"

The song was a hit as always. There were many Centipedes and Doctor fans in the crowd. As the Doctor himself looked down upon the crowd from the stage, he scanned left and right to try and count heads. It only looked like 800 to 1,000 people at best. Not at all like Spud Burger promised. Oh well, just make the best of it, he thought, as he prepared to play the next song.

As he strummed his guitar, he hit his overdrive pedal. This gave a spike in the line of his already high output pickups and caused sparks to shoot out of his amps, with some sparks settling on the dry hemp in the wagon. It went unnoticed for some time as it gently smoldered all by itself on the side of the stage. The crowd saw the sparks and cheered, thinking it was part of the stage show. Soon everyone slowly got a buzz as the hemp wagon smoldered. The band played on.

"Ach! I feel funny here. A little lightheaded. Now it is time for 'Soar into the Sun'." Once again the crowd raved and waved, but they were also getting more mellow at the same time. The enthusiasm was not the same and the Doctor noticed.

Agents Sparrow and Crow were feeling it too. A relaxed, totally in control feeling. Fans from the audience took notice of the two agents after they both put on their sunglasses when the spotlights were interfering with their buzz. People were pointing and taking pictures of the two characters, a Blues Brother on each side of the stage. Crow was first to start posing and interacting with the fans. Soon after, Sparrow was feeling the spirit of the moment and was waving and posing for pictures.

During the guitar solo, the hemp wagon burst into flames and massive billows of smoke floated away from the wagon in various directions. Marlon got a big blast of the smoke cloud right into his face while he was selling merch. "Yeah, that's what I am talking about," he said. "I want to see the joint that hit came from."

Jeb noticed that he, too, was feeling at ease during the show. Not being able to see the stage from behind the tour bus, he was unaware of the massive fire right next to the stage.

The Doctor was feeling the heat from the fire and said, "Yah, guys, it was getting a little cold up here, but you made too big of a fire. Who is ready for 'Slap the Virgin'?" The crowd signaled that they were indeed stoned and ready for the classic Centipedes song. The Doctor played the iconic beginning riff as more smoke drifted over the audience.

Agents Sparrow and Crow were no longer buzzing but in an all-out paranoid stoned moment. They both were breathing hard, looking across at each other. They met backstage and stared at each other for what felt like minutes but were only seconds. "Now what? I think I am baked," said Agent Sparrow.

"Yes, I don't know what to do. I don't smoke weed. What do we do? I can't stand there. I am starting to freak out."

"Thes, mee thoo, I am dirsty, my thongue is sticking to my mouth."

"Let'th get wather," said Crow. The two of them walked to the concession stand and bought two bottles of water, which they each chugged till empty and then bought two more bottles. "That's better! What now? I am still kind of freaking out."

"It felt good to walk over here. Let's keep moving, it has to wear off soon."

"We have to be able to see the stage." Crow agreed and the two agents spent the rest of the concert walking around the stage continuing to inhale the burning hemp wagon, which was now completely inflamed. Billy Utters unhooked the horses and decided to let it burn since it was far enough away from the stage and posed no harm to the concert. He took a couple of deep breaths of the burning bales and sat back and watched the Doctor on his stage.

After the show and a lengthy meet and greet, they were finally finished. The band went back to rest on the tour bus. Neusy and Hocker had an easy night as no breakdown of equipment was needed since there was a second show scheduled for the next night.

The very stoned Doctor, Neusy, Marlon, and Jeb were sitting in the tour bus lounge discussing the night. The other guys went to sleep in their bunks, being drowsy from the effects of the weed. Cal Crabs decided to pitch a tent outside and hang out with other hippies but refrained from smoking weed. Although he unwillingly was stoned because of the burning hemp wagon.

Cal was talking with Billy Utters, who was extremely honored to have the Doctor play on his stage. "What a great show. When I contacted Spud Burger to ask if the Doctor would play my festival, I expected him to say no way. He told me that all it would take is to pay him a signing bonus of two thousand and pay the Doctor five per night. Shit, I was willing to pay three times that amount. That Spud is a good man."

"Not everyone thinks that, my man," said Cal. "Be careful with Spud, and he should not be getting any signing bonus for the acts that he books. He gets his percentage of the contract and that is it."

"Wow, OK, I did not know that. This is the tenth year of the Hemp Fest but only the third year that we have had bands play, and none as big as the Doctor. Mostly local bands. Tomorrow should be another great day. We have a Grateful Dead metal tribute band and the same blues band that we had tonight."

"Cool, I dug that band. They were good. Hey, I got to ask, but why am I feeling stoned? Did you guys make a bonfire? I heard some talking."

"That was genius. It was actually an accident, but I think that it's OK. I'm going to make that a thing now. Not the burning wagon, but a bonfire during show time with the extra hemp bales."

"OK, bro, you're crazy, man."

Inside the bus the Doctor was pacing. "Achh! I'm exhausted! I need to sleep!"

"Well, you know where your room is," remarked Jeb.

"Yeah, man…you know where your room is," repeated Neusy.

"Don't be a smarty!" said the Doctor as he opened the refrigerator.

"Do you have the munchies, Doctor?" asked Neusy.

"Nein, nein…I am just browsing around."

The Doctor didn't find anything of interest in the fridge. He started opening the cabinet doors. Nothing special there. He even looked in the silverware drawer. No, nothing there. He spied the two boxes of cold pizza left over from the day before. Nah, don't want that.

"I think you are stoned out of your gourd!" said Jeb.

"Achh! I am very tired, but I want to have a little snack. I don't like that word: gourd. My head is a very complex organ."

"I think what is in the head is an organ and not the head itself?" asked Jeb.

"You have a point," agreed Neusy, still feeling stoned.

"You guys are a lot cooler tonight, more mellow, on my level now. Haaa you even said organ…haha," said Marlon.

"Speaking of organs, I have to drain mine," said Neusy to the laughing Jeb.

As Neusy got up to walk to the restroom he said, "Now what are you doing?"

The Doctor started again, opened the refrigerator, closed the refrigerator, opened the cabinets, closed the cabinets, opened the silverware drawer, closed the silverware drawer. He looked at the pizza boxes again.

"Achh, nah! There is nothing to eat."

"The Doctor has the munchies! The Doctor has the munchies!" chanted Neusy while Jeb and Marlon chuckled and leaned on each other.

"Achh! You three are like children in the kindergarten."

The Doctor repeated opening and closing things for twenty minutes, never finding satisfaction. "Why don't you eat some pizza? It is a musician's favorite food in times like this," said Neusy as he disappeared into the restroom.

"Achh, that couldn't be good today."

"Well, you didn't find anything in the fridge that you can eat, a lot of meat and other people's stuff in there."

"I'm so hungry now. I want to eat something. ACHHHH!"

"Oh, go on, Doctor! Have a slice of pizza, it won't kill you," Jeb said. The Doctor opened the box and stared at the day-old pizza. It didn't look too bad. All vegetarian, of course: bell peppers, mushrooms, onions, black olives, and tofu pepperoni. The Doctor reached for a slice. Not too bad, he thought as he finished it. Maybe another. He grabbed the second piece, and it too was gone.

"AWW! That's nasty! I would never eat day-old pizza, especially since it wasn't refrigerated," laughed Jeb as Neusy returned from relieving his organ.

"Yah! Yah! Have your stupid jokes und laughs."

"You guys are funny," said Marlon. "My organ hurts from laughing."

"Your organ hurts me every time I look at you," said Neusy, and they all laughed except the Doctor.

"Yah, you guys with the jokes," said the Doctor as he left the lounge.

Chapter 26

The next day, Hocker and Neusy searched for something to eat in the row of food trucks. Everything looked and smelled great right down to the fresh apple and berry pies. They had everything from BBQ, pizza, specialty sandwiches, pancakes with maple syrup as well as boiled lobsters and crabs with butter, to things that smelled good but neither Neusy nor Hocker had seen before. A culinary heaven! As they entered the area, the Doctor was right there, eating pancakes and licking his lips.

"Are you enjoying those pancakes, Doctor?" asked Neusy.

"Oh, yah! This maple syrup is out of this world. Wunderbar in the highest level!"

"That's nice! Well, it's too late in the day for pancakes for us, so Hocker and I will continue to look for something real to eat."

The Doctor made a face of disapproval as he knew their meal would include some type of dead animal. Hocker and Neusy continued, walking past many types of cuisine prepared in contrasting but distinctive ways. "Fuck it, Neusy! Let's have BBQ ribs! I can't even pronounce half of what these trucks are serving," whined Hocker.

They walked along the path and found a vendor that had a huge smoker out in front of the food truck. The smoker consisted of many levels and was one of the most beautiful things the boys had ever seen. The aroma brought them in for a closer look. "The Maine Station BBQ, this looks great!" said Hocker.

"Anything coming out of that smoker, has got to be amazing. Look at how that thing is smoking! OK, I'll grab some beers from that booth over there and order me the same BBQ plate as you are having, Hocker," said Neusy.

Happy Harvest Gold Lagers would be the first choice, specially brewed for the festival. Neusy got two beers poured into plastic sixteen-ounce cups. He sipped on one as he walked back to find a table. Hocker had finished ordering and was waiting off to the side until his order number was called out. Finally, his number was called, and he grabbed the plastic tray with the two loaded-up plates and went to sit with Neusy at the table.

"Oh boy, oh boy! Look at these ribs!" exclaimed Hocker, drooling. Neusy sipped on his beer; the joys of eating with Hocker.

The boys were enjoying their time off but not as much as Marlon. Marlon took his free time to explore the festival. One of his favorite pastimes and there was a whole festival dedicated to it. Marlon was in his element, pure heaven. Better than any dispensary he had seen. There were at least two dozen booths with just weed. Freshly harvested weed. He browsed around and then stopped at one called Nature's Best. He was impressed that they had a strain that was fluorescent green. It looked like it would glow in the dark. "Hi, I am interested in that one there," said Marlon with a huge grin on his face to the man at the booth.

"Yes, that's Scary Steven," said the man wearing a T-shirt with a large marijuana leaf on it.

"Why do you call it that?"

"Because after some people smoke it, they claim to see things and become frightened."

"Wow! I'll take a quarter."

"That will be $50."

The man took Marlon's cash and handed him a green plastic bottle. Marlon walked away. He stopped at another booth. This booth had solid purple buds. Marlon was intrigued.

"Do you like that?" asked the old hippy.

"It's…it's…just so…beautiful."

"It's called Purple People Eater," replied the man. "Because people that smoke it get the extreme munchies. The urge is so great to eat that if they were in the jungle stranded, they would be enticed to eat anything they found, including other people."

"Give me a quarter of that. I love eating!"

"That will be $50."

"Can I get two of those pre-rolled joints as well?"

"Sure, that will be $10 for those."

The man took Marlon's cash and handed him a purple plastic bottle, along with the two joints in their own bottle. Marlon sparked one of the joints and took a couple of puffs. Instantly, his mind expanded, and he had the extreme munchies. He hurried himself over to the food truck area, he was craving something sweet. He found a truck that specialized in cream puffs. He bought four and began to eat one. "So good!" he said out loud with cream all over his face. Two hippies gave him the thumbs up as they passed him. He walked down the path eating a second cream puff and walked right into a stranger, the puff smashing into his face. "Oh, sorry about that!" Marlon said to the tall man.

"Marlon?"

"Yeah, who are…hey I know you, don't I?" Marlon said.

"You bet. Agent Crow, here."

Agent Sparrow stood next to him. "Are you stoned, Marlon?"

"Well, of course, this is the Hemp Fest, isn't it?" said Marlon.

"What is that all over your face?" asked Agent Crow.

"It's a cream puff. They're great," replied Marlon as he scraped a little off his face with his finger and offered it to Agent Crow, who politely declined. Marlon licked the cream off his finger.

"You should try getting more of it in your mouth next time," said Agent Sparrow.

"You guys look funny! Where are your suits? I didn't recognize you," Marlon asked the two agents. They looked out of place to him, both dressed as hippies in tie-dyed shirts and blue jeans, but with well-cropped hair and sunglasses.

"We thought we would change our look and try and fit in," said Agent Crow.

"Yeah, no one can call us the Blues Brothers now," replied Agent Sparrow.

"Right on, that's what this whole festival is all about. Let yourself go and be free," said Marlon, wiping more cream from his face.

Jeb spent the day advancing the next week's shows. He contacted the promoters and venues and, along with Cal, came up with their schedule. He was setting up the merch booth when Marlon returned with a joint in his mouth. The Maine Lobster Broilers Blues Band had just started their set and Hocker and Neusy were back on stage waiting for the set to end. The band was on the bus preparing for the show. A man in a tie-dyed T-shirt approached the merch table.

"Sorry, we are not quite set up," said Jeb.

"It's me," said Agent Crow.

"Whow, agents, you look quite different. First time I have seen you out of your suits."

"We had such a relaxed sleep. It was incredible, so we decided to look the part today."

"Right on, agents, carry on."

The agents walked away, and as they rounded the bus a tall man wearing a Pipewater Dreams Real Estate Agency T-shirt brushed into Agent Sparrow.

"Fucking idiot, why don't you watch out where you are walking," said Ellis Pipewater.

"Hey buddy, it was an accident," said Agent Crow. "You came around the bus not paying attention."

"I'm trying to listen to the band, assholes," said Ellis, and he walked away into the crowd. He had just scored a four pack of pre-rolled joints of top-shelf indica buds called Alien Stargazer Blueberry Dreams. After smoking one before his altercation with the agents, he was feeling good and found a spot to sit up against a tree where he immersed himself into the sounds the Maine Lobster Broilers Blues Band were creating on stage.

After their set, Billy Utters walked out on the stage to loud screams from the crowd. He was their god. A man that could pull off a festival like the Hemp Fest had this countryside full of worshipping stoners; content, mellow and stocked with enough weed to last well into the fall months.

"Well, alright, thanks for making this weekend the most successful since we started this tradition ten years ago," said Billy. "Let's hear it for the Maine Lobster Broilers Blues Band. Aren't they great? They have played the festival now for the second straight year." The crowd applauded; Ellis Pipewater was standing up, pumping his fist and giving chest bumps to the tree he was just sitting under.

"I hope that next year we can have this next artist, who will close the festival, come back, and play again. But before the Doctor hits the stage, we are going to light that pyramid of hemp bales over there and create the first planned bonfire of the festival. A tradition that will be replayed next year on every night. Ready guys, light it up." The crowd screamed as two men with torches started the bonfire.

The Doctor and the Surgeons were on the stage ready to play. Tommy took a deep breath of the passing smoke. The Doctor looked at him and said, "Yah, Tommy, you already play behind the beat. You don't need more of that," as a wave of smoke engulfed the Doctor. "Perhaps we will be OK. We are ready now, Mr. Utters." As he looked out into the audience, his eyes started watering, and through the smoke he could see what appeared to be a man chest bumping a tree on the left side.

"OK, ladies and gentlemen. Now is the time. Please welcome for a second night in a row, the Doctor of Dynamics, Jurgen Weislangwolf!"

The crowd was already stoned before the bonfire was started, and they did applaud, but most were waiting for the music to start again.

"Yah. Hemp Fest. Here we go, one more time for you."

Agent Sparrow on stage left was completely engulfed in a cloud of smoke while Agent Crow on the opposite side was getting micro blasted.

The man chest bumping the tree stopped. "The Doctor," he shouted. "Who is the Doctor? What happened to my blues? I don't need no doctor."

"Yah," said the Doctor, "that is a song, but not one of ours. Here is 'Bitchy Wife'."

Ellis Pipewater stood there watching the stage and smoked his second joint of Alien Stargazer Blueberry Dreams. When the song ended, the audience clapped. Not a lot of screaming from the twice-stoned crowd. It was more of a polite clap. The Doctor liked the sound of that; it was motivating to him until Ellis shouted, "Doctor, where is my blues? You suck! I could play better than you. Next year I will sponsor this festival and make sure you are not on the bill."

The Doctor stood there and listened. He channeled his inner calm.

"Nobody listened to the Centipedes when I was in—"

Suddenly the loud man screaming was silent. The Doctor looked at Tommy and nodded. Tommy hit his hi-hat and they played "Soar into the Sun." The show continued uninterrupted for the next hour and a half. The agents held their positions on the stage, other than to purchase water to sooth their suddenly dry mouths.

When Ellis Pipewater woke up, he was tied up once again, his hands behind his back and his legs folded under his body. He could not move a muscle. Scaggz stood over him, covering him with dried marijuana plants that were on a pile next to the bailing machine that Ellis Pipewater now found himself laying on. Once Scaggz had the conveyor belt loaded, he walked over to the ignition and started the machine. They were only a hundred yards behind the stage, but no one heard the machine rumble to life with the Doctor playing at maximum volume. Ellis now saw his fate. He tried to push himself from the conveyor belt, but the more he moved, the tighter he seemed to be bound.

Scaggz moved over to the lever. Ellis could not say a word. He closed his eyes when Scaggz pulled the lever and the belt began to move.

"You could have made it home tonight," said Scaggz. "But you're just another narcissistic piece of shit. No one will miss you." Scaggz walked away as he heard the machine breaking Ellis' bones, then spitting out a hemp bale that had Ellis folded in half with his knees over his head and legs bent back over to his waist.

After another lengthy meet and greet, the crew broke down the stage and loaded the equipment and merchandise back into the trailer. The last hemp wagon ride was boarding, and Marlon wanted to go on one final ride. Jeb told him one ride and return. They must leave on time for a scheduled border crossing into Canada. The next stop is a show in Ottawa in two nights. Marlon agreed and went on his ride. The ride returned after five minutes when someone on the wagon saw a bale of hemp with a head sticking out of it and legs in an unnatural position to the head.

The agents were called but there were not many people left at the festival. No one seemed to have seen anything and the agents determined that they were beyond baked, and it was hard to hold a conversation. They asked the local police to help and take statements, claiming that they needed to search the grounds for clues. The local police handled the interviews while the stoned agents walked the grounds and found the cream puff stand that Marlon had raved about earlier in the day.

The band and crew were cleared to leave, and they did.

"Jebsy, what do you say?" asked Cal.

"I say we are a bus."

"Hang on everyone, we are rolling!"

Chapter 27

Liam Gagnon stepped off the private jet in Ottawa. As he stepped onto the tarmac, heads turned to admire this cunning, handsome, and light-on-his-toes detective. Wearing a custom-fit navy-blue suit with perfectly groomed hair that did not give in to the wind blowing as he walked across the tarmac, his gait garnered respect.

Liam was a crime solver. Sixteen years with the Royal Canadian Mounted Police (RCMP). Now he was a freelance inspector, hired by countries worldwide for his nontraditional ways of crime solving. For the last six years he has been awarded the International Golden Handcuff Award for his ability to turn dead cases into solved crimes. His four Platinum Baton Awards are most ever awarded to one agent for his always adapting innovative techniques. London, Frankfurt, New York, Montreal. The RCMP and INTERPOL, among others, have hired him either to consult or lead investigations for their toughest crimes.

Liam shook hands with the superintendent from the RCMP. He was handed a folder and keys to the waiting federal SUV parked in the adjacent hanger. As he approached the vehicle, the door was opened by a uniformed police officer who also shook his hand. Liam entered the vehicle and read the file. Not much… Murders following a tour that is now in Canada. The Doctor, Jurgen Weislangwolf, he was quite aware of, having grown up a huge fan of the Centipedes and the main reason he contacted the RCMP and volunteered to work this case. The Doctor, being his all-time favorite guitarist, cannot have a legacy of murders following his tours. This would stop, right here, right now in Canada.

The file went on to include pictures of all the band and the crew members on tour with the Doctor. Liam memorized every detail of the file after he arrived at his hotel. The file gave all details of the tour, including the FBI agents that have been working on the road with the Doctor now for the second tour. The Doctor was not expected in town for a day. This gave Liam time to properly prepare.

After studying the file, he went down to the bar and had his favorite drink. Whiskey, neat. He browsed the internet on his phone and found more info on everyone that was on the tour, other than Marlon, who there was just nothing online other than a social media page with selfies posted on an hourly basis. He ordered his second whiskey when his phone rang.

"Inspector Gagnon, this is Border Agent Hayes here at the Coburn Gore border crossing. There were instructions that we should call you when the Jurgen Weislangwolf tour crosses into Canada."

"Yes, Agent Hayes, thank you. Have they crossed? Is all well?"

"Yes, Inspector, they are in Canada. Quite a colorful bunch. Apparently, they just played the Hemp Fest and we had to confiscate some marijuana, but other than that, they were clean."

"OK, thanks again, Agent Hayes." Liam ordered another whiskey that he took with him back to his room, sipping the amber liquid as he read the file one more time before he went to sleep.

The bus finally arrived in Ottawa after their once again near disaster at the border with Marlon and his weed. But being that everyone was still stoned from the bonfire, they got through it without any feelings being hurt.

Now they were at the Guantanamo Bay Club. The name alone should advise that one should proceed with caution. The club was run by Warden William Barton, who viewed himself as the warden of the facility.

Patrons who got too drunk and started fights got thrown into solitary confinement until the show was over and weren't let out until closing time. They got to listen to the show but couldn't see anything. The rooms were cages similar to jail cells, but each one only had a built-in seat, toilet, and sink with barely enough room to stand. In front of the steel bars but out of reach from those within the cells were black curtains that were drawn, making the room completely dark except for a two-watt LED nightlight built into the rear wall. Not exactly the ideal concert experience, but because of the notorious strict rules in the house, there rarely were any occupants. Another thing that was not tolerated was that the Warden was never to be contradicted; this, too, would land you in solitary.

The Warden had the security personnel dress like prison guards and hired some tough brutes. Part of the job description was to enjoy roughing up unruly guests.

The club was fairly new, and the band and crew had no idea what to expect. Jeb looked the club up online. What he found were pictures of the security guards throwing VIP guests in orange jump suits into solitary with the description, *Many people really want to let loose on the weekend after a tough week at work. Drinking is one of those ways to let loose. Getting drunk can sometimes be criminal. And for those who want to take that to the extreme, then the Guantanamo Bay Club is the place for you. A safe place to blow the lid off your stressed life.*

A proud moment to be a VIP; guests got orange jumpsuits, and for an extra $50 they could be beer-boarded, advertised as a new way of getting drunk. The VIP experience included a ball-and-chain mosh pit. At the end of the night, the Warden would draw raffle tickets; ten lucky VIPs got pardoned and attended a meet and greet with the evening's artist.

Jeb and Neusy walked up to the club entrance and arrived at iron bars preventing them from entering. Jeb shouted through the bars. A tall, ugly, uniformed guard approached the bars. "Yeah, what do you want?"

"I'm Jeb, the tour manager for the Doctor. We're here for the load in."

"Wait here! I have to ask the Warden. Nobody comes in or goes out without the Warden's say."

"OK, we'll wait." Jeb looked at Neusy with the WTF look. Neusy returned the just-another-stupid-themed-club look.

The guard returned. "OK, you guys are approved! Let's get it done!"

"Hey, Hocker, let's go!"

Hocker, standing back by the trailer, grabbed a speaker cabinet with the Doctor's amp head on top and rolled it toward the door. Neusy went back to the trailer and grabbed the bass drum case. Marlon grabbed some merch boxes. They all went in and out until everything that was needed out of the trailer was inside the club. Hocker and Neusy attended to the stage set up as usual. Jeb and Marlon looked for a suitable place to set up the merch booth.

The Warden came out of his office to meet Jeb. "Hello! I'm Warden William Barton."

Jeb laughed at the introduction. They apparently took the theme of the club seriously. "Hello, I'm Jeb. I spoke with you earlier."

"Yes, I was expecting you. And it's a good thing that you guys are on time; I run a strict camp here."

"Well, we like to be on time. Where can we set up the merch table?"

"Over there is fine, next to the guard tower."

Jeb and Marlon looked where the Warden pointed. There indeed was a ten-foot-tall guard tower with a spotlight up top. Marlon carried a box of T-shirts and followed Jeb toward the tower. The Warden said as they walked away, "You know I get twenty percent of everything that sells in this place. That includes T-shirts, beer koozies, CDs, DVDs, cigarettes, and conjugal visits."

"Hey, wait a minute, I thought we agreed on ten percent," replied Jeb.

The Warden snapped his fingers and one of the huge guards walked over to his side and said, "No one contradicts the Warden!" The guard pulled out a set of cuffs and looked at the Warden, who put up his hand signaling to wait.

"OK, whatever you say," replied Jeb.

Hocker was setting up the drums with Neusy attending to amps and connections up on the stage. They were more interested in reading the sign over the bar to see what kind of beers they might enjoy after the set up was completed.

Early Parole IPA 5%

Stool Pigeon Ale 5.5%

Oops… I Dropped the Soap Lager 6%

Prison Riot Red Ale 9%

Don't Get Shanked IPA 8%

10 Year Sentence Pale Ale 10%

Solitary Confinement IPA 11%

Electric Chair Malt Liquor 15%

Beer Boarding $50 for 10 minutes

Beer Enema $50 for 5 minutes

VIP Orange Jumpsuit package: *mosh pit access, and a chance to meet and greet with tonight's band* $100.

In the front of the stage there were twenty iron balls with chains with a shackle on the end. Each ball was six feet away from the next. VIPs could be shackled to a ball and mosh in a small orbit around their own ball without making contact with another patron.

"What are you going to have, Hocker?"

"Maybe an Early Parole, I don't want to get too fucked up yet."

"I'm thinking of having a Stool Pigeon. I don't want to get too fucked up either."

"What's up with the beer boarding and the beer enema? I never heard of shit like that before."

"I guess it goes along with the theme of the club. Being tortured by beer, I think I could do that. I can't see how that is any kind of torture. You want to try, Hocks?"

"Maybe the beer boarding. I think I'll pass on the enema."

"Maybe we can get Marlon drunk enough and give him an enema."

Hocker burst out in laughter. "Yeah, that's funny shit, maybe we can."

"Let's see if we can talk Jeb into it. Give Marlon the night off. He really doesn't need Marlon to help with merch sales, anyway, Jeb is the real salesman. Marlon just likes to talk and drink free beers."

"We'll give him some free beers tonight!"

As they looked around, they saw everything was painted in institutional pale green with a red stripe running midway around the perimeter of the building. The fifty-foot bar was centered in the building and there were two guard towers in the rear corners. Between the two towers were eight declining boards seven feet long. They had restraining straps on each side. On the left side of the left tower were three holding cells. There were another four cells on the side wall near the restrooms. On the right side of the right guard tower were three rooms. Each room had an inversion table and a machine next to it that looked like a pump connected to a beer keg and a hose with a nozzle on one end hanging off a hook.

From outside Jeb heard a man yelling, "What do you mean we can't come in until doors open? We are Agents Sparrow and Crow." They both held up their badges on cue. "Let us in…now."

The security guard looked at his list. "Sorry, guys, you are not on the list."

"Not on the list? We are part of the tour. We are FBI. Have you not heard about the trouble that this tour has been having?" said Crow, holding up his badge once again.

"Boys, you're in Canada, you realize that, right?"

"Unbelievable. We want to see the manager," insisted Crow.

"OK, but that will not end well."

After ten minutes, Warden Barton appeared with four other guards. "What is it you wanted to see me about?"

"Your guy here is an idiot. I don't know where he gets his authority, but that guy needs better training," said Crow as they both held up their badges.

"Well, the warden here runs the show," said the Warden.

"Well, this warden then is an idiot."

The Warden nodded at the security guard, who nodded back and put his key into the gate's lock.

"OK, this is much better. You guys should be respecting us as agents." The agents stepped towards the gate as the gate opened. Four pairs of hands grabbed them and dragged them into the club.

"I am the warden here. You guys will cool down in solitary until show time." The agents were dragged to separate cells on the side of the club.

Neusy summoned the band in, and they entered for soundcheck. The Doctor walked in and had a look around. Getting a funny feeling about what prison life was like, he was not liking what he was seeing. The vibe was all wrong. He did not like such things as prisons and torture camps.

The Warden saw him walking around and approached him. "Who are you?"

"I am the Doctor."

"I am Warden William Barton. I run this show."

"Achh! Where is the dressing room?"

"It's back there next to the left side of the stage."

The Doctor wandered back to have a look inside and then returned to the Warden a bit upset. "I don't see my special food ready."

"Yeah, I have some special food for you: powdered eggs and Bisquick muffins, with creamed chipped beef."

"Achh! That sounds terrible! I don't eat meat. Where are the vegetarian pizzas, ranch dip and chips, und my red wine? If I don't get these things, I don't play."

"Are you contradicting me…eh?" The warden snapped his fingers; …two guards came over. "This inmate is talking back to me. A little stay in a cell ought to make him more reasonable." The guards grabbed the Doctor and hauled him off and locked him in a cell on the side near the agents.

"WHAT? WHAT ARE YOU DOING?" yelled the Doctor.

Jeb came running over to the Warden. "What happened? Why did you lock up the Doctor?"

"He started contradicting me. I don't like that."

"Can't you let him have an early parole or something? I'll have a talk with him."

"No, sir! He gets one hour in there to help him remember who the boss is around here. But since he is the headlining act, I will let him have a complimentary beer while he sits."

Jeb walked back to the table to set up the merch with Marlon. He told Marlon to be careful in this place and that the Warden was a real prick.

Scaggz, outside the gate, looked in after the band entered and heard the entire conversation. He sent a text to Jimmy and told him that he would not be entering the club, and to watch the manager.

Jimmy, now on stage, read the text while he was waiting for Tommy to rearrange his drum kit that Hocker had set up. "You get many text messages, Heinz?" asked Tommy.

"Yeah, this one from a friend back home."

"They must be so happy that you are OK. That must have been difficult being abducted like that last year."

"Yes, it was horrible. The food was the worst part." Jimmy sent a text back to Scaggz: *The Doctor was put into a holding cell by the manager who calls himself the Warden.*

Scaggz replied, *Send me a pic of this guy.*

Jimmy could see the Warden from on stage talking to his security guards. He took a picture and sent it to his brother.

Scaggz was parked in the parking lot across the street. He was unsure what he was going to do. He took a nap and awoke when a dark-colored SUV pulled into the parking lot. He watched Inspector Gagnon exit the vehicle and walk across the street. Scaggz followed in the shadows.

There was a short line of people waiting for the doors to open. Liam walked to the gate, showing his credentials to the security guard. "I am Liam Gagnon, special investigator." The guard instructed him to wait.

A minute later the guard returned with the Warden and opened the gate. "I am William Barton, I run this place. It is an honor to have you in our establishment. Being in law enforcement for twenty-five years, I know exactly who you are and your reputation. I was told you would be joining us tonight. Can we take a photo together that I can hang on the wall here near the entrance?"

"Hi, William, yes of course." The Warden leaned in and there was a flash. "Wow you don't waste any time."

"Yes, Liam, we run a very efficient unit here. Come with me into my office and we can work on security detail for the evening."

Liam followed. He watched the soundcheck, minus the Doctor, and when he inquired where the Doctor was, the Warden informed him that he was in solitary, same as these two that looked like the Blues Brothers. Liam found the agents' cells. "Hi, I am Liam, you must be Sparrow and Crow, we talked on the phone a few days ago."

"Yeah, I am Agent Sparrow and in the other cell is Crow."

"It seems the two of you have gotten yourselves in a bit of trouble. I will see what I can do." Five minutes later a guard came over and released the agents from captivity.

The Doctor heard the agents being released and started causing a ruckus, yelling from his cell. Jeb walked over to him and peered between the bars.

"Jurgen, keep it down. That guy is a real prick. We need to get through the night and get paid, so calm down. Remember India. Feel the peace."

"Yah! You are right, Jeb. Feel the peace."

Liam introduced himself to Jeb and said sorry that he was not able to call but was watching their progress at the border. He told Jeb that he would be around all evening. If anything seemed odd to let him know.

Jeb shook his hand, said, "I hate fucking border crossings," and walked away.

The Doctor sat on the floor in the lotus position and meditated. Jeb secured him a glass of red wine. Just before show time, a guard walked over and let the Doctor out of his cell. "Your time is up! I hope you learned your lesson," said the guard.

"Yah! I sure have! This is the last time I will play at this place."

"Don't let the Warden hear you say that, or you won't play at all," snapped the guard.

"Guten Abend, Ottawa! This is our first time to the Guantanamo Bay Club und we are going to do some 'Jailhouse Rock'." The Doctor started the famous riff from the Elvis classic and Nathan went into his best Elvis impersonation. The crowd dug it! The Doctor had a mean tone on the Universe Guitar and custom Galactic Amp. "Ach, yah! I'm glad that you liked that one. Now we are going back in time, back to 'Nails in my Coffin'." The crowd screamed in absolute glory. The VIPs in front chained to their balls were running around trying to crash into each other, but the chains were too short, and they were stopped just inches from their neighbor.

In the back of the club the beer boarding had begun. People were being strapped down on the declining planks as guards poured buckets of beer down their stomachs until it rushed onto their faces. With their open mouths, they would try and drink as much beer as they could within a ten-minute period. If they got too drunk and couldn't function, they would be placed in a holding cell with others until they could maintain.

Hocker, standing near the merch table, put his arm around Marlon and said, "Hey, buddy! I want to buy you a drink."

"Are you feeling….okay?"

"No, really…let's go to the bar. I feel like a shot of whiskey, do you want a shot with me?"

"OK, why not." Marlon knew it was unusual for Hocker to be nice to people but was willing to take him up on his offer. "Jack Black for me, what are you having, little buddy?"

"Crown Royal."

The bartender gave them their pours. "Ahh! Nothing like Uncle Jack!"

"Nothing like Crown, buddy."

"Oh, yeah? Let's do a taste test. I'll order two more, this time we'll switch. You do the Jack and I'll do the Crown."

"OK, let's do it!" The bartender gave them their second pour. This went on a few more times and then they both were feeling tipsy. "Hey, Marlon, I want to treat you to something you have never had before."

"Yeaaah…whaaat'sss that? Hocker, old paaal. I really like you!"

"Let's have one more drink and I'll tell you about it." The bartender gave them their seventh pour. Hocker motioned Marlon to follow him. Marlon stumbled along behind Hocker. He was much drunker than Hocker. Because of Hocker's size, he was a master of drinking people under the table. "This way, little buddy."

Marlon followed Hocker beyond the bar, sipping his whiskey. Hocker pointed at one of the doors to the right of the guard tower. "In here, little buddy."

There was a cute girl in a guard outfit. "Hello, what's your name?"

"Marrrlon!"

"Well, come in and take off your pants and lay on this table."

Marlon had no idea what was happening, but he didn't care. A pretty girl was asking him to take off his pants and lay on a table. Why not?

Hocker said, "I'll wait outside for you. Have a nice time!" He chuckled as he left the room.

Marlon took off his pants and laid down on the table as he was told to do. The girl fastened clamps around Marlon's feet. He didn't think much of it.

Then she said, "Are you ready?"

"Yeaah, baby…I'mmm ready when yooou are."

She flipped him upside-down on the inversion table and the blood rushed to his head.

"WAAHHHHHH!"

"Now baby, here comes the surprise." She grabbed the hose with the nozzle off the hook and she inserted it into his anus. Then she turned on the pump and it injected the beer.

"OOOOHHHHH SHHIIIIT!" Marlon didn't know what to do. He hung upside-down on a table with a constant flow of beer. He could only take about three minutes of it and begged the girl to turn it off.

She did. Then she flipped him back upright. "How do you feel, baby?"

"Woooow…baaaby, I'm soooo fuuucked up! Whaaat the hell laws thaaat?"

"That was your beer enema! You friends paid for it."

"IIII neeeverrr had anything liiike that in myy life… I fiiink I roove you!"

"Wow, you are really relaxed," said the girl.

Marlon smiled at the woman that became a vision of two.

Scaggz could hear the entire show from the parking lot. The warden guy would get his later. He found a pizza restaurant nearby and walked back to the club with a large pepperoni.

The security guard at the gate said, "You can't bring a pizza in with you."

"No, I am delivering for Inspector Liam Gagnon."

The one guard said, "Nobody works here with that name."

"He ordered the pizza," said Scaggz. "He was being a bit of an ass if you ask me. But he said to make sure that someone gets him right away."

The second guard said, "It's that guy that walked into the back with the Warden. The one you took a picture of for the wall."

"Oh yeah, I remember, that guy was smooth. I'll go get him."

"OK, thanks," said Scaggz. "Can I leave it here with you? I have another delivery to make."

Liam walked to the entrance and was given a pizza by the security guard that had fetched him. "I did not order a pizza. Open the box but be very careful."

The security guard opened the box; the three of them looked in. The guard said, "Oh, pepperoni, just how I like it."

Liam said, "I was afraid of something like this." On the inside of the top of the box Scaggz had written, *Welcome to the tour inspector. Enjoy the pizza. I will see you soon.*

After the show, Scaggz watched the crew load out the equipment and one by one get on the bus. He read Cal's lips through the window of the bus: *Are we a bus?* He could see Jeb up front nod and then he read Cal's lips again. *Whoooo, we are rolling.* The bus was on its way to Montreal.

The parking lot emptied. Scaggz found a couple of vehicles parked behind Guantanamo Bay Club. The most expensive one was a newer-model Chevy Tahoe. He figured that must be the manager's vehicle and waited behind the dumpster for the employees to exit. First were what looked like bartenders, then two female prison guards. A few large men exited and then only the Tahoe remained.

Scaggz waited patiently until a half hour later a man appeared and walked to the Tahoe. He opened the door, not hearing Scaggz walk up behind him. "Are you the warden?"

"Haha, yes, I call myself that. I am the manager of the club. What can I do for you?"

BAM! The blue Stratocaster brought the Warden to the ground. After ten minutes, he awoke. He was groggy, but he could make out Scaggz sitting in the passenger seat of his SUV. His head was throbbing, and he could barely move his neck. When things became a little more in focus, he realized that his head was caught in the driver's side window. The door was closed, and his head was inside but the rest of him was outside. The window was as far closed as it could go without cutting off his breathing or blood to his brain, but tight enough so that he could not remove his head. He tried to reach in and open the window, but the car was off, and the window did not move.

Scaggz held up the key fob. "The window will not open unless the car is on. Now, Warden, you are in my prison. I hope you will be comfy tonight. I'll leave the key over by that dumpster, but that is too far away to start the car. Someone will find you in the morning. I hope you have learned your lesson."

The Warden said, "What the fuck? Don't leave. I can give you money. I have the deposit for the bank right here. Please let me out."

BAM! Scaggz hit the Warden in the forehead with the Strat. "Wrong answer. Have a good evening, I have to get to Montreal."

Chapter 28

The venue in Montreal was a multi-story club called Layers. On the top floor was a karaoke club, which opens for happy hour and stays open all night until 2:00 am. Top Layer, as it was called, always brought in a full house of interesting people ranging from industry singers and retired stars to cross dressers and cabaret dancers. The Doctor was playing in the Under Layer, the main room on the ground floor.

Liam arrived at Layers early, having read in his file that the tour preferred loading in around 3:00 pm. He sat and watched from a distance, taking in the crew and band members and what they all did during this time. He observed the bus arrive early by twenty minutes and Cal Crabs exit, stretching as he walked off the bus. Jeb followed and looked around the street, then disappeared into the venue. Next, Neusy walked out with Hocker and Marlon right behind. They walked around the back of the bus and opened the trailer, then disappeared inside.

Jeb returned and all the equipment and merchandise were loaded in. The trailer was closed and locked and then the crew all went into the venue. One by one the band exited the bus. Heinz walked down the street and so did Tommy. Torsten walked out, and five minutes later Nathan walked out, looking into windows of the shops as he walked away. A taxi arrived and Cal was whisked away to his hotel to get some much-needed rest.

The area that the club was situated in was an older area of Montreal called Le Village Gai. It was the part of town that was mostly gay. There were all sorts of shops, restaurants, and bars lining the street. Liam, on his way to Layers walked past Nathan who was looking in a shop window and taking pictures.

Jeb walked off the bus and Nathan immediately walked over to him, grabbed him by the arm, and said, "Jeb, come with me, I want to show you something." Jeb followed and Nathan brought him over to the store he was taking pictures of.

"What is all this?"

Jeb looked in the window and said, "Well, it looks like a store that sells dicks." He was looking at the window display of penis-shaped items of all kinds. There were lamps with penises, glasses and plates with penises, a penis-shaped picture frame, penis-inspired furniture, penis mouse pads, and all sorts of statues made of different material. Wood, metal, plastic penis statues. "Let's go in."

The pair walked in. There were more items with penises. T-shirts with penis designs and different sayings—Jeb saw one that said, *What's for Dinner? Guess.* Then on the back was a plate with a penis on it. There was another one with a unicorn jumping over a rainbow with a penis-shaped horn. They walked to the rear of the store, passing a penis couch and ottoman and various statues of all sizes. Jeb noticed as he continued to the back of the store that hanging on the wall right at eye level were a half dozen computer mice and all sorts of kitchen items: towels, potholders, plates, mugs, glassware, silverware. There were penis-shaped wooden spoons and a penis-shaped pasta server. Nathan was walking right behind, taking pictures one after another.

Then, down the other side to the front door, he stopped right past the counter in the rear of the store where the owner was standing. There in front of them was a life-sized wooden sculpture of a beautiful woman, painted almost lifelike. She was naked, with small but attractive breasts and blonde hair past her shoulders. One arm was in the air and the other was down her side, holding her twelve-inch penis. "Look, a chick with a dick," said Jeb.

Upon hearing this. the store owner came around the counter and said in an annoyed tone, "A chick with a dick? How can it be a chick if it has a dick?"

Jeb grabbed Nathan and pulled him towards the door, and they walked back to the venue. When they arrived back inside, Neusy and Hocker had the stage set up and Marlon the merch set up.

It was almost time for soundcheck when Agents Sparrow and Crow walked in. Tommy and Heinz soon followed. Jeb had some concerns when Tommy walked up to him. Now what?

"Hey, Jeb, we are in the gay part of town. Heinz and I went for coffee. We were getting all sorts of looks walking down the street."

Heinz agreed. "Yah, this is very interesting over here. I had someone blow a kiss at me."

"Well, that explains a lot," responded Jeb. "OK, let's get the soundcheck over with."

Under Layers was the main club in the building, a large club with high ceilings and a small balcony in the back. With a capacity just under 3,000 people, this was the largest room that Spud had ever booked for the Doctor, thanks to the fact that a special guest was announced. One that, when his name was released, caused tickets to immediately sell out. They held back revealing that Sludge would be on the bill until one week prior to the show. Just as was expected, the show went from having 123 tickets sold to being sold out. When fans called Layers and complained as to why Sludge was not announced on the bill when the show was announced a month earlier, the answer they received asked them why they did not buy tickets one month earlier. It was great marketing.

Spud had enough sense not to book another city the next night, keeping it open. When the initial show sold out, a second show was announced with Sludge on the bill. The only difference was the price of the tickets. The second night would cost four times as much as the initial night. Spud created demand and was now reaping the benefits with his profit. The contract he signed with the Doctor and Sludge was the same for each night. But the contract with the venue was different. The Doctor had no idea, once again victim of Spud Burger's deceitful business practices. Sludge was overjoyed to be on the bill with the Doctor and was promised that he could join the Doctor each night on "Slap the Virgin." It took a long time to convince the Doctor, since he disliked jamming with other artists on his classic songs. Jeb finally convinced him that if he played "Slap the Virgin" with Sludge as an encore he would play to a full house, as opposed to the 123 people that bought tickets to only see him.

The stage was large with plenty of space to have Sludge's crew set up their gear in front of the Doctor's once the Doctor's soundcheck was complete. Sludge arrived early to watch the Doctor's soundcheck but was disappointed that the Doctor sat it out. He stayed seated at the larger of the two bars that were at the rear of the club. Jeb was standing there next to the bar in the merch area with Marlon.

Marlon said, "Wow, this place is huge. I bet we will have all sorts of people buying us free beers tonight. Look at all this space they gave me to set up the merch."

"Yes, this is a nice venue for once. Listen, if Sludge's people want you to sell merch for them, tell them no, unless they give us a percentage," instructed Jeb.

Sludge, hearing this, approached Jeb. "Hi, Jeb, nice to see you again. I was hoping to watch the Doctor soundcheck."

"He rarely shows up for soundcheck. Glad you guys got on the bill. I was hoping it would be for a few shows, but two nights here is not bad."

"Yeah, we just squeezed this in. We leave for Europe right after to start our own tour. This is kind of a warmup for us. But an honor just the same. Don't worry about our merch. We don't have any; it's all in Europe for our tour. We rented the equipment for these gigs. Everything of ours is there in Europe."

"Really, no merch? I have an idea. Marlon, take Sludge's picture."

Marlon walked around the front of the table where Sludge was standing. Sludge backed up, not knowing what was going on. Marlon snapped a couple of selfies with Sludge in the background.

Jeb continued, "I have done this in the past. We make up tour cards—Sludge and the Doctor—with the dates. Probably get twenty bucks each. I will split that with you."

"Does not sound like it is worth it," said Sludge.

"I will make up 1,000 cards. We can sell all of these if we have almost 3,000 here each night and you have no merch. They will sell."

"OK, I get the ten grand, no matter what. Then we have a deal… I have to go set up my gear. We did not bring any crew or tour manager. We are using Europeans for this over there, so we are on our own here."

"Deal," said Jeb as Marlon took the picture of Sludge. Then another selfie with Sludge, this time standing next to him that he posted to his social media page before Sludge walked up on the stage. Jeb uploaded the solo photo of Sludge to his computer and along with the tour promo pic for the Doctor's tour, created a single image. He contacted a print house nearby and had the cards printed and delivered for a cost of $500.

"When anyone asks if we have any merch for Sludge, tell them the only Sludge merch is the tour card. I ordered them 8x10 inches so it will look nice," said Jeb. Marlon smiled and nodded his head in agreement while checking how many thumbs up he had already received from his latest upload.

Chapter 29

Scaggz parked his VW in a public lot a ten-minute walk from the venue but near a variety of stores. He needed two disguises, one for each night. He would sleep in the van and use the gym across the street to shower. He found an assortment of wigs in one of the stores and purchased a shoulder-length blonde wig. On his way out, when the clerk was not watching, he grabbed a blue bandana and tossed it in his bag. He had a leather jacket in the van that would help create the image. He decided he would leave his beard for this show but would shave the beard and leave the moustache for tomorrow's. Also, for tomorrow's show, he still had a travel spray bottle of his tanning spray and would spray his face and hands.

But for tonight, blonde hair, bandana, leather jacket, and what is this? As he passed a consignment shop, there in the window staring at him was the final piece of his disguise. Scaggz brought the newly obtained items to his van. These would be special shows, important to get in early before a large crowd. He rested, then changed into his disguise.

Scaggz arrived at Layers right as Sludge was doing his soundcheck. Standing outside of Layers, careful not to be seen, he stepped into the lobby where a notice on the ticket window informed him that the show was sold out. He peered inside the venue until a man dressed in the most perfectly fit suit with impeccable hair approached him. "The doors do not open for another half hour," said Liam Gagnon.

"Oh, no problem, I'm just excited, big fan," said Scaggz.

"Yes, I am as well. See you later at show time," said Liam, who went back to standing next to the metal detectors he had ordered for the shows.

Scaggz needed a way to get in. He did not expect a show featuring the Doctor to be sold out, and from the look of what he just witnessed it would be more difficult to get in without a ticket. He left Layers, walked around the corner of the building, and ran into a sign stating that there was *Karaoke Tonight* with an arrow pointing up the awning-covered stairs. He walked up the stairs and found the entrance to Top Layer. He went inside. They had just opened and already had a decent crowd. He walked up to the bar and ordered a beer.

He took in the room: a small stage up front with a mic on a stand, TVs on both sides of the mic, next to the stage was a DJ station that was used for the karaoke. The bar ran down the side of the room and low cocktail tables filled the entire lounge. He saw a door to the left of the bar and strolled over to glance at what was behind it. The sign on the door indicated that the door led to the restrooms. He opened the door and was in a small hallway with two restrooms, both with a man and a woman symbol on them. Between the restrooms was a sink, a soap dispenser, and a dryer. A dead end, Scaggz walked back to the bar. He sat there a moment drinking his beer when the bartender asked him, "Would you like to order one of our happy hour appetizers?"

"Food?" asked Scaggz. "You serve food here? Of course, happy hour and all."

"Would you like to see the menu?"

"Yes, I would," said Scaggz. He looked at the menu but was more interested in where the food was prepared. He scanned the room again. There was another door off the bar to the right, but behind the bar. No one had entered through there since he arrived, he assumed that was only an office. When the bartender came around again, he asked her, "I am with the band playing downstairs, can I get my food to go? Also, is there a way that I can get down there without walking outside?"

"Sure, you can go through the office behind me, then down the steps into the main office and Under Layer is right there."

Jeb and Neusy were at the bar drinking a Jester's Hog Blood Orange Wheat Beer that was recommended to them by the club manager, who introduced himself as just Harry. He also informed the two beer connoisseurs that the other house beer was one they would also enjoy, the Unicorn Horn Lager. They tried that after.

"Is that Harry guy your contact? He seems very nice, a bit of a beer pusher," said Neusy.

"No, I don't know who he is, but the free beers are nice. The promoter is a woman that I only had contact by email; her name is Francesca. She said she would not be here as she had another show at a theater across town and could not make both tonight. She said she would be here tomorrow so we will settle both shows then."

Marlon was digging watching Sludge soundcheck. This was the biggest star he had ever spoken to and was watching from up close. He had followed Sludge from the merch booth to the stage like a puppy looking for love. When soundcheck ended, Jeb watched him talk to Sludge as Hocker walked over to the bar and asked, "Where is my beer?"

"Don't know, it wasn't my turn to watch it," snickered Neusy, and he and Jeb clunked glasses.

"Asshole," said Hocker, and was given a beer from Harry. "I got one without your help. So, Sludge offered me another hundred each night to help with his equipment. Easiest hundy I ever made. I load his shit backstage and then back on stage tomorrow. He said the brothers would help."

"What brothers?" asked Jeb.

"His drummer and bass player are brothers. They are from the band Ratson."

"No shit," said Neusy. "Those guys are great."

"I don't know them," said Jeb.

"Dave and Timmy Roberts? Never heard of them? Dave is a drummer, he goes by Schlagger."

"Still never heard of them."

"The bassist is an asshole," said Hocker. "He was ordering me around like I was his bitch. I almost fucking leveled him. Obnoxious fuck."

Neusy was surprised to hear Hocker call someone else obnoxious. He took a sip of his beer; Jeb could see him smiling.

Marlon came over and said, "Sludge is amazing. We talked, he showed me pictures of his son, I showed him pictures of my kids. I can't wait to see his show. He promised he would give me one of his double-billed caps!"

Neusy ordered another Unicorn Horn and rolled his eyes. Jeb nodded and ordered one as well.

Liam came over and said, "It will not be easy for your stalker to get in. I have metal detectors in the front and Sparrow and Crow watching the back doors, along with a couple investigators from the Mounties in the back and another two, up front with me. Where is the band? I would like them to stay inside tonight and not leave for the bus till after the show."

"We will let them know. Neusy, can you send them a group text?" Neusy agreed with a nod. "I think it will be OK, the green rooms are terrific here. We have three large rooms ourselves fully stocked, with showers as well. I think they only gave Sludge one, but technically he is opener for these shows."

"Yeah, that is unbelievable," said Liam. "How did you manage that?"

"He offered, apparently a big fan," said Jeb, but Liam's attention drifted to the servers walking in the front entrance. They were all smiling at the handsome inspector as they passed him.

"Five minutes until doors," said Harry and then disappeared.

Scaggz received his to-go order and was shown the way to the office behind the bar where a walk down the steps led to the office downstairs just as the bartender said. He did this carefully, navigating the dark steps leading down to Under Layer. He opened the door at the bottom of the steps and was surprised by Harry sitting at the desk. Harry looked up at this blonde-haired man with blue bandana, wearing a leather jacket and black kilt.

Scaggz stopped and said, "Hi, I just went to get something to eat, they said I can come back this way. I am with the tour."

"Ah," said Harry, "that explains it. Just through there." He pointed to the double doors at the end of the long room. "Be careful, it's a little dark."

Inside, people were starting to enter. Scaggz timed it right. He walked to the merch booth and was talking with Marlon when he overheard Hocker at the bar next to them talking to Jeb.

"The singer, Nick Baronson, is cool, he was telling me about his main band. I have heard of them. They are called Feculence. Yeah…but that fucking bass player. I asked him to be careful not to step on the Doctor's cables and he said, 'This is not my first rodeo, douchebag. You be careful not to mess with my shit, then we will be OK.' That is what he said to me… Can you believe it? He then said, 'Don't fuck up the settings on the bass rig when you move it.' I said to him, 'I thought you were helping move the shit, is what Sludge told me.' And that asshole told me the only thing he is helping after the gig is helping himself to a beer backstage… Fuck him."

They ordered one more beer before getting to work, and with a clunk of the glasses shouted out, "Fuck him!"

Jeb returned to the merch booth and Marlon said, "That guy in the black kilt bought me a beer. I got it down! I will be drinking free beers all night."

The venue had filled up and it became difficult to walk around. Marlon was busy selling merch and receiving free beers. Jeb's plan was working. They were selling tour cards to many of Sludge's fans. He calculated that they should sell out. Easiest mech money he had ever made. He was pleased with the extra money that the tour would earn, since the Doctor always had unexpected and unnecessary expenses.

The band minus the Doctor were all standing by the merch booth as well. They wanted to watch Sludge. Nathan, Torsten, and Heinz were standing in the back with Jeb. Tommy shouted, "I can't see a fucking thing without my glasses, I am going backstage."

Liam came over and reported, "Most everyone in and no issues both up front and in the back. A couple small pocketknives we confiscated, one guy had a travel can of hair spray from in his pocket, but for the most part clean."

Jeb gave him the thumbs up as the lights went off.

An orchestral arrangement started, and then a recorded intro. "From the dawn of creation to modern society, one thing still exists—SSLUUDDDGGGGE!"

Under Layers came alive. The sound from the audience was deafening. The stage was one of the most modern of the whole tour: arena-grade lighting, smoke, and lasers. Sludge came out with his double-billed cap. Men were pumping their fists and women were screaming. Sludge was wearing a custom shirt just for the show that said, *Sludge's Dream.*

He walked to the mic and played the first chords from the Petunia and Amo classic, "Leaving the City." He then announced, "Ladies and gentlemen, Nick Baronson." The audience screamed again as Nick walked out on stage and sang the classic verses to the song.

Marlon walked back into the room after smoking weed outside and joined Jeb at the merch booth. Sludge was well into the first song, jumping up and down. There was a break in the song and Sludge flipped around his double-billed cap. The audience went crazy. Marlon screamed. The Austrians looked at each other and nodded. Sludge ended the song with Marlon yelling "SLUUUDDDGGGE" as loud as he could.

Sludge went into another less known song from Petunia and Amo, but the audience knew exactly what he was playing, and sang along. Marlon didn't recognize the song but was humming along with the audience.

Sludge then played several songs from his first solo album, *Sludge from Hell.* This got the audience going. Sludge jumped up and down with Marlon in the back jumping up and down with him. During the song "Dark Angel Gone," Sludge played the solo that won him solo of the year in Guitar and Amp Magazine. Marlon jumped up on the merch table. He grabbed one of the tour cards and was waving it over his head along with the music. When the solo ended, he screamed again. The people in the back of the venue looked over. They saw the tour card and came over. Marlon sold a few dozen cards to the people in the back. Jeb liked what he saw.

Marlon, back on the table, was watching the most exciting guitarist he ever saw. He was pumping his fist. Sludge, up on the drum riser with his fist in the air, had Marlon mimicking what he was watching. Sludge held his fist in the air and the drummer went round on his kit. Then, in perfect timing, Sludge jumped off the riser, and when he hit the stage, the song ended and Sludge flipped his cap sideways, so the brims were over each ear, his guitar held over his head. The audience erupted and were stomping their feet. The Austrians hugged each other as that was the coolest thing they had seen a guitarist do.

The audience continued to stomp their feet; it sounded like a stampede. Marlon stomped on the merch table. He was crushing CDs and DVDs as they shattered under his feet. Key chains went flying off the table. Sludge walked over to the mic. "Thank you. WOW, you guys are loud."

Marlon held up the tour card and yelled, "Sludge is God!"

Sludge pointed at Marlon and said, "I see you, my new buddy."

Everyone turned around and looked at Marlon. He fainted backwards and fell off the table. Torsten was fanning him with the tour card when he woke up. He grabbed the card and jumped back onto the table.

Sludge went on. "We have a couple of new songs we want to play and then another Petunia and Amo song."

They went into a song off the new album. During the song, Scaggz made his way through the audience to the front of the stage. He unplugged Timmy Roberts' bass cable from the effect boxes he was using positioned at the edge of the stage. Sludge looked over when he realized something was wrong with the bass. Timmy was yelling and pointing at Hocker, who walked out and plugged the cable back in. As Hocker walked past Timmy, he pushed Hocker out of his way. Hocker turned around and was about to knock him over, but Neusy stopped him.

Sludge announced, "OK this is it, our final song. Then I will see you all later for my dream of playing with the Doctor.

This is Petunia and Amo's classic, 'My Dog Tannenball'." It was Petunia and Amo's biggest hit from their first album.

Towards the end of the song, Scaggz unplugged Timmy's cable once again. Timmy screamed at Hocker, who once again went to plug in the cable. This time Scaggz removed the bass fuzz effect and ran back into the crowd. Liam was watching what was going on and tried to make his way to the stage, but the people were packed in too tight, and he only made it halfway there. Scaggz managed to run backstage, not being seen as all eyes were on the stage trying to see who the culprit was unplugging the cable.

Hocker plugged in the cable to the remaining effects and the bass was once again heard, but not the same sound. It was very clean and did not sound like the song anymore. Timmy was furious. He kicked his bass amp, next to where Hocker was standing, and when the song ended, he abruptly left the stage, bumping into Hocker as he left.

During the intermission, Liam was able to get to the stage. Hocker explained what went on. Liam said, "The guy in the black kilt, I saw him before the show."

Sparrow and Crow came out from backstage, and Sparrow handed Liam the bass fuzz box and said, "One of the employees in the back said I should give this to you. He said you will know what to do."

Liam looked at the effect and said, "Why would I know what to do? I don't know anything about these things. What did the guy look like?"

Crow interjected, "He was a cool guy, talked to us a minute then said he had to go. He had blonde hair and wore the coolest black kilt."

Chapter 30

The next morning there was a buzz about the tour. Playing two gigs in the same venue has an advantage. No set up, just walk in and all is done. A quick soundcheck at 5:00 pm and they were set.

Neusy and Jeb spent the day in Montreal. They sat in old town and discussed the upcoming dates. There was a buzz. The show the night before had made the news. There was a clip of the Doctor and Sludge jamming. They made a big deal out of it. Sludge's return to the stage after years off, right here in Montreal.

People were talking about the show in the pub the pair stopped at for lunch. "How is the Old Town Musty Porter?" asked Neusy as he sipped his Horse Underbelly Red.

"Yeah, it's good. What a show last night. Crazy time. I wish they all could be like that."

"Well, another tonight and then on to the typical Doctor shows. Listen to these people, though, they are talking about the show. We did good."

"Yup, let's get through tonight. We got to keep Marlon under control. He turned into a little fan boy."

"What about Hocker? He wants to kill that bass player… Haha…there is something enjoyable about watching someone give him the mental bitch slap," said Neusy.

The pair finished their beers; it was time to head to the venue for soundcheck. As they exited the pub, a VW Kombi drove down the street slowly looking for a place to park. "That reminds me of the tour in India. What a fun time that was," said Neusy as they watched the VW drive by.

They made it back to the bus, and as they entered Cal said, "Boys, good evening. I heard it was quite the show last night. Marlon can't stop talking about it. He has been watching Sludge videos for the last half hour back there." They looked past Cal and saw Marlon watching a video and moving his phone around, showing the band sitting near him. No one was particularly interested; they were each busy with their own phones.

Jeb said, "What would we all do without these phones?"

Neusy nodded in agreement, and they walked aboard.

"Are we a bus?" asked Cal.

"Everyone is up here except the Doctor. Is he in the back?"

"Nein, he went shopping," said Nathan.

"We have five minutes if you want to be on time," said Cal.

After five minutes Cal fired up the bus and said to Jeb, "Your call. I can come back and pick up the Doctor after. It's only ten minutes away."

Jeb replied, "Let's go be on time since Sludge still has to set up and soundcheck after us."

"Fuck Sludge and his band. Especially that asshole bass player. I am going to fuck him up today if he gives me shit. Did you see him walk into me after the show yesterday? He almost went flying off the stage. He came around later with a beer in his hand and was checking that I didn't change the settings on his amp when I moved it. I am going to fuck with it while he is on stage tonight. Watch, he says anything to me, and I will do it."

Cal chuckled. "He has been like that the whole time he got on the bus."

"Yeah, fuck him," replied Hocker.

Cal put the bus in gear and inched forward; there was a loud bang on the side of the bus. Cal stopped and opened the door. The Doctor was standing there with a shopping cart full of more items for his back room. "Yah, you were leaving without me? Nein, that is not acceptable. Did Jeb not check to see if I was in the back?"

"We knew you were not here. We are on a time schedule. You got the text that Neusy sent out. So you knew. Crabs was going to come back but we need to get to the soundcheck."

"Yah, you know I hate these things. I will not soundcheck tonight. The ICU will be getting a facelift. Help me bring these things in the bus."

Jeb walked down the steps and saw the cart filled with more stuffed animals, a new mirror, lamps, plants, curtains, and pillows. Jeb carried it all on the bus and into the back. Neusy gave Jeb the I-don't-know-how-you-deal-with-this-asshole look. Jeb looked up towards the heavens.

With the ICU now loaded up, Cal drove to the venue. They walked in and Francesca the promoter was waiting for them. She said, "Hi are you Jeb? I am Francesca."

"Yes, I am, and this is Neusy. If you need anything, either of us can help you. We are looking forward to another great show," said Jeb.

"Yes, it was quite the night last night. I am looking forward to watching it tonight, although I was shocked that you guys wanted four times the money for the second night."

"What?" said Jeb. "The tour is getting the exact same amount. Let me guess, you had to send the difference in a deposit prior to the show."

"Yes, we have the remainder in cash for the two shows for you."

Then both at the same time said, "Fucking Spud."

They laughed and Francesca hugged Jeb. She smelled nice and her smile got his attention. Neusy watched and gave Jeb the go-for-it look. Jeb, while still embracing Francesca, smiled and gave him the way-ahead-of-you look.

"OK, if you need anything, you met the manager yesterday. He will be around all evening. I must leave, go home, and shower. I stayed across town yesterday. I had another show, but this was the place to be." She walked away in her tight blue dress and looked over her shoulder at Jeb as she left the room.

"Oh boy, Jebsy… A tall redhead with an ass like that. You better watch yourself."

Jeb adjusted his crotch and walked to the merch booth. Marlon was at it, boxes opened, and the table set up again. "Sorry about the crushed merch yesterday. That Sludge is something."

Jeb said, "Let's be a bit more professional tonight. But waiving the tour cards was a good idea."

The band started soundcheck and Sludge walked in with his band. Marlon sprinted over to him and said, "Dude, you were incredible last night. You're the coolest dude I have ever watched."

"Thanks, my friend! I saw you going nuts last night. I love the energy," said Sludge, and then to Jeb, "That was a career moment for me last night jamming with the Doctor. Next time out let's schedule more shows or a full tour."

"That would be great. Let's see what happens next time out. I will certainly be in touch," said Jeb as Sludge walked away. In his mind he went over a few things. A new booking agent, with Sludge on board, was their chance to get away from that thief Spud Burger. This made him smile.

Neusy saw the smile and said, "You thinking about the redhead for later?"

"No, thinking about dumping that pirate Spud Burger who's stealing money from us left and right. With a Sludge and Doctor tour we can do this. Although Francesca puts a smile on my face, as well." Jeb showed Neusy lots of teeth. Neusy laughed.

"That's great….but I never want to see that again," said Neusy and they both laughed.

Neusy walked to the bar where the manager, Harry, was setting up. He was about to order a couple of beers for him and his touring partner when the soundcheck ended and Hocker shouted, "FUCK YOU! You move it yourself. I am done helping you!"

Jeb turned and was moving when Neusy gave him the I-got-this nod.

"You're getting paid to be our stagehand. Do your job!" said Timmy, the bass player. He then threw a pick at Hocker as Neusy arrived up on stage.

Hocker took a step towards Timmy. Neusy got in front of him and put his hand on Hocker's chest. Hocker stopped and said, "Oh you're lucky Neusy stopped me or off the stage you would have gone. $100 for the night is not worth dealing with his shit. I am only working for the Doctor tonight." Liam walked in through one of the metal detectors and the alarm went off just as Hocker added, "You better be looking all around tonight, I will fuck you up," thinking that he was going to change the amp settings when Timmy was playing. Then to Neusy he said, "That son of a bitch pushed me and said, 'Now go set up my amp and don't change any settings.'"

"Don't sweat it. Like you said, you're not doing that job tonight," said Neusy. He looked at Sludge and added, "Your guys are on their own tonight, we can't have this escalate."

Jeb watched as the scenario unfolded. He did note to himself that at least Liam was more cognizant with what was going on. Sparrow and Crow were nowhere to be seen.

When Neusy came back to the merch table, Jeb said, "That was a good way to deal with him. Your calmness is always an asset. Listen, do me a favor tonight, don't leave Hocker's side. Shadow him as to be his conscience in case he decides to do something stupid."

"You got it. What about stoking the fire if he decides to fuck with the amp while the show is going on?"

"Well…that? Why not…don't encourage him. But if he does decide to do it, that bass player had it coming."

"Time for a beer," said Neusy to Harry, who handed them each a Dragon's Lair Smoked IPA.

"Try this one, boys, it is locally brewed with a hint of spice from habanero pepper extract."

They looked at each other, and with a nod of the head that said why not, they each took a sip. "Wow, that is actually refreshing in a weird way," said Neusy. Jeb agreed and they both took a second sip.

Up in the balcony overhead was Scaggz. He managed to enter again through Top Layer, which had opened right before soundcheck, and made his way down before anyone entered the venue. He was watching the bass player Timmy closely as he applied his spray tan from the travel can he had in his pocket. He walked over to the metal railing and looked at his reflection. The tan was perfect, his hair now colored black. He had gotten a perm and color earlier in the day at a hairdresser near the venue. He shaved his beard as planned, leaving his moustache, which he also colored black. He had his Doctor shirt from the tour last year and wore black cargo pants. He waited up in the balcony until the doors opened, and with people in the venue it would be easier to walk around unnoticed.

Sludge played the identical show from the night before. Marlon was able to control himself and not destroy merchandise on the table. He refrained completely from jumping up on the table. Jeb thought he was under control until Sludge played "My Dog Tannenball." He then grabbed two tour cards and started running through the crowd, bumping into people since there wasn't really any clearance. But once he started going, the audience gave him the space. They parted like the Red Sea. Marlon was running and jumping with a tour card over his head in each hand.

Backstage, Hocker and Neusy were drinking a beer. Hocker said to Neusy, "I know Jeb put you on my ass. I'm kind of glad because I was yelling at that asshole and that inspector was watching. But I will tell you, I am going to turn up his amp. I am going to max out the fucking thing. Hope it blows. I think that is what he was so worried about."

"OK, big guy, just take it easy up there. Don't get into a fight with him. The last thing we need is you going to jail up here in Canada."

"You got it," said Hocker, and he left the room with Neusy following him.

Sparrow and Crow were in the corridor backstage looking at a video of some tropical beach with nude sunbathers when Neusy said to them, "Hocker is going to play a prank on the bass player." The agents looked up and followed immediately. They had only heard about road pranks and now they had their chance to participate in one. Although this was more of a vicious message Hocker was sending.

Behind the bass amp up on its speaker cabinet, Hocker reached around and turned the volume knob until it stopped. The bass was loud. It reverberated in the bass drum, causing a buzzing sound. Sludge looked over and could see Timmy playing with the knobs just as the bass cut out and smoke started rising from the amp. Hocker, with a smile on his face, stood there. Timmy was unplugging and plugging cables. Nothing worked. The emptiness of the missing bass killed the song and Sludge stopped playing. He announced, "Looks like we have a little trouble. We will get it fixed and start again."

Scaggz used this time to slip backstage while no one was watching once again. He found Sludge's green room with the large Sludge logo printed on paper hanging on the door. He walked in and took off his backpack. He looked around the room. He saw the food spread and helped himself to celery and dip. There was an ice bin with cold drinks in the ice and some beer. A small refrigerator was next to it. He opened the door. "Ha, they make it too easy for me." He pulled out the six pack of beer with a note on the front that said, *Timmy's beer do not touch.*

Scaggz opened his backpack and pulled out three vials of rat poison concentrate that he had made himself to keep rats away from his camp sites. Each vial of poison would last him weeks. He really had no idea what it would do to a human, but that's the fun of it all. The poison was made of concentrated bleach, ammonia, and snake venom that he himself extracted from venomous snakes in the different areas where he had camped. Today's special had snake venom from the Mojave Rattlesnake and the Western Diamondback. He would bait the rats by putting a couple of drops on leftover food. The poison was so toxic that it would kill the rats within minutes by causing their bodies to bloat and choke off their breathing.

He then pulled out a bottle capper that he purchased at a home brew shop in Montreal. The capper had two handles that, when pushed down, caused the crimped part of the cap to wrap around the top of the bottle. Scaggz carefully removed all the caps of the six bottles. He poured out a little beer then poured half a vial of the poison in each. Carefully, he placed the caps back on the bottles and used the capper to secure them around the top.

Scaggz exited the green room as Timmy plugged his bass in Heinz's bass amp and Sludge again started playing his last song. Timmy looked over at Hocker and was screaming, but with the music he could not be heard. Hocker gave him the middle finger, then he and his entourage went backstage again. As Scaggz passed the agents, he snapped a selfie with them and said, "What are the Blues Bothers doing here?" No one recognized him as he walked away.

During intermission, Francesca was at the merch booth talking to Jeb. She was all made up, wearing a pink top and jeans. Her red hair was up in a bun. Marlon was watching Jeb and talking to fans. "What I can really use is a beer, does anyone here want to get me a beer? I will let you take a picture with me. The Doctor's merch dude."

Jeb smiled at Francesca and she said, "Is your partner there always that outgoing and forthright?"

"Yes, he is starting to come out of his shell. You look very nice."

"Awe, thank you, Jeb. You look…well, the same as before, but very handsome. I love your hair. You had it up earlier; I didn't realize it was that long. It's quite sexy," she said as she ran her fingers through it.

"Wow," said Jeb. "Talk about being forthright. But please, don't stop. I'm getting aroused."

"That's OK…because I am too," said Francesca just as she stopped. "Later, when you have time, I have a forty-year-old bottle of port wine from Portugal that was given to me last year by the manager of the Portuguese band Galinha Gritando. Let's share a glass."

"That sounds good to me. Once the Doctor is on stage and going for a while, I usually have time as nothing needs to be done and all positions seem to be handled." Jeb looked at Marlon; happy that he was on the tour so he could break away. "Galinha Gritando…that's a band, huh? What is the translation?"

"Screaming chicken," she said, and kissed Jeb on the cheek. "I have to go and get some work done. Look for me in the office later."

"Whooohooo. Jeb you are lucky," said Marlon. "I want to get that kind of action as well."

There was more shouting on stage. "You are a fucking idiot," Timmy yelled at Hocker. Hocker just looked at him and laughed. "Now guess what, shithead? I don't need that amp, it was a rental and we have other equipment in Europe. So I don't give a shit. Have fun moving it. I am going to drink a beer." He flung another pick at Hocker.

Neusy, who was tending to Tommy's drums, walked over to calm Hocker. But Hocker was calm. "Don't worry, Neusy, I will gladly move that with the embarrassment that guy had to go through. It was beautiful to watch."

Liam watched the entire Sludge set from up front and now made his way back to the merch table. There were several women at the bar that came over and wanted to talk with Liam. Jeb raised his eyebrows and Liam said, "Yeah, that happens everywhere I go. I was watching up there. Quite interesting what your man Hocker did. He worries me a little. How long has he been with you?"

"He has been with us for years…I think this is our fourth tour together. He is harmless. A loud bark, as they say."

"Well, we will see." Liam turned to the half dozen women who were younger than most fans at a Doctor show.

Jeb liked the idea of playing with Sludge, it brought in younger people. Widened the audience for the Doctor.

"Ladies, let's go over to the bar." Then he winked at Jeb.

"Whew," said Jeb to Marlon. "I'm glad that is over. Maybe we leave Hocker home if we tour with Sludge next year."

"The Doctor and Sludge?" Marlon could not stand still. "I am in. Damn, that would be amazing. I bet I could get laid on that tour." Then, in a louder voice to the fans around the table, "OK, I am out of beer."

The Doctor opened his set with a couple of songs from his post-Centipedes band, Darkened Moon. First was "Arctic Shock," followed by "From Puddle to Pond." Sludge stood on the side of the stage, filming the show with his phone. Two nights in a row with the Doctor. This was his idol growing up, and now he was standing twenty feet from him, watching every note.

"Yah, you like Darkened Moon songs, yah?" said the Doctor. "Well, I am not going to play one now. But later, perhaps. Now we will play 'Bottom of the River.' This is a classic from the Centipedes."

The show was going well. Jeb went backstage to check on everything and to make sure things there were going well so that he could steal a little time with Francesca. He managed to make his way slowly through the crowd. He entered the backstage area.

Timmy was pacing the hallway chugging a beer. He threw the empty bottle in the trash can, disappeared into the green room, and emerged with a fresh brew. "These are mine," he said out loud. Then he slammed another beer and again retrieved another.

Neusy approached Jeb and said, "All under control back here. Timmy seems content with getting drunk. I think Sludge made him talk to Hocker. But he said he was going through a tough time. I guess his wife left him for Sludge's last bass player."

"Yikes!"

"Yeah, I know. Hocker is out there and Timmy back here, so I think we are over the hump with that situation. Half a show remaining, then we are out of here."

"OK great, I am going to go spend a little private time with that Francesca. She invited me into the office for a drink."

"Yeah, buddy…have fun," said Neusy.

Jeb entered the office, but Francesca was not there. She had put the bottle of port on the desk. Jeb walked around the room. There were souvenirs and posters from many of the acts that had played Under Layers in the past. He admired it all. He found himself walking up the stairs to Top Layer to see what it was like. At the top of the steps, he was in another office. He walked through the doors and was behind the bar. When the bartender looked at him, he said, "Sorry, I am with the band playing downstairs. I am just taking a break and wanted to check this out."

"Sure, can I get you something to drink? You can sit at the bar, just walk around there."

"Sure, I'll take the house beer. The spicy one. The Dragon's one." She handed him a beer and he watched the karaoke. There was a man in drag singing "It's Raining Men." Jeb watched and the people seated at the tables were singing along. What a great vibe, he thought. The song ended and the man in drag seated himself back at the bar and a woman, or was it a man? Jeb could not tell, but this person started singing the Doobie Brother's song "Jesus is Just Alright."

Great upbeat song. Jeb finished his beer in record time and was hoping Francesca was back in her office. He stood and asked the bartender, "Is it OK I go back down through the office?"

"Of course, just walk around the end there and come back here."

Jeb walked around the bar and a man wearing a white sleeveless T-shirt stopped him. He put his hand on Jeb's chest. Jeb looked up in surprise at what this man was doing. The man said, "Come with me."

"Huh?"

"Yes, you, come with me." He grabbed Jeb's shoulder and was pulling Jeb with him. "I have money, it will be alright."

Jeb punched the man as hard as he could in his shoulder and said, "Get the fuck away from me." He walked around the bar and through the doors and down the steps.

Francesca was in the office behind the desk. "Wow, you were upstairs? I'm glad you came back down here, sexy."

"Yeah, it's quite the room up there."

"It is colorful, for sure."

"I got propositioned by this guy."

"Awe, that's because you are so handsome." Francesca opened the bottle of port wine, poured two glasses, and walked around in front of her desk. "Let's sit on the couch."

Jeb followed as instructed.

They sat and took a sip of their wine. Francesca said, "I wanted to kiss you from the second I saw you this afternoon."

Jeb put down his glass and took Francesca's, placing it as well on the table in front of them.

She moved over and they embraced, kissing softly. Jeb could smell her perfume. The scent filled his nose, and he was lost in the moment.

Outside on the stage he could hear the Doctor say, "Yah, und now it is that time again. Sludge will come out and jam with me. Sludge, where are you? Oh, I see, you are here already. We will play 'Slap the Virgin'." The crowd screamed, the Doctor played, and Sludge joined in. Neusy was on the stage to the side with Hocker when Timmy came stumbling past them.

"Fucking drunk," said Hocker.

Timmy was clenching his throat and started to spin in circles.

Neusy said, "There's something wrong with him."

Timmy, out in the middle of the stage, dropped to his knees. The Doctor stopped playing and the band followed. Timmy stood up again, then spun around and just stopped. He fell over backwards with his head catching the end of the drum riser with a THUD.

Sparrow and Crow were looking at videos backstage of beaches they wanted to visit after the tour, unaware of what was happening on stage. "A shorter set tonight," Agent Crow said as he heard the music stop.

Liam made his way to the stage. He had his flashlight out and shining it into people's eyes so they would move apart for him. He walked up on stage and over to Timmy. He felt for a pulse, but there was none. "He's dead," said Liam. He was scanning the area. He looked over at Hocker and said, "We are going to talk." Behind Hocker off the side of the stage, he saw movement.

Scaggz stopped and looked over; Liam was looking right at him. Liam did not recognize the dark-skinned man but did recognize his eyes. He never forgets a person's eyes. It was the man wearing the kilt the night before. But why was his skin darkened? Liam stood up and said, "I need to talk with you as well."

Scaggz moved quickly, close to the wall where there were not as many people. Liam jumped off the stage. Scaggz started running, pushing people out of his way. Liam made his way over to the wall as Scaggz disappeared through the double doors into the office. Jeb and Francesca were now lying on the couch. They jumped up when the door slammed open. Jeb was only in his underwear and Francesca was covering her breasts, but still had her jeans on.

Scaggz looked at them, then ran up the steps to the Top Layer's office. The door opened again with a loud slam. Liam looked at the two half naked people and said, "Did he go up there?"

"Yes," said Jeb as Francesca screamed.

At the top of the steps, Scaggz looked around the room. Mounted on the far wall was a ladder with a sign that said *Roof Access*. Scaggz was turning the knob on the hatch to the roof when Liam entered the room. At the same time Liam saw him, Scaggz disappeared through the open hatch. Liam climbed the ladder and climbed out onto the roof. Scaggz was trapped at the corner of the roof, no other building reachable if he jumped.

Liam slowly walked towards Scaggz. "I need to talk to you about that man lying on the stage." Liam got closer.

Scaggz looked down. It was too high to jump. He was cornered. He had a vial left in his backpack but did not know if he could reach in and be able to throw it at the inspector. If it got into his eyes or mouth, that would do it. Scaggz reached around, and as Liam approached, jumped over the side of the building. Liam ran to the edge in time to see Scaggz slide to the ground down the water drainpipe and look up. Unsure how he was able to do this, Liam decided not to try.

Inside, the room was in a shutdown. The Mounties had it locked down. The agents were on the stage inquiring what had happened when Liam climbed back up. He approached Hocker and said, "What can you tell me about that guy I just chased."

Jeb and Francesca were coming out of the office. Jeb looked up on the stage and saw that someone was down with his head on the drum riser. He approached the stage with Francesca holding his hand.

Hocker was saying, "Nothing, I've never seen him. Hey, I was standing here the entire time. I had nothing to do with that. That guy was an asshole. I didn't like him, but I didn't do anything."

Neusy said, "I was with him almost the entire time, and when I was not with him, I was backstage and Timmy there was back there at the same time."

Jeb, up on the stage now with Francesca terrified holding his arm, said, "I had Neusy stay with Hocker in case. To make sure he wouldn't do anything stupid, and just in case something did happen that we had eyes on him the entire time since you heard him make the threat earlier."

"Thanks, really? You wanted eyes on me?" said Hocker.

"Just be happy that I did. He is OK, isn't he? I mean, how could he have done anything? Neusy was with him," said Jeb.

Neusy gave him a downward nod. Jeb looked down and zippered his jeans.

"Well," said Liam. "I know you will be in Toronto tomorrow as you have a show there in a couple of nights. I will see you there. I know that guy I chased had something to do with this. His eyes were the same as someone I saw yesterday. I never forget a pair of eyes. Everybody is free to go. Do you have a small copier?" he said to Francesca, who just nodded while looking at the dead bass player on the stage. "OK, please get it and bring it to the front doors." He then stepped up to the mic and announced, "You all may leave. The remainder of the show is canceled. Have your ID or driver's license out when you leave, and we will make a copy."

Sludge pulled the forward brim down over his eyes. He sat next to his fallen bass player and said, "Right when I was jamming with the Doctor. Timmy, your timing always sucked, but I will miss you."

Heinz stepped behind his bass amp and sent a text. *Johnny, the inspector recognized you from yesterday, he knows you were in different disguises, but he is still in the venue. You are OK. Maybe you should not go to Toronto.*

The show must go on. I have a plan.

Chapter 31

The tour spent the night in Montreal. They all slept on the bus. Jeb bought another night at a hotel for Cal and decided that it would be best to leave in the morning as opposed to after the show as was scheduled. With a day off in Toronto prior to the show, it did not cause any delays in travel.

Cal got the bus to Toronto without any issues. No one seemed to want to stop for the entire drive. The mood was somber on the bus after the death of Sludge's bass player. Everyone but Hocker and Marlon were silent. Hocker, because he disliked Timmy immensely, and Marlon was just in awe as a newfound fan of Sludge.

Neusy and Jeb were sitting up front on the journey, the two making an outline for their second book of tour stories and working on the schedule for the next few days. "I'm not sure if the Doctor will ever be granted another visa to play the US if this nonsense does not stop," said Jeb.

"This Inspector Liam seems to have his shit together. He did discover that the guy in the kilt fucking with the cables the first night was the same as the dark-skinned guy that he chased out of the building. That on its own is amazing as the two looked nothing alike," replied Neusy.

"Yeah, it makes me wonder how many times this guy was right under our noses, and we just didn't know. If you think about all the people we meet."

Marlon, sitting near, added, "That guy in the kilt bought me a beer. Man, I hope the Doctor can tour again next year.

Do you think it will be with Sludge? That sucks his bass player got killed like that. Sludge is amazing, wow, a whole tour with him and the Doctor."

"That bass player was a pretty big dick, that's all I have to say on the subject," said Hocker.

"See, he is purposely getting right in next to us. He is either just fucking with us or he uses it to get info on our schedules. It's funny he knows where we always are," said Jeb.

Neusy was staring out the window watching the scenery whisk by. There were lots of trees and a lake in the distance. Letting his mind go and processing his thoughts, he said, "You know, what you said a moment ago, that with all the people that we meet? How many times has this guy talked to us? It could be anybody. He was in the kilt the night before. I think he had long blonde hair…I remember a beard. Then yesterday he had dark skin…dark hair but no beard. With all the people that we don't know and just meet, how do we know anyone is really who they say? Think about it, last tour he played in that band, remember? He sent the agents that message on their beer bottles. Right there, two nights right under our noses. He is constantly changing looks… Do you know who else had dark skin but a dark beard as well?"

"Jeetu," said Jeb. "But you don't think that was possible that he was with us the whole time in India?"

"I am just saying there is that possibility."

The Doctor entered the front lounge looking for something to eat. He opened the cabinets and found nothing. "Achh, why do we not have anything for me to eat?" He opened the refrigerator and found a bag with two hard boiled eggs. He put an entire egg in his mouth, and after swallowing it, said, "Yah, this is very good that Sludge wants to tour with us next year."

"At this point I'm not sure," said Jeb. "He said that before his bass player got murdered on your tour."

"You see, Jeb, this is where you must contact him after the tour." He went to put the second egg in his mouth, but it dropped to the floor. He picked it up, ran water over it in the sink, and said, "He did say that he wanted to tour, so it is your job to see we do this. We would play to larger crowds. Why is it you look at me like that? I bet you would have thrown that egg in the trash, yah?"

"Do you realize how disgusting this bus floor is? Do you know what is on that floor? Every men's room from every place we go, a little comes back in here on our shoes."

"Yah, you Americans like to waste food. I am going back to sleep."

After the six-hour bus ride, they arrived in Toronto. The mood picked up slightly. The Doctor was looking forward to playing in Ocean's Blue Sea Cave. The new venue opened a year ago and already was an internationally acclaimed venue. It was the new hot spot in Toronto. Previously on the spot was a small local bar called Ocean's Blue. It was a local spot for blues music. When the owner died, his children, with investors, decided the land was more valuable than the actual business and that they would do something grand, and that's exactly what they did.

Ocean's Blue Sea Cave was now known all around the world as the club to go to in Toronto. The interior of the 6,500-square-foot club was something to be seen. During the day it was a seafood restaurant, and after 9:00 pm it became a dance club and concert venue. The original Ocean's Blue still existed in the rear of the newly constructed club. They were able to build the new structure around the old building, keeping the smaller intimate room for local bands while larger bands or dancing was going on in the main club.

The entrance to the club, once the gate was opened, looked like the opening to an ocean cave. Inside, it felt as if one was in a cave. The floors were a brilliant blue that mimicked water. The way that light illuminated the floor from underneath made it appear to ripple. The walls and the ceiling were made of artificial rock of all different heights and thicknesses. In the walls all around the club were large fish tanks that contained all sorts of different saltwater fish in all sizes. The bar in the center of the club was triangular and designed like a coral reef, with more fish tanks all about that included live coral in them.

The Doctor had seen pictures and videos online and this was certainly another highlight of the tour. He instructed Jeb to make sure that a lot of pictures were taken so that they could use on their website. Spud Burger did good, getting them booked in Ocean's Blue Sea Cave.

Cal parked the bus at the hotel where they would spend the night. He said, "Whooohoo, we are here, boys, let's think positive. I may even come down to the show tomorrow. I want to check out the club."

Jeb booked three rooms, one for Cal to sleep and the other two for the band and crew to use as shower rooms. Cal walked off the bus to check into his room and rest while the other occupants waited for Jeb to bring keys back so they could begin to use the rooms to shower. Most would use the rooms in the morning and spend the day exploring Toronto. Once Jeb brought the keys back to the bus, he said, "Make sure when you are done with the room that you put the key back here on the table so it's available for the next person." Then he walked off the bus and Neusy joined him. The two would spend the day away from the tour and the needy people involved, enjoying their day off. They decided that they would visit the Hockey Hall of Fame and then go to have some beers and dinner. They both were looking forward to dinner at a brewery called Blades, which was owned by an ex pro hockey player.

About an hour after they left the bus, Marlon realized that the only one remaining on the bus was Hocker who noticed the puzzled look on Marlon's face and informed him, "They went off to the hall of fame and dinner."

"That's weird, why didn't they ask me? I would have gone."

"Those two are like that sometimes, on an off day they disappear. I don't care, I just want to chill and sleep. They want their alone time so fuck them."

"Now I don't have anything to do," said Marlon, and he walked off the bus. He took out his phone and opened his marijuana dispensary app called Budz. He located two nearby and decided to explore what they had to offer.

After filling his pockets with various products consisting of pre-rolled joints, loose marijuana, and a couple of gummy edibles, he walked the streets of Toronto and soon came upon a brewery that advertised food. He smoked one of the joints and entered Blades Brewery. He recalled hearing Jeb and Neusy mentioning it on the bus ride into town. He sat at the bar and ordered a beer while admiring the large, curved bar brightly lit by LED lights that changed colors. Not realizing it was a hockey stick that changed colors representing all the NHL teams, he became engrossed with his phone, not looking at anyone.

After the Hockey Hall of Fame, Jeb and Neusy arrived at Blades. They took seats at the opposite side of the bar from where Marlon was seated, not seeing him with his head down looking at his phone. Behind the bar was the brewery, they watched the brewers clean the tanks. Blades was starting to fill up for happy hour. After ten minutes, they were finally asked what they would like to drink.

Jeb said, "I almost died of thirst I waited so long. But I'll take the Zamboni Spiked Tire Red Lager."

"And I will have the Goal Post Amber," said Neusy.

After another five minutes they received their beer. Marlon noticed them sitting at the bar and walked over. "You guys left me on the bus and now you're ignoring me in here?"

"We didn't even see you here. What are you doing here?" asked Neusy.

"I was walking around and saw this place."

Jeb stood up and said, "Let's move to the table behind us." The three of them quickly sat at the table. Jeb and Neusy looked at the menu and five minutes later were approached by a server and asked what they wanted to eat. They both ordered cheeseburgers while Marlon declined any food and continued to look at his phone.

"What's wrong, Marlon," asked Neusy.

"I miss my kids. My daughter sent me a text telling me how much she misses me."

"You should eat," said Jeb.

"I'm not hungry."

"Look at all the women in here. This place is great," said Jeb. "We should get some of these ladies to sit with us."

"Yeah, let's go for it, look at those two that just walked in," added Neusy.

"I'm not in the mood," said Marlon.

The women were approaching the bar, and as they walked past the table, Neusy said, "Ladies, there are no seats at the bar, but we have three right here for you. Why don't you join us?"

While they were not beautiful and slightly overweight, there was something nice about the way they carried themselves. "Hi, I am Julie," said the first woman, who pulled out a chair and sat down. She had bright blue eyes and brown hair. She wore just enough makeup to highlight a pretty face. "This is my childhood friend, Maddy. We grew up together in Montreal, then I moved here. She comes and visits every six months."

"It's nice to meet you. I am Neusy, that is Jeb, and the one over there not paying attention is Marlon."

"Nice to meet you ladies," said Jeb. Their food arrived and Jeb ordered a round of beers for the table and shots of

Canadian whiskey all around. "Help yourselves to some fries. Marlon, you too, you should eat."

"No, I'm fine," said Marlon as he buried his face in his hands.

"Awe, what's wrong with him?" said Maddy as she put her hand on his shoulder.

"He's in a bad mood. I don't know what's going on. We're on a rock tour and have been living on a bus. I think he is just tired," said Neusy.

"Oooh, a rock tour?" said Julie. "Do I know the band?"

"His name is Jurgen Weislangwolf. He used to play with the Centipedes," said Jeb, but he knew that the name did not mean anything to these young ladies.

"I don't know him," said Julie. "You ever hear of him, Maddy?"

Jeb gave Neusy the I-knew-that-was-coming look. Neusy replied with a nod, signaling what did you expect with younger women.

"No, but Marlon, tell me about him."

Marlon kept looking at his phone, not engaged with what was going on at the table. He said, "Look, here are my kids. My daughter just texted me a while ago telling me how much she misses me."

"Awe," said Maddy.

The beers and shots arrived. Neusy said, "Marlon, wake up, let's do this." They all lifted their shots, touched glasses, and downed the whiskey. "Can we get another round of those?" Neusy said to the server. She indicated she would bring them in a couple of minutes.

"That's nasty," said Marlon. "Why did you make me do that?"

"Because you need it," said Neusy. He took a sip of his beer, and it was half gone. "We should get another round of these as well."

Jeb agreed. "Yes, we should. That burger was good. Marlon, I am telling you that you should eat, or you will get fucked up."

"I am not hungry. I'll have another beer. Can you bring us all another round of beers?" Marlon said to the server when she brought the round of shots. Maddy was whispering something in his ear that no one else could hear. Marlon shook his head and sipped his beer.

"OK," said Julie. "Whoohoo, let's do this shot."

They all held up their glasses and once again downed their shots of whiskey.

"Awe, that is good."

"Yeah, it's good," said Neusy. "Are you starting to feel better, Marlon?"

"I have to go to the bathroom," said Marlon and he left the table.

Julie motioned to Marlon walking away. "is he always that much fun?"

"No, usually we can't get him to stop talking," said Jeb, and then to Maddy, "Where are you going?"

"That beer is going right through me; I need to go to the ladies' room."

"OK, I'll go with you." The ladies stood up and were gone.

"That was interesting," said Neusy. "Let's get one more beer. I want to try the Shoot the Puck Stout."

Jeb nodded and Neusy ordered the beers. When they arrived, they were in a glass that had a small hockey puck on the side of the glass that was sitting in an indent in the glass making it appear as if the puck was going through the glass. "This also is interesting. Cheers."

They sipped their stouts as Julie came back to the table. "Where is Maddy?" asked Jeb.

"She is still in the bathroom. When she gets back, we need to go. We have reservations at the Italian restaurant around the corner."

"OK, we probably should get back to the bus soon. We have to work again tomorrow," said Neusy.

Twenty minutes later, they were still sitting at the table. Neither Marlon nor Maddy had returned.

"I wonder where they went?" said Jeb. He took a sip of his beer and Marlon appeared. "Where have you been?"

Marlon, grinning with a smile he could not keep down, said, "Dude, I was in the bathroom."

Five minutes later Maddy came back. She said to Julie, "Ready?"

"Yes, we have to go, guys." Maddy leaned over and whispered once again in Marlon's ear.

When the ladies left the table, Marlon said, "Oh my god. That was amazing. Nothing like that has ever happened to me. Dude, I walked out of the men's room, and she was waiting for me. She pulled me into the ladies' room, and we went into the stall. I had her up on the baby changing table. Shit, I can't believe that."

"Sir, please stand up," said a voice from behind Marlon. The officer had his hand on Marlon's back and said, "Put your hands behind your back. You are being arrested. We received a complaint from the manager here saying that you were in the ladies' room having sex."

"But…but…that woman was in there, where did she go?"

"The manager only pointed you out. He said there was a woman, but she left. You must come with us," said the officer, and he and another officer walked Marlon out of the restaurant.

Chapter 32

The next morning the Doctor was rummaging once again for food. "Yah, always no food for me," he said as he opened the refrigerator door a second time. "Ah look, we have ranch dressing." He took out the ranch and found someone's leftover salad. "Yah, you looking at me again. You Americans waste food. I will eat this salad." He squeezed a large amount of ranch on the salad, though Jeb was sure there was dressing already on the salad. "So, Jeb, tell me what is happening with Marlon."

"He was caught at a brewery yesterday having sex in the bathroom and got arrested."

"Yah, that is so disgusting. I will have a talk with him."

"The good news is that this club is open for lunch so we can load in early and tend to Marlon after," said Jeb.

"Yah, I want to look at the venue. Remember to take the pictures."

"Yes, I will have Marlon take some pictures."

"Ha, if he gets out of jail," said the Doctor. "I want Neusy to take these pictures."

"OK," said Neusy. "No problem."

Torsten and Nathan came out of the sleeping area and Torsten announced, "Yah, I will go use the shower now."

"Me as well," said Nathan.

"Together?" asked Jeb.

"You're always funny," said Torsten. "Only if you join us. Are there not two rooms?"

"Yes, of course," said Jeb.

"Your humor is not that funny," said the Doctor, and he went back to his room.

At noon, Cal started the bus and asked, "Are we ready, are we a bus?"

"As much as a bus as we will be. We're just going to load in. Sorry to get you out here early, but Marlon got arrested so we need to take care of that later."

"Not a problem. I will bring the bus back to the hotel after and the boys can finish showering. The little guy is in jail? What did he do?" He put the bus in gear, and they drove the block and a half to the venue.

"Sex in a bathroom of a brewery."

"Men's room sex? I hope not," said Cal.

"Crabs, no…god, some chick he just met. It was in the ladies' room."

"Right on, the little guy scored!"

Jeb, Neusy, Hocker, and the Doctor walked inside the venue. "Wow, this place is incredible," said the Doctor while he watched some large fish swim past him in one of the tanks.

"Hello, I am Justin, I guess you guys are with the band playing tonight? You're a little early."

"Justin, I am Jeb, we emailed each other. Yeah, sorry, we were parked up the street all night and were hoping we can load in early, figuring you guys are open for lunch."

"This is the nicest place we are playing on the tour; I love all these fishies," said the Doctor.

"OK, do we load in that door back there?"

"Oh, no," said Justin, "you are not booked in this room. We have dancing in here tonight. One of our biggest nights all week. You guys are booked into the original Ocean's Blue. The entrance is on the side of the building. I'll open it up for you. Some Inspector Liam said he wanted to get in there early, too. He said he has a metal detector being delivered."

"What?" said the Doctor. "We will not play in here?"

"No, sir, follow me. I'll show you where you load in."

They followed Justin through the back door into the original club. He turned on the lights and illuminated what was one of the dirtiest venues they have ever seen. The small stage up front was covered with what looked like parts for a lighting system. "I'll have that moved off the stage. We keep spare parts for the main stage up there on that stage."

The bar was short and had seashells embedded in the surface. As they walked on the carpet near the bar, their feet were sticking to it.

"Fucking disgusting place," said Hocker.

The bar appeared to have just been shut down the day before without cleaning. There were rings remaining on the bar from whatever was served before they closed. There were a few tables scattered around that had the same patina as the bar. Half the lights hanging from the ceiling were not working and the stage looked like there was no real PA system, just a couple of small speakers on stands mounted on either side of the stage.

The Doctor looked around and said, "Yah, I will not perform in here. Cancel the show," and he walked out.

Jeb ran out after him.

"Why are we in that small room, Jeb?"

"I don't know, but you probably would not fill the big room. They have that dance thing tonight, is why."

"Why does Spud do this? You tell him never book a room like this again. I will not play."

"Look, it's just one night. Just play the show, play a shorter set or whatever just to get through. Yes, it sucks, but we play the show and collect the money. It's a decent paying gig. It would be worse if we leave and don't get paid."

"Yah, I don't like it, but this makes sense… I will play the gig. But you tell Spud that any other shows like this I will not play."

"OK," said Jeb.

A dark SUV entered the parking lot at a faster-than-safe speed. It stopped right next to where Jeb was standing. The driver's window opened and smiling, Liam said, "Did you guys lose something last night?"

Jeb looked at him confused as nothing was lost. The passenger door opened, and Marlon jumped out. "Dude, that was the best night of my life."

"Lucky for you guys, I have friends everywhere. My buddy on the force called me after your guy kept talking about the tour. I went down there, and we went over to the brewery and sorted it all out with the manager. No charges, your boy got lucky twice. He spent the night in my hotel room."

"Guys, best night of my life. I never did anything like that before. In the bathroom, in the stall. It was insane. Then Liam let me stay in his suite—it wasn't a room; it was bigger than my apartment. I had my own room, and then he had these women come in and we got massages. It was totally sick."

Jeb looked at Liam and said, "Thank you, I guess. We, or at least Marlon owes you one. You're in a suite? Lucky you, we are stuck on the bus."

"Well, being freelance has its advantages. The pay is much better; if you know what I mean," said Liam, winking at Jeb. "By the way, snake venom killed Sludge's bass player. It was in his beer. He finished five, but we had the last one tested."

"Great," said Jeb sarcastically.

They all walked inside. Liam said as they entered, "I am expecting another metal detector; look out for the delivery guys for me."

"You got it," said Marlon. "What an awesome night, thanks!"

Cal drove the bus around to where the smaller club had an area to load in. He spotted Jeb and said, "Not all that exciting back here, but shit, up front that place is insane. After I nap, I am going to check out the club. I bet there is going to be all sorts of women there tonight."

Tommy walked off the bus and into the venue, his eyes still not all the way open. He looked around, squinting, and then said, "I thought tonight was that fancy club, what are we doing here in this piece of shit?"

"It's this shit hole tonight," said Hocker. Tommy turned around and went back out to the bus for more sleep.

They loaded all in and could not set up the stage. The bus rolled back to the hotel with the crew waiting for the stage to be emptied off so they could begin set up. So much for the early load in.

Chapter 33

Heinz grabbed the key off the front table of the bus and headed to the hotel room's shower. He stopped at the hotel front desk and asked if there was a message. Scaggz said if anything came up, he would leave a message for his brother at the front desk of the hotel. Scaggz decided that using the phone to text should only be a last resort moving forward. He told his brother not to send texts anymore unless necessary. The Inspector was smart, and he didn't want to make any mistakes with him watching.

Relieved that Scaggz was doing OK, he went to the room to shower. When he finished, he reached for his towel, which was not there. He opened the shower curtain, and sitting on the counter was Scaggz, still dark skinned with the dye only a couple days old, holding the towel. He threw it at his brother.

"What the hell are you doing in here? You scared the shit out of me."

"I have some things for you. It was too close the other night. That inspector almost caught me, and with my skin like this, I can't be seen till this crap wears off. Does he have any idea who it might be that he chased?"

"No, not at all, just that it was the same guy from the night before that was wearing the kilt."

"Whew," said Scaggz, "that is good. I have a good plan to hopefully send him away. At least for a while. I will find a guy outside the venue, before the doors open. I will leave you a message on the back of the trailer. Somehow, I will put one of the empty vials I have in his pocket, make it look like he was carrying it."

Heinz was drying himself with the towel as Scaggz continued. "Jimmy, in this bag here is the blonde wig. Put it on. If he is drinking a beer, knock it out of his hand. Then apologize and buy him a new beer, dropping the contents of this full vial into his beer. I am hoping that the inspector finds the empty vial and figures he somehow accidentally poisoned himself."

"That sounds like a long shot. What if he's not drinking a beer?"

"Then buy two, start drinking one, and put the venom in the other. Walk up to him and tell him that you can't find your friend who you bought the beer for. Give it to him and make something up."

"I don't know, this doesn't sound like the best plan."

"I promise you I will only do this if I find the perfect guy, otherwise we move on to the next show. OK, Jimmy?"

Heinz looked into the bag and took out the wig. He then put it back in the bag with the small vial of venom. "OK, anything that does not look right, we abort."

Scaggz smiled and said, "OK great, it's a deal. Look for a note at the back of the trailer." Scaggz then walked out the same way he entered and climbed down from the balcony.

"First Marlon with Sludge, and now it looks like Marlon has a crush on the inspector," said Neusy. The stage was finally cleared; he and Hocker were setting up the equipment.

Hocker looked over at Marlon, who was helping Liam position the metal detector inside the door. Marlon could not stand still. He was excited to be around his new role model. "Ha, yeah, look at him. Well, he better start helping out over here soon. I don't think Jeb will be too happy. Hand me that cable there."

"Here you go. Jeb is fine. Liam helped us out with getting Marlon out of trouble yesterday. Marlon is growing. Remember last year? He was a bit of a pussy."

"He still is a pussy, but one who got arrested for fucking in a bathroom."

The Austrians walked in. Torsten said, "Where are the fish tanks? This place looks different online."

"We got fucked," said Hocker. "Go look inside the other room. It's a nice place, but they got us back here in the shit hole."

They walked around through the connecting door and ten minutes later returned. "Yah, that is nice," said Torsten. "I hope the Doctor knows we are playing in this room. Are we ready for soundcheck?"

Neusy said, "He knows and all is OK, Jeb fixed it with him. We are just about ready. Tommy was adjusting his drum kit, which Hocker set up incorrectly."

Outside, Scaggz was walking around the venue and came across a couple dozen people waiting in a line for the ticket window to open. Scaggz had purchased a pair of tickets the day before as he developed his plan. He walked from the front of the line to the back twice and no one fit his model needed for the plan to work. He stood at the back of the line when a voice behind him said, "Is this the line to purchase tickets for the Doctor's show?"

Scaggz turned around and he was looking right into the eyes of someone that could almost be his twin, as far as height and eye color. "I am not sure. I think it might be for entrance to the show. I just came out early because I wanted to hear the soundcheck. I am a huge fan," said Scaggz.

"Cool, me too. I love the Doctor. I missed him last year because the tour was canceled. I am just happy they made it to Toronto. I wanted to hear soundcheck as well."

"You don't have a ticket?"

"No, I was going to buy it at the door."

"You're in luck, I have an extra." Scaggz pulled the pair of tickets out of his pocket.

"Awesome, how much?"

"Ah, you can just have it, otherwise it would go to waste."

"Thanks," said the stranger. He took off his backpack and put the ticket inside the small pouch on the side. "I have a bunch of things that I want him to sign. Some CDs and an old tour program that I brought."

"That's cool, can I see?" The stranger opened the main compartment of the backpack and pulled out the tour program. Scaggz took it and flipped the pages. "I haven't seen this in years. It's from the Centipede days."

The stranger was proud of his souvenir. "Yeah, I had it all these years and now it will be perfect with the Doctor's signature on the cover."

Scaggz put the program into the man's backpack, and as he did, he dropped the empty vial in with it. He then grabbed the backpack and said, "Here, let me help you put it back on." The man turned around and Scaggz put it back over his arms. He then said, "I have to go take a piss, can you hold my spot?"

"Sure, bro."

Scaggz walked past him and said, "Thanks," as he patted the backpack in a gesture of thanks. Unbeknownst to the stranger was that Scaggz used that distraction to drop the near-empty bottle of Tanover also into his backpack.

Soundcheck ended and the doors opened. The stranger looked around for his new friend, but he was nowhere to be seen.

The band was back on the bus, resting with soundcheck over and the doors open. There was an opening band scheduled to play, but when they showed up and found out that they were not playing in the main venue, they went home.

"No opening band tonight, Heinz," said Neusy, walking around the bus to go back inside the venue. Jimmy, behind the trailer, jumped back, taking the note his brother left him. He read the note and it described the stranger. Jimmy nervously went back inside the venue. It was filling up and hard to see with the limited lighting. He finally found the person that his brother had described—same height, similar hair to his brother, tucked up under a beanie. Perfect. He was standing by himself, and he was actually drinking a beer. Scaggz's plan may work.

Jimmy went into the men's room and put on the wig. He walked out but the stranger was not where he had been; he spotted him ordering another beer. Jimmy walked rapidly to where the stranger was paying for his beer, and when he turned around, Jimmy swiped his hand and knocked the beer out of his hands. "Oh, I am so sorry," he said to the stranger.

"It was an accident, don't worry. I'll just get another one."

"No, I will buy you one. It was totally my fault. Where are you going to be standing?"

"I was standing over there but there are people there now."

"Well, go find a spot, it's filling up quickly," said Jimmy.

The stranger walked away, and Jimmy purchased a couple of beers. He drank half of one in a single sip. He was nervous but needed to do what his brother wanted. When the bartender turned her back, he grabbed the second beer, turned around so that other people standing at the small bar would not see, and poured the vial of venom into the beer. The beer foamed; he looked around the room. Liam was busy at the front doors.

Sparrow and Crow walked in from the venue next door after figuring out the dance night had nothing to do with the Doctor. Sparrow was moving towards the stage. Crow went to the door to help Liam. Jimmy finished his beer, careful so that Sparrow would not see him. He walked over to the stranger and handed him the laced beer.

"Thanks, bro, that was nice," said the stranger, unaware that those would be his final words spoken.

Agent Sparrow found Jeb and said, "Liam would like all involved with the tour to be inside. He does not want to have to watch for them outside."

"OK, I'll have Neusy text them."

"I'm on it," said Neusy. "Oh, there's Heinz, he's already in here coming out of the men's room." Jimmy had ditched the wig in the trash can and re-entered the small club.

Marlon was selling merch and watching Liam bring people in through the metal detector. "Did I mention how great last night was? In the ladies' room. How cool was that?"

Cal walked in. "Boys, it is sick next door. The room is packed and the women are just amazing."

"I will have to go check it out," said Marlon smiling, now that he had become a player.

"Well, see you guys, have a good show. I'm going back next door, it is waaayyyy more interesting in there. You wanted to leave at eleven tomorrow morning, right?" said Cal.

"Yes, we have the border, which should be no problem. We should be in Buffalo in time for load in at three." Marlon started to follow Cal until Jeb added, "OK, I'm not paying you to be next door."

Dejected, Marlon returned behind the merch table. "I'm thirsty, does anyone want to buy me a beer?" said Marlon just as the Doctor walked up on the stage.

The lights went off in a very unspectacular way. People stopped talking and looked at the dimly lit stage. "Yah, Jeb, where are the lights? Well people, welcome. I wish we were in the other venue next door, but this is where we are. Here is the song 'Soar into the Sun'." With the small PA system, it was not loud enough to keep up with the volume of the Doctor's amp. It was the Doctor playing, with the rest of the band and vocals in the background.

The song ended and the crowd applauded also in an unspectacular way. The Doctor was not channeling any of their vibes. Neusy looked at Jeb and gave him the he-is-not-happy look. Jeb returned the now-we-have-to-listen-to-him-complain-later nod. The Doctor went right into the next three songs and did not say a word.

After the sixth song he said, "Sorry, I am just not feeling vibes up here, I will try harder. Here is an old one called 'Missed the Bus'." A loud scream was heard from the audience. Not the entire audience, just a woman screaming really loud. The Doctor said, "Yah, I hear you! It is terrible in here."

The woman screamed again, but this time it sounded more panicky. Liam ran to where she was screaming. He had his flashlight out. The Doctor was watching, not knowing what was going on.

Liam yelled, "Sparrow, Crow…get the lights on."

They were looking down at a man with a backpack that had collapsed to the floor. He was clearly dead, there was no pulse.

Liam turned to Crow and said, "Get these people away from here. The Doctor is done for the night. Call this guy." He handed Crow a business card from his friend and detective in Toronto.

Liam dumped out the contents of the backpack and immediately saw the bottle of tanning spray. He moved around a couple of CDs and there was the empty vial. He put it into a plastic bag and waited for the police to arrive.

"Hmmm, initially it looks like he must have ingested some of that venom by mistake. I want to have any beers and all drinks that are in the back tested to see if he put some back there. Nobody drink anything! It is a little odd that he would drink one of his poisoned beers. He was drinking from that cup there, it looks like. I am thinking that he possibly got some on his finger and then on his cup."

Liam checked the back and declared any drinks back there off limits. Hocker had grabbed one and was taking a sip when Liam entered the room. Liam lunged and knocked the beer out of Hocker's hand.

"Relax, it's just a fucking beer."

Liam replied, "We don't know if they are poisoned."

Hocker coughed slightly at the mention of poison. After an hour, the body was removed.

"Wow, that is how the stalker died. By his own sword, so to speak," said Crow.

Sparrow added, "His overconfidence with that venom is my guess." Crow was looking at hotels in St. Martin on his phone. Soon they would be on the nude beach.

As the body was being taken away, Liam opened the corpse's eyes, but with all life gone was unable to determine if this was the same man that he had seen in Montreal in disguise.

Chapter 34

Jeb walked back to the bus from the hotel feeling good after showering. Cal fired up the bus, wanting to leave on time. "What a night last night, Jebsy. You guys had some excitement, but damn, on the other side I was quite excited too. Got involved in a foursome. Two sisters and a best friend. All I will have to say is that we certainly got our money's worth out of that hotel room you got me! Are we ready? Are we a bus?"

"Let me check," said Jeb.

"No," said Hocker. "Fucking Marlon is not here. He's inside, I think. Inspector Liam was there, and Marlon was following him around. Also, the Doctor went to get something to eat with Nathan and Tommy. He was complaining how bad the gig was and that there is never anything for him to eat on the bus."

Neusy walked out of the sleeping area and joined Hocker and Jeb. "I couldn't sleep, Torsten was watching his tablet and giggling loudly. I woke up and looked and he was watching old cartoons."

"Great, well, we are stuck here for a while it seems. Where is Heinz?"

"He is lying in his bunk, curtain open, just in his underwear."

"What a great fucking morning," said Hocker.

"Here comes Marlon," said Neusy.

"Don't let him off the bus again," said Jeb. "Cal, how are we looking?"

"We are a half hour late now, about a two-hour drive with a stop at the border. With the last few border crossings over the past two tours, anything can happen with you guys."

Marlon entered the bus. "Look, I got all these pictures with Liam." He showed his phone to the guys. "He gave me one of his ID cards. They are like business cards but he calls them ID cards. See, he has his picture on there and it says that he is freelance used by international forces. He is cool. It's too bad he's not coming along."

"Did you get rid of any weed that you have?" asked Neusy. "Border crossing today."

"Oh shit, I am going to go outside and smoke it."

"Here are the stragglers," said Cal. "You better be quick and lose whatever you don't smoke."

Marlon walked off the bus as the Doctor and his breakfast mates arrived. Jeb and Neusy were watching. Marlon fired up a joint and started coughing uncontrollably. They looked at each other and smiled. The Doctor took the joint, smoked a few tokes, and then came on board. Neusy and Jeb looked at each other and then looked up.

"Yah, why do you too look at me like that? It's just a little puffy on the pot. It was terrible sound in there yesterday. Did you tell Spud no more of these type clubs?"

"Not to mention that someone died," said Jeb. "Yes, I emailed him this morning and he replied that it was the only offer he received in Toronto. We did get paid fairly well, and we sold a bunch of merch until, yet another show was cut short."

"Yah, but this one was OK to cut short. If Bea calls, don't answer it, she has been calling me all morning, but I don't want to deal with her." He made his way to his room.

"I hope that pot smoke did not get up here on the bus, I want to sleep now and that shit bothers me," said Tommy as he passed by, already working on removing his pants.

"Jebsy, get your guy outside, he is getting Nathan stoned now. I want to leave," said Cal.

Jeb opened the door and said, "Let's go, and drop any leftover joints on the ground. Nathan has to sing tonight so not such a good idea that he smokes." They did as they were told and started laughing when they got on the bus. They sat in the lounge and looked at each other, laughing uncontrollably.

"So we are a bus now, correct?"

"Yes, Crabs," said Jeb. "A kindergarten bus, it seems."

Cal pulled out of the club parking lot where they stayed the night at Liam's request while he completed his investigation.

Hocker opened a beer. "Fucking alright!"

Jeb's phone rang. He looked at the number. It was from the States but not recognizable. Thinking it was a promoter, he answered it. "Jeb…where is Jurgen? He is not answering my calls."

"Bea? What number are you calling from, aren't you in Austria?"

"Yes, but I am using an internet phone now to save money on calls to the US. Much cheaper than using my cell when I need to talk to Jurgen. Why is he not answering my calls? I keep calling him and he never picks up. I called him over twenty times yesterday and today another dozen times. I really need to speak with him. I went to put ketchup on my hamburger, and we are out. He knows that when we use something up, that the rule is to replace it. I had to throw the hamburger out. I could not eat it without ketchup. And we are all out of soup. I wanted soup and he finished all of them. I don't know what to do. We don't have any ranch, he used that up as well. I bought five bottles and I went to make a salad yesterday and we had no more. I can't live like this."

Jeb put the phone down on the table. Hocker started handing out beers. "Guys, there are still a bunch of beers; we got to get rid of those too. Not allowed to take across." Hocker passed one out to Marlon, Nathan, Jeb, and Neusy. Heinz came into the lounge dressed again, to everyone's relief, and Hocker handed him one as well.

"What is this?" asked Heinz as he took the beer.

"It is a fucking toast," said Hocker.

Jeb said, "Guys, you all have been solid this tour. Now that the stalker is dead, that is all behind us and we are headed back into the States with no agents or inspectors tagging along. Cheers to all being behind us."

They all touched bottles and in unison said, "Cheers."

Jeb picked up his phone and Bea was still going. "We have no tampons and three of us are on our periods now. He has not sent any money back in a couple of weeks, can you talk to him? I really don't know what to do. I also went down into the basement, and he and Dr Spiers have all this equipment they were using, these creepy tanks. Please Jeb, can you talk to him?"

The Doctor emerged from the back looking for some more to eat. He opened the cabinet and found a bag of candy. Jeb said, "Phone call for you," and handed him his cell phone.

"Nein, I don't want to speak to Bea."

"Too late."

The Doctor said into the phone, "Yes, Bea… Yah… OK, Bea… Yes… I see… Yeaaah, OK." He hung up and handed Jeb the phone back.

Jimmy was looking at a text that Scaggz just sent him. *That was close but I think we threw them off. I will be watching, can't take any more chances on this tour.*

Hocker chugged his beer and opened another. By the time they got to the border, they had finished all the beers remaining and the empties were in a bag ready to throw away after they stopped.

"OK, Jebsy, go wake everyone up that is sleeping. We are at the border. Nothing stupid this time, please, guys," said Cal.

The stop was just as expected, but this time it would be easy. Heading back into the States should be no problem. All visas in order for the Austrians, and the Americans all had their passports, which Jeb held in his hand as the border patrol officer entered the bus. He took the passports and said, "Any alcohol or cigarettes that were purchased in Canada?"

"No," said Jeb. "The passports and visas should all be in order."

"Did I ask you if they were in order? I will look at them. Are you sure there is no alcohol from Canada on the bus? Because it smells like a brewery in here. Also, you better not be trying to sneak any pot back across the border."

"No, nothing," said Jeb.

"Why does it smell like beer?"

Hocker picked up the bag of empty beer bottles and tossed it at the feet of the border patrol agent. "Because we finished all the beer while we were in Canada." He grinned as large of a smile as Neusy had ever seen on him.

The border agent did not find any humor in this action and said, "OK, I need you all to come with me inside. You too, driver."

"Yah, why can't we just stay on the bus? I want to sleep," said the Doctor.

"Don't make this worse," said Jeb.

They all followed the border agent into the building and were instructed to wait in the seating area while the border agent searched the bus and taught these guys how to properly cross the border. Another hour passed; the border agent never actually set foot on the bus. He came around and said, "Next time don't be such a wise ass. You're all free to go."

Behind the wheel of the bus in his barber chair, Cal said, "We're still an hour from the club. You will not be there for your 3:00 pm load in, but I'll do my best."

Scaggz waited for the bus on the US side of the border, and as the bus passed him by, he followed behind. "Boy am I going to miss those agents, but I will see them again soon. I should send them a post card from Buffalo."

Epilogue

The Doctor returned to Austria with his band, the Surgeons, just happy that they were able to complete the tour without any more killings. The prospect of touring in larger venues with Sludge next time pleased him. But for now, he would have to deal with Bea on a daily basis. Without the clones, it means that he will have to pick up odd shows to earn the extra money that he needs to keep his family fed.

His girlfriends, after the last tour, realized that he did not have enough money to support them and his family. With no money, they had taken an interest in the new up and coming guitarist Mathew Zolton, who was all over the internet and social media and goes by the name Fishbowl.

Fishbowl had quite the following, playing in clubs twice as large as the Doctor and selling out every night. He got his name when one night in high school he decided to put a fishbowl over his head and attach a pair of sunglasses to the front of it before he got on stage at a local bar. It stuck and he now wears it at all shows. He plays alone on the stage with backing tracks. His tours are super simple, with just him and a tour manager. He can afford the women. He has women in all major cities, and with the Doctor's ex-girlfriends, never is lonely.

The Doctor did not like Fishbowl. Not because he was with most of his girlfriends, he does not really care about that all that much, but because Fishbowl, in his opinion, is a hack and the fans are fooled by his average playing. But yet, Fishbowl was all over social media and all the magazines. The Doctor was sickened by it.

When the Doctor's phone rang and he saw it was his good friend and inventor Trenton Towers, he answered it hoping Trenton had good news for him on a new invention. "Hi, Trenton."

"Hi, Doctor. Hey, I am just sitting here in my lab with Fishbowl. I am doing some work for him. He wants to have an automatic effect board, but he was telling me that he is a huge fan of yours and I said, 'well let's call the Doctor, he is in my contact list.' So here we are."

The Doctor threw the phone out the open window and picked up his Universe Guitar. He strummed out a chord progression, which motivated him to record his first album in over ten years. The ideas were flowing, and he would soon begin recording. But first he needed to pen a shopping list of all the items that Bea insisted he replace.

Jimmy was now living back in Austria as Heinz. He was giving guitar lessons at a local music school and content with his slow-paced life. The Doctor would tour again. He was loving life in Austria. He could eat whatever he wanted and not wait for his brother to bring home the rodent of the day.

After a few months, Heinz was recruited by the classic Austrian metal band Dismissed. They had many hits in the eighties, including the anthem "Brains on the Street," and now they have re-formed. They needed a new bass player and the Doctor recommended Heinz. They will also be entering the studio to record a new album, but first they have a small tour as a warmup of ten shows. He did not tell Scaggz about the tour, as he did not want his brother following along.

Nathan and Torsten went back to their regular lives. Torsten continued to get requests to record keyboard tracks on various bands albums. He also had an offer to go out on the road with Dismissed. They also needed a keyboard player, but Torsten declined as he wanted to spend more time in Austria composing what hopefully will become his first solo album.

Nathan tried to form a new band but was unable to find willing participants. He played the coffee shop once a week with his acoustic guitar, watching the women walk in and out. His drought with the women was now continuing at home. To earn extra money, he started painting houses and has become quite good.

Jeb and Neusy had enough material to complete their second book of real-life touring stories. They did submit both books and now are published authors. They started a production company that bands coming to the States could hire. They would provide everything—bus, backline of equipment, crew, tour manager, and merchandise. An all-in-one tour production company. They have had many inquiries and the idea seems to be one that will be lucrative for them.

Bands coming from overseas liked the idea of not having to bring anything but themselves and having it all worked out for them. Their first clients were the band Dismissed. The ten-day tour was a success and now they have three more tours planned. But they were leaving a space in their schedule for the Doctor and Sludge next year.

Cal Crabs moved to Toronto so that he could spend his nights at Ocean's Blue Sea Cave. After three months he got the call from Jeb and has steady work driving the tour bus. He now calls Toronto home and is living on the bus parked at different locations around town.

He also has been playing guitar more and going to open mic nights. His old touring buddy, Johnny Scaggz, called him and visited him in Toronto. The two played guitar on every open mic night they could find. Finally, Cal got the owners of Ocean's Blue to hold an open mic night that he would host in the original club. He was doing well with it, and they added a second night every week.

Agents Sparrow and Crow returned to Los Angeles almost as heroes. Their peers congratulated them on apprehending the Jurgen stalker, although they did absolutely nothing, but still they managed to end the killings. They no longer were the brunt of as many jokes. They still got the occasional "Hey Elwood, where is your brother Jake?" remarks, but now as the agents that solved the two-year crime spree, they were taken a little more seriously.

The agents decided long before their return to Los Angeles that St. Martin was calling. They booked a hotel right off one of the larger nude beaches and spent a week laying in lounge chairs under umbrellas on the beach, sipping funny looking drinks.

Scaggz invested in a case of Tanover and followed the agents to St. Martin. Being a nude beach, Scaggz had to use the tanning spray on his entire body. He had to spray every patch and crevice of his body. He wasn't sure that he liked his penis being dark, but it sold the disguise. He positioned himself near the naked agents so that he could hear what they were talking about daily. When they went in the ocean or to the bathroom, Scaggz would hide their sun block. The agents both were getting sunburned while spending a fortune on sun block.

Scaggz was happy to read on the bottle of tanning spray that it was water resistant but found that when he emerged from the ocean his tan was always a shade lighter, and he needed to spray himself again. He was glad that he brought the entire case with him.

The naked people on the beach were nothing like what all the videos and hotels showed on the internet. After a week on the beach, the agents were happy to return to Los Angeles away from all the ugly people and the naked dark-skinned man with the ever-changing tan that seemed to always be nearby.

A Special Dedication

As the stories of this book came together, the ideas flowed and before we knew it, we had a complete story. All through the process of writing and discussing the plot, we kept being drawn into conversations about several people that have passed away and hold a special place in our hearts. The writing was fun and at times goofy but we would like to be serious for a bit and pay a special dedication to the following people that have touched us throughout the years.

Steven Hulberg - Kent: You really did live the rock and roll dream, tour manager, bassist, army medic, and mortician. Your humor was just as bizarre as mine and your stories and inspiration were monumental in finishing our first book. I miss your ultra-baritone, announcers voice, sure to be the life of any party. Your quick wit and vivacious life were second to no one. I miss your 6'10" ass! Why did you leave me in this place to rot?

Jeff: While we only met minimally in person, we communicated multiple times over various subjects, your review and kind words regarding our first book touches my heart and you will always be in my thoughts.

Stephen Eggers - Kent: We had been pals since high school, both guitarists that played out of home stereos because we couldn't afford a proper amplifier. You and I shared many years of writing inspired music together. Original beyond original. I still have hundreds of hours of our creations on hard drives. Every time I listen to a piece, you are always there. Besides music, you and I had the most insane sense of humor and ridiculousness. I wish you could have been here to read our first book, Are We A Bus? I know that you would have laughed your balls off chapter by chapter.

Jeff: Steve, the times that you, Kent and myself, hung out were always a fun time. Your reaction to our stories were motivational to our writing. I wish we could have spent more time together.

Kim Kalouria - Kent: You, Jeff, and I we very like-minded in every way. We also bonded with you at various tour locations while we were on the road with artists. You were a great guitarist and a good soul to be around. Some of your humor was utilized in our second book. We think that you would have enjoyed reading our books. Then you would have said That Kent and Jeff are out-of-their-minds!

Jeff: Kim, we spent many times talking into the late night. It was always a highlight of any tour when we got to cross paths. Your humor was always a welcome part of my life. The last go around, it was not the same without seeing you on the road! I miss you and think of you often, many times replaying that crazy car ride to get the late night burger.

Elliott Rubinson - Jeff: Elliott, thank you for being an important part of my life for many years. Your calls and inspiration is hugely missed and still hear our conversations and discussions every day! The laughs we shared over a variety of subjects was a highlight every time we spoke. I think you would enjoy reading and laugh hard while reading our books. As we were writing the first book over the years your encouragement was motivational.

Kent: I was fortunate to be friends with you for a short time, Elliott. I had much respect for all your accomplishments, starting your musical instrument business out of a small apartment in New York and building it into a mega company, and being a seasoned bassist that was able to play professionally on tour with many famous musicians that you admired as a fan in your youth. I was honored to help set up your bass equipment for the show or run to the store to pick up a last minute libation for you before the concert evening was finished. You were very personable and had a great sense of humor. Many of our conversations together helped Jeff and I stay motivated to complete our book. I will always be eternally grateful that you located the very last Sky Guitar in the USA and that I was able to purchase. I wish you could be here to enjoy the humor of our books. I know you would be laughing page by page.

Also in the

Mayhem and Melody series:

Are We A Bus?

www.ingramcontent.com/pod-product-compliance
Lightning Source LLC
Chambersburg PA
CBHW051436190726
48289CB00001B/215